A MESSAGE
TO THE CHARNWOOD READER
FROM THE PUBLISHER

Since the introduction of Ulverscroft Large Print Books, countless readers around the world have confirmed that the larger and clearer print has brought back the pleasure of reading to an ever-widening audience, thus enabling readers to once again enjoy the companionship of books which had previously been denied to them due to their inability to read normal small print.

It is obvious that to cater for this ever-widening audience of readers a new series was necessary. The Charnwood Series embraces the widest possible variety of literature from the traditional classics to the most recently published bestsellers, and includes many authors considered too contemporary both in subject and style to be suitable for the many elderly readers for whom the original Ulverscroft Large Print Books were designed.

The newly developed typeface of the Charnwood Series has been subjected to extensive and exhaustive tests amongst the international family of large print readers, and unanimously acclaimed and preferred as a smoother and easier read. Another benefit of this new typeface is that it allows the publication in one volume of longer novels which previously could only be published in two large print volumes: a constant source of frustration for readers when one volume is not available for one reason or another.

The Charnwood Series is designed to increase the titles available to those readers in this ever-widening audience who are unable to read and enjoy the range of popular titles at present only available in normal small print.

THE SONG OF THE RAINBIRD

When Kate Carswell arrived in Nairobi, at the turn of the century, to find that her fiance had been killed in suspicious circumstances, common sense demanded her return to England. But Kate already felt the stirrings of a deep and abiding love of East Africa. This is the story of Kate's life in a pioneer country, and of the farmers, hunters, civil servants and missionaries who made up her life there. The story of her fight for justice in a colour-conscious community; of her half-caste adopted daughter, Patsy; and of James, Patsy's son, forced by circumstances to join a Mau Mau gang.

BARBARA WHITNELL

THE SONG OF THE RAINBIRD

Complete and Unabridged

CHARNWOOD
Leicester

First published in Great Britain 1984 by
Hodder and Stoughton
London

First Large Print Edition
published February 1985
by arrangement with
Hodder and Stoughton
London
and
St. Martin's Press, Inc.,
New York

British Library CIP Data

Whitnell, Barbara
The song of the rainbird.—Large print ed.—
(Charnwood library series)
I. Title
823′.914[F]   PR6073.H653

ISBN 0-7089-8244-1

Published by
F. A. Thorpe (Publishing) Ltd.
Anstey, Leicestershire
Set by Rowland Phototypesetting Ltd.
Bury St Edmunds, Suffolk
Printed and bound in Great Britain by
T. J. Press (Padstow) Ltd., Padstow, Cornwall

Part One

1906–1921

1

KATE felt conspicuously alone in the ship's saloon. She was surrounded by fond families talking brightly to disguise the sadness of parting, making small jokes that seemed in some cases to tremble dangerously close to tears. Only she, it seemed, was leaving England unmourned.

No, no—that was untrue. For hadn't Aunt Sophie risked her brother's fury to accompany her niece to Victoria Station? She had twisted a damp handkerchief in her gloved hands all the way from the vicarage, and her over-long nose had grown red and had twitched as it always did under the stress of great emotion.

"You will write, Kate dear? We shall be so anxious to hear." Standing on the station platform, Aunt Sophie had been forced to bring the handkerchief into more active play, dabbing her nose vigorously. "Such a long way! So many dangers! You will be sure to take good care of your health, won't you, dear? Eat sparingly, especially *fats*, and do try to avoid red meat, it's so heating to the blood. And Kate, wear a hat at all times, I implore you. The perils of the sun's rays are very great, I have it on the best authority. Dear Mr. Lambert was a missionary in Nigeria

1

for many years, so knows exactly what he's speaking of."

"East Africa is different," Kate said, not for the first time.

She fought down a guilty feeling of impatience and leaned from the window of the Southampton train to touch Aunt Sophie's cheek with genuine affection.

"It was good of you to come," she said. "I hope things won't be too bad at home."

"Don't think too harshly of your father. You must realise that he only wishes your happiness."

At this Kate smiled and nodded and said nothing. There was nothing more to say, for the arguments had raged, on and off, for the past two years, rising to a crescendo this past month, ever since Edward's letter had arrived saying that at last he had saved sufficient money for Kate to join him.

"A marvellous business opportunity has opened up for me," he had written. "I am to become a partner in a firm of gunsmiths."

"It won't last!" Kate's father, the Reverend Carswell, vicar of the church of St. Philip and St. James in Bayswater, was scornful, exhibiting none of the charity which he urged upon his fashionable congregation Sunday by Sunday. "When did that young coxcomb ever stick at anything? He's never done an honest day's work in his life. You're a fool, Kate, if you think he can ever bring you happiness."

2

"I love him," Kate replied.

Nothing had moved her. The obligatory morning prayers had become laced with petitions, imploring the Almighty to show her the error of her ways before it was too late. Embarrassed maids had smirked behind their folded hands, drooping lids fluttering with the drama of it all. His sermons, thundered from the pulpit, were overwhelmingly concerned with filial duty and the respect in which virtuous children should hold their parents. A cold, angry silence pervaded the vicarage like the chill of winter, causing Aunt Sophie to scamper about the house looking pink and frightened and apologetic, dropping small objects and showing a marked tendency to burst into tears.

If Kate had expected a softening on his part when the time came for a final leave-taking, she was to be disappointed.

"You are no longer my daughter," he had said, his strong-featured face looking as if it were carved from granite. He sat unmoving behind the desk in his study, as if she were a stranger.

"You won't even wish me happiness?"

"You are behaving in a way that is undutiful, un-Christian and unforgivable."

For a long moment she had returned his look, noting the harsh lines that ran from nose to mouth, the slate-grey eyes that were totally without warmth.

3

"I'm sorry, Father. I had hoped that we could part more amicably than this."

He had already picked up his pen and turned from her.

"Goodbye," she said. Then, when there was no response from him, she left the room, knowing as she closed the door noiselessly behind her that it was for the last time.

She was free!

In spite of the sour taste that this parting with her father left in her mouth, excitement soared. So many times she had fought and lost. So many battles had ended with triumph on her father's side, frustration and rebellion on hers.

Above all things, she had longed to teach: she had never wanted anything else, not since the days when she had ranged her dolls and stuffed toys in line and chanted the twice times table at them.

The headmistress of her school had begged Mr. Carswell to allow Kate to continue her studies, even as far as university. Yes, yes, she agreed —perhaps it was a little revolutionary, but the twentieth century had just begun and for some years now women had had the chance of higher education. Kate was exactly the type of woman who would benefit.

Mr. Carswell had been appalled. Blue-stockings were a disgrace to their sex— unfeminine, strident, constitutionally unsuited to

4

prolonged mental effort. The mad-house was their inevitable destination.

"Then perhaps you would consider a college for the training of teachers," Miss Hackett had suggested. "Kate has an undeniable gift. She is a born teacher, I feel certain."

"My dear Miss Hackett!" Mr. Carswell's amusement was patronising. "There is no *need* for my daughter to teach."

"But there is a need," Kate had said to him afterwards. Dramatically she had laid a hand on her bosom. "There is a need here, father."

"Then continue with your Sunday School class, child. Girls of your social standing do not take paid employment. Besides, your duty is here, with me, helping with parish duties until such time as we find a suitable husband for you."

She had endured the best part of a year of paralysing boredom before being rescued by the only man in London who had the power to stand up to her father—the Bishop of the Diocese.

He had called on church matters, had stayed to tea, and had talked, among other things, of the difficulty his sister, Lady Farrell, was having in finding a suitable governess for her three little girls.

"Since Miss Featherstone left—a charming young woman, Miss Carswell, I'm sure you must remember her, she was a regular attender at St. Philip and St. James—my sister has found it

5

impossible to find a young lady of the same calibre to replace her."

Kate did remember Miss Featherstone well—had, in fact, held several conversations with her, in the course of which she had learned that the Farrell household was a delightfully happy, easygoing establishment where the governess was treated with friendliness and courtesy. But His Grace was still talking.

"There is no shortage of applicants, of course, but my sister is anxious to find someone who is lively and intelligent—in short, someone who can make learning a pleasure."

"I could," Kate said, as she offered a plate of scones.

"My dear young lady—"

"A preposterous suggestion—"

The Bishop and Kate's father spoke simultaneously, but it was to the Bishop that Kate addressed herself, sinking down on a low stool beside him, holding the plate as if it were some votive offering.

"Would your sister consider me?" she asked earnestly, two spots of colour appearing in her cheeks. "I know I am young and without experience, but Miss Hackett could tell you how much I loved helping with the younger children—"

"And Kate's Sunday School class grows more popular every week," Aunt Sophie put in

6

proudly, subsiding uneasily as she caught her brother's speaking glance.

"I feel sure my sister would think you most suitable," His Grace said, beaming down at her and thinking what an appealing little thing she was. "The right background—of excellent education—a Christian home. I shall mention the matter to her this very day—if your father has no objection?"

Kate turned to smile innocently upon her father.

"Oh, how could he object? Lady Farrell is such a good friend of St. Philip and St. James—"

And good for a sizeable offering in the collection plate every Sunday, not to mention the fact that Sir William was becoming a force in the Government. How, indeed, could Mr. Carswell object?

That was one battle in which she had been the victor and she thanked heaven for it every day of her life, for the Farrell family were every bit as amiable as the departed Miss Featherstone had said. Kate had settled down with them immediately, becoming an integral part of their household, sleeping there from Monday to Friday and returning home at weekends. Entering the doors of the vicarage each Friday evening seemed to her, whatever the weather, like passing from sunshine to shadow.

The three girls—Marjorie, Dorothy and Maud —were lively and responsive, and intelligent

7

enough to keep her on her toes. They were no angels, but all three of them were open and warm-hearted, as indeed was their mother.

There was much coming and going in the house, with Sir William's position as Parliamentary Under-Secretary involving a great deal of entertaining. Lady Farrell held an At Home each Wednesday afternoon, and often upwards of a dozen people would call. Sometimes Kate and the girls would be summoned to the drawing room to meet the guests.

It was on an occasion of this kind that she met Edward Matcham. He had been brought along by a certain Angela Winterton, who was, perhaps, not quite a lady but was smart and amusing enough to pass as one. She had taken him up with a view to engineering a meeting for him with some theatrical producer, for, as she told Lady Farrell, the dear creature looked like a Greek god and could sing very nicely as well.

He was about to sing very nicely as Kate brought the girls into the drawing room, and Lady Farrell motioned them to sit down and be quiet. He was, Kate thought, the most beautiful young man she had ever seen—fair-haired, fresh-faced, features nobly proportioned. There was an air of great good humour and self-confidence about him, but his smile died as he began to sing, for the ballad was a sad one concerning unrequited love and early death.

The banal lyric was exactly the kind that

8

normally Kate would have mocked unmercifully and it was with inward amusement that she composed herself to listen to it with the required amount of reverence. Then, towards the end of the third verse, the eyes of the singer turned towards her and the words were suddenly charged with meaning, the dying fall of the cliché-ridden music heart-rendingly significant.

She looked away, confused; but inevitably she turned back, for the magnetic force was irresistible. After the song was over she knew that his gaze turned again and again towards her, though she sat in a corner as demure as any governess should be.

A few days later he contrived to be in the park as she escorted the girls to their dancing class. She had only to see him for the rest of the world to fade away. She was conscious only of his smile and of the strange, disturbing behaviour of her own heart.

Kate knew instinctively that her father would disapprove of Edward and she embarked somewhat guiltily on the secret meetings he suggested. Inevitably she was drawn into lies and evasions to account for her late return home on Friday evenings or for being required by Lady Farrell on a Sunday afternoon, and her conscience troubled her. Not enough to stop the meetings, however, for she was totally under Edward's spell, unable to believe her good fortune in being singled out by such a charming, handsome young man.

She had never met anyone like him. There was a rakish tilt to his hat and a sparkle in his eye. He made her laugh as she had never laughed before. He surprised her with small, unexpected gifts and introduced her to hitherto unknown delights: the Music Hall, a coffee stall near Covent Garden, the rural attractions of Richmond Park where they kissed and kissed and kissed again.

And now she was leaving everything and everyone she had ever known to join him in a foreign country, in spite of her father's implacable anger, the arguments, the tears. All had come to this conclusion.

A forceful voice from close at hand broke in on her thoughts.

"Wool next to the skin," said the stout, grey-haired woman at the next table. She was addressing a young woman of about Kate's own age. "Never forget how rapidly Ronnie takes a chill."

Kate stood to leave the saloon intending to see what was happening on deck, and as she did so her eyes met those of the young woman. They exchanged a brief glimmer of amusement and for a moment Kate felt less solitary.

Outside there was still much activity. Cranes were winching goods into the hold and porters carried the trunks of late arrivals up the gangway.

A tall, blonde woman was coming aboard with a small boy in her arms, looking smilingly at the length of the ship as if the sight of it excited her. Kate was included in the orbit of the smile and she returned it shyly, envying the unknown woman's air of assurance.

She looked at her fob-watch. Sailing was not for another hour. She should, perhaps, go down and begin unpacking her clothes in the cabin she was to share with another occupant so far unknown to her, yet she felt diffident about staking a claim to either of the bunks or wardrobes without consultation. She would stay on deck, she decided, just for a little longer.

It still seemed unbelievable. This is *me*, she kept telling herself, about to sail for Africa.

Edward's determination to try his fortune in the British East African Protectorate had grown steadily with his apparent inability to carry out his father's instructions to "settle down to a steady job, boy." His hatred for the idea of an office desk had prompted his flirtation with the theatre, but Angela Winterton had proved a sore disappointment to him and her introductions had yielded nothing. There were titles dotted along the branches of his family tree, but as the younger son of a younger son neither they nor any money had come his way. The situation was getting desperate.

"You might just as well throw me over," he said to Kate in a rare fit of gloom one summer day when they had taken a picnic into Richmond Park. He was lying on his side, his chin resting on his hand. The sun had brought a flush to his cheeks and it glinted on the gold in his hair.

"Do you want me to?" she asked fearfully.

He reached out to clasp her arm.

"God, no! You're the best thing that ever happened to me, Kate—but of what use am I to you or anyone else?" He sighed and turned over to lie on his back. "I want nothing more than to marry you, Kate. I'll make you happy, I swear it —but how? What am I to do?"

"Don't worry so," Kate said. But she worried, too.

It was a few days later that he first mentioned emigrating.

To Australia? Kate asked.

"No, Africa—British East Africa. BEA everyone calls it. A fellow I met yesterday was telling me all about it. It sounds wonderful—a whole new land of opportunity."

"They built a railway, didn't they?" Vaguely she remembered her father fulminating about the waste of taxpayers' money.

"That's right!" Edward's face was alight with enthusiasm. "Imagine it—what a wonderful, crazy thing to do! Who but a visionary could plan a railway going right through the heart of Africa, over desert and mountains and lion-infested bush, all the way from the ocean to Lake Victoria."

"Why did anyone bother to do such a thing?"

12

"Partly because of national prestige, partly to help stamp out the slave trade. Now the railway is there, the Government has to make the land productive to help pay for it. Land is going dirt cheap, I'm told, and is incredibly fertile. You can grow anything on it—anything at all."

"But you're not a farmer!"

"I could learn to be. Or I could be something else. There's a new town growing up—Nairobi, they call it—and there must be a thousand opportunities. I could go and make a place for us, Kate."

Kate could hardly believe him to be serious; it was another pipe-dream, like going on the stage. In this she was wrong. There was something in the concept of this new country that had captured his imagination and he did not let the subject rest. He sought more information and reported to her over muffins and cream cakes in a back-street tea-shop.

"There are sailings twice a month from Southampton," he said, a lock of golden hair falling over his brow as he leaned over the table eagerly. "And my father's agreed to stake me to the tune of a hundred pounds. The fare is only forty-eight, first class. Old Uncle Wallace says I can have two tin trunks and a pith helmet that's mouldering in his attic. They're all as pleased as punch to be getting rid of me, it seems—all except Mother, but then mothers are like that,

13

aren't they? I mean, one loves and reveres them but should never be tied to their apron strings."

Kate watched the bright face and the movement of his lips and she felt a clutch of fear. If not the end, she thought, it was the beginning of the end. He would go away, would meet new people and have new experiences and he would never, never send for her, no matter what he said now—

"When may I call on your father?" he asked. "Since we're talking of families—"

"My father!"

A new terror. Kate looked down miserably at the table, biting her lip, imagining the icy rage, the biting sarcasm.

"I have to meet him some time," Edward said reasonably, "if we are to be officially engaged before I leave England."

"You don't know him," Kate replied helplessly. But there was a shaft of brightness in the thought that Edward actually wanted to make their relationship official. Until that point there had been a vagueness about the future which she had not dared to probe.

Her father's reaction had been all that she had expected, with Edward being sent packing with his tail between his legs.

"We don't need his approval," Edward said afterwards. "You're over twenty-one, after all. I shall send for you, Kate, I swear it. Just keep the faith, as I will."

14

He had gone, and there had been weeks when it was hard to keep the faith, for letters were not frequent. It was all too easy to imagine him charming some other woman. Night after night Kate lay awake, her tortured imagination picturing scenes no less graphic because the background was unknown to her.

By day she concentrated on the children and her work, and life returned to the dull round it had been before she met Edward. Whether letters arrived from him or not, she wrote constantly and sometimes it seemed to her that her life only had meaning because she reported it to him.

When his letters did arrive—addressed always to Lady Farrell's house in Eaton Square, for the virtuous Mr. Carswell would have destroyed them—they were as full of plans for their joint future as ever, even though things had not worked out entirely as he had planned. He had found that the streets of Nairobi were not paved with gold—in fact, he wrote, they were not paved at all and in the dry weather were inches deep in dust, while in the wet they were a sea of mud. And land was not quite so easy to get hold of as he had imagined. Oh, it was cheap all right, but capital was needed for anyone to have a chance of success and farmers were beset by all sorts of petty rules that complicated their lives. Accommodation, too, was hard to come by.

Kate thought she detected disillusionment, but by his next letter he seemed more cheerful.

15

He had found friends, was sharing a tent in a temporary camp set up for intending settlers, was casting around for business opportunities.

His next letter was full of even more buoyant enthusiasm after a chance encounter with an Irishman in the bar of the Norfolk Hotel.

"He's looking for a man who can shoot straight to go with him after ivory. Now, dearest, I may not have many talents, but no one can deny my ability with a gun! Ivory fetches a high price and Brennan seems to know all about elephant hunting. It's quick and easy money, he says, so I think this trip is just what I need. It will give me sufficient capital to establish myself so that you can join me."

Edward and the Irishman had gone into the bush which meant an agonisingly long period without letters. When he finally returned to the comparative civilisation of Nairobi he wrote that money from ivory was neither so quick nor so easy as he had imagined, but yet another opportunity had opened before him.

"Christy Brennan is an amazing fellow," he wrote. "I've never met anyone quite like him. He has a real Irish temper that blazes like a rocket at times, but mostly he is the best of company and he knows everything there is to know about hunting. He keeps very mum about his past. All I know is that he was in the Boer War and has a scar to prove it. He has asked me to join with him, wet-nursing big-game hunters who come

16

out from Europe. He says it's a very quick and easy way of making money . . ."

No talk now of a business in Nairobi. The months came and went, and Kate's hopes fluctuated. But at last, eighteen months after his departure, the letter telling her that the waiting was over had arrived. The hunting safaris had paid off, he had sent money for her passage, their happy future was assured. He now, quite definitely, was going to settle down in partnership with a friend, running a shop that was to sell hunting rifles and safari equipment. Meantime, Christy had asked him to go on one last elephant hunt. Just a little more easy money wouldn't come amiss.

This time the term had made her smile. It had been a long road, she thought now as she leant on the rail of the ship, but her faith had been justified. In a little more than three weeks she would be with Edward again, a lifetime of bliss in front of them.

There was a small commotion on the gangway below her and she craned to see the cause of it. A porter carrying a cabin trunk on his back had apparently collided with the stout, black-clad woman who had delivered the advice regarding the wearing of wool, and now neither could pass in the restricted space. Outraged words floated upwards. Behind her Kate heard a subdued giggle and she turned to see the young woman who had smiled at her as she left the saloon.

"I offer no prizes for guessing the outcome of that battle," the girl said. "There—the poor man is having to back all the way down again. My heart goes out to him!"

Kate laughed.

"You sound as if you may have lost a battle or two yourself in the past."

"Yes, indeed." The girl joined her at the rail. "Still," she went on with a smile, "I've won the war."

"War?" Kate raised her eyebrows questioningly.

"I must introduce myself. I'm Louise Hudson and that rather terrifying lady is my mother-in-law. The relief—oh, the relief of leaving her behind!" Mrs. Hudson threw back her head and laughed delightedly.

"Your husband is already in BEA?"

"He went six months ago. Oh, she was furious, simply furious! Not only because he finally left her apron strings, but because he has actually bought a grocery business. She simply can't get over it. Every time she has looked at me for the past few months she has shaken her head more in sorrow than in anger and has asked what on earth can have come over him. No Hudson has ever been involved in trade, you see. That's supposed to be one in the eye for me, because my father was a pharmacist with his own business. The implication is that I have dragged Ronnie down to my level."

18

"Can she really be as bad as that?"

"Oh, worse—much worse! My dear—" and here Mrs. Hudson leant towards Kate as if to confide a horrendous secret— *"she makes the maids polish the broom handles*. There!"

Kate laughed, amused both by the words and the girl's expression. She had a small, piquant face and a twitch to her lips that seemed to indicate that there was much in life that made her laugh. A fashionable straw hat with pink ribbons tilted forward on her dark head.

"So you're not sorry to leave England?" Kate asked.

"Sorry? I'm delighted!"

"What about your own parents?"

"Both dead, alas. My father many years ago, my mother quite recently. We don't seem a very long-lived family on my side. There are times when I wish I could say the same for the Hudsons!" She caught her underlip between her teeth. "Oh, what a dreadful thing for me to say! Now if my esteemed mother-in-law is run down by a cab-horse it will be on my conscience for the rest of my life. Please tell me, what is your name? You haven't introduced yourself yet. I'm hoping against hope that you're Miss K. Carswell."

Kate looked surprised.

"Yes, it happens that I am."

Louise Hudson extended her hand.

"Then we're cabin-mates. Oh, the relief! I was so afraid that Miss K. Carswell would turn out

19

to be that stringy lady in the cocoa-brown dress with eyes like a blood-hound. I'm sure she must be a missionary, don't you agree? Only someone with her mind firmly fixed on higher things could go around looking like that. Shall we toss for the top bunk? I'm afraid I've brought far too many clothes with me, but I promise to keep them under control. Shall we go below and sort ourselves out?"

This process was enlivened by a running commentary from Louise, from whom conversation seemed to flow as effortlessly as water from a mountain stream.

"Have you been on board ship before?" she asked, shaking out one dress after another and cramming them into the totally inadequate cupboard provided. "I never have, but I do know that one never dresses for dinner on the first night, and walls are called bulkheads and the left-hand side of the ship is called the port side. I can remember that quite easily, for I have a left-handed cousin in the Navy, and he is most frightfully fond of port. You know—" suddenly she stopped talking and faced Kate, clasping a pale-green afternoon dress to her bosom— "you are to promise me one thing, if we are to share this tiny space happily for the next three weeks. Whenever you feel I am talking too much, you are to tell me very firmly to be quiet. I can be very trying, I am the first to admit it. My tongue runs away with me, which doesn't mean that I'm not interested in listening to all that you have to say. Why, you've hardly said a word yet! Tell me, are you travelling out to relatives?"

"I am to be married," Kate said.

Putting it into words seemed to give this incredible idea substance, and joy flooded through her. The unbelievable was happening. After all this time, she was on her way to Edward.

It was rough in the Bay of Biscay and the number of those passengers able to take their meals was cut by two thirds. Louise, Kate, and the tall blonde lady with the small boy were among the few who still presented themselves in the dining saloon, and because they were much of an age and travelling without male escorts, it was natural that they should gravitate together.

Louise and Kate were impressed by the other woman's cool beauty and had christened her 'Her Serene Highness'. Now they learned that she was Mrs. Meg Lacey, that her son was called Colin and that he was just two years old. Her husband, she told them, owned a coffee farm in a district some ten miles from Nairobi called Kiambu.

"He went out in 1901," she said. "Now, five years later, the coffee is just coming into bearing. It doesn't do to be in a hurry if you're going to be a farmer."

"You must tell us absolutely everything," Kate demanded, less shy now that blonde beauty had proved herself disposed to be friendly. "Men

21

leave out all the most important things, like how on earth one bears to wear corsets in the heat and are spine pads really necessary? And what about shopping? And how does one communicate with the natives?"

"One learns Swahili," Meg said. "All the different tribes have their own highly complicated languages, but Swahili is being adopted as the lingua franca."

Kate resolved there and then to sign up for twice-daily lessons with an elderly missionary who had offered his services for this purpose to anyone who cared to avail themselves of them.

"As for shopping," Louise said. "You must, of course, patronise Ronnie's store. He tells me he has a good supply of tinned and dried goods and is hoping to arrange for a farmer to bring in fresh foods daily—vegetables and dairy produce, and so on. His mother is convinced we shall be social outcasts."

"She's wrong—and that's part of why I like the place," Meg said. "People value you for what you are, not for your pretensions or the size of your bank balance. Which, I may say, is just as well, for Hugh and I haven't a bean to bless ourselves with. We seem to live on hope, heavily subsidised by our bank manager."

When afterwards Kate looked back on that voyage, she could remember only the laughter and the comradeship. The cockroaches in the cabin were an annoyance but had no lasting memorial. It was the fun that stayed with her: the gully-gully men at Port Said, who made chickens appear and disappear from the most unlikely places, and the camels and fuzzy-haired negroes at Port Sudan.

Her regard for Meg Lacey deepened with each day that passed. There was a quiet, good-humoured strength about her. Her dark grey eyes were warm and reflective in a face that was beautiful not only because of the regularity of its features and the generous curve of its mouth, but also because of the glow that seemed to come from within. Kate found herself revealing more and more of her own personality to this sympathetic, perceptive listener and from her she absorbed a tantalising picture of the life she might expect in Africa. Meg did not minimise the hardships and challenges, but she could not disguise the deep love she had for the country.

Kate made friends with Colin, too. He was a rather serious small boy with his mother's eyes. He was of a conversational turn of mind and Kate took such pleasure in his company that inevitably her mind turned longingly to the time when she and Edward might have just such a son.

Louise was all froth and bubble. Kate never quite brought herself to tell her to be quiet, as she had been directed, but there were times when she came near it. Towards the end of the voyage she felt sure that she must know every last detail of Ronnie's courtship, proposal and their subsequent marriage, and she had a day-to-day knowledge of Mrs. Hudson's ménage, complete with details as to dress, temper, and taste in food.

"I don't know how you stand it," Meg remarked on one occasion. "She's a dear, I know, but she talks even more than Colin. Does she go on all night?"

"I've become adept at going to sleep while she's still in full spate, and she never takes the smallest offence. She really is the most amusing creature. I shall miss her—"

She broke off, met Meg's eyes, and laughed.

"Well, perhaps I shan't miss sharing a bedroom with her, under the circumstances, but I shall miss you both in your different ways. I've enjoyed it all so much."

"We'll meet again, never fear."

At last they awoke one morning to find Mombasa there before them, its white beaches palm-fringed, the sea overlooked by the old Portuguese fort. Letters awaited them from their menfolk. Meg smiled over hers and folded it away, saying nothing, but Louise, as always, was more communicative.

"Oh, poor dear Ronnie! The farmer who was going to supply the dairy products has let him down. Isn't that the worst possible luck? He says he has to work terribly hard to make any money because more and more Indians are opening shops, and they live on the smell of an oil rag. What a curious expression! Still, he's managed to buy a little house for us not far from town. I'm so excited! I'm quite sure he will be the most tremendous success, Indians or no Indians."

Kate did not take in her words for she was reading and re-reading the letter she had received from Edward.

"I hate to end my association with Christy on a sour note," he had written, "but we had the father and mother of an argument last night and he accused me of things I can never forget. I believe I told you that he had a temper—well, I was certainly right! I thought for a few moments that he had murder in mind.

"I had imagined that we were friends, but it seems that this is not so. Never mind. This is the last safari I shall make with him and all I can think of is that you will be with me soon.

"I hope this letter reaches you. I am writing it far from civilisation and shall give it to a runner who will place it in a cleft stick and take it all the way to the Post Office in Thika. My darling, I wonder if you have any idea how primitive this country is? I pray that you will feel at home here and promise to do all that I can to make you happy."

Oh, surely he must realise how easily that would fall within his powers?

She dismissed the part about the quarrel with Christy Brennan. She had never cared for the sound of him—he with his Irish temper and his assurances about quick and easy money. Edward was better off without his friendship.

Kate, Louise, Meg and Colin stayed overnight at the Grand Hotel, Mombasa, and the following day they caught the train to Nairobi.

It was a long, hot and exhausting journey. Once away from the lush greenness of the coastal strip, dust caked their skin and made their hair coarse and brittle to the touch. Colin grew fractious and Kate told stories endlessly to entertain him.

Outside the carriage window unrolled a scene which Kate could never have imagined, even though she had read so much about the country. Elephant, rhino, ostrich and buck of all kinds could be seen beside the railway line, and near-naked tribesmen stood, blanket on one shoulder and spear in hand, under a shimmering burden of heat.

At night they stopped at a dak bungalow for a meal, then slept on the bedding that had been unrolled for them in the carriage. Gradually the train snaked uphill to cooler altitudes, and the scenery changed dramatically. In place of the red dust of the desert there were now plains on either side, stretching for mile upon mile, burnt by the sun to a light biscuit colour and dotted with acacia thorn trees. Here there was an even greater profusion of wild-life—enormous herds of pretty animals with flicking tails that Meg told them were Thomson's gazelles, hundreds of zebra and

26

still more wildebeest, all grazing together at perfect peace with each other.

"I wonder why it is," Kate said meditatively as at last they were approaching Nairobi and the number of natives that could be seen had increased a little, "that one isn't at all embarrassed by the sight of a naked black man? They look so much more *finished*, somehow."

Louise giggled.

"Come now, Kate! They're not exactly naked."

"Well, if you're under the impression that those blankets actually hide anything, you're either short-sighted or too modest to look."

"Never let it be said! Oh my stars, will you look at that?"

The train was slowing to a halt. It seemed impossible that the gruelling journey was at last over, but though they had longed for it to come to an end, the sight that met their astonished gaze was enough to make the newcomers wonder uneasily what they had let themselves in for.

Outside the window, ranged on the ramshackle platform, was a solid phalanx of ochre-smeared natives, some with the usual red blanket slung from one shoulder and others in the more ceremonial garb of monkey skins and ostrich feathers. All held spears.

Even Louise was silenced and turned to look apprehensively at Meg, her eyes round and fearful in her dust-streaked face.

"Meg—they're not *hostile*, are they?"

27

Meg laughed.

"No, simply curious, the same as all the Europeans. Everyone comes to meet the train. Oh—there's Hugh! Look Colin, there's Daddy. Wave to him. Hugh, Hugh, we're over here."

A tall, khaki-clad figure with a high-domed, balding forehead was pushing through the crowd towards them, and from another direction—altogether smaller and swarthier, but also dressed in khaki—came Ronnie Hudson. Squealing with delight, Louise jumped down into his arms.

Kate stood on the step of the carriage, looking this way and that, while the noise seemed to swell around her, the lines of Africans breaking and re-forming as passengers climbed down from the train. All was bustle and confusion. The rickshaw men shouted for custom and attempted to make off with the luggage that was being unloaded. Whiteclad Indians accosted travellers shouting the virtues of the transport that was waiting outside. Reunions between friends were accompanied by shrieks of joy.

In all of this there was no sign of Edward.

Unreasonably, a feeling of panic took possession of her, a feeling which she did her best to quell. There must be a hundred reasons for his non-appearance, she told herself. It was just a question of waiting.

But what would she do, where would she go, if he did not come? Of course he would come! She was being foolish.

"Miss Carswell?"

She heard her name and quickly turned to see that a young, dark-haired man in some sort of official uniform had approached her unnoticed and now stood close beside her.

"Yes?"

She looked at him with eager enquiry. The feeling of panic returned, redoubled, as his blue eyes shifted away from her uneasily. He had pink and rather prominent ears, she noticed, and he passed his solar topee nervously from one hand to the other.

"Yes?" she said again, when still he did not speak. "Where is Edward? Have you a message from him?"

The stranger moistened his lips with his tongue.

"Would you be kind enough to come with me, Miss Carswell? I have something to tell you."

Kate could feel the blood drain from her face

"What is it?" she whispered. "Is it bad news?"

The man blinked and nodded.

"It is all most regrettable . . . I can't tell you how very sorry . . . please be good enough to come this way . . . "

His very incoherence seemed to make everything plain.

"Bad news," Kate said again, and swallowed convulsively. "How bad?" Her hand fastened on his arm. "Tell me now, is he dead?"

Hugh was swinging Colin up into his arms, Meg was embracing a friend, Louise was babbling, pulling at her arm, saying that she had to meet Ronnie. Voices filled her ears as numbly she stood there, her eyes fixed pleadingly upon the young man, begging him to deny her fear.

It was a shooting accident, the man told her. No one had been to blame. It was the sort of thing that happened regularly here. Edward was dead and buried.

It had happened ten days before, he said. Ten days.

Events blurred and kaleidoscoped from that moment. She did not cry, not then, though Louise did so and Kate felt mildly outraged about that. What gave her the right to cry when she had never known Edward?

Meg and Hugh stayed with her; there was talk of finding an hotel room, but for some reason there were difficulties. There was a race meeting, the town was full. Someone suggested the hospital. Nothing really penetrated the paralysing grief that surrounded her like a fog.

At the hospital a kindly doctor gave her something to drink. Meg, a nurse, an orderly faded in and out of the room, led her towards a bed, speaking kind words to her.

It was a relief when at last everything dissolved into blackness and the voices stopped.

2

KATE struggled towards consciousness to the sound of more voices, high-pitched and carefree. For one moment she thought they belonged to Marjorie, Dorothy and Maud.

It was a dream, she thought with relief. A dark and frightening nightmare. What can the children be thinking of, to make such a noise?

Her eyes opened to the reality of the bare white room, its brightness dimmed by the folds of the mosquito net hanging from its circular ring above her bed, and the thread of those comforting thoughts snapped, brittle as a twig. The voices she could hear were not those of the Farrell girls, but of some African women who were planting a lawn in the garden that surrounded the hospital. Dimly she remembered them from those confused, kaleidoscopic scenes of the evening before.

It was true, then. All true. But a nightmare for all that. The events of the previous day flooded back to her, and she buried her face in the pillow that smelled of damp and insecticide, unable to bear her grief.

For a long time she wept, shuddering and helpless, and was glad that no one came near;

31

but at last she was drained of tears. Curled into a ball she cowered inside the net, feeling that it sheltered her from the world outside, never wanting to leave it.

The sun was shining. She could see it slanting in through the white-curtained windows, making a pattern on the bare walls, but there seemed no warmth in it. She felt cold—cold right through.

What was she to do? Go back to England, to face her father? It was unthinkable. She couldn't bear the prospect of it.

Memories of the previous day returned to her. She remembered the nervous young man and the kindly doctor who had administered the draught. But now she was awake again, and the pain was as bad as ever. Did he have another draught, and another and another, she wondered? Was there a medicine in existence that could possibly take this agony away? What was she to do? Of what use was she now to anyone?

She could see a movement in the room outside the net and a nurse was there with an African orderly beside her, who untucked the net and deftly twisted it into a neat coil, tying it into a knot where for a moment it swung above her head. There was breakfast—fruit and toast and coffee. She saw the pinky-gold paw-paw oozing moisture and despised herself for the twist of hunger she could feel. It was wrong that she should have an appetite for food when Edward was dead.

"How are you this morning, dear?" the nurse asked. She had a pale, kind, long face like a sad horse, Kate thought. She considered her reply lengthily, and when she spoke her voice was polite and neutral.

"Quite well, thank you."

The nurse smiled mournfully, revealing two long, sad teeth.

Sun streamed through the window and the singing of the women seemed to reach a climax.

"They love to sing," the nurse said.

Meaninglessly, Kate nodded, her mouth full of paw-paw. What did she care if they sang or if they were silent? She was untouched by them. She wished the well-meaning nurse would go away, but she appeared to think it necessary to make conversation.

"It's nice to see the sun," the woman said. "You'd hardly believe it, but we've had quite a lot of dull weather recently. You get that, in July and August. Next month is more settled."

Why wouldn't she stop? Didn't she realise that it hurt to think of a shining new morning just beginning, while somewhere, miles away, Edward lay sightless?

Her thoughts veered away from him, fastening on another name which no one had so far mentioned. Christy Brennan, Edward's guide and

33

mentor. Where was he when this accident happened?

Before she could pursue this thought, Meg was in the room and they clung together.

"We want you to come to the farm with us," Meg said. "Hugh and I have been talking— you're in no fit state to decide what's best to do, whether you should go or stay. You need time to recover. Please come. Yes, really, we are both perfectly sure—both Hugh and I. We want you to come."

"I don't want to be a nuisance."

"You won't be, I promise. You can come and be peaceful, or you can come and work. There are a thousand things on a farm that you can do, or not do, just as you please. Just come, there's a dear. Think how delighted Colin will be to have his precious Kate to stay with him!"

Meg helped her to dress and gather her things together. A cart pulled by two oxen and already loaded with luggage and farm supplies stood outside the hospital, but a few minutes before they were ready to leave, a khaki-clad figure on a bicycle wobbled into sight up the rough driveway. It was the same government officer who had met the train, still looking ill-at-ease.

He leaned the bicycle against the steps which led to the verandah on which Kate and Meg were standing and, apparently striving hard for a show of normality, approached them, putting his hand

34

out to Kate with a jauntiness that he patently was far from feeling.

"Andrew Honeywell," he announced. "I did introduce myself yesterday, but I don't suppose you took it in. I just popped in to see how you are today, offer my services in arranging a passage home, that sort of thing."

"Miss Carswell is coming to stay with us at Kiambu," Meg said.

"Oh, that's good—most kind, Mrs. Lacey. At a time like this one needs one's friends."

"Where's Christy Brennan?" Kate asked suddenly.

"Brennan?" The question caught him by surprise and his pale blue eyes widened. "He's gone up country again as far as I know. He came back to report the accident and went off again immediately."

"Was he the only witness to the accident?"

A trace of wariness came into Honeywell's eyes.

"I believe so. Except for the gunbearer, of course. Why do you ask?"

"I was interested to establish that the report came from his unsupported word."

Honeywell shifted awkwardly.

"Miss Carswell, Mr. Brennan was Mr. Matcham's friend and there was no reason in the world to doubt him. His report was quite clear. They had been following a wounded lion who jumped Brennan from the cover of thick bush and in the resulting confusion the shot went wide

35

and hit Mr. Matcham instead of the lion. It was a tragedy, but nobody's fault. I'm quite sure that Mr. Brennan's version of events can be trusted."

"Except that he and Edward had quarrelled. I received a letter at Mombasa that told me that much. Perhaps they weren't such good friends any more."

There was a moment of silence, then Honeywell cleared his throat awkwardly. When he spoke, it was defensively, a barely perceptible edge of irritation in his voice.

"I don't think there can be any doubt about what happened. You're understandably upset, Miss Carswell, and you have my most sincere sympathy, but unfortunately these things happen in Africa."

"Some people might find that attitude very convenient."

Meg moved forward and took her arm.

"Come, Kate," she said gently. "Hugh is waiting with the cart and we really should be on our way. Give yourself a little time—"

"What kind of man is this Brennan?" Kate stood her ground, resisting the pressure to move. "Edward told me very little about him, except that he had an unpredictable temper."

Meg and Andrew Honeywell exchanged glances.

"There's no harm in the man," Meg said. "I'm sure you'll meet him soon enough. Leave it now, Kate. Mr. Honeywell knows where you will be

36

staying and if Brennan turns up again he can be told where to find you."

"I should be grateful if you would do that," Kate said.

"Come, dear, we must go." Meg increased the pressure on her arm. "We have a long journey ahead of us and still must collect Colin from the hotel. I left him with a friend, but I'm anxious to get back."

"Of course. I'm sorry. Forgive me." Kate nodded and smiled an empty smile towards Honeywell before yielding at last to Meg's touch and walking down the verandah steps.

3

KATE'S grief was like a dark pit in which she was isolated from the life that went on all around her. Each morning when she awoke it was there, waiting for her. Inside it, nothing had any reality except Edward's death, herself least of all. She felt strangely empty of emotion as if she had gone beyond the point of feeling anything.

"I wish she could let go," Meg said anxiously to Hugh.

"She's not the letting-go sort."

"I have to stand by and do *nothing*!"

"What can we do? We can only wait, and be here."

Meg knew he was right. She looked after Kate's creature comforts and waited for the time when she would come back to life. She found her one day standing before the house looking towards the distant hills, slow tears coursing down her cheeks.

"Oh, Kate, Kate!" said Meg, putting her arms around her. "How can I help you?"

Dumbly Kate shook her head.

"It's so beautiful," she said after a moment. "Do you know, I'd hardly noticed?"

Over to the left on the lower slopes of the farm

were the established coffee bushes, their leaves green and glossy, and beyond them were the infant seedlings still several years from coming into bearing. To the right, the land rose towards thickly wooded slopes which were the haunt of leopard and lion and a thousand smaller creatures.

In the far distance purple mountains were smudged against the sky; so much sky, so many clouds. It was the clouds that gave the farm its name—Mawingo Farm.

"So beautiful," Kate said again. "Oh Meg, what am I to do? What's to become of me now?"

"There's no need to make decisions yet."

"You've been so kind, you and Hugh."

"If only we could do more! We do understand how you feel, Kate."

"No one can understand," Kate said, the words tight with pain. "It's like—like being lost in a dark place where no one can come near and there's nothing but emptiness."

She was crying again and this time Meg made no comment but allowed the tears to flow without question, feeling that only they could ease the pain of Kate's loss.

In some way they did seem to presage her slow return to life. There came a time when she found herself appreciating the clarity of the air and the colours of the flowers that rioted over the posts of the verandah, and even laughing at Colin's antics. In fact it was Colin who tugged her back to life more than anyone else. He made no allowances for her grief and could not comprehend why she should be other than the interesting and amusing companion she had been on board ship. She stopped Meg from curtailing the demands he made on her.

"He's good for me," she said.

She had been at Mawingo farm for almost three months when Hugh brought a small packet back from the Post Office for her. She turned it over in her hands curiously.

"Who on earth can this be from? It has a Nairobi postmark, but it's not Louise's writing—"

"May I suggest you open it?" Meg said.

The envelope contained banknotes—quite a thick wad of them, stained and tattered, wrapped around with a brief letter.

"Dear Miss Carswell," it ran. "All Edward's effects have been returned to his mother in England. This is money which was owing to him after our last safari and I know he would want you to have it. I send it to you with my sincere sympathy."

Kate raised her eyes from the page.

"It's signed 'Christy Brennan'. What do you make of that, Meg?"

Meg shrugged.

"What is there to make of it? It seems straightforward enough."

"Perhaps it's conscience money."

40

"Oh, Kate! You're not still thinking Christy might have had a hand in Edward's death?"

"I wish I knew why he and Edward quarrelled. Edward wasn't at all a quarrelsome sort of person. Meg, you've met him, haven't you—this Christy Brennan? What is he really like? Am I being foolish?"

Meg hesitated for a moment.

"I—think so," she said slowly. "Christy is something of an enigma, I admit, but not a malevolent one. He can be brusque and outspoken and he doesn't suffer fools gladly, but for all that he is likeable."

Later she recounted the conversation to Hugh when they were in their reed-lined bedroom. Hugh was already in bed, watching her brush her long golden hair by lamplight in front of a mirror.

"I feel I didn't tell the whole truth," she said. "There is a—a kind of violence about him, isn't there? Yet it seems pointless to raise all sorts of suspicions when there's no basis for them."

"And nothing can be proved, one way or the other."

Meg turned from the dressing table and looked towards her husband.

"That sounds as if you think Kate could be right about him."

"Brennan's a complex character," Hugh said after a moment. "On the whole I think I like and trust him, even though it amuses me to see him swaggering down Government Road decked about with his bullet loops and his hat on the back of his head. I think it amuses him, too. He doesn't take himself too seriously. Kate's right about his temper, though. I once saw him in a fight at the Norfolk that made the place look like the final scene in *Hamlet*. I always thought Edward Matcham an unlikely partner for him— not that I met the chap more than once, I have to confess."

"Why was he an unlikely partner?"

Hugh shrugged.

"Perhaps Matcham had qualities that were hidden from me. He seemed—oh, how can I express it?—a lightweight. A great deal of surface charm, but not the sort of man one would choose to rely on."

"Kate says he was an excellent shot."

"That explains the partnership, I suppose."

"She adored him. Would they have been happy, Hugh?"

"Who can tell? One thing I'm sure of—Kate is worth a dozen Edward Matchams. Meg, have you ever known anyone go *at* things like Kate? It's almost as if now she's decided to start living again, she's determined to make up for lost time. She rides really well now. She simply refused to be beaten by that obstinate little pony and this afternoon I heard her conversing in very creditable Swahili with Njuguna."

Hugh paused and raised his head to look at his wife.

"Woman, come to bed! Do you propose to sit there all night?"

"I'm coming." But still Meg stared blindly into the mirror. "I don't quite know why," she said, "but for some reason I dislike the idea of Kate harbouring suspicious thoughts of Christy Brennan."

Hugh laughed softly.

"I've always heard he's considered irresistible to women. Is it the scar or all that Irish blarney?"

Smiling, Meg rose and came towards the bed, the lamp in her hand.

"It's a good thing I'm happily married," she said.

Lying sleepless in her bed at the other end of the house, Kate could hear the sound of their conversation and their soft laughter, even though their words were indistinguishable. There were other noises in the night—the screeching of a tree hyrax from the darkness outside and the constant chorus of crickets. Nearer at hand something rustled in the thatch above her head.

So much life going on, she thought. But what of me? Somehow I must claw myself back into the mainstream of it all. But how? Where? Shall I use Edward's money to return home?

All her instincts shrieked out against it. She thought of her father—of the joyless, self-congratulatory welcome she would receive from

43

him if she went trailing back. Surely there was something she could do here?

Meg urged her to stay. She liked her company and valued her help with Colin and the garden. She had become more than useful, too, at the daily clinic on the back verandah at which farm workers presented themselves with burns and sores and fevers.

"If I really were going to stay here," Kate said one morning when they were clearing up after finishing with the last patient, a small boy who had been badly burnt in a hut fire, "I should learn Kikuyu. Most of them still have to struggle with Swahili, don't they?"

Meg shot her an amused glance.

"You could learn Kikuyu in the morning and Masai in the afternoon," she said.

"Mock me if you must," Kate replied with assumed dignity. "One of these days I'll surprise you."

"I'm fully aware that anything you set your mind to, you usually carry out."

Kate sighed.

"My mind is something I should prefer not to discuss. It keeps coming to a different conclusion several times a day."

"Stay," Meg said, knowing that it was her future Kate was referring to. "You could become a governess here just as well as in England."

"Perhaps."

As October drew to an end, Hugh became

worried about the non-appearance of the short rains. Each evening the clouds gathered and threatened, but there was no rain and the Laceys feared for their coffee bushes.

One night Kate woke to a strange sound, quite unlike anything she had heard before. A sibilant rattling filled the air and for a moment she felt quite sure that the awaited rain had at last begun; but then she realised that her first impression was wrong. There was no splash or whisper of life-giving water, but rather a dry and menacing rustle. She lit her lamp, thrust her feet into slippers and hastily tied her dressing gown, growing more anxious as she became aware of a dog's frantic whines.

She opened her door which led to the small sitting room to find Hugh on the opposite side of it, Meg close beside him.

"Stay where you are," he shouted. "It's *siafu*."

He lifted the lamp on to a high bracket and Kate could see the thick black rope which lay across the floor—a rope which writhed, a rope totally composed of ants.

Dilly, the labrador, slept by the fire with her three new puppies. Now she stood whimpering in agony as the ants swarmed over her and already the pups lay limp and dead beyond anyone's help.

Hugh rushed across the room and grabbed Dilly, shouting for Meg to fetch Njuguna. The pups were a lost cause but with prompt action the mother might be saved.

45

"That's Africa for you," Meg said the following morning.

The ants had passed through the house and moved on. There was no way to stop them, no method of diverting them, and, while Meg and Hugh both mourned the loss of the puppies, they were resigned and philosophical. It had happened before, quite recently, only then it had been a clutch of valuable baby chicks that was destroyed; no doubt it would happen again.

Kate found it hard to accept. In a way it seemed to her that here was a parallel to Edward's death; everyone accepted it calmly and unquestioningly, attributing it entirely to the unavoidable dangers posed by the country. They shrugged and said, "That's Africa for you." The waters of Africa have closed over their heads, she thought sadly —Edward and the puppies alike.

The unexpected arrival of John and Olivia Rowley who called in at tea-time the following day caused a pleasant diversion. They were close neighbours who lived a mere five miles away across the valley. Olivia was a gossipy, amiable woman who liked nothing better than to arrange her friends' lives for them and it soon became clear that she proposed to do some arranging for Kate's benefit.

"My dear, you're just the person I wanted to see," she said, taking the chair next to her. "We were in Nairobi yesterday, and who should I run in to but Mrs. Druce. You know her, don't you,

46

Meg? She's the dragon who runs the little school for girls on the Hill. There are only a handful of pupils. People are so utterly stupid about the climate, don't you agree? So many still insist it's unhealthy for children, though I've never seen a bonnier child than your Colin—"

"You were speaking of the school?" prompted Meg gently, seeing Kate's expectant eyes fixed on Olivia.

"We fell into conversation over tea and it seems that she is quite desperate because she has an old mother in South Africa—my dear, just imagine how ancient *she* must be!—and she wants to visit her. But if she does, she'll have to close the school. So *I* said that I knew the very person who could take it over for her as a sort of locum and she practically fell on my neck!"

"You mean I could do it?" Kate asked. "I'm not qualified, you know."

"I doubt very much that Mrs. Druce is. Her husband was a Railway man but he died a year or two back and she stayed on to run this school in her house. The Hill Academy, it's called—such a grand name for half a dozen girls in a back room! What do you think, Kate? She seemed delighted to hear of you and I promised I would get you to write to her."

"It sounds interesting." Kate's eyes were bright. "If you think I'd be capable of it."

"Of *course* you would!" Olivia said, not having had more than a few minutes' conversation with

Kate in her entire life. "And I told Mrs. Druce so. She really was most awfully pleased. She was telling me how she hopes to enlarge the school eventually, perhaps even take in boarders whose homes are up country, so probably once your foot was in the door, Kate, she'd want it to stay there. *And* she's getting on in years. It won't be too long before she retires altogether and then Kate would be the headmistress. Just imagine! You'd have to move to new premises, of course—"

"Olivia, what a perfect farmer's wife you make," Hugh said, laughing. "You really are the supreme optimist! Here you have Kate as headmistress of a large and flourishing girls' school before she's even set foot inside the door."

"Or met the present incumbent," said Kate.

"Oh, there won't be the least bit of a problem, I'm sure. Mrs. Druce was positively desperate when she spoke to me. I'm sure she'd simply *jump* at Kate." Olivia looked around with a puzzled expression. "I can't see what's so funny in that. Seriously, Kate—what do you think? You will write to Mrs. Druce, won't you? I assured her that you would. I said we could take you in to meet her the very next time we go, which John tells me will most likely be next week because the plough we were hoping to pick up today hadn't arrived."

"It's certainly worth looking into," Kate said cautiously.

She rode with Hugh the following morning to

the Post Office. Hugh was in good spirits for at last there had been a shower of rain and all the signs led him to think there was more to come.

Their way led through a forest track where raindrops glinted like diamonds on spiders' webs. The world looked bright and new-washed and Kate found balm for her soul in the beauty of the day. They passed through a glade bright with butterflies where a small bushbuck froze at the sight of them, his velvet nose quivering before he leapt off into the undergrowth with high, springing bounds.

Overhead, monkeys crashed unseen through the trees, making their strange, explosive, smacking sound, and suddenly Kate knew with certainty that in spite of everything that had happened to her—in spite of the blackness of the pit and the grief that had numbed her for so long —it was here, in Africa, that she wanted to stay.

There were bird songs in the forest all about them, but one made itself heard more clearly than most—five descending, liquid notes, repeated in the same sequence time after time. She turned in the saddle and asked Hugh the name of it.

"It's a rainbird," he said. "At least, that's what everyone calls it. In fact it's a type of bulbul, I believe."

"It sounds very sad. Birdsong in a minor key."

"Not at all." The path widened a little and he rode forward to come alongside her. "Rain isn't sad in Africa. It's a blessing that we long for.

49

Whenever I hear the rainbird I know that seedtime and harvest isn't going to vanish from my particular patch of earth. You should regard it as a message of hope."

"A sign that life goes on?"

He smiled at her.

"As it will for you, Kate."

"I know," she said on a sigh. "Part of me knows it, anyway."

"You're young—twenty-four, isn't it? You have two thirds of your life yet to live. You'll meet someone else you can love. You won't mourn for ever, believe me."

Kate said nothing and for a few moments they rode in silence.

"You know, I don't think you're right, Hugh," she said at last. "Edward was everything to me —all the love and fun and colour I'd ever known. I don't think I shall ever feel for anyone else what I felt for him. I don't *want* to feel it! I'd rather be self-sufficient, not dependent on anyone else."

"We're all dependent on someone else! You'll love again, and you'll be loved, too. With your looks—"

"My *looks*?" Kate turned and looked at him, laughing with genuine amusement. "I've never thought a lot of them. Next to Meg I feel like a common daisy compared to a whole spray of orchids. No—tea-roses, I think. Orchids are too cold."

"Meg is—Meg," Hugh agreed. "Admittedly

50

incomparable, at least to me. But you can be beautiful too, Kate, given happiness and animation. I've seen it recently."

"Oh, Hugh! Such exaggeration!"

But she smiled nevertheless, momentarily forgetting the drift of their conversation.

"I know you're strong and self-reliant," Hugh went on, drawing her back to it. "But you're a warm and affectionate woman—"

"Hugh, everyone laughed when Olivia talked about how one day I would be the headmistress of the school, but don't laugh at me now, I beg you. I can't think of one thing I should like more in life." She clenched her hand and laid it on her heart, unconscious that it was the same gesture she had used years before when describing her love of teaching to her father. "There is a feeling *here* that says this is what I was meant to do. I've been told I'm a born teacher, and I believe it. I don't think any man will come between me and this ambition now that Edward has gone."

"I see."

"You don't approve?"

"I think it a pity—but you have to follow your own destiny."

She smiled at him gratefully.

"I can never thank you and Meg enough," she said. "You've been wonderful friends to me."

"Just be happy."

51

The path narrowed and Hugh fell behind her again as they both rode on in silence, lost in their own thoughts.

4

THE hunter stood on the edge of the forest in the foothills of the great, snow-capped, twin-peaked mountain which the Kikuyu knew as the home of the god Ngai.

It was the hour before sunset when every colour and shape seemed to be intensified in the clear air. Each leaf, each blade of grass had assumed a great importance in its own right, and there was a stillness abroad as if the spirits of the night were taking time to admire the perfections of nature before blanketing them with darkness.

They had camped the previous night, he and two peers of the realm, on the open, inhospitable heathlands which, at eleven thousand feet, had been so icy cold that none of the party had slept very much. They had risen before dawn and slithered downwards into the belt of bamboos where the trees rose grandly above them like the nave of some great cathedral, but where underneath the fallen branches clogged their path. Piles of steaming elephant dung had indicated that the huge animals were very near. At times it was possible to hear the rumbling noise that they made, but they had not gone in search of the beasts for they had already shot as much as their licence allowed. The safari was over.

They had done well, those noble gentlemen. It had been physically demanding, as all foot safaris were, but they had not complained. Hats off to the playing fields of Eton, Christy Brennan said dryly to himself. Now they were content to sit on their folding canvas chairs before the blazing fire, glasses of whisky in their hands, to relive the best moments of the day. He had become superfluous.

He stood looking down on the cluster of round, thatched-roofed huts which he could see below him. His expression was dark and brooding, his hands thrust deep into the pockets of his stained khaki trousers. Yet, although there were deep lines etched from his strong, straight nose to the line of his mouth, his face bore a look of cynical amusement, a look caused by the way a livid scar bisected his left eyebrow, giving it a permanently quizzical lift.

He was not amused. He was thinking of Edward Matcham.

What a fool the man had been—what a weak, irresponsible, fool. One moment he had sworn that it was the safari he loved and that no girl existed who could make him give it up, and the next he would be wallowing in sentimental tears over a letter from the poor deluded female he had left behind him.

He'd been an amusing companion, one had to admit that. He was good with the clients and able to make pleasant conversation. All things to all men, Christy thought—and women, too. But criminally weak.

A man was coming up the steep path from the village and Christy straightened.

" *Jambo*," he said.

" *Jambo, bwana. Habari?*"

"*Mzuri. Habari yako?*"

The civilities had to be observed. The routine questions had to be asked and answered, and Christy curbed his impatience until they were finished.

At length he was free to reach the essence of the conversation.

"Is the girl still in the village?" he asked.

"No, *bwana*. She ran away."

"Where has she gone?"

"Nobody knows, but it is thought that she made for the town. The moon has come and gone twice since she left, but no one has heard news of her."

"Her father has not pursued her?"

"She is dead to him."

"And you? She is your sister!"

The man's eyes flickered and focussed on something beyond the hunter.

"*Mimi vili vili,*" he said. "To me, also. The day it happened our mother found a crack in her cooking pot. Three of my father's goats sickened and died. There is a *thahu* on Wambui. My own wife is with child. It is right that Wambui should leave the village."

55

Christy's jaw clenched and his eyes blazed.

"She will become a prostitute," he said. "Because you turned her from home."

"*Hapana*. She saw the *thahu*. Spirits came to her and told her to be gone."

Angrily, Christy swung away from him, fists clenched inside his pockets. Holy Mother, he thought—I could kill him, so I could.

"*Kwenda*," he shouted over his shoulder. "Get away from me."

"*Bwana*, what of the *askaris*?" the man asked.

"The police? They are not concerned with this. God help me, I told them it was an accident."

The two men looked into each other's eyes. The African's were flat, brown, bloodshot from the smoke that filled his hut day and night. Christy's were a light grey, so clear that he had been given the name *Bwana Macho Maji*, the *bwana* with eyes of water. To the man standing before him they seemed as cold as the snow that covered God's mountain, as menacing as the flash of a spear held in the hand of a Masai warrior.

Uncertainly, he turned to leave, feeling Brennan's gaze like chips of ice between his shoulder blades. It would, he thought, be prudent to sacrifice a goat.

It was a physical effort for Christy Brennan to hold his anger in check as standing on the hillside he watched the man descend towards the village. Then, suddenly, his anger evaporated, changing instead to the bitterness of self reproach. The lines in his face deepened as he looked down towards the cluster of huts.

"And am I not to blame? Father, bless me for I have sinned."

The words sprang to his mind unbidden and impatiently he turned to stride towards the camp. Damn it to hell, he thought savagely, am I never to outgrow this accursed Catholic conscience? The guilt's not mine. I won't accept it.

"Halloo—Brennan!"

From afar he saw the younger of his clients stand up, waving a bottle over his head. A drink: that was what he needed. He quickened his long-legged stride.

Kate Carswell erupted into the lives of the girls of the Hill Academy, charged with enthusiasm for a return to what she considered her natural element. Suddenly mothers found that their daughters were happily tripping off to school with every appearance of delight instead of dragging themselves there as a matter of duty.

Mrs. Druce had been a stickler for discipline and deportment, for learning by rote and repeating-after-me. Her formidable presence filled the classroom with an atmosphere of terror-stricken foreboding.

Things were different with Kate. She embarked on each day's teaching as if it were a voyage of discovery. She could be as severe as the next teacher about talking or giggling in class, as one or two rash spirits found out to their cost, and any thoughts that because of her youth liberties might be taken were soon dispelled. But severity was hardly ever needed. Soon the girls were vying to please her, enjoying this change from the old regime with delighted incredulity.

Geography lessons spilled over into history lessons and sometimes developed into political discussions. Literature sprang into life and laughter was commonplace. Two or three of the girls fell desperately in love with her, and it became the fashion to have tendrils of hair falling on to the forehead, because that was the way Miss Carswell wore hers. Mothers were pestered for braid-trimmed boleros, for that was what Miss Carswell wore.

Parents were impressed, and as for Kate, her return to the occupation she loved accelerated her rehabilitation in a way nothing else could have done.

The house—rectangular, raised on stilts, surrounded by a verandah and roofed in corrugated iron—belonged to the Railway Company, to whom Mrs. Druce paid rent. It suited the Railway to let her continue to live there, just as she had done while her husband was alive, for now there was a cluster of houses on the Hill and many of the newer employees had wives and families, unlike in previous years when the Protectorate had catered for lone men, pitting strength and spirit against an inhospitable continent. To be able to say that a school was available represented a considerable inducement to many, however limited the education it offered.

The bungalow seemed enormous and very lonely after the comradeship of the farm, especially in the evening after the girls had gone. Kate thanked heaven that she always had a good deal of preparation to do and that she was surrounded by neighbours who were disposed to be friendly. There was a great deal of social life —a constant round of dinner parties and other gatherings to which she was invited as a matter of course.

Even so, she still kept the photograph of Edward by her bed and looked lovingly at his handsome features each night before she slept, even talking to him sometimes in a way that, had she been entirely honest, she would have admitted was impossible during his lifetime. He had never been the most attentive of listeners and had never understood the fascination her job held for her. He had been easily bored by talk of it and she had quickly learned to notice the tell-tale signs and to steer her conversation into other channels. But now he had become the best listener in the world.

By the time Kate took over the school the short rains were over and so, indeed, was Christmas. This was the hot time of the year, with the start of the day bringing a pale blue sky that grew steadily deeper in colour until at noon it was hard and bright, making the red of the hibiscus flowers and the canna lilies almost painful to the eye. In the evenings it softened again so that the pink, feathery tips of the gum trees were etched against an expanse of palest lemon as the sun set over the hills that Kate could see to the west across the plain.

She was not far from town. She bought a bicycle and regularly braved the pot-holed, unmade roads to ride to the shops—shops that seemed to increase in number almost daily. Edward had been right about that. Government Road now had only a handful of vacant plots along its frontage and could boast a hardware store, a cornchandler's, a milliner's and a dress-maker's. There were hotels, too: the Norfolk, the Stanley, a Temperance Hotel, and bang in the middle of Government Road an establishment known as Millie's, which was a boarding house catering for the dozens of single men who passed through the town. Millie, people said, was no better than she should be, but she had become an integral part of Nairobi and was a familiar figure about the town, driving a buggy painted in scarlet and yellow, her comfortable figure clad in frills and flounces, her hair an improbable shade of auburn.

Trees had been planted opposite the Norfolk. No one could call the town beautiful, but the authorities were doing their best with the material at their disposal. There was a Club a little further out where cricket was played and pink gins consumed, and a Railway Institute for public meetings and amateur stage shows. Rickshaws plied for hire. Everyone knew everyone else and was aware precisely who was in love with whom and if anything was likely to come of it.

Women were in such a minority that one would have had to be plain indeed not to excite a romantic interest in the bosom of one of the lone, frustrated men who had come seeking their fortune. Kate had hardly set foot in the town before she was besieged with admirers. She smiled and was friendly, in a sisterly sort of way. Not one of them so much as penetrated her protective outer layer.

The dust was choking and all-pervasive in town, but less troublesome on the Hill. Insects, Kate found, were more of an annoyance. She hated the thick-bodied sausage flies that blundered into the lamps at night, and learned to walk with her toes curled up to avoid the jiggers that burrowed under the skin and laid their eggs there.

She never could get used to sharing the room with a number of transparent lizards who lived high up on the walls and darted after the flies and mosquitoes that came within their orbit, even though she appreciated the service they performed. Perhaps the spiders were even worse. There was one which appeared nightly in the corner of her bedroom—long-legged, hairy, inimical. She was glad of the net which protected her from more than mosquitoes.

To go out to the long-drop in the garden once darkness had fallen was something that took courage and an urgent necessity. The rustlings and scrabblings in the little outhouse seemed to shout aloud the presence of unimaginable dangers. In spite of which, she was surprised once or twice by the realisation of how natural this life had become to her and how much she was enjoying it.

School finished early on a Friday and one hot afternoon in February, Kate took the opportunity to ride into town to buy buttons and thread. And while she was so close, she decided to call into Ronnie Hudson's store to see if anything new and exciting had come into stock. It behoved one to keep an eye on the shops even when one was not actually in need of anything, otherwise it was all too easy to find that some longed-for luxury had arrived one day and been sold out by the next.

There was little business being done at that time of day. Most housewives went to town in the early morning, houseboys trailing behind to carry their *kikapus*, and at this hour the only other occupant of Ronnie's shop was a tall, dust-stained figure in khaki trousers and gaiters of buffalo hide, a leather waistcoat and a slouch hat, set at a rakish angle. A blue scarf was knotted about his throat and he was liberally decorated with guns and bullet loops.

The archetypal White Hunter, Kate thought—successor to Allan Quatermain and determined to outdo him if at all possible. Would Edward have looked like that? She smiled a little at the thought, turning away to survey Ronnie's rather poorly stocked shelves as she waited for him to finish serving his colourful customer.

The transaction was quickly finished and the man turned to stride out of the store, giving Kate an appraising glance as he left. She affected not to notice. There were too many men giving too many appraising glances in this town and she had quickly learned that indifference was the only defence.

Ronnie laughed at her, his brown eyes knowing, white teeth gleaming under a neatly clipped moustache.

"Don't pretend you didn't notice him. All women do." The voice was sly, hinting at a familiarity which Kate had no wish to acknowledge.

"Really?"

Kate was aware that her tone was frosty and forced herself to smile in a more friendly manner. This was, after all, Louise's husband, and Louise was a close friend. It was a disappointment that, try as she might, she could not like Ronnie Hudson. Even his name annoyed her. Ronnie was a name for a small boy—an affectionate diminutive which should surely only be applied to someone for whom one felt some kind of fondness. She would so much rather have been able to call him Ronald.

She approached the counter with a can of meat in her hand. Ronnie seemed in no hurry to serve her and instead walked round to her side of the counter, leaning against it with his arms folded, looking at her through narrowed eyes.

"You know who that was, don't you?"

"Should I?"

"Most people do. That was Christy Brennan. I should have introduced you, shouldn't I? I'd forgotten for the moment that he was your late fiancé's partner."

Kate shook her head.

"No," she said. "I don't think I want to speak to him now. Not here, like this, at any rate."

Ronnie was watching her, his hot little eyes alight with speculation.

"It's sometimes best to forget the past."

"I'm sure you're right."

"No one can mourn for ever."

"Perhaps not. Ronnie, I'll take two of these—"

"Life goes on." He leaned towards her. "I think about you a lot, Kate, all alone in that house with only those silly girls for company. It's all wrong, you know. It's time you noticed there are other men in the world."

Kate frowned at him.

"Men like Christy Brennan?"

Ronnie moved a little closer.

"I wasn't thinking of him. I was thinking of me."

"You?" Kate stared at him, totally bewildered.

"You know what you remind me of? You're a Sleeping Beauty, waiting for the kiss of the prince to wake you up." His hand fastened on her arm, pulling her close to him. "You're not going to wait for ever, are you? Don't you know that I'm here, whenever you want me?"

She looked at him in open-mouthed amazement before pulling sharply away from him.

"You must have taken leave of your senses!"

"I've seen you looking at me—"

"Only in your imagination. I think I'll forget the tins of meat, thank you." She made for the door, but stopped and turned before reaching it, hating the sly smile that was still on his lips, hating the thought of this man coming anywhere near her. "I'll forget this ever happened and I suggest you do the same. Louise is one of my dearest friends. Don't ever, *ever* speak to me like that again."

His smile grew a little broader, but it was not one which suggested amusement. He said nothing in reply but watched her go in silence, still leaning indolently against the counter. "Sanctimonious little bitch," he said softly to himself when she had gone.

Poor Louise, Kate thought, as she went out

into Government Road. Was he like that with everyone?

And then she forgot Ronnie for her next call was at the Post Office where the flag flying from the roof indicated that the mail had arrived. There was a letter for her with a South African stamp.

Her heart sank. Mrs. Druce wrote frequently, seemingly totally unable to allow the school to pass completely from her hands, and every time Kate received a letter from her she realised afresh how empty was her dream of being able to stay on at the school once its rightful headmistress returned. Her methods and outlook were as different from Mrs. Druce's as chalk from cheese.

She saved the letter until she was sitting down to tea on her verandah. Seconds later, all thought of tea forgotten, she was running down to Louise's house with the letter in her hand, bursting in on her friend almost incoherent with excitement.

"Guess what, guess what," she cried. "Louise, she doesn't want to come back at all! Isn't that the most marvellous thing?"

"Who? What? Sit down, for mercy's sake, Kate! What's happened."

"It's Mrs. Druce. She's written to say she's getting—getting *married*, can you believe it?— and do I want to buy the goodwill of the school plus all the equipment! *Do* I? Oh Louise, I'm so absolutely thrilled! She can't surely charge very

66

much for those tables and chairs and out-of-date books."

"Married!" It was this aspect of Kate's news that had apparently impressed Louise most. "Never say that the age of miracles is past, Kate."

"She remarks that the gentleman in question is 'not in the first flush of youth but is one of nature's gentlemen, well established in a comfortable situation', which I take to mean that he is rather old and of little education or breeding but well provided with this world's goods. Whoever he is, I love him myself, to the very brink of adoration. The school is *mine*, Louise—can you believe it? I only hope I can afford to pay what she wants."

"You have a little money, haven't you?"

"Only very little."

"And there's always the bank. Everyone in this entire country lives on an overdraft, Ronnie says. We certainly do."

"I'm determined to get hold of it somehow. I'm dining with the Bowdens tomorrow—if I have a chance I'll talk to Mr. Bowden."

Even Kate, who was inclined to take a jaundiced view of her own appearance, realised that she was looking well next evening. Excitement had brightened her eyes and brought a creamy flush to her cheeks. She felt light—almost weightless, as if she floated on air, which perhaps was fortunate as after dinner the entire party was

67

to proceed to the Railway Institute where a gala ball was to be held.

Mr. and Mrs. Walter Bowden were delighted with the way she had discovered talents in their daughter, Clara, which neither of them had suspected, and they had from the first taken Kate under their wing, asking her frequently to join their parties for numerous social events. Mr. Bowden seemed the obvious person to turn to for advice on financial matters, since he was the Chief Accountant of the Railway Company.

A trap was sent round to transport her the short distance to the Bowdens' bungalow and she could tell from the sound of voices as she climbed down from it that at least some of the other guests had arrived. She wondered what single man would have been invited for the specific purpose of squiring her, and ardently hoped that it was someone with a gift for conversation. She guessed that it might be Andrew Honeywell, the young government officer who had been given the unenviable task of breaking the news of Edward's death to her. He had seemed very attentive to her lately, in a deferential way, and was quite friendly with the Bowdens.

The last person she expected to see was Christy Brennan. The day before he had looked like a wild man, dust-stained and dirty. Yet here he was in white tie and tails, his hair a little ragged perhaps and hanging far too low upon his collar, but for all that a distinguished figure—even a dominating one, for he towered above the other men and seemed the focus of attention among men and women alike.

The strange, light eyes sharpened as she was introduced, but he gave no hint that he had heard her name before, which Kate found disconcerting. He bowed over her hand, not smiling. Or was that a smile? It was hard to tell, his face seemed so full of odd planes and lines and contradictions.

At close range he was obviously younger than the impression she had gained from Edward's letters, no more than twenty-eight or nine: only a few years older than Edward himself, in fact. Yet Edward had deferred to him and it was not hard to see why. There was an unmistakable air of authority about him, the scar which bisected one eyebrow giving him a look of sardonic amusement.

"Such a pleasure to meet you, Mr. Brennan." Kate's voice was composed enough, but beneath the surface she felt nervous now that she was face to face with the man at last. "Edward told me so much about you in his letters."

"Ah, Edward," he said obscurely. "Sure, wasn't that the most terrible tragedy to befall a man? I thought it likely you would have left for England by this time."

How convenient that would have been for you, Mr. Brennan, Kate thought drily. All loose ends would have been neatly tidied away. Was that the reason for sending the money?

They parted to sit on opposite sides of the room and Kate quickly became engaged in conversation with Mrs. McTavish, a thin, sandy-haired lady with an over-genteel Edinburgh accent whose daughter was about to join the Hill Academy. They were soon joined by Mr. Bowden who announced immediately that he, too, had received a letter from Mrs. Druce and would do all he could to facilitate such financial arrangements as might be necessary to enable Kate to take over the school.

"For the Railway Company has reason to be grateful to you, my dear," he said. "As indeed we all have. Do you hear the good news, everyone? It seems that Miss Carswell is a permanent fixture at the Hill Academy."

It was gratifying that this announcement was greeted with universal pleasure and cries of congratulation.

Christy was placed next to her at dinner.

"I have to thank you for sending me the money," Kate said under cover of the general conversation.

"And why wouldn't I, at all? Wasn't it Edward's money, earned fair and square? He'd not have wanted me to hold on to it."

A man with a face like that shouldn't speak with a voice that sounds like a caress, Kate thought.

70

"You seem the most popular lady in town," he went on after a short pause. "I must confess you are not at all as I expected."

"Oh?"

"I saw the photograph Edward carried. Sure, the face of it would have decorated a chocolate box very nicely, with never a hint to be seen of the determined chin and the chill in those pretty blue eyes."

"My appearance is hardly your concern," Kate said stiffly.

Christy sucked in his cheeks and glinted a smile towards her as if her hostility amused him. Kate drew a deep breath, determined to seize an opportunity which might not occur again.

"Mr. Brennan, why did you and Edward quarrel?"

"I see." He looked at her measuringly, still smiling faintly. "So that's the way of it, is it? How would you be knowing about that?"

"Edward wrote to me. There was a letter waiting for me at Mombasa."

"Well, didn't he give the reason for it?"

"Edward was a gentleman who wouldn't want to blacken the name of a man he had regarded as a friend. He merely said that the friendship was over, which was a circumstance that saddened him."

"Well now, it would do, wouldn't it?"

It was impossible to know if he was laughing at her. She had never known such a contradictory

71

set of features. He continued his meal with every evidence of enjoyment, saying nothing. Then he turned to her.

"Miss Carswell," he said. "Edward Matcham and I were two very different people and we argued frequently. An Englishman and an Irishman closeted together, night after night— sure, we argued. He made me angry with his upperclass superiority; I made him angry with my lack of respect for established ways. Even so, we shared almost two years' companionship and got along reasonably well. Now why in the world would you be looking at me as if I was something the cat wouldn't want to drag in? Would you be thinking I was glad when he died?" He looked at her, not smiling now, his voice low and angry, audible only to her.

"It had occurred to me." Kate's voice was equally soft. "The report was, after all, your unsupported word."

His eyes seemed to bore into her and she turned away from him, suddenly afraid that she had gone too far. There was a violence about the man. She could sense an ungovernable fury that seemed about to explode.

Unexpectedly, he laughed.

"Holy Mother," he said softly. "I've been called a lot of things in my time, but never a murderer." He pronounced it 'murtherer' and on his lips the word sounded faintly comical.

"I hope in your school you take full advantage

of the opportunities offered for the study of Natural Science," said the gentleman on her other side. Kate turned to him with relief, finding that he was an authority on butterflies, the study of which was his main interest in life. Gratefully she listened as he dwelt on the many varieties to be found in the area, happy that he demanded nothing of her but silent attention.

When at last he turned to reply to a remark from his other neighbour she heard Christy's voice in her ear once more.

"You must believe whatever you choose," he murmured. "It's not in me to protest my innocence."

She looked at him and he returned the look, an enigmatic expression on his face.

Damn the man, she thought. I'm no further forward. He could be guilty of the darkest crimes or innocent as a babe.

"Miss Carswell." A voice from across the table claimed her attention. "Will you be making changes when control of the school passes to your hands?"

It was Mr. McTavish speaking. Kate hesitated for a moment, her thoughts in some confusion.

"I'd like to expand, of course," she said. "But so far I've had no time to make plans. Firstly I want to find someone to teach art and music; I'm sadly deficient in those skills myself."

"You've made history and literature come alive for our Clara," Mr. Bowden beamed.

"They are my favourite subjects, I admit. One thing has been bothering me, though once more I haven't had time to think it out clearly." She frowned as she spoke as if pursuing something that was hard to define. "I can't feel happy that we ignore the culture of the country we're living in."

"Culture?" Mrs. McTavish looked bewildered. "There's no culture here. No *native* culture, that is, though I must confess I have seldom seen a more *pairrfect* production of *Iolanthe* than that performed by the Railway Dramatic Society last month."

There were murmurs of agreement round the table.

"The Kikuyu do have a great many interesting traditions," Kate said diffidently.

The butterfly expert turned to look at her in amazement.

"Most of which are best left in obscurity, my dear young lady. It's they who must learn our ways."

"Tell us more of what you have in mind, Miss Carswell," Christy said. His voice was deceptively innocent, smooth as cream, and Kate stepped into the trap.

"It seems wrong to me that we should superimpose our mode of life on the natives without making an attempt to understand their very deeply held beliefs. Oh, I don't mean we have to emulate them— just try to understand

74

them. I've had long conversations with my houseboy—"

"He speaks English?" Christy's expression was one of surprise.

"I've become fairly proficient in Swahili and I'm struggling with Kikuyu."

He looked at her thoughtfully. The other faces were turned to her as if fascinated, waiting in shocked disbelief for her to continue.

"They have a very rigid moral code within the tribe, I find," Kate went on rapidly, hoping to appease her listeners. "I cannot see that ignorance of their ways can possibly be of advantage to young people growing up in this country. I should like, if possible, to teach my girls to respect what is good in their beliefs."

"I hope you will teach them that they are nothing less than the salt of the airth," burst out Mrs. McTavish, her neck as red as a turkey cock.

"You're very young," said the butterfly collector, "and very new to this country. Some of the tribal customs are quite unspeakable."

"Lord Delamere might agree with Miss Carswell," Christy said, coming unexpectedly to her rescue. "He has his Masai herdboys in his house every night and swears they are his favourite companions."

"Yes, well . . ." Even Mrs. Bowden, who thought ill of no one, seemed unimpressed by this invocation of the noble lord, though he was the acknowledged leader of the settlers as well as

75

being the sharpest thorn in the side of the Government. "Lord Delamere is doubtless a very worthy man, but we all know that he is eccentric to a degree. Come, ladies, shall we leave the gentlemen to their port? I feel quite sure we can rely on Miss Carswell to continue in the same excellent way as she has begun . . . which reminds me, my dear, Clara was most insistent that I should extract from you, by fair means or foul, the name of the Indian tailor who makes your blouses."

Kate blessed Mrs. Bowden for her kindness and tact, but in spite of them she was conscious of a slight chill in the atmosphere as the ladies waited for the gentlemen to join them for coffee. She was relieved when voices and laughter heralded their arrival.

Christy made straight for the sofa on which she sat.

"Camouflage is the first rule of survival in the wild," he said, sitting down beside her. "I'm after thinking you must learn to be less open."

She gave him a small, sardonic smile.

"If I remember rightly, Mr. Brennan, it was you who urged me to state my views."

"Sure, it's an argumentative, trouble-stirring devil I am. Can you not see how I could have quarrelled with Edward?"

"All too easily."

He seemed to study her closely. Kate returned his look with a level, appraising one of her own.

76

"I think I underestimated you, Miss Carswell."

"Sure now," Kate said, in a parody of his own accent. "Wouldn't that be a silly thing to do?"

He smiled then, amusedly and frankly, and Kate saw that his whole face seemed to change as he did so. No longer did he look enigmatic and unknowable. She was glad when Mrs. Bowden rounded them all up to proceed to the Railway Institute.

Here, in a hall decorated by the ladies of the committee with festoons of ribbons and flowers, a Goanese quartet—four swarthy little men in tight suits—ploughed their way through waltzes and two-steps, polkas and cotillions with unflagging energy. As always, women were greatly in the minority, and of this minority, single girls represented only a small proportion.

For this reason Kate was besieged from the moment of arrival. She noticed that Christy was dancing with Mrs. Bowden but thereafter he was not in evidence on the dance floor and she assumed he had gone to the bar.

Men were in such a majority that this defection was hardly noticed, still less remarked on; yet for some reason Kate felt annoyed by it, a reaction she admitted to herself made no sense at all. She had as good as called him a murderer. It was hardly surprising he showed no desire for her company.

However, she found on her return from a boisterous military two-step with an officer of the

King's African Rifles that Christy had returned to the fold. The quartet began a waltz tune and he rose to his feet, turning to her with an elaborate bow.

"Would you be doing me the honour?" he asked.

"I've already promised this one—"

"Sure, simply because I haven't an inch of gold braid to dazzle you with!"

"Mr. Brennan, you know quite well that's not the reason."

She hardly understood how, in spite of her protests she found herself sedately circling the floor with Christy looking down at her with a broad grin compounded of triumph and devilry.

"This is unforgivable of me," she said.

"As unforgivable as accusing an innocent man of murder?"

"If he is innocent."

His laughter was unaffected and amused.

"Now, there's a dilemma for you!"

"Why did you quarrel?"

"I've forgotten. It wasn't important."

"Edward told me you had a violent temper."

"Now isn't that the truth?" Still smiling, he appeared to be enjoying himself. "You'll know, then, that we fought often."

"This must have been different. There was never a quarrel significant enough to mention before. I can't believe it was as unimportant as you make out."

"Then don't believe it. Concentrate on the dance."

The music changed and quickened and the hand that had been lightly touching her waist tightened. She held herself ramrod straight, but the rhythm of the music was insistent and suddenly every movement of her body seemed in harmony with his. She could feel herself relaxing within the circle of his arm—could feel herself swinging against him as they spiralled on and on in a dance that seemed to be without end. Suspicion was lulled, thought was suspended. There was just the music and this unexpected oneness.

When it stopped they stood without moving, their eyes locked together. Her breathing had quickened. She felt unsure of herself, slightly traitorous, a little angry. Slowly Christy smiled.

"Thank you, Miss Carswell," he said.

Abruptly she turned to lead the way back to their table, disliking the triumph she felt sure she could discern in his face.

5

NO one ever dreamed that the railway camp would develop into a town.

It had been sited on the flat plain close to the swamp because on this place an engine could be turned round. A few miles further on and the operation would be impossible, for here the line would have to ascend the steep Kikuyu escarpment if it were to fulfil the planners' dream and link the Indian Ocean to Lake Victoria.

A forward base had to be set up somewhere. This place close by the river known to the Masai who lived in the area as the Uaso Nairobi seemed convenient, if unhealthy. It was swampy and riddled with malaria, and the soil was black cotton which meant that drainage was impossible.

Quite obviously, it was far from ideal, merely the only option. But then it hardly mattered, for no one would stay there once the line had pushed on into the highlands beyond the Rift Valley, would they?

Meantime, people had to live. Tents were pitched, corrugated iron workshops were thrown up. Temporary tin shacks housed the Indian coolies brought from their motherland for the purpose of labouring on the railway—the lunatic line, as people called it. And when some of those same Indian coolies decided to break away from the railway and invest their savings in shops and businesses, it was easy enough for them to put up a few more corrugated iron hovels and lean-tos. After all, they were only temporary.

The European railway officials formed a club. Tents were replaced by frame houses with iron roofs only marginally more substantial. An enterprising Englishman opened a store and an hotel where it was possible to buy a drink.

A group of White Fathers from France built a church and introduced coffee bushes to the country. The British Sub-Commissioner, a Mr. John Ainsworth, whose headquarters had hitherto been sited at a place called Machakos halfway between Nairobi and the coast, eyed the growing shanty town with interest. It was rapidly overtaking Machakos in size. Clearly, the seat of government would have to be moved, the Union Jack carried up country to be planted firmly over this ramshackle sprawl of buildings which were proving to be not quite as temporary as everyone had at first imagined.

The Railway Company, who had so far been monarchs of all they surveyed, were less than pleased. They had their own health and police departments, and a fire-fighting system. They were damned if they were going to be shouldered into second position. They settled themselves firmly into the Hill district and glared somewhat balefully at Mr. Ainsworth, across on the other hill above the river.

The Masai and the Kikuyu tribes, both of whom inhabited this area, were traditional enemies; sometimes he wondered wearily if Railway employees and government officials were destined to fulfil a similar role.

And then came the settlers, individualists to a man.

Andrew Honeywell, the Sub-Commissioner's young assistant, shook his head ruefully as he stared out over the growing town. Nairobi! Was there ever such an ugly place? He had left his airless little office for a few moments to try to catch a breath of air on this stifling day in February.

His gaze rested on the Hill—the residential district which he could see just beyond the worst of the corrugated iron jungle swimming in a haze of heat and red dust. The prospect was more pleasing here, for gardens were growing and the stark lines of the bungalows were softened by sheltering trees and shrubs.

The cynical expression in his eyes melted.

She was there—and she was staying! Never mind the wretched settlers, arguing over the Land Ordinance, and never mind the natives, growing restive about paying their Hut Tax. Never mind the increase in stock thefts and the difficulty in persuading the Kikuyu to turn up to work for European farmers, though naturally all these things were blamed entirely on the Government. Nothing mattered except Kate, and the fact that she was on the Hill and was kind to him and listened to his problems and ambitions. Brickbats from settlers, slighting words from the Railway bosses, they signified nothing.

He would need patience, of course, for he knew that there was still no room in her heart or mind for anyone but Edward. But memories, even the most fervent, eventually faded. At the crucial moment, he would step forward.

"Honeywell!"

An irascible voice dragged Andrew back from the realms of make-believe where he dallied with Kate, dazzled by hope. He stood to attention and tugged at his jacket to straighten it.

"Coming, sir," he replied briskly.

Somewhere in the noisome huddle of buildings that constituted the Indian quarter, Christy Brennan was searching. The odour of spices vied with the stench of urine and the strange, indescribable, unforgettable smell of dust—not pleasant, exactly, but not unpleasant either.

He entered one dark, open-fronted shop after another. She was here somewhere, he had been told.

He had wasted a great deal of time in this sleazy jumble of alleys, which had seemed the obvious place for her to run to. He had questioned scores of people, repeated her name and her description and the location of her village over and over.

Some said they had heard of her. Some said they had seen her. At last a small, sullen prostitute had given him the information that although the girl had lived for a time under that very roof, she had now gone.

"Gone where?"

"She is no good." The girl had twined herself round him, rubbing her body against his. "I am better. Take me."

Christy picked her up like a child and set her down several feet away from him.

"Where did she go?" he asked again.

The girl pouted.

"Njombo will beat me if you do not give me money," she said.

Christy reached into his pocket and gave her two rupees.

"Now tell me," he said. "Where is Wambui?"

"In the house of an Indian."

He frowned in disbelief.

"Why?"

"Her time is near," the girl said. "Her belly is great with child."

"Holy Mother!" Christy's face looked as if it were carved from stone.

"Njombo has no use for her now."

"So he threw her out."

"He was angry. She must have been with child before she came here, and all know that a *thahu*

84

will enter the body of any man who lies with a pregnant woman."

"Where did she go? What Indian do you mean?"

The girl laughed.

"Ay—ee, you are so fierce! I have heard of you. You are *Bwana Macho Maji*. Why do you want that girl? She is sick."

"What Indian?" Christy insisted. "Is she in the bazaar?"

"Who knows where in the grass a doe will hide herself when she gives birth?"

Christy put his hand once more in his pocket and the girl's eyes flickered.

"I will give you this," he said, holding a coin at arm's length. "And as much again tomorrow if you tell me the truth."

"She is in the bazaar," the girl said sullenly, her gaze fixed on the coin. "More I do not know."

He tossed her the coin, and thankful to be gone lifted the tattered curtain at the door to go out into the dust-filled track between the tin hovels that led him to Victoria Street. Oblivious of his surroundings, he strode to the Indian quarter.

Pregnant. He had not known that. He counted backwards over the months and his mouth tightened. It fitted. He had to find her.

In and out of the shops he went, down evil-smelling alleys and into the backs of dwellings so dirty and foetid that he longed for clean air to breathe and the feel of a cooling wind on his face.

It was at the back of a tinsmith's shop that he found her. She was sitting passively on the floor with her enormous belly resting on her legs which stuck straight out in front of her. She was nursing a large-eyed Indian child, while several more sat with her on the floor.

He squatted down beside her.

" *Jambo*, Wambui," he said, his voice soft.

She stared at him, her eyes flat and opaque.

"Wambui, I have searched for you everywhere. I have come to help you."

Still she looked at him and said nothing. Christy turned to the little Indian tinsmith who had followed him into the room behind the shop.

"What is she doing here?" He had addressed the Indian in English but switched to Kiswahili when it became obvious that the Indian did not understand him.

"I have given her a roof while she looks after my children." The man jerked his head towards the ceiling. "My wife has another." A thin wailing could be heard from the upper regions as if to support his words.

Christy turned back to the girl. Her face, on a level with his own, was that of a child—a beautiful, smooth-faced child with exquisitely modelled features, nostrils gracefully flared, a rounded chin. It was a face that accorded oddly with the grotesquely swollen body.

"Wambui," he said. "You must go home. I will see that you are cared for while you have the baby, and then you must go back. Here, in the town, there is nothing for you."

Her eyes widened and she began to shake. Christy put his hand on her shoulder and she recoiled slightly.

"You can be purified," he said. "I personally will speak to the *mundu mugu*. I'll buy a whole flock of goats."

Still she did not speak.

"In her head she is sick," the Indian said scornfully.

Christy stood up and peeled notes from a wad taken from his wallet.

"Keep her here," he said to the Indian. "Treat her well and there will be more for you. I have to leave Nairobi tomorrow but at the end of the month I shall be back, and I shall want to see her well, do you understand?"

The man's eyes widened at the sight of the amount in Christy's hand.

"*Ndio, bwana*," he said, dipping his head, over and over in an excess of affability. "She will be as my own child, *bwana*. In all honesty I say this, as Allah is my witness."

Christy grabbed a handful of the shirt the man wore outside his ragged *dhoti* and lifted it until he was standing on tip-toe, the whites of his eyes gleaming.

"If she is not," he said. "I shall know how to treat you."

87

He shook the man slightly, dropped him back on to the floor, and strode out into the street.

6

THERE were times in the still watches of the night when Kate had doubts. It seemed an act of sheer effrontery, she told herself wildly. Her experience was limited, her qualifications nil. Who was she to think she could take on a school, not on a temporary basis but as its permanent headmistress?

"It couldn't happen anywhere else," she said to Louise one Saturday morning when they were taking coffee together on the Hudsons' verandah. "In England it would have taken me years to get to this point."

"You've proved yourself already," Louise said encouragingly. "I haven't heard one voice raised in disapproval."

"Not one?"

"Well." She struggled for honesty. "There are those who say that you are perhaps a little radical in your thinking, but no one doubts your ability as a teacher." She moved to pour the coffee and a shaft of sunlight fell on her face.

"What's wrong with your eye, Louise?" Now that Kate could see her friend clearly it was plain that she was in some discomfort. Louise, however, dismissed it.

"A bite, that's all. It's already a great deal

better than it was. Will you ever get used to these strange insects, Kate? Somehow I doubt that I ever will."

"I'm fortunate, I think. My flesh can't be as succulent as yours. They seem to leave me well alone."

She sipped her coffee, still looking speculatively at Louise, thinking how pale she looked.

"You are well, aren't you?" she asked at last.

Louise smiled at her.

"Perfectly." She looked at Kate with her lips pressed together. "Oh Kate, I wasn't going to say anything, but you know me, I'm not the least bit of use at keeping secrets. Promise me you won't tell a soul? It's far too early to make an announcement, but I can't help being pleased, whatever Ronnie says. And after all, you are my dearest friend—"

"Louise, what *are* you talking about?" Light dawned on Kate. "It's a baby, isn't it? You're going to have a baby! Oh, how absolutely lovely. You must be thrilled. What does Ronnie say?"

The glow faded from Louise's face and it struck Kate afresh that she had changed considerably from the plump, pert, smiling girl she had known on board ship. She put it down to the symptoms of pregnancy.

"You know what men are," Louise said. "It doesn't mean the same to them. Ronnie wants a child," she added hurriedly, "I wouldn't want you to think that he didn't—but he's worried about money. I keep telling him that it's early days yet, it's bound to take time for him to become established, but he's worried about the Indian traders. They don't care how many hours a day they work—"

"And they live on the smell of an oil rag!" Kate laughed a little as she spoke, for this had become a cliché which was applied to all Asiatics at all times.

"It's true, they do. Ronnie says it's unfair competition. He'd give the whole thing up if he could. It seemed a good idea at first—a bit of a lark, someone like him opening a store, but he didn't realise all the work that was involved. He's not used to it, you see."

"And the Hudsons were never in trade."

This reminder of her mother-in-law failed to draw a smile from Louise.

"The baby's due in July," she said. "I'm sure Ronnie is pleased, deep down, and as far as the store goes, I expect things will get better soon. It will just take time."

Kate agreed that undoubtedly things would improve, hoping that she had injected a sufficient amount of conviction into her voice. The truth was that she had heard whispers in the town about Ronnie Hudson—how the store was often shut when it should have been open, how it was almost always possible to find Ronnie propping up the bar of the Norfolk Hotel. Perhaps a baby was just what he needed to make him wake up to his responsibilities.

A few weeks later Meg and Hugh arrived for a short stay, mainly for the purpose of collecting a pair of Shorthorn cows in milk that were due to arrive from England. When Meg broke the news that she, too, was expecting a baby in August, Kate clapped her hands in delight.

"Isn't that the loveliest thing?" she cried. "Meg and Louise both having babies, Hugh expecting Shorthorns, whereas I'm celebrating the birth of a bonny, bouncing school."

Hugh studied her smilingly across the width of the verandah.

"It's wonderful to see you looking so well," he said. "Tell me, Kate, this wouldn't have anything to do with young Andrew Honeywell, would it? One hears rumours even in darkest Kiambu."

"Sheer nonsense!" Kate was both amused and mildly outraged. "He's a friend, nothing more. By the way, I have invited Louise and Ronnie to dinner tonight. I thought a party was called for, now that we have so many things to celebrate."

She had hardly spoken to Ronnie since his conversation with her in the shop. She avoided him whenever possible, but this was an occasion when his presence was forced upon her. Louise was looking forward to seeing Meg again and of course it was impossible to ask her without also inviting her husband, much as Kate would have preferred to do so.

In spite of this, Kate was delighted at the thought of giving a dinner party in her own home. She had inherited Kamau, the cook, from Mrs. Druce, along with the house and school, and he was as pleased at the thought of entertaining as she was. He and a young relation divided the work of the house between them, but it was Kamau who ruled the roost—and not only in the kitchen, Kate sometimes thought ruefully.

He was a slight man with a long, bony face which had the ability to look both more tragic and more jubilant than any other face Kate had ever seen. From the first he had been impressed by Kate's extreme youth and had questioned her about her strange lack of family. Where was her *bwana*? he had asked. And her mother and father?

Only her father was alive and in England, she told him. Kamau clearly thought this inexplicable, and in this he would have had something in common with Mr. Carswell, whose sole comment upon the news of Edward's death was to say that God moves in mysterious ways and that He obviously did not intend Kate to live in Africa. Kate had torn the letter up and had been unusually stern with her pupils for an entire day.

Kamau looked after Kate well, as if trying to compensate for her solitary state. Sometimes his protectiveness was irksome. If she walked in the garden without a hat, he would rush out with her *terai* in his hands. When all she wanted to do was relax in a chair, he would be beside her, stuffing cushions behind her back.

Mrs. Druce had taught him to cook, and had taught him well. The kitchen was a smoke-blackened little outhouse which Kate was content to leave entirely to him, and she was constantly amazed by the range of dishes he was able to produce from these unlikely surroundings. The prospect of having guests for dinner made his expression grave and sphinx-like. He washed and pressed his newest *khanzu*—the long white garment that was the uniform of house-servants —to do justice to the occasion.

It should have been a happy one but from the moment that Louise and Ronnie arrived it was obvious that things were not going to be easy. They were an hour late and plainly Ronnie had already been drinking heavily. He was in a spiky and argumentative mood, flatly contradicting Louise's lightest word, drawing attention to the fact that she seemed to have lost her looks now that a baby was on the way, putting in sly, malicious comments about anyone whose name entered the conversation. Kate felt nothing but relief when at last they left.

"Poor, poor Louise," Meg said, when Kate returned after seeing the Hudsons from the premises. "I had no idea he was quite so objectionable."

"Remember how bright and vivacious she was

on board ship?" Kate sank down in a chair feeling able to relax for the first time that evening. "It worries me when I see how much she's changed."

Hugh inclined his head, as if listening to something outside the window.

"If they're walking home, they'll get wet," he said. "That should cool friend Ronnie down, perhaps."

"Rain!"

Meg's face lit up, and she, too, turned towards the window. The light curtains gusted inwards. The sound was a mere whisper, but it increased even as they looked delightedly at each other. Drops pattered on the iron roof as the scent of water on parched earth invaded the room.

"Heaven send that it's falling on my coffee," said Hugh.

There were lion about. Christy could hear them grunting from somewhere across the river, and once there was a roar that cut across and silenced the smaller and more insistent night noises, as if all nature held its breath with awe for a second or two.

Tomorrow he would stake out a kill—unless by good fortune he was able to find the lions own prey to which they would certainly return. Either way it would mean a sleepless night as he and the Americans kept vigil. It went without saying that they wanted above all things to shoot a lion; but they wanted a buffalo and a leopard and a fine pair of tusks, too. It was his job to make sure the customers were satisfied.

He could hear them talking softly in their tent. They had been pleased with their day. The oryx which the younger man had shot had been a particularly good specimen.

The porters, too, were happy—full of meat, drowsy and contented. They were also talking, going over and over the events of the day in the manner which was entirely their own, one voice dominant, the others answering him like a Greek chorus, strophe and antistrophe.

Christy sighed. Was all the world at peace except him? If he had any sense, he told himself, he would turn in and go to sleep, yet he was restless, unwilling to desert the star-filled night.

What was he to do about Wambui? Why should the fate of one unimportant African girl plague him in this way? No one else lost any sleep over her. Distractedly he rubbed his hand against the side of his face, rasping the beard that was beginning to grow.

Even her family seemed to feel nothing but relief that she had left the village.

She had been such a lovely girl—shy and submissive, of course, as they all were, but with that extra flash of spirit, that love of life, which had made him single her out long ago when she was a child. He had loved to play tricks on her and make her laugh. Her enormous eyes would dance over the hand she clapped to her mouth,

96

and Chief Muthengi would shoo her away as if she were one of the scrawny chickens that scratched in the dust.

Angrily he picked up a stone and pitched it down into the ravine.

"I am *not* guilty."

The words seemed to be dragged from him, he uttered them with such harsh intensity. There was no reply but the continuing kwark-kwark-kwark of the frogs.

The image of Kate Carswell came unbidden to his mind. What, he wondered, would she say? He smiled sardonically. There would be no room for doubt in her mind. Her verdict would be 'guilty'.

And she would be right, one half of his mind said. Aren't we all the guilty ones—all of us who stride like a Colossus over this continent, not looking upon whom we place our feet?

What sort of foolish thought was that? Civilisation had to come to the country one way or another. Inter-tribal wars had caused death and frustration for centuries, and men's lives were shadowed from cradle to grave by ignorance and superstition. It was foolish to speak as if the coming of the white man was anything but beneficial to a continent still held fast in the dark ages.

Yet his unease persisted. He gave a short laugh as he thought of Kate. It was the cause of wry amusement to him to wonder what Edward

Matcham would have made of her. Sure, he'd have turned in his grave, Christy thought, if he'd heard Kate's little speech on the night of the dinner party.

The lion roared again and the very stars seemed to tremble. There were clouds beginning to obscure them now from the south-west which could spell trouble for the safari, even though the farmers in the highlands would be pleased. He lifted his head and sniffed the air. It's my guess, he said to himself, that it's already raining in Nairobi.

It drummed on the roofs and fell in torrents on the sticky black soil until the whole town was waterlogged and the unpaved streets so clogged that carts lurched and foundered in the glutinous mud.

Social life of necessity slowed down. *Memsahibs* stayed at home and sent their servants to market. The hitherto dry and dusty earth sucked greedily at the rain and drooping bushes became green again.

Kate was almost oblivious to it, except where it impinged on the life of the school. Even with strict rules about changing shoes, mud was tracked everywhere, and it was tedious for the girls to have to spend their free time amusing themselves on the verandah instead of strolling in the shady garden.

There was so much occupying her mind. Each

day brought books to mark and lessons to prepare, but she had other long-term schemes too. There was the problem of finding a suitable assistant so that she could enlarge the school, and the necessity to do something about music and art teaching.

Andrew, ploughing regularly through the mud to see her, provided a ready ear for all her dreams, and if sometimes he merely sat and watched her talking rather than paid attention to every word that fell from her lips, she failed to recognise the fact. She felt charged with energy, as if the rain had brought new life to her as well as to the gardens of the bungalows on the Hill.

"I thought a badminton court would be a good idea," she said one day as they sat by the log fire together after the girls had gone home. She was leaning forward with a slice of bread impaled on a long fork and the room was filled with the smell of toast mingling not unpleasantly with that of Andrew's wet trousers which steamed gently in the warmth of the fire. "There's a flat expanse of grass towards the bottom of the garden. And it suddenly struck me, Andrew—there's no reason on earth why we shouldn't grow at least some of our own vegetables, is there? We've plenty of room, but no kitchen garden at all—"

"Watch the toast!"

"Oh dear—never mind, I'll have this bit. No, really Andrew, there's no need to be a martyr! Oh well, if you insist. Anyway, I've told Kamau to find extra help in the *shamba* so that we can get things planted quickly before the rains finish. The problem is that I'm so ignorant about such things . . . Could you possibly be a dear and get me some pamphlets from the Department of Agriculture? They must have information about the best way to go about it."

Yes, yes, yes, Andrew nodded, his ears glowing in the firelight as he crunched his overdone toast. Yes, he would find out all he could about growing vegetables, and he was quite sure that somewhere he would be able to find information about the dimensions of a badminton court, and yes, the moment the rains stopped he would contact the Officers' Mess of the King's African Rifles where he was quite sure they had a little machine for making white lines on sports fields. And yes, he would certainly organise some transport to bring the two boxes of books that had arrived at the station up to Hill Academy. And he smiled beatifically when Kate thanked him warmly and said that she didn't know what she would do without him. Even as she thanked him, she reproved the small devil of amusement that lurked within her at the sight of those effulgent ears.

Ears, she told herself severely, are unimportant. They had nothing whatsoever to do with true worth, which is what Andrew possessed in abundance. He was a good friend and she was truly fond of him.

100

She was unaware of the fact that she dominated his every thought, that he felt more alive than he had ever done before simply because she seemed to need him and because she shared her thoughts and plans with him. He thought her smile the loveliest thing he had ever seen, and would have written poems to her eyebrows had he been able to string together two original thoughts. He loved her vivacity and her vehemence, and at night, tucked under the mosquito net in his narrow bachelor bed, he burned with desire for her. One day, he thought. One day when Edward Matcham was only a faded memory, he would tell her of his love, and if there were any justice in the world, she would surely turn to him.

Of all this, she was unaware, just as she was unaware of the African girl in the dark, damp lean-to at the rear of the Indian's shop who, on a heap of rags, was labouring to bring forth her baby. The rain which fell unceasingly was coming through the roof in several places and the air succeeded in being both cold and stuffy.

Panting with effort, eyes wild and un-comprehending, Wambui moaned softly, the cries mounting to a climax as the child struggled to be born. As if in answer to her cries, the door swung open and, holding a lamp above his head, the Indian peered into the room. For a moment he watched her, his face without expression, and then he withdrew. This was woman's work. He was tempted to leave her, to forget about her until

101

morning, but then he remembered the wildness in the strange eyes of the man who had charged him with her care.

Resignedly he went in search of help.

The safari had turned towards the plains of Serengeti and had escaped the worst of the rain, but on the way back it fell upon them relentlessly and the going became so difficult that at Kisumu Christy suggested that the Americans should take the train back to Nairobi. It left him free to take a steamer across Lake Victoria and press north. The fancy had taken him to shoot crocodile on Lake Kyoga with only Juma, his gunbearer, for company.

August was over when he rode back into Nairobi and the weather was beginning to warm up after the months of cloud. He put up at the Norfolk, as always. The usual crowd was in the bar, full of the usual hot air—the old Etonian with frayed cuffs to his jacket, the barrack-room lawyers, the impecunious but often noble farmers, the get-rich-quick boys, the newcomers still starry-eyed and gullible. Each one a politician, Christy thought cynically, listening to their fulminations about the Colonial Office, the Land Ordinance, the formation of a Legislative Council to do away with the iniquity of taxation without representation. And always there was the labour problem which had been discussed uphill and down dale for months. Surely, the farmers said, Government, having invited them to the country to sink their capital into land, had a duty to ensure that a sufficient supply of labour was available? What was the use of land without men to work it? With a word of encouragement from District Officers, the natives would flock to the farms: without it, they would sit on their backsides as they had always done. And as for the idea of allowing Indians to buy land in the highlands—Goddamit, there was suitable land in plenty for them, but not so many square miles that were suited to European settlement.

Christy pushed himself away from the bar and took his beer out on to the verandah. He had heard it all before and would doubtless hear it again. The contrast between the silent, empty country he had recently left and all those yammering voices seemed suddenly too great to be borne, though the sight that met his eyes on the verandah seemed just as incongruous.

His lips curved into a smile of pure enjoyment. He had almost forgotten how good a woman could look with tended hair and flower-decked hat. The curve of an English-rose cheek looked almost edible to him after his months in the bush, and the sound of female voices was like music.

There were tables along the verandah, and interspersed with officers of the King's African Rifles and farmers in bush jackets and shorts reaching no further than the knee were finely dressed ladies in silk dresses and shady hats.

There were others in high-necked blouses and sensible skirts, wearing pith helmets or double *terais*. Some were in riding habits. In short, it was the usual Nairobi mixture, leavened with the gun-toting tourists who were now beating a path to this Garden of Eden where the unsuspecting animals waited patiently, all too ready, it sometimes seemed, to be turned into nothing more than trophies on library walls. Suddenly Christy felt a little sickened by it and wondered how long he would be satisfied to continue with it all. He blinked in a bemused sort of way. This scene now before him was a world away from the bush which had so recently been his home.

A hand waved at him from halfway down the verandah and he recognised Meg and Hugh Lacey, both looking in his direction. He walked towards them, tankard in hand, and accepted the invitation to sit at their table.

"It takes a while to adjust to all of this," Christy said, looking around him. "I can't get used to the way Nairobi grows each time I take my eyes off it."

"You've been away some months, haven't you?" Meg asked.

"Indeed I have. What's gone on in my absence?"

"Meg's had a baby girl."

Christy lifted his tankard to her.

"Congratulations, Mrs. Lacey. May she grow up to be as beautiful as her mother."

"Such blarney!"

"Devil a bit of it, I promise you."

No, not a bit, Christy thought as he looked at her. He liked Meg Lacey. There was a calm sweetness about her that made him think of peaceful, comfortable things, like soft beds and the smell of bread baking.

"And the farm?" he asked.

Hugh shrugged.

"Par for the course," he said. "The coffee has cutworms and my two new Shorthorns died of rinderpest. Still, the bank manager doesn't appear to have lost faith in me. I have a stay of execution."

"It was awful about the Shorthorns—" Meg began.

Hugh reached out and covered her hand with his own.

"I'm so sorry," Christy said. "But you can cure the cutworms, can't you?"

"One of my errands today was to buy poisoned bait for the moths. I'll give them a meal they won't forget. Did you hear that over two hundred Dutchmen from the Transvaal arrived last month, complete with wagons and oxen? They've trekked up towards Uasin Gishu. I hope it's a good idea. I can't somehow see them improving the labour situation, can you?"

He broke off and rose to his feet. "Ah, here's Kate, at last."

Christy rose too, and bowed a little warily as Kate joined them.

"Miss Carswell."

"Mr. Brennan. How nice to see you again."

Kate's voice was pleasant and showed no trace of the sudden flutter of nerves she had experienced as she had stood at the end of the verandah and seen that Christy was sitting with the friends she was about to join.

She had not seen him since that night at the Railway Institute. Nine months after the event, she had largely forgotten it for there had been many other similar evenings. The uncomfortable moments at the dinner table were only now recalled with wry amusement at her own naivety, for events had made it plain that as far as school attendance was concerned her words had done no permanent damage. The main, lasting memory of that night was the strange abandonment with which she and Christy had danced together, and the thought of it filled her with a feeling of distaste that she could have so forgotten herself with a man she half suspected of killing Edward. She was determined that such a thing would never happen again.

Yet as in answer to Meg's questioning he spoke of the land he had left so recently, her attention was caught in spite of herself.

"Sure, it's the space I love," he was saying. "The wide, wide plain, burnt lion-skin yellow,

106

and the thorn trees. Did you ever look at a thorn tree? There's not a more gracious sight."

"You're a poet, Mr. Brennan," she said coolly.

"Not I. But there are times when I wish that I was one, though I can't imagine any doing justice to Africa. You should see more of it, Miss Carswell. You can't call the verandah of the Norfolk Africa, nor yet a bungalow on the Hill."

"My experience isn't entirely confined to Nairobi. I've been to Kiambu and once to Ngong with Andrew Honeywell and the Ainsworths."

"And how is the estimable Andrew Honeywell?"

"Why don't you ask him?" Kate said. "He's about to join us."

Once again Christy rose to his feet, but this time after a polite greeting to Andrew he did not sit down again. He begged the party to excuse him and left them to return to the bar.

"Quite a looker, isn't she?" a voice said in his ear. He turned to find Ronnie smiling at him with a slyness he found distasteful.

"Who?" His voice was dismissive.

"The school-ma'am. Miss Carswell." He spoke the name with a sneer, as if it were something Kate was not entitled to.

"Sure, any woman looks good when you've been in the bush as long as I have."

Christy turned away to order another beer, angling himself away from Hudson. He knew him only slightly, but enough to know that he was a

dull and boring man who could, after a few
drinks, turn into an aggressive nuisance.

"I shared a tent once with Edward Matcham,
before he went into the hunting business with
you."

"Is that right?"

"She doesn't know the half of it, does she?"

Slowly Christy turned, not indifferent now, his
eyes suddenly blazing. Ronnie faltered a little
before their intensity.

"She's not going to, either." Christy spoke
softly, menacingly.

Ronnie's eyes flickered with a look of defiance.

"The girl died," he said, after a moment.

"What?" He had all of Christy's attention now.
"What girl?"

"You know. God alone knows what her name
was, but you spent long enough searching for her.
They say she had a baby girl. Very pale skinned,
they say."

"Is the child alive?"

Ronnie gave a short laugh.

"What's it to you, Brennan? Is she yours?"

Christy's hand closed around Ronnie's upper
arm with a vice-like grip.

"I want an answer, Hudson."

Ronnie shrugged himself loose.

"For God's sake, man! Yes, she's alive, as far
as I know"

"Who told you?"

"I have my contacts. I don't confine my

drinking to this bar, you know. There are places in the bazaar where it's cheaper."

"If I ever hear that you've spoken of it—"

"What's the fuss, old boy? What does one sickly little *nusu-nusu* matter, one way or the other? Who cares who fathered it?"

Without answering, Christy elbowed his way past him. Ronnie stood and watched him go, a thoughtful expression on his face.

Kate was telling Meg and Hugh about Gerard Phelps.

"I haven't met him myself, but Andrew says that he's an accomplished artist and taught at a school in South Africa for some years. He seems just what I'm looking for to come to the school two afternoons a week."

"You may not think him suitable," Andrew cautioned her. He had experienced mixed feelings about introducing Phelps to Kate. He knew how badly she needed someone to teach art, and longed to earn her gratitude by producing the very man; yet it went against the grain to encourage any other masculine caller at the Hill Academy. He was having a bad enough time with the new Government doctor who seemed ready to drop everything at the hospital and rush to the school at the merest whisper of a bee-sting or turned ankle.

"I shall soon see. He's coming to see me tomorrow morning."

"What sort of age is he?" Meg asked.: "You don't want all your silly girls falling in love with him."

"Oh, they're bound to do that unless he has two heads and a humped back. Girls of the age of Agnes McTavish and Clara Bowden are capable of dreaming themselves into any situation, particularly girls with so little mental resources—"

"But the man is forty," Andrew said with horror. It had been the one factor that had tipped the balance in favour of Gerard Phelps. No man so old, he felt, could possibly attract a woman as young as Kate. Now she was talking of fourteen-year-old schoolgirls!

"Careful, Honeywell," Hugh said, looking amused. "Some of us are coming up the home straight, you know."

"As long as *he* doesn't fall in love with any of my girls, I shall be satisfied," said Kate. "And he's had experience in a girls' school, Andrew says, so I imagine he knows what he's about. Certainly the testimonials he sent me were excellent."

"Have you had any luck in your search for an assistant?" Meg asked.

Kate shook her head sadly.

"Not yet. Isn't it maddening? I can't expand until I have the right person to help, and I've several letters from up country asking me if I could arrange accommodation for pupils. I know the demand is there."

"The right person will come along, I'm sure. I'm so glad it's all going along so well otherwise. One hears such good reports." Meg smiled at her, pleased for her sake.

"I don't know where I'd be without Andrew," Kate said. "I ought to take him on the staff as an odd job man."

"If what I hear is true," Hugh said, "he's tipped for somewhat higher things than that."

"What a place this is for rumour." The ready colour rushed to Andrew's face, but he looked delighted nevertheless. "I can't imagine where you get your information," he said. "I do my job, that's all."

Kate leant forward to pat his arm.

"And you do it beautifully, Andrew. Can't you see him, Meg, when he's wearing his Governor's helmet and feathers? I shall be telling my girls in quavering tones, 'I knew the great Sir Andrew Honeywell when I was young. He drew me a diagram of the life cycle of the frog which was the finest I ever saw '—and there you'll be, quelling riots singlehanded and turning the desert into wheatfields and having everyone mopping and mowing at your slightest whim."

"Kate!" Andrew contrived to look embarrassed but pleased at one and the same time. "What nonsense you talk."

"It's not nonsense at all. I know perfectly well

111

that you're going to be a success, Andrew. You're so conscientious and dependable."

It was this comment that persuaded Andrew to take the bull by the horns when finally Kate had taken leave of Meg and Hugh and they were on their way to the Hill in the little mule buggy he had lately acquired.

"Kate," he began somewhat nervously. "I don't know where Hugh obtained his information, but for once rumour was right. Mr. Ainsworth has told me that he has strongly recommended me for promotion. This is strictly between us," he added hastily. "You won't mention it to anyone, will you?"

"Of course not, if you ask me not to. But Andrew, that's wonderful news. No more than you deserve, though. Does it mean that you'll have to move from Nairobi?"

"I gather not—at least, not at the moment. For which, I may say I'm very thankful."

The buggy lurched along the dirt road between ruts and potholes and neither of them spoke. The flat plain stretched out endlessly to the left of the track and almost unseeingly Kate watched a herd of Thomson's gazelle browsing calmly in the grass, their tails twitching with agitation as if they had a life of their own.

Instinct told her that some sort of declaration was about to be made and she blamed herself bitterly. For some time now she had been aware that Andrew was becoming too attached to her, but it was a problem which she had shelved. She had continued to treat him with a breezy friendliness which she had hoped would tell him more clearly than words that her feeling for him was far from romantic. Now she suddenly realised that the time for breeziness had run out.

"Kate—if I—*when* I get my promotion, will you marry me? You must know that I adore you. I've wanted to speak for so long, but I knew it was too soon. Perhaps it's still too soon, but truly I can't keep silent any longer. I know how you feel about the school. I wouldn't dream of wanting you to give it up—I could help you even more than I do now. Please, please say that you'll consider it. Don't turn me down straight away."

"Oh, Andrew." They had turned into the track leading upwards now and were going at a slower pace. "Oh, Andrew," Kate said again miserably.

"What does that mean?" Hopelessness was expressed in every line of Andrew's face.

"It means I like you and I hate to hurt you. I value your friendship, Andrew. Along with Meg and Hugh, you're probably the best friend I ever had—but I don't think I can marry you—"

"You don't *think*—?" He was clutching at straws.

Kate bent her head.

"I know I don't talk about Edward any more. Anyone could be forgiven for thinking that I've forgotten him and that the school is the only thing I care about. But it's not like that, Andrew. I loved him in a way I'll never love again. He was everything in the world to me and I'll never forget him—never be able to replace him."

Andrew swallowed with difficulty.

"I see," he said, as if his throat were suddenly paining him.

Kate turned and put her hand on his arm which was as stiff and unyielding as a piece of wood.

"Andrew—dear Andrew, don't be hurt. Don't be cross. You've been so good to me—"

"Please!" Angrily he shrugged away from her. "I don't want gratitude."

"No." Kate replaced her hands in her lap and looked down at them again, picking unhappily at the seam in her glove. "I'm so sorry, Andrew. I wish we could still be friends."

For a few moments Andrew sat in silence, nervously biting the inside of his cheek.

"I've never asked a girl to marry me before," he said with sudden violence.

"I—I—" helplessly Kate looked about her as if seeking inspiration. "I'm very honoured," she said.

"Rats to being honoured," he snapped, a small boy on the verge of tears.

Sudden hysterical, traitorous laughter welled up inside Kate and she looked down at her hands again, concentrating hard on quelling it.

"I'm sorry," she said again.

Andrew shook the reins, his mouth set and determined.

114

"I'm not giving up," he said at last. "I'd like to say 'to the devil with you', but I can't. We'll still be friends, if that's what you want. But just be warned! I'm not giving up."

He brought the buggy to a halt outside the house and they looked at each other. Kate smiled, briefly and nervously.

"Well," she said, and stopped. She cleared her throat and began again. "Well, thank you, Andrew."

"For bringing you home or for asking you to marry me?"

"Both, I suppose. Truly, I'm aware that it's the greatest compliment—"

"Oh, for heaven's sake! Don't say any more, Kate."

He sat staring woodenly in front of him, not leaping out to help her to the ground as he would normally have done. Kate gave him a last, guilty look and climbed down without assistance.

"Come and see me again soon," she said.

He looked at her unsmilingly, turned the buggy and lumbered off down the hill.

7

HE doesn't look forty, Kate thought, covertly studying the man who sat opposite her in her small sitting room. Though on the other hand there was a network of fine lines about his eyes and a sprinkling of grey in the hair over his ears.

He was a small, spare man. His hair was dark and close curled, cut very short to reveal a neat, round head. Looking at his face one was, she thought, more than usually conscious of the skull beneath its covering of skin, yet he was a good-looking man if one liked men's features to be on a miniature scale. Speaking for herself, Kate did not find him attractive though he was amiable enough. He smiled easily and often as if he were anxious to please. Kate felt strange, being in such a position of power over a man so much older than she.

"Do you hope to find work as an artist in Nairobi?" she asked. "I'm afraid the very best I can offer is two afternoons' employment."

"I realise that. It will suit me perfectly. Of course I shall hope to get commissions—portraits are my speciality—but I'm not fool enough to think I shall make my fortune that way. I've always been interested in photography as well as painting and I'm setting up in business in Government Road. I'm negotiating for a corner of Dobbie's shop as a studio. With a small amount of teaching, I'm hoping I'll be able to keep the wolf from the door."

"Your recommendation from the school in Cape Town could hardly be better. What made you choose to come here, Mr. Phelps?"

He shrugged.

"Wanderlust. A longing for change. I was intrigued by the thought of a new country—"

"As so many of us are."

They smiled at each other, polite but uneasy. He's shy, Kate realised suddenly, and with the realisation her own confidence grew. I am the mistress here, she thought grandly but with a degree of amusement at her own pretensions.

She asked to see the pictures he had brought with him in his portfolio and was immediately entranced. Sketches of faces tumbled out on to the table before him—faces old and young, black and white. All were drawn in charcoal with swift, economical strokes. All looked as if at any moment they would begin speaking, crying, laughing, singing.

"You're a *real* artist!" she said as if amazed.

He threw back his head and laughed unaffectedly and the tension drained away from the atmosphere.

"I know."

"Then what on earth are you doing wasting

117

your time taking photographs and teaching children?"

"Because even real artists have to eat and pay the rent. Unless one paints those sort of pictures —" and at this he nodded towards the framed prints of highland cattle that hung on Kate's walls —"it's hard to turn an honest penny."

Kate looked guiltily around the room.

"They are quite dreadful, aren't they? They belonged to my predecessor, Mrs. Druce. I hated them with a passion for the first few weeks but did nothing about them because I expected Mrs. Druce to come back. And then I became so busy I stopped noticing them. That brute over the whatnot was my especial bête noire."

"I'll paint you something to replace them if you like."

"How kind of you! I should like that very much. Meanwhile we ought to discuss terms. I thought perhaps ten rupees each afternoon?"

Mr. Phelps professed himself agreeable to this and she rang for coffee to seal the bargain, excited and pleased because it seemed that the plans she had for the school's future were one by one coming to fruition. She said as much to Mr. Phelps.

"If only I could find someone to assist me with the younger children, I'd be overjoyed," she remarked casually as she poured the coffee. "My numbers continue to grow, but unless I can get help it's going to be impossible for me to cope with the age range, still less will I be able to take a few boarders which is my eventual aim."

"Have you met Miss Skinner?" asked Mr. Phelps.

"No. Is she a newcomer?"

"Only a little less new than myself. She's staying at the boarding house where I'm living at the moment, together with her brother and his wife and family. They've come out to settle—they've already bought land in Naivasha, I understand, but of course there's the usual delay with the Land Office about getting title to it. Miss Skinner travelled with them to help with the children—they have five, no less. She's a qualified teacher. She was telling me so only last evening."

"And she proposes to stay here?"

"I believe so. She said yesterday that she was attracted to the country. Strictly between us, I think she has been somewhat overwhelmed by the attention she has received from certain military gentlemen."

"I'm not surprised. Am I to take it that she's a young lady?"

"Oh, yes. No older than you are yourself."

"And qualified! How perfectly wonderful. How I envy her!"

"Froebel, I believe."

"*Froebel*! Exactly the qualification I should choose myself. Mr. Phelps, if I wrote her a letter, would you be kind enough to deliver it for me? I think I must meet Miss Skinner."

"I'd be glad to," he said.

Kate withdrew for a few minutes to write the note, and when she returned to the sitting room she found to her surprise that Louise had arrived and, with her baby in her arms, was sitting very upright upon the sofa.

"Kate, please forgive me," she said. "I had no idea you had a caller—"

"My dear Louise, I'm glad to see you. Mr. Phelps and I had concluded our business—have you introduced yourselves? Mr. Phelps, this is my dear friend Mrs. Hudson. We travelled out together over a year ago."

"Yes, indeed." Gerard Phelps half rose and bowed towards Louise. "Mrs. Hudson has already made herself known to me."

"You'll join us in coffee, Louise?"

"Thank you. A cup would be welcome after my walk. The baby is only tiny, but you'd be surprised how heavy she gets."

"She's beautiful." Kate went over and gently pulled aside the shawl to look into the baby's face. "I must introduce Miss Julia Hudson too, Mr. Phelps."

"I've already paid my respects. You must be very proud of your daughter, Mrs. Hudson."

"Oh yes, indeed I am."

Louise sat with her head bent and a smile on her lips. There was a calmness and a ripeness about her which was new since the baby's birth. She had sailed through the experience with little

120

effort and had taken to motherhood as if it were a state she had been preparing for all her life. To the artist sitting across the room she looked rather like a Renaissance madonna.

He finished his coffee, cleared his throat a few times as if unsure what was expected of him, then rose to his feet.

"Thank you for the coffee, Miss Carswell. So kind. I shall look forward to seeing you next week."

"You won't forget to deliver my letter?"

"No, no." He patted his pocket. "I have it safely here. Miss Skinner shall have it the moment I get back." He bowed again towards Louise. "Goodbye, Mrs. Hudson. Goodbye, Miss Carswell."

"Funny little man," Kate said lightly when he had gone. "He's terribly shy. I hope I've done the right thing in taking him on. He's an excellent artist, but somehow I don't quite know what to make of him."

Louise seemed to be studying her baby's face, only half-attending to what Kate was saying.

"What did you think of him, Louise?" Kate asked.

Smiling, Louise pondered the question for a moment.

"I think he's rather sweet," she said.

Christy Brennan was a nomad. What few possessions he had, he stored in a box at the

Norfolk Hotel and it was brought home to him what a long time had elapsed since he last looked into it when he opened it and saw the rectangular, tissue-wrapped package lying on top of various other letters and papers he saw fit to keep in it.

He took the package and opened it, knowing what he would find beneath the paper but curious to see it once again. Framed in tarnished silver, the face of Kate Carswell looked out at him.

He sat down on the bed and stared at the sepia photograph. It was like her, he could see that—yet it was not like her at all. It was, as he had said to her a year ago, a face which could have happily adorned a chocolate box. There was a strength and a determination about the original which was entirely lacking here.

He would take it to her. He had meant to return it, ever since the day he had discovered that it had been left out of the parcel of Edward's effects which had been sent to his mother, but it had gone from his mind. Now he was conscious of a feeling of anticipation—a feeling of relief, as if he were glad to have discovered a good reason for going to see her.

"And aren't you the prize idiot?" he asked himself as he re-wrapped the photograph. "What's to be gained by it?"

He didn't know. All he knew was that for some reason Kate had stayed with him since that meeting on the verandah of the Norfolk Hotel. He had looked at Meg Lacey and thought her beautiful and the sort of woman who would bring peace to a man. But it was Kate's mobile, lively looks he remembered.

He presented himself at the bungalow just before four o'clock which was generally recognised as an acceptable time for a gentleman to call upon a lady, and was surprised to find that the school was still in session. For some reason it had not occurred to him that it would last beyond noon.

"I'll wait," he told Kamau, and was shown into the sitting room.

The afternoon was warm and all doors and windows were wide open. He suffered the sitting room as long as he could, but the sight of the verandah and the garden beyond it beckoned him and after a while he walked out with the intention of finding somewhere less oppressive to wait.

He came to rest on the stone steps of the verandah which led down to the garden and settled himself in the shade of its projecting roof, realising as he did so that now he was almost a part of the class that was taking place in the room that was at right-angles to the main house. The windows were wide open and Kate's voice came to him clearly. He could see two childish, attentive heads, both turned away from him, both frozen in an attitude of stillness.

He recognised the half-forgotten story of Esther. It was almost at an end now, almost at the point where Haman would receive his just

123

deserts and where Mordecai would triumph over him. Even from a distance he recognised the drama in Kate's voice and could see that the two small girls framed in the window were in spirit miles away from Nairobi and were there, with Queen Esther in the court of Ahasuerus.

There was a collective, long-drawn out sigh from the girls inside the classroom as the story came to an end. Kate's voice changed its tone as she returned them to the present day and gave instructions about lesson preparation.

There was movement and a banging of desks and scraping of chairs. Christy rose and stepped inside the verandah, where he was standing when Kate came through from the classroom.

She stood stock still as she saw him.

"I didn't know—"

"How could you? Your houseboy showed me inside to wait."

"I see." Flustered, Kate ran a hand over her hair. She indicated some books she carried. "Excuse me—I must just get rid of these."

The girls were leaving through another door. He could hear their voices calling to each other.

"Come *on*, Nellie—you are a slow-coach—"

"Wait for me. Don't go. Mama says you're to wait for me."

"Well, hurry then."

Kate was back on the verandah. She looked cool and composed now.

"You will have tea, of course? Kamau, *lette chai*."

"I was impressed," Christy said, without preamble. "I wish someone had told me stories from the Bible like that."

"How can one fail with a story like Esther? It has everything—rags to riches, the bad man punished, the good man rewarded. It's always been one of my favourites—and it has the advantage of being uncontroversial. I received something of a rap over the knuckles from some of the parents the other day by implying to the children that in my view Jonah wasn't really swallowed by a whale at all."

"He wasn't?"

"Well, I don't think so. I don't think we're meant to take it literally at all. I believe it to be an allegory and that what we were meant to understand from it was that God arranged for Jonah to go away somewhere completely on his own to give him a chance to think things out."

"You make God sound like a celestial Thomas Cook."

Kate laughed amusedly.

"Oh, what a dreadfully irreligious thing to say."

Christy looked at her with delighted amazement. At the Bowdens' dinner party she had been intense and didactic, exhibiting unmistakable hostility to him. On the verandah

125

of the Norfolk she had seemed remote. Now suddenly he was seeing a warm and lively woman.

"I've often thought of what you said at the Bowdens'," he said abruptly. "I hope you weren't discouraged by the way the others contradicted you. There was a great deal of truth in it."

"Thank you. I expressed myself badly, I'm afraid."

"I imagine Jonah won't be the only thing to bring you a rap over the knuckles if you forge ahead with introducing lessons in African traditions."

"I've learned tact since then. I impart information so that they hardly realise it—besides, I realise now that it's not facts the children need so much as a new attitude. I have this dream about educating my girls to grow up unfettered by prejudice, clear-eyed and open-minded. I'd like them to shun the second-rate in whatever culture it may be found. Heaven knows, there's much that is second-rate in our own culture."

"You mean, we're not the salt of the airth?" His imitation of Mrs. McTavish made Kate laugh again.

"Not always," she said. "Not all of us."

There was silence between them as Kamau, white-robed and wearing a dedicated expression as if he were high priest of some religious sect, brought in the tea things. He placed them on the small table beside her, and in the silence Kate had an opportunity to feel astonishment at the ease with which she was sitting and conversing with Christy Brennan.

He caught me off-balance, she thought, excusing herself. I still can't trust him.

"Milk and sugar?" she asked.

"Please—and strong, so that you can trot mice across it."

She laughed once more, and looked at him quizzically as she handed him the cup.

"What did you come for, Mr. Brennan? I don't think it was merely to make jokes."

"I have something to give you." He put the cup down and took the white-wrapped package from the pocket of his bush jacket. "I found this in my box of papers. I'd quite forgotten I had it. I thought you might like me to return it to you."

Kate took the package with a puzzled look but had only half unwrapped it when she recognised it for what it was. She made no sound, but her hands froze in mid-action.

"Look at it," Christy said.

Slowly, as if dreading what she would see, she continued to remove the paper. She shook her head slowly and sadly as she looked at the face revealed within it.

"Was I ever like that?" she asked. "I look such a child. I've aged a hundred years since then."

Christy gave a burst of laughter.

"You look a hundred times better."

"I'm a different person." She looked up at him with a frown. "What a horrid thought. Perhaps

Edward wouldn't recognise me if he were to see me now."

"Do you think of him still?"

"Of course." She sounded amazed that Christy could think of asking such a question. "How can you imagine that I wouldn't?"

The air had chilled again. Kate looked at the photograph once more, then put it down on the table beside her with an air of finality. In silence Christy sipped his tea, then put the cup down with a resolute expression on his face.

"It wasn't only the picture," he said. "I wanted to talk to you."

"Oh?"

Damn the woman—she's cold and remote again, Christy thought. Sure, I was an idiot to come. Didn't I know that from the first?

He looked at her, gnawing at his lip as if choosing his words carefully, but when they came they tumbled from him in a torrent as if he had wanted to say them for a long time.

"Kate—I find I dislike the notion that you're suspicious of me." He leaned forward, as if forcing her to pay attention to him. "At the Bowdens' dinner party I said to you that it wasn't in me to protest my innocence. You angered me then and I was in no mood to argue my case— sure, it wouldn't have done me the least bit of good, would it? You were upset—not prepared to listen. But time has passed now. It surprises me that I should care about anyone's opinion, but

128

the fact is that I do. I didn't kill him, Kate. We quarrelled, it's true, and there was bad blood between us at the end, but I didn't kill him."

Kate sat back in her chair and looked at him measuringly.

"Perhaps not. Yet my every instinct tells me that the whole truth has never been told. It was not a simple accident, was it?"

"There's no reason you should think that, at all."

"Yet you quarrelled. What about, Mr. Brennan?"

"I don't propose to tell you."

"Then why should I believe you?"

"Because I am an honest man."

His eyes seemed to blaze at her and for a moment she found it impossible to look away. She realised with surprise that she wanted to believe him.

"Mr. Brennan—"

"Could you not manage to call me Christy? Everyone else under the sun does."

"Christy, then. Suspicion bloweth where it listeth. It's hard to rid oneself of it if it's taken root."

"Do your best, girl," he urged her. "Do your best."

Reluctantly her eyes seemed drawn again to his. They seemed to have an almost hypnotic effect on her.

"I'd like to believe you," she said.

He smiled suddenly, his expression changing the angles and planes on his face so that Kate realised that Meg was not far short of the mark when she described him as 'devastating'.

"Then there's a chance for me," he said.

Hope Skinner received the invitation to call on Kate with delight.

She had never intended to stay in East Africa. She had agreed to accompany her brother and his family because her sister-in-law was a poor sort of creature who could never have managed the journey on her own. John Skinner had begged his sister to help, foreseeing all too clearly a voyage in which he himself would be called upon to amuse the children and attend to their needs. This was not something he had ever done, and he had no intention of starting now.

It had suited Hope to agree to his request. Since qualifying at the Froebel Institute of Education two years previously she had forsaken the modest provincial comfort of her parents' home in Swindon to teach in London, a place which seemed to hold out the promise of a fuller life. Its glamour had faded rapidly, however, when she found she was expected to teach in an area more dingy and poverty-stricken than she had ever imagined.

Disillusion with city life was not the only reason she was glad to leave England. She had been brought up to attend the Methodist Church

130

and she still did so after she had moved to London. For an entire year she had gazed longingly over her hymn book at the handsome profile of Sydney Marchbanks, son of the local bank manager, and considered that she had received clear indications that the interest was reciprocated.

When his engagement was announced to a fashionable young lady in quite another part of town, her self-esteem received a devastating blow, so that she hardly knew how to face the congregation or her colleagues again, for she had spoken often of him, giving the impression that marriage was a distinct possibility.

After this disappointment her reception in Nairobi had amazed and delighted her. She had a slim, girlish figure and golden hair, but was aware that her nose was too long and thin and her eyes protuberant. To the men of Nairobi these factors were unimportant. She was by no means unattractive and had the bloom of youth on her cheeks; best of all, she was unattached.

Within a week of her arrival she had been to a reception in the Officers' Mess, a soirée at the Railway Institute and had received no less than three invitations for a Halloween Dance at the Nairobi Club. Sydney Marchbanks was banished from her mind for ever.

She dressed very carefully for her interview with Kate, determined to make a good impression, and took a rickshaw to the Hill

Academy. It was something of a let-down to find the place so small and the headmistress hardly older than she was herself—and not even qualified, as she admitted frankly.

"But if I were qualified, I should like above all to be Froebel trained," she said warmly, ushering Hope to a chair on the verandah. "I've read Herr Froebel's books on education and find them so sensible and practical. You were lucky to have parents who believed in education for women! My father thought me rather unnatural to want to become a teacher."

"How many girls do you have here?" Hope asked.

"Ten—from nine to fourteen. It's not many, but with only one teacher and an age range of that size it's quite enough. I have numerous enquiries all the time about taking more, particularly younger girls, but without an assistant I haven't been able to contemplate it. My idea is that you should take the nine to eleven-year-olds—or perhaps we can even reduce the starting age to eight. I am confident we could count on a class of at least ten, which would leave me free to concentrate on the six older girls. Do you play the piano, Miss Skinner? You do? Oh, that's capital! We shall be able to have singing lessons now—that is, of course, if you decide to join me."

Hope smiled enigmatically. She had made up her mind to take the job before she met Kate and

132

had heard nothing to persuade her against the idea. Quite the reverse. There was an almost childish openness about this unlikely head-mistress that suggested a pleasing deference to her undoubted qualifications. Nevertheless she did not show too much enthusiasm.

"Would I be expected to live at the school?" she asked.

"Eventually, yes. Before too long I should like to take a few boarders. I thought of having a wooden structure built at the bottom of the compound just beyond the badminton court to house two classrooms—the Indian *fundis* throw them up in no time at all—then the present classroom in the house could be converted to a dormitory. It could hold six beds very adequately. Come—let me show you the geography of the place and then we must have a real chat about our aims and ways and means. It will be wonderful to have another teacher to discuss everything with. I can't tell you how grateful I am to Mr. Phelps for telling me about you."

Hope smiled again, a gracious smile tinged with the merest touch of condescension.

"I'm sure we shall work together very well," she said.

8

SOMETIMES Andrew Honeywell reflected rather bitterly on the contrast presented by his service career and his personal life. In one he appeared to grow in authority while in the other he behaved, he told himself, like nothing more than a puppet which was jerked about at the end of a string, capering to someone else's whim.

Three full years and several proposals later he still pursued his path of dogged fidelity. Many times a week he vowed that he would stop behaving like a love-sick schoolboy, but Kate had his heart and there seemed little that he could do about it. He continued to trail up to the Hill Academy to take tea with her and with Hope Skinner who, unfortunately, was always present now that she had taken up residence at the school, and was as ready as he had always been to leap to do Kate's bidding.

By July 1910, many of Kate's plans had come to fruition. The first few boarders had occupied the old classroom, as Kate had planned, but soon their numbers had increased to the point where it was necessary to turn that room into a common room and to add two more dormitories. A low wooden building down by the badminton court held the two classrooms, plus an extra room that was used as an art or music room, for now Miss Jukes, the daughter of the vicar of St. Stephen's, came twice weekly to give piano lessons.

Just as the teaching personnel had increased since the school's inception, so had the domestic staff. Kamau now worked solely as cook, and his nephew, Karioki, had been promoted to houseboy and was in turn assisted by another young relative, Mwangi by name. Another Mwangi worked in the *shamba*. To avoid confusion, the younger, smaller Mwangi was christened Mwangi *Kidogo*—Little Mwangi, a name soon shortened to Mwangidogo. For all his lack of inches, Mwangidogo was an excellent worker, soon far outstripping Karioki in industry and intelligence, though Karioki was a smiling, amiable rogue for whom Kate felt a great affection. She counted as one of the happier sights of Nairobi life that of Karioki and Mwangidogo, sheepskin pads attached to their feet, gliding over the red cement floor of the verandah like some bizarre music hall turn.

Hope Skinner now occupied a bedroom on the opposite side of the house to Kate's own, and if in some ways she had proved a disappointment, there was no fault to be found in the way she taught the children under her care. Kate had been amused at first by the way in which she had flaunted her superiority in the matter of qualifications. For the first few weeks Hope had not been backward in telling Kate where she was going wrong, and while Kate was always ready for discussions and questioning—of her own methods as much as anyone else's—she had no intention of surrendering her authority to this newcomer who seemed quite sure that her ways were always best.

The close camaraderie Kate had hoped for had failed to materialise. It was not that they quarrelled. They were, in fact, very polite to each other—Kate even more polite than Hope, for she had learned from bitter experience that Hope was quick to take offence and had no discernible sense of humour. Still, they rubbed along satisfactorily, if rather joylessly.

Kate saw less of Louise these days with both of them busy in their different ways, but she did not realise how long it was since their last meeting until by chance she came face to face with her in town one day and was struck by the change in Louise's manner.

She seemed pleased enough to see Kate and chattered as unrestrainedly as before, but her eyes were restless as if she were looking for someone and Kate detected a brittle nervousness that seemed unnatural.

"You are all right, aren't you, Louise?" she asked diffidently. It was hard to put a finger on what was amiss.

"Oh, perfectly! Never better!" Louise laughed breathlessly.

136

Kate remained unconvinced and made a point of calling to see her at tea-time on her next half-day.

If she had thought Louise's manner odd in town, it seemed doubly so on this occasion.

"Why, Kate—such a surprise! I didn't expect —never mind, it's lovely to see you. Come in, come in."

She gave the impression of hovering nervously on the threshold of the room beyond the small, enclosed verandah.

"How strange life is," she went on. "Day after day I see no one and now I have not one but two visitors on the same afternoon."

With a nervous laugh she ushered Kate inside and a figure rose from a chair as she did so.

"Mr. Phelps!" Kate said, striving to appear cool and unsurprised. "We meet again."

Only the previous afternoon they had taken tea together after his bi-weekly art class. Louise's name had never been mentioned between them since the day of his interview and Kate had no idea there had been any contact between them.

Gerard Phelps smiled and blinked and gave a little, ducking bow. He looked both hunted and guilty, Kate thought.

"Such a warm day, Miss Carswell—just passing—knew Mrs. Hudson would be kind enough to offer refreshment—"

"Gerard wants to paint my portrait," Louise said, as if in further explanation of his visit.

First name terms, Kate noted.

"Any artist would," she said smoothly, taking the chair that Louise indicated. Gerard cleared his throat, consulted his watch.

"If you'll excuse me—time I was going—"

"Please," Kate said. "Not on my account."

"No, no. Another appointment."

Louise returned from showing him out looking flustered, and Kate hardly knew whether to be amused, shocked or sympathetic. Gerard Phelps! Such a harmless, quiet little man! She reproved herself for jumping to conclusions, remembering all the times that Andrew had taken tea with her; yet the atmosphere seemed full of awkwardness and intrigue.

"Did I interrupt something?" she asked.

"Of course not," Louise replied stiffly, picking up the tea-pot to pour Kate a cup of tea. Then, the cup only half-full, she set the pot down with a thump. "Oh Kate," she said, her wide eyes tragic. "What on earth am I to do?"

"About having your portrait painted?" Kate's voice was light and teasing.

"No, of *course* not! I mean about Gerard."

"You're—you're in love with him? You're serious?" Kate stared at her in disbelief. She was quite ready to believe that Ronnie Hudson was the most unsatisfactory husband a woman could have, but as the object of a *grande passion*, Gerard Phelps seemed singularly unlikely.

Louise's eyes filled with tears.

"Of course I'm serious," she said. "We both are." She drew a handkerchief from her sleeve and dabbed at her eyes. "Oh, I know people have their flirts, Kate, and heaven knows I've had my chances. What woman hasn't in this town? But this is different. What am I to do? I don't love Ronnie any more—he's unkind and even brutal at times, but he is Julie's father—"

As if on cue Julie toddled in from where she had been playing on the back verandah, but for once Louise ignored her.

"And Gerard is practically penniless," she went on. "Not that I *mind* that, but it means we just can't go away together somewhere—and even if we did, Ronnie would come after us. He's terribly jealous, though I can't imagine why for he shows no sign of caring for either of us, Julie or me—"

She broke down into helpless sobbing and Kate moved swiftly across to put her arms around her, not at all amused any more but horrified at the depths of misery that Louise was revealing to her. Julie, thumb in mouth, looked on silently.

"Does Ronnie know about Gerard?" she asked.

"Oh no, no!" The thought appeared to terrify Louise. "Heaven knows what he would do."

"Then surely it's madness to let him come here."

"We had to meet. There were things to discuss. It's so difficult, finding opportunities."

"You've certainly been discreet. I haven't heard a whisper."

"I've wanted to confide in you, Kate, but Gerard thought it better not to involve you because of the school and his job—"

Yes, the school, Kate thought grimly. There must be no scandal to harm the school. She pushed the thought from her. It was Louise's happiness that mattered at this moment.

"I sometimes think if it weren't for Julie, I would kill myself—"

"Hush, Louise—don't say such things." Kate cast an anxious look at the child. "You loved Ronnie once. Isn't it possible to—"

"No, no. Everything between us is dead. I didn't know him—I had no idea of the sort of man he is."

But Gerard Phelps! Kate still found the idea incredible. Then she remembered his quick, shy smile and the gentleness of his manner. Perhaps it was not so difficult to understand his attraction for Louise.

Resolutely, Louise dried her eyes and took Julie on her knee.

"There is no answer," she said despairingly, rubbing her cheek against the child's soft curls. "If it was only myself, I'd go away with him— anywhere—and somehow we would manage. I'd find a job of some kind. It wouldn't *matter*. But with Julie to consider things are different." She gave a short, mirthless laugh. "Don't worry, Kate. I didn't mean what I said about killing myself. I'd never leave Julie to Ronnie's tender

140

mercies. I'll just go on, one way or another, getting through life the best way I can."

Kate stayed for a little longer but left long before the time that Ronnie might be expected home. She walked back to the school, deeply affected by Louise's desperation, remembering with sadness her infectious gaiety and optimism on board ship. It had all gone, every bit of it, so that she seemed, quite literally, a shadow of the girl she had been, all colour drained from her. Ronnie Hudson had a lot to answer for.

It had become accepted practice that in July at the end of every school year, a prize-giving ceremony was held in the school garden in the late afternoon, after the heat had gone out of the sun. A convenient grassy bank made a good platform, and Kate—dashingly dressed in tailored green silk and a hat of cream straw that tilted up at one side—looked down from her seat and felt an undeniable thrill of pride. There was something reassuringly established about the look of the school now; a feeling of permanence.

After she had given a brief report of the year's activities—diplomatically thanking everyone in sight—she introduced the guest of honour, Mr. Villiers, the General Manager of the Uganda Railway. He rose from his chair and announced his intention of saying a few words.

His interpretation of the word 'few' was, Kate thought, something upon which others might take issue. She schooled herself to keep a look of polite interest on her face as exhortation followed exhortation, cliché followed cliché. He had a mannered method of delivery and a flowery turn of phrase. He dwelt at length on the noble men and women who had brought enlightenment to the barbarous savages; touched upon the inspiration and civilising influence of a truly refined woman; urged the girls before him to take up the torch of duty and service and, forgetting the dangerous nonsense talked of woman's equality, to fulfil their God-given role of inspiring their menfolk to deeds of greatness.

"And whatever life and the future may hold," he cried, clearly working up to a climax, "may you keep ever before you the noble precept: for God and Empire!"

One hand was raised above his head, finger pointing heavenwards. Unbelievably, it was over. Applause rang out and everyone smiled with relief. Prizes were distributed and refreshments served.

"It all went marvellously," Andrew said afterwards, pouring sherry for Kate and Hope who collapsed into the verandah chairs after everyone had gone. "The parents seemed delighted."

"What a pompous old bore Mr. Villiers is," Kate remarked, accepting the sherry gratefully. "Why you put yourself through the ordeal of coming I can't imagine, Andrew. Time enough when you're a parent yourself."

"I was representing the Governor," Andrew said stiffly. It was as good an excuse as any. Even to himself he hated to admit that he could not keep away from Kate. "Actually, I thought there was much in what Mr. Villiers said."

"Oh, *Andrew*! It was the most dreadful poppycock—"

"I have to disagree. I know you think me pompous, too, but I happen to think that we do have a noble duty here."

"Bringing the benefits of civilisation to the barbarous savages?"

"Of course. How else can one feel?"

"Oh, it's not the duty I question so much as the so-called benefits."

"So-called? *So-called*?" Andrew's face grew red. "How can you question that? You know as well as I that many of the native customs are bestial. Of course our ways are superior."

"Oh, I know—I know. Killing twins at birth and putting the old people out to die and female circumcision—how could one defend it? But think of their old moral code, Andrew. Long ago, if one Kikuyu struck another or killed someone, they knew they had done something dreadfully unclean. They knew that they and their whole family would be cursed if reparation wasn't made, either to the man they had harmed or to his family. But now what happens? They're hauled up before the beak and likely as not they go to prison. They can't see the sense of it. They don't see why Kingi George should give them free board and lodging, and in that way while our ways might be best for us I'm not entirely convinced that they're best for them."

"They have to be educated. This is, after all, a white man's country now—"

"We came, we saw, we lusted!"

"And made it productive. And put a stop to the slave trade."

"That apart, are they really better off? I mean in their terms, not ours."

"Should they be allowed to kill each other off in tribal wars? To live in fear of the witch-doctor? You're being deliberately provocative, Kate."

Kate dropped her head back against a cushion and closed her eyes.

"As I am so often," she said. "Poor Andrew! It's just that I took such a dislike to that pompous little man that if he'd said the sun rose in the east I would possibly have disputed it. Doesn't it ever strike you, though, that by insisting on our ways we're imposing something second-hand and alien on what was once a proud culture? No? Oh well, I'm too tired to argue. I must go and see that the girls are having their supper."

"I thought they'd all gone home for the holidays."

"Three are staying until tomorrow—then six

144

whole weeks of blissful sloth at Mawingo! I'm so looking forward to it."

She got to her feet reluctantly and left the verandah, and for a moment Andrew and Hope sat in silence, Hope with down-bent head, smiling secretively.

"Dear Kate," she said after a moment. "She has such strong views. I'm sure I wish I could express myself so forcefully. There are so many occasions when I find myself not *quite* in agreement with her, yet somehow I can't find the words."

"She gets carried away," Andrew said awkwardly.

"Oh, *yes*! Really, I can only laugh, she makes such wild statements. I don't believe she means half that she says. For myself, I found Mr. Villiers' speech very moving."

Andrew took out his watch and frowned at it.

"I have a dinner engagement. I really should be going, but I promised Kate I would check over some figures for her."

"You're much too good to us. I was teasing Kate the other day about how much she takes you for granted."

"Would you make my excuses to her?"

Hope smiled brightly at him, showing no trace of the annoyance she felt at the way he apparently disregarded her words.

"Of course."

"Tell her I'll call tomorrow—no, that won't

145

do. I have to be at Government House. The following evening, then."

"Certainly. Good night, Andrew. I, at any rate, appreciate everything you do for us." She followed him to the door. "Do you know," she said as he reached the threshold, "do you know, Andrew—it sounds silly, perhaps, but when Mr. Villiers was talking of the British being the most noble race on earth, I had this tremendous urge to leap to my feet and say, 'There—look—there sits the most noble Britain of them all!' And I would have pointed to you, Andrew."

Andrew, pausing with his hand on the doorknob, ducked his head shyly. His ears grew pink.

"Oh, I *say*! That's coming it a bit strong, Hope."

"I—I suddenly felt I had to tell you."

"Most kind. Quite wrong, of course—I do my job—anyone else would do the same—" Shyness defeated him completely. "I really must go. Have a pleasant holiday."

"Thank you. I shall be visiting my brother and his family at Naivasha."

By the time Kate returned to the room, Hope was sitting down once more with her ankles crossed, the little smile in place.

"Andrew had to leave," she said. "He said he would come the day after tomorrow to check the figures."

"Bother! I'm leaving for Kiambu tomorrow.

146

Never mind, you'll be here until Saturday, won't you?"

"That's right," said Hope.

Hope was involved in amateur dramatics and left after dinner to bicycle down to the Railway Institute to a rehearsal. Kate sat alone by the fire, too tired to do more than dream, the dreams taking a familiar direction: the school she would build one day. It would be a *proper* school, she thought, with entirely new premises specifically designed for the purpose. And girls would emerge from it ready to question old dogmas and face a world without prejudice.

The sound of someone knocking at the front door roused her from this agreeable reverie. When she found Christy Brennan outside, she was not entirely surprised. He made a habit these days of dropping in unheralded whenever he was in Nairobi.

"Would ye ever be giving a poor wanderer a drink?" he asked, his smile white in the darkness.

Kate was glad to see him. She had forgotten her suspicion of him—or almost forgotten. She relished his conversation for its unconventional attitudes, its edge of humour, the knowledge that, like herself, he was not afraid to question the outcome of the policy of settlement.

Even after all this time she knew little more of his background than what she had learned from Edward's letters. There were many years unexplained and unaccounted for, vast secret expanses of time that remained locked away.

"What an hour to come calling," she said, nevertheless opening the door wide to let him in.

"I couldn't come earlier, Kate. It was after sundown when I got in from Thika."

"Was it a good safari?"

"One of the best. What a country it is! I shall have to take you some time."

"How could a poor school-ma'am afford your prices?"

Without asking for his preference, she poured whisky and added water.

"May God bless you," he said, taking the glass. "I could possibly consider reducing the charge."

"I'd love to see the mountain," Kate said, serious now as she sat down again by the fire. "From the distance it looks magical."

"It's cold up there," Christy said. "So cold it sears you to the bone. You go up and up through the forest and then you're out on a bare, windy plateau that feels like the top of the world. But then you know it's not, because sometimes, if you're lucky, the clouds drift away and there's the mountain high above you, looking like every mountain in the world ought to look—delicate and pure and covered with snow."

"That's the Celt in you speaking. Andrew told me it's 'awfully jolly'."

Christy gave a grunt of laughter.

"How is the worthy Mr. Honeywell?"

148

"Very well. He was here today, at the prize-giving—and oh, Christy, you should have heard Mr. Villiers' speech!"

It was a joy to recount it to someone who actually laughed at her mimicry and was not moved to disapprove of her levity.

"I'm afraid I upset Andrew—but really, how can one take such pompous rhetoric seriously?"

"What did our Miss Skinner think?"

"Miss Skinner's views were as usual. She invariably agrees with the last speaker. I don't doubt that the pair of them tut-tutted over me the moment my back was turned."

"She's a snake in the grass, that girl. Seriously, Kate, I've seen the strangest expression on her face sometimes when she's been looking at you. She'd stab you in the back if she could. I don't trust her."

"Feelings of distrust aren't always rational," Kate said gently. "As you, perhaps, are in a position to know more than anyone. Hope and I get along reasonably well. Understandably, she has something of a chip on her shoulder, because I'm the headmistress while she has the qualifications—"

"Qualifications aren't the be-all and end-all. Hope Skinner couldn't organise a Temperance Society. It's your personality and initiative that have made the school a success."

"Bless you, Christy—that's music to my ears.

I was thinking of the school's future when you arrived."

They talked of the school of her dreams which in turn led to discussion of affairs of the day. Eventually Christy rose to go.

"Thank you for coming," Kate said. "It's good to speak to someone who doesn't disapprove of my unconventional opinions."

"Namely Andrew Honeywell?"

"Among others."

"Are you going to marry him? The whole town knows he's been madly in love with you for years."

"The whole town must mind its own business —and that goes for you, too. The school fills my life quite adequately."

He was laughing at her and she grew mildly irritated.

"You men!" she said. "You can't imagine that any woman can be happy without being tied for life to some member of your own sex. Stop laughing at me, you infuriating creature! I'm perfectly satisfied. My school is enough for me."

"Oh, Kate, Kate—so the school is enough, is it?" Now she was not sure if he were smiling or not. "Now isn't that a terrible thing for a lovely young woman to be saying, at all? What am I to be doing with you?"

As if in answer to his own question he bent down and covered her lips with his. For a moment she fought against him, but as his arms came round her she found it impossible to resist the sheer physical release that his kiss awoke in her. It was as if a door had opened upon a whole world of pleasure that she had firmly put away from her when Edward died. For one brief moment she felt as if she had rediscovered something that made life delightfully simple—as if all she had to do was to surrender her will to his and there would be no more complexities, no more worrying decisions, no more loneliness.

There was the sound of Hope's key in the lock and with it she returned to her senses. She pulled herself away from him, breathing rapidly.

"It's very late," she said. "You really ought to be going."

He looked at her and did not move.

For a moment she looked back at him warily, on the defensive, sure that he would be laughing at her again; but he smiled gently and for a moment held a finger against her cheek before bidding her good night.

At Mawingo she always slipped back into the routine of the farm as if she had never been away.

There were a few changes since her first visit. The coffee trees were larger now and a further acreage had been planted in defiance of the disease which had decimated the previous crop. The outbreak of rinderpest seemed to have died away and Hugh had borrowed money from the bank to build up his dairy herd.

The house had a corrugated iron roof now in place of the rustling thatch and two wings had been added at right-angles to the main building to accommodate the growing family. But the land still rose and fell in wooded ridges towards the distant hills and the majestic clouds still sailed like galleons—white and purple and grey—in the vast blue bowl of the sky. Jasmine rioted over the verandah and the garden was bright with hibiscus, plumbago, allamanda and bougain-villaea.

"Kate, come and see my garden," Colin implored her, pulling at her skirt. "And my preying mantis. You can have it in your room tonight, if you like."

"Your generosity overwhelms me," Kate said, hugging him.

"You will ride with me tomorrow, won't you? I've got a new pony since you were here last."

"I can't wait to see it."

"I'm glad you're here."

Kate was glad too, and rode frequently over the farm with Colin and played with Janet and helped Meg with the daily clinic. And at night when the chill mist surrounded the house and the log fire crackled on the hearth she sat and talked of many things with Meg and Hugh, delighting in their company and the friendship which never seemed to diminish in spite of long absences.

"I hear nothing but good things about the school," Meg said. "How I wish you could take

152

boys! I can't bear the thought of Colin going away to prep school, but what's the alternative? Dashed if I'll let him go at eight, though, no matter what other stiff-upper-lip mothers do." She pulled a face at Hugh, as if daring him to disagree with her. He smiled back in return.

"Be thankful Janet is a girl," he said. "At least Kate can have the pleasure of educating her when the time comes!"

Inevitably they talked of Louise, though Kate had not breathed a word to another soul of what she had discovered.

"She's so desperately unhappy, Meg," she said. "As who wouldn't be, married to Ronnie Hudson?"

"I seem to detect a few reservations about this Gerard Phelps. Could he make Louise happy?"

"She seems to think so. Oh, he's pleasant enough, and I suppose has a certain quiet charm, but he has so little to offer, really. No money and no—" lost for words Kate waved her hand vaguely—"no *gumption*! Louise needs someone strong to lean on—"

"And Ronnie needs someone strong to punch him on the nose. I do see what you mean. Poor Louise. I do hope things work out well for her."

Kate had been at the farm three full days before she realised that she had left Edward's photograph behind in Nairobi. It gave her a shock to realise that his memory was no longer with her every moment of every day. Hugh had foretold it, she remembered, the day they had heard the rainbird, but she had not believed it. Paradoxically the realisation that he had been right made her sadness return in some measure. She mourned Edward's death no longer, but she mourned the fact that she had ceased mourning. She had thought herself strong enough to be faithful unto death; now she was not so sure. Something strange seemed to be happening to her.

She discounted the thought that Christy's kiss might have something to do with it. He was a byword in Nairobi. It would not surprise her to learn that he had gone straight from her house the other night into the arms of some other woman: Millie, or the doctor's wife who was said to be attracted to him, or perhaps some wealthy, aristocratic client, seduced by his colourful appearance and persuasive charm. Many women smiled upon him, yet all recognised the fact that in spite of their smiles he walked alone.

Yet something had awoken desire in her. Perhaps it was the sight of Meg and Hugh, walking along the grassy track to the house, fingers entwined; or playing with Colin, or lifting Janet in her arms. For whatever reason she began to yearn for—what? A man's touch?

One morning she awoke having dreamed of Andrew, and the details of the dream were quite clear to her. He had come to the verandah where they had sat together so often and said, "It's time

154

to tell you. I married you secretly while you were asleep in hospital, the day you arrived in Nairobi."

In the dream it seemed that Kate remembered that this was so; and she had turned to him with happiness and relief. When she awoke the feeling of peace was still with her.

Andrew, she thought. And then: Andrew?

The thought of him took hold of her slowly. Walking with Meg, she spoke of him.

"Meg, what would you say if I were to marry Andrew?"

Meg turned an astonished face towards her.

"Marry Andrew? Kate, you can't!"

"Why not? I'm really very fond of him."

"But you don't love him. You're always making fun of him."

"Only in the most affectionate way. He's been a good friend to me, right from the beginning."

"Friendship is one thing, marriage is something else."

"I should have thought it made a good basis. Meg, I shall never love again as I loved Edward. Either I settle for someone I respect who loves me, or I give up for ever the chance of having children of my own. I got angry at Christy the other night for saying that the school wasn't enough—but in a way he was right. Seeing Colin and Janet I know that I want more."

"Don't rush into anything," Meg cautioned.

Kate laughed.

"Rush! Andrew's asked me to marry him half a dozen times. It amazes me that he keeps coming back for more. Don't look so worried, Meg. He's a good man. I like him."

"But there has to be an attraction—" Meg remained unconvinced.

Increasingly as the days went by Kate felt sure that she felt that attraction. There was, she remembered, something rather vulnerable about the nape of Andrew's neck and a sweetness about his mouth. She dreamed of the future and could see no flaw in it. He had said many times that the school could continue as before. They could build a cabin in the garden for Hope or any other assistant they might have.

Meanwhile she was happy to dream away her weeks on the farm, hearing news from Nairobi with as much detachment as if it had come from another planet. There was talk of a rickshaw strike and news of a fire in the bazaar, quickly contained by the new fire engine.

"What a metropolis it's becoming," Meg said, as she turned the pages of the paper. "Hugh, there's an article here about ostriches. The feathers are worth a lot, you know."

"We're in the wrong area. They need a lower altitude."

"I'd rather be here," said Meg.

With surprise Kate realised that she would rather be in Nairobi. She had enjoyed every moment of her stay but had now come to the end of it and felt strongly that it was time to get on with her life.

She found there had been changes in the town even in the short time she had been away. There were street lights now, and the grand, wide avenue that bisected Government Road at right-angles was well advanced. And there were more rickshaws than ever, in spite of the rumours of a strike.

"Ugly old place," Hugh said teasingly. He had driven her back in the bullock cart and smiled at her air of delight at being back.

"It feels like home," she said.

Hope was back at the school before her and greeted her with unaccustomed warmth and a long account of how she had passed the holiday. Her sister-in-law, it appeared, was being difficult. She didn't like the country—never had, not from the first. She did nothing but find fault, Hope said. Really, it was a relief to be away from her.

Kamau, Karioki, Mwangi and Mwangidogo all greeted her with enthusiasm. The jacaranda tree by the classroom block was in flower and she could smell the yesterday-today-and-tomorrow bush through the open door of the verandah.

It was so good to be back. She wondered how long it would be before Andrew came to see her.

"Did Andrew come round to look at those figures?" she asked Hope.

Hope's face seemed to close up.

"No, he didn't. He sent word to say that Mr.

Ainsworth was sending him to Mombasa unexpectedly."

Kate was content to wait. One thing she felt sure of in this life was that Andrew would be finding his way to the school before long.

Two evenings later he came. School was not due to start for another week and Kate and Hope were busy drawing up a new timetable when he put in an appearance just after tea. He was in good spirits, beaming with pleasure because Kate was back in Nairobi.

She felt an unaccustomed shyness at first, as if he could see into her mind. Apparently he noticed nothing. Hope stayed in the room with them and the conversation touched on nothing more personal than Andrew's experiences in Mombasa and the possibility of starting a kindergarten class at the school.

Hope was passing on some of Herr Froebel's words of wisdom on the subject when pandemonium broke out outside the house.

"What on earth—?" Kate sprang to her feet and ran to the small window that looked on to the drive. "Someone has arrived—but what can all that shouting be?"

Kamau appeared in the doorway.

"*Memsabu,*" he said, looking agitated. "*Bwana na taka wewe.*"

"Which *bwana?*" Kate asked.

"Kate," a voice yelled over the screams. "Will you come and help me, for the love of God?"

158

"It's Christy!"

She went outside swiftly to find Christy looking more flustered than she had ever seen him before, a small and struggling child in his arms.

"Come on, darlin'," he was saying to her. "Would you ever stop that wriggling about, now? Kate, what am I to do with her at all? Can you not help me, woman?"

The child was thin and slight and slippery as an eel. She had a small, triangular, coffee-coloured face streaked with dirt and tears, and her wild hair stood out stiffly round it.

"Christy, what on earth have you got here? Who is she?"

"A waif and a stray."

Carefully he put the little girl down on her feet, grabbing at her as she darted away from him.

"No you don't, darlin'. Stay still, now. Say hallo to the nice lady."

Kate knelt down and turned the child to face her.

"Hallo, little girl," she said softly. "Don't be frightened. We're here to help you."

"Divil a word of English she knows," Christy said. "If we could speak Gujerati we might get through to her."

"Gujerati?" Her hands still on the child's shoulders, Kate looked up at him in surprise. "But she's not Indian, is she?"

"No. Half white, half Kikuyu—but she's been brought up by Indians in the bazaar. There was

159

a fire there the other day and two people lost their lives."

"I read about it."

"It was the man and his wife who died. Their children were saved and relatives have taken them but this poor mite was a foster child and nobody wanted her at any price."

"How do you come to be involved?"

"There's no time to be telling you now. I knew her mother and her grandfather. 'Twas all a tragic tale, with me fool enough to pay out money to the Indians to keep her."

The child seemed to have quieted and Kate picked her up in her arms, wrinkling her nose at the stench that came from her.

"My goodness, she's high," she said. "These clothes should be burnt. What are you doing with her now, Christy?"

"Trying to find her a temporary home till I can fix her up with one of the mission schools. No one else seems to care whether she lives or dies, and I shall be off before dawn."

"Let's take her in—there, there. Shh, dear, keep still now. She's terrified out of her wits, poor little thing. How old is she?"

"Around three years old. Three and a half, maybe. How good you are with her, Kate. I felt as if I was carrying a wild animal."

Kate and the child preceded him into the house where Hope and Andrew greeted their arrival with astonishment.

"Don't speak loudly," Kate cautioned them, "and sit very still. The child is frightened to death."

"What a frightful odour," Hope said faintly.

"I think we ought to feed her before we think of giving her a tub," Kate said, speaking softly. "I wonder what she would like? Something sweet, perhaps. Hope, could you please go and ask Kamau for some bread and honey and a little warm milk?"

The child had buried her face in Kate's shoulder, one enormous, terrified eye peeping out at this strange world in which she suddenly found herself.

"You can't be thinking of keeping her—" Hope began. She caught sight of the look in Kate's eye and went out in the direction of the kitchen.

"What's her name, Christy?" Kate asked.

"Sure, I've no idea at all. D'you think you could keep her, Kate, just till I fix her up at the mission?"

"Brennan, this is too bad." Andrew, having sat tongue-tied with horror at the sight of the child, suddenly found a voice. "You can't ask this of Kate. She has her school to run—"

The child began to wail.

"Andrew, please keep your voice down," Kate said evenly. "The child is very frightened. Long-term plans can wait."

161

"What on earth do you imagine the parents of your pupils will say?"

"Andrew, *please* be quiet!"

"Certainly." He got to his feet. "I was on the point of leaving anyway."

Kate looked at him sadly. This was going to be the evening when she let him know, subtly but unmistakably, that if he cared to propose again he might possibly be accepted. She smiled at him. There would be other nights.

"Come again, Andrew," she said.

"Charity begins at home," Hope said.

"I've always thought that one of the silliest maxims."

Kate was not being polite any more. Her patience with Hope was all but exhausted.

"It's all very well—"

"In what possible way does the temporary presence of this small child bother you, Hope?"

"It's all wrong. She shouldn't be here. She smells."

"She does not. I scrubbed her myself, three times. She's as clean as you or I."

"There are places for those sort of children—"

"Which Christy is going to find. Hope, she's tiny, she's alone and she's afraid."

"He should have made other arrangements for his little bastard—"

"*Hope!*"

Hope's colour rose.

"Well, what other explanation could there be?"

"He knew her mother, he said."

"I'm sure he did. Intimately, I imagine."

"Does it matter? Christy brought the child to me because he knew he could count on me to treat her with compassion. I couldn't live with myself if I turned her away. It's not as if I expect you to look after her. When I'm busy Mwangidogo will see to her. He was absolutely marvellous tonight when I was bathing her—I could never have managed without him. And do you know, Hope, she actually laughed once she'd got used to the water! She really loved it. I thought it quite remarkable to get a response like that so quickly."

"Andrew was right. The parents won't like it."

"You do them an injustice, I'm sure. Most of them work hard for charity."

Hope sniffed and took herself off to bed, returning in only a few minutes to say that a letter had arrived for Kate earlier but that in all the excitement she had forgotten to mention it. She'd put it on the desk, she said.

It was from Gerard Phelps—a brief note saying that for private reasons he was forced to leave Nairobi and that he regretted any inconvenience this might cause.

"As well he might," Kate muttered grimly. "Where am I to find another art teacher before the beginning of term?"

That was a minor worry, however, compared to Louise. Where did she fit into this? Had Gerard removed himself rather than continue to love her from afar? Did Louise cherish hopes of joining him?

Kate found time to go and see her the following day and learned that things had come to a head during the six weeks she had been away from Nairobi.

"We realised it was impossible to go on the way we were," Louise said. "In a way, I suppose I—I pushed him into going, for it seemed that he was content to let things slide. Oh, he loved me—it wasn't that—but he's altogether more *resigned* about things than I!"

"So where has he gone?"

"To Salisbury. He has friends there who can help him find a job. He's a talented photographer, you know, as well as an artist. He was sorry to leave you in the lurch, Kate—but you must blame me, not Gerard. I gave him an ultimatum. Either he took positive steps to make a life for us, or I would stop seeing him altogether. Here comes Julie—no more talk about my affairs! She's getting altogether too knowing. Tell me about your new charge, Kate. Have you thought of a name for her?"

Kate laughed.

"Hope thinks I'm mad, but I'm calling her Cleopatra," she said. "Patsy for short, which seems a little more suitable for a child and has a touch of the Irish about it which should please Christy. There's a strangely imperious beauty

164

about her which reminds me of the Serpent of Old Nile. You know, Christy is a surprising person, isn't he? Do you know that he's been paying for that child's support ever since she was born? I don't know the full story, of course, but I should have thought him too casual a person to stick at something so doggedly. A huge, once-and-for-all gesture would seem so much more in character."

"Yes," Louise said, without expression, and fell silent.

There was something about the quality of the silence that made Kate look at her curiously.

"Do you know something that I don't, Louise?"

"Of course not," Louise said hastily. "Come here, Julie—show Aunt Kate your new dolly and all her lovely clothes."

Patsy had a quick intelligence and rapidly charmed all but Hope and Andrew.

"It's a preposterous thing for Brennan to ask of you," Andrew said, his blue eyes hard with outrage.

"Why? She doesn't put me out at all." Kate smiled down at the child and stroked her curly head. Patsy kept her eyes fearfully on Andrew as if she could sense the hostility that flowed from him.

"I don't understand why he should bring her here. You're altogether too soft-hearted, Kate.

165

You should think what this could do to the school, never mind the child herself."

"You mean that for her own good I should have turned her from my door?"

"I mean it's no favour to allow her to become accustomed to a European way of life. And as for the school, whatever you think, the parents are not going to like having a half-caste child here. One may not approve of their attitude but one has to face facts."

Kate studied him for a moment, her face expressionless.

"And what becomes of our duty to the native that everyone talks about so piously?"

"It must be tempered with common sense, obviously."

"I see."

She looked down at Patsy and gave a short laugh that ended in a sigh. It was not really amusing, the death of those fantasies she had woven at the farm. How wrong she had been! In her need she had taken the figure of Andrew and superimposed a creature fabricated from dreams.

"I'm a very foolish woman," she said to him sadly.

"Thank heaven you've seen sense! I'll make arrangements with the Scots' Mission—"

"I was thinking about something quite different. No, Andrew. Patsy will stay here until Christy collects her, as I agreed."

Across the room Hope lifted her eyes from her needlework and with a barely perceptible shrug exchanged a sorrowing, suffering glance with Andrew.

9

" *M EMSAHIB!*"

Kate turned from the blackboard, textbook in one hand and chalk in the other, and looked with a frown towards Kamau who stood hesitantly in the doorway of the classroom. Such interruptions were not encouraged.

"*Ndio?*"

"*Iko shauri, memsahib.*"

Inwardly Kate smiled. Of course there was a *shauri*. There was always a *shauri* about something, for the word covered a multitude of events and meant a fuss or crisis of some kind. It could indicate anything from a shortage of sugar to a fight to the death.

"*Shauri gani?*" she asked him. "What kind of *shauri*?"

"A very bad *shauri, memsahib.*"

Resignedly Kate sighed, looking from the book to the board and then at her class.

"Girls, continue with the work you're doing. I shall be back shortly."

It was, Kamau told her, a *shauri* of the *Memsahib* Hudson. Her houseboy, Kiriri, had come down from her house to say that she was ill and needed *Memsahib* Carswell to go at once.

"Now?" Kate looked perplexed. "Is it that serious? She knows that I am teaching—"

"*Memsahib*, Kiriri said that it was a very bad *shauri*. He said he did not know if the *memsahib* would live or die."

Kate questioned him no longer but took the hat he held out to her and with a brief word to Hope, who was not at all pleased at being interrupted in the middle of explaining the intricacies of long division, she set out for Louise's home.

She was worried by the thought that Louise might be seriously ill. While all the Europeans insisted rather too emphatically that the Protectorate was a perfectly healthy place to live, there was no doubt that malaria was endemic, while plague and rumours of plague continued to emanate from the bazaar.

The Hudsons lived in a tiny, airless house made entirely of corrugated iron, once painted white but now leprous with age. The plot on which it was built had been cleared but never cultivated, beyond a half-hearted attempt at a flowerbed close to the front steps where a few dispirited petunias hung their heads. The coarse grass was knee high. Kate picked her way over the rough path that had been hacked across it.

Nobody was about. The small living room was dark after the glare of the sun outside, and seeing no one Kate called Louise's name.

"Kate?" Louise's voice came thinly from the

bedroom, which led directly from the living room. Swiftly Kate went in search of her, hurrying to the bedside.

"What's wrong?" she asked with concern. "Have you a fever, Louise?"

"It's not that."

Louise's voice sounded strange and Kate peered at her more closely. The curtains were drawn across the one small window and the room was shadowy.

"What is it? Your face—has there been an accident? I can't see you properly." She turned and drew the curtains back a little. "There, that's not too bright, is it? Are you in pain?" She looked back at the bed and gasped, falling to her knees by the side of it.

"Oh, Louise! Oh, my God! What happened to you?"

Slow tears were seeping from the swollen eyes over the purple contusions that disfigured Louise's face.

"Ronnie," she said.

"*He* did that?"

Louise nodded. She moved uneasily under the thin blanket.

"I think perhaps I have broken a rib. Something is very painful."

"You must get a doctor—go to the hospital. Louise, the police should know of this—"

"No, no, no." Louise reached out and grasped Kate's arm. "I couldn't bear the disgrace of it,

170

Kate—people knowing what he was like. And it would all come out—everything about Gerard and me—"

"But you need treatment."

"They would only strap me up. You could do it just as well. There are bandages in the cupboard. Please help me. I've always managed on my own before."

"This has happened before? Louise, what sort of monster is he?"

Louise did not reply but continued to cry, slowly, soundlessly and helplessly.

Kate fetched the bandages and did as Louise asked her, biting back further comments until she had finished.

"Where's Julie?" she asked as she worked, suddenly realising there was no sign of the child.

"I told Kiriri to take her over to Mrs. Jarvis next door, first thing this morning. I sent a message to say I had a fever."

"There," Kate said at last. "I hope that's all right. I can't leave you here, though—suppose he comes back—"

"He was drunk when he did this, drunk and mad with jealousy. Gerard has been writing to me from Salisbury to the address of a friend of his in town, but somehow the letter miscarried. The friend himself was ill and another man picked up his mail from the Post Office, and seeing a letter addressed to me thought it had been addressed wrongly and helpfully delivered it to Ronnie at the store."

Louise began to cry again.

"Heaven alone knows why he should care," she said between sobs. "He's always complaining because we're an expense to him and a drag on him. He said such awful things about Gerard—such terrible, terrible things. You know how good and honourable he is; he's the kindest, gentlest man in the whole world—"

"Hush, dear. Do try not to upset yourself so much. I'll make you a hot drink, shall I?"

There was a small paraffin stove on the back verandah which was used for such things, though the rest of the cooking took place outside. Kate, waiting for the kettle to boil, stared unseeingly at the porcelain water filter that stood in the corner, its tap slowly dripping.

What a strange and inexplicable thing love was, she thought. Louise obviously saw things in Gerard that were hidden to her, though in the light of Ronnie's behaviour it was easy to see how his very mildness must have made him seem doubly attractive to Louise. She shook her head, still hardly able to believe that any so-called civilised man could have inflicted the injuries she had seen. Yet now that she thought about it there had been other occasions when she had noticed odd bruises and cuts, always lightly dismissed by Louise. Why hadn't she left the man ages ago?

172

Sheer practical considerations, of course. Running away from a man in Africa cost money.

She made tea, put cups on a tray and was about to take it through to the bedroom when to her dismay she heard Ronnie's voice outside calling to Kiriri.

She could not remember having felt so frightened, but after a moment's hesitation she straightened her shoulders, picked up the tray and walked through the living room towards the bedroom. Ronnie was already entering at the front door.

"What are you doing here?" he asked curtly. "She's been crying on your shoulder, has she?"

"If she has, it's not without reason."

"Get out." He moved to take the tray away from her. "We don't need your interference."

"I'll just say goodbye to Louise."

"You'll give me that and get out now." He seized the tray and set it down on a brass-topped table with such force that the cups rattled. "You're to blame for all of this. I hold you entirely responsible."

"*I* am responsible?" Sheer indignation made Kate forget that she was frightened. "Why should you think that?"

"You employed that bastard. You encouraged them to meet."

"Ronnie—Ronnie—" Louise's weak, anguished voice came from the next room, but her husband ignored it.

173

"I suppose it gave you some kind of satisfaction, did it? An old maid like you, with no man of her own."

"Never for one moment did I encourage Louise," Kate said coldly. "Though I don't blame her in the least for looking elsewhere."

"Shut your mouth!" Ronnie seized her shoulders and thrust his face in hers so that the mud-coloured, bloodshot eyes were unpleasantly close. "If you think I'm not a better man than that namby-pamby little art master of yours, you're wrong. No wife of mine needs to go whoring after every Tom, Dick and Harry."

"I wonder why Louise has always thought you too much of a gentleman to be in trade?" Kate's voice was contemptuous. "You have the mind and manners of a guttersnipe."

He flung her away from him and she landed awkwardly against a chair.

"You nigger-loving little bitch," he said softly. "Of all the people in the world to look down her nose at me!" He gave a short, mirthless laugh. "At least I'm not a traitor to my own kind."

Kate stood up, her face pale.

"I'm going, Louise," she called, so that she could be heard in the bedroom. "I'll come back later."

"You will not."

She had moved towards the door but Ronnie seized her arm and forced her to a standstill.

"You'll never come to my house again."

She looked at him coldly, hiding her fear.

"With you in it, I've no desire to."

"Bitch," he said again, pure venom in his voice.

"Please let go of my arm."

He took no notice of this but stood looking at her with an ugly smile on his face.

"Such a pity I'm not the gentleman Edward Matcham was," he said, a note in his voice that Kate did not understand.

"I can agree with that."

"Of course." His grip tightened. "But I daresay I could tell you some home truths about that *gentleman* that would make you change your mind. He was fond of little black girls, too, you know. Very fond. But his reasons were quite different from yours, I fancy."

"I don't understand you. Let me go."

"I could tell you some interesting things."

"Nothing you could say would ever interest me."

"No?"

He released his grip and Kate took a few paces towards the door.

"That nigger *toto* Christy Brennan foisted on you," Ronnie said to her back view. "Matcham was the father."

Kate froze, then turned slowly towards him.

"You're despicable," she said. "There's not a word of truth in that."

"Ask Christy Brennan. He knows. He'll tell

175

you that the superior, gentlemanly Mr. Matcham had a *nusu-nusu* bastard." He began to laugh. "And the joke is that you're looking after it."

"Ronnie, how could you?"

Louise had somehow struggled to the door of the bedroom and was supporting herself against the jamb.

"She had to know some time."

"It's all lies," Kate said forcefully, but she faltered a little as she looked at Louise's face and saw the truth there. She licked her lips which had become strangely dry.

"I must go, Louise," she said, not looking at Ronnie. "Will you be all right now?"

"Yes. I'm so grateful to you for coming, Kate."

Blindly she began her walk home. There were long-tailed mousebirds wallowing in the dust on the track, but she did not notice them. The pungent scent of leleshwa bushes rose from the ground, disturbed by her passing, but she was unaware of it.

Once away from the house she clung to the scaly trunk of a blue gum tree, her eyes closed as if in thought.

She was not thinking. There seemed no room for thought in her, no ability to concentrate. She felt lost and disorientated, as if there were no certainties any more, nothing to hold to.

The class, she thought. I must get back.

With an effort that seemed almost superhuman

she pushed herself away from the tree and walked on.

Christy stood with her in the garden and looked towards the Cape chestnut tree. In the pool of shade beneath it, Patsy sat with three of the younger boarders who were weaving a chain of marigolds to hang around her neck. Beyond, four girls were playing badminton, skirts and pigtails and shuttlecock flying.

"I don't understand," he said. "I've made arrangements at Kijabe. They're expecting her."

"I want her to stay."

"Is it the sun that's affecting you, at all? What in the wide world can you be thinking of?"

"I know who her father was, Christy."

She heard him draw in his breath sharply.

"Who told you?"

"Ronnie Hudson."

The quick anger flared in Christy's face.

"That sly, sneaking bastard—he had no right—"

"I provoked him."

He looked at her, then nodded slowly with a kind of grim humour as if understanding how this could be. He lowered himself to the steps of the verandah.

"Come here and sit beside me, Kate. Sure, I can't see for the life of me why you should think this is necessary."

"I felt numb when I heard—I still do. Only this thought seems to make sense to me."

"You're in no state to make decisions."

"Sometimes it's right to behave instinctively. I mean to keep her, Christy."

"It might not be the best thing for her, you know. The problems would be enormous."

"I realise that."

"She's not your responsibility."

"I feel that she is. Why should she be the one to suffer through Edward's lust? She's a lovely child: quick and responsive and affectionate. And talking of responsibility, why did you feel the need to bother with her?"

"I felt in some way to blame," he said, after a long pause. "The mother was little more than a child herself, and I'd known her from my first safari, long before I knew Edward. She was shy but she trusted me. There was a spark of— something, I don't know, how can one explain personality? She grew up proud and graceful. Her father trusted me, too, and whenever I camped near the village he would send her up with gifts for me. I shot a lion once—a man-eater, that had taken a woman from his village—and from then on we were bosom pals."

He reached up and broke off a twig from the shrub that grew beside the verandah steps, absently stripping it of its leaves.

"Go on," Kate said.

"He would send her up," Christy repeated, "with never a thought that she was in danger."

When he paused, she looked at him again.

"This is all tied in with Edward's death, isn't it? What happened, Christy?"

His hand rasped along the side of his chin in a characteristic gesture of indecision.

"It's not an easy story to tell, Kate. Perhaps too much has been said."

"I must know!"

The words seemed wrung from her by force, and the children under the tree turned momentarily to look at her.

"I must know," she said again, quietly. "Surely you understand, Christy? I've spent years of my life mourning for Edward. Was I mourning for someone I never really knew? What sort of a person was he?"

Slowly he shook his head.

"What am I to tell you? I don't know the answer myself."

"*Did* you kill him?"

"Holy Mother! Would you ever stop going on about that? No, I did not. The girl's father did."

"And was never brought to justice because of the story you told."

"Justice? *Justice*? All my sympathies were with him. His justice was good enough for me. At that point I *could* have killed Edward."

"*Why*? Oh, I'm not condoning what he did, Christy, but I can't believe that your life has

179

been so pure that you can condemn Edward so virtuously. If the girl was a willing party—"

"She was not, Kate. She was not. I didn't want to tell you, but you go on and on at a man—"

The colour drained from her face.

"He—forced her?"

Christy, elbows on knees, was staring down at the stone steps, his face savage.

"It was rape," he said bitterly. "And the fault was partly mine for I knew what way his mind was shaping. You don't spend months in the bush with a man without knowing him through and through. I knew he was at the camp alone, I knew the girl would come, but I was too blinded with the lust for ivory to think it important."

Kate's fingers were pressed to her lips, her face stiff with horror.

"Oh God," she whispered hoarsely. "Oh God! How horrible—unspeakable—"

Christy gripped her arm.

"Look at them, Kate," he said, nodding towards the children under the tree. "Perhaps you're right to think of keeping her. They don't seem to mind her, do they?"

"*Mind* her? Of course they don't mind her. Children don't bother about a colour bar, unless the adults make them aware of it. Oh, Christy!" She looked at him tragically as, only momentarily diverted, she returned to the thought of the enormity of Edward's crime. "How can I trust anything again?"

"He had his good points, Kate. His crime was to see the girl as less than human. He would never have raped a white girl." He dropped his own soft accent and adopted the clipped tones of the English upper classes. "It wouldn't have been cricket."

"The girl's colour made the crime worse, if anything could do that. He was in a position of trust and authority."

"In all fairness to the judicial system here, the law would have seen it that way, too. Most people would. Kate, Kate—don't look like that! There's no point in dwelling on it; it's the future that matters now." He looked once more at the children under the tree. "It's good to see black and white so happy together, isn't it? Perhaps there's hope for this country after all."

"So help me," Kate said grimly, "I'll do what I can to make sure that there is. I'm more determined than ever now to keep Patsy with me and to educate her so that she's a—a living bridge between the races." She brightened a little as the grandeur of this concept came into focus in her mind. "Wouldn't that be a wonderful thing, Christy? She's a bright, intelligent child and when she finally takes her place in the school it wouldn't surprise me in the least to find that she does better than many of the Europeans. Surely, if only a handful of girls accept her as a person in her own right rather than a representative of another race, then I shall have done something worthwhile?"

"Don't minimise the difficulties."

"I'm not, I'm not! Oh, why does everyone have to be so pessimistic?" She was sitting up straighter now in a purposeful way, the colour back in her cheeks. "I will bring Patsy up as my own child. After all, the chances are that I shall never have another—"

"How can you know that? That's a ridiculous thing to say?"

"I don't think so. I'll educate her so that she'll be right there in the forefront, helping to lead this country out of the dark ages. Think of the contribution she will be able to make! Think of all she'll be able to do for the status of women!"

"Sure, the poor child!"

"She won't suffer. I'm fond enough of children to make sure she's a normal little girl before she's anything else—but think, Christy! It's an exciting prospect, isn't it? Oh, I've always thought teaching the most important, fascinating job in the whole world, and this makes it more so."

"Planning a child's future isn't always a good idea. Didn't it break my old mother's heart when I wouldn't go into the church, the way she hoped?"

Kate hugged her knees.

"She'll grow up strong and self-assured, able to compete on equal terms with any white girl in the Protectorate."

"I wish you well." Christy uncoiled himself from his position on the steps and got to his feet.

He stood for a moment looking down at her. "You can't live on dreams, Kate," he said softly. "And you can't regulate other people's dreams, either."

"The school is a reality, not a dream. I've seen it grow, term by term, just as I planned it. You laughed when I said that it was enough for me, but I meant it, Christy. Oh, I've such plans for the future!"

There was a cry from the badminton court.

"Oh, I *say!* Good shot, Lilian."

"Hey, it's my turn to serve—"

Christy offered a hand to pull her up.

"I don't remember laughing," he said, when she was on a level with him. His strange, contradictory face was unreadable, the misshapen eyebrow asking a question she did not understand. "Sure, Kate, I felt more like crying, and that's the truth of it."

10

THE world seemed to narrow down for Kate, so that only Patsy and the school had any reality for her. She went through a period of intense depression which she could only compare to the initial period of mourning. At that time she had been sad because she had lost Edward: now she was sad because she had lost her conception of him.

And not only that. She had lost confidence in her own judgement. She had loved Edward, only to discover that he was not worthy of her love. She had foolishly tricked herself into believing that she could love Andrew, only to discover that it was nothing but a fantasy. More amazingly, Louise had loved Ronnie once. Was it all a huge, cosmic confidence trick?

She disengaged herself from the social events that took place around her, partly because it was difficult to get away in the evening now that she had Patsy to care for, and partly because she had lost interest in them. She longed for Christmas and her visit to the farm as if this would provide a cure for her spirit as it had done before, and in some measure she was right. It felt like easing off tight shoes to immerse herself in the practical tasks on the farm, to laugh with Meg and read to the children. She was grateful for the loving acceptance she found there, both for herself and for Patsy.

Naturally she confided in Meg. It would never have occurred to her not to do so.

"It's a pity you had to hear of it," Meg said, after she had unburdened herself. They were sitting beside the fire on Christmas Eve, wrapping presents. The children were in bed at last, and Hugh was out attending to some *shauri* on the estate. "I think Christy was wrong to bring Patsy to you, in a way. He must have realised there was a danger of your finding out the truth."

"He had to make a decision in a hurry, and I'm thankful he did. Patsy is very important to me now, Meg."

"I can understand that. She's a lovely child, and bright, too. Her vocabulary is quite astonishing considering she knew no English less than four months ago. I'm afraid I discovered Colin teaching her a very rude word last night."

Kate laughed.

"Little wretch! She picks up anything quickly, especially things one would rather she didn't. It's good of you to have us both like this, Meg."

"As if we would dream of your spending Christmas anywhere else!" Meg studied Kate for a moment as she struggled to enclose a doll in an inadequate piece of wrapping paper. "Here—you need a bigger sheet for that. Take this piece. Besides," she went on after a moment, "I think you need a change of scene. You've had a trying time."

Kate sat on the rug before the fire, the paper in her hand but the doll temporarily abandoned.

"Yes," she said. "Yes, I have felt low. I've been so worried about Louise—and then there's the question of Hope. She really is becoming a trial."

"But you've always said how good she is!"

"She's a competent teacher, but to live with—that's a different matter. We were never kindred spirits, as you know, but we had worked out a perfectly satisfactory mode of life together. Now, although there's been no open quarrel, I can feel hostility coming towards me in waves."

"Because of Patsy?"

"I suppose so. She didn't want me to take her and has consistently refused to take the slightest bit of interest in her. She's evolved the strangest system of pretending that Patsy doesn't exist. She never calls her by name, never directly addresses her, never hands her a toy that's fallen. I don't understand it. I've never asked her to put herself out in the smallest degree because of Patsy. Her life isn't affected by a jot or a tittle."

"Maybe she'll get married and leave you," Meg suggested.

"Which would create other problems: but even so, I'd welcome it almost as much as she would. I find her infinitely depressing."

186

"I suppose she's spending Christmas in Naivasha with her brother and his wife?"

"Not this time," Kate said. "She opted to stay in Nairobi."

Actually, Hope had had no option since her sister-in-law had produced a string of excuses for not inviting her to the farm, but naturally she had no intention of revealing this to Kate, whom she saw leave the school with relief and pleasure.

She liked the feeling of having the house to herself. Her first action was to go to Kate's room and look around it. She opened a few drawers incuriously and shut them again. They held little interest for her because she had already been through them very carefully and had read the few letters Kate kept: the annual, stilted note from her father; a longer, but no more informative epistle from her aunt. She had been more interested in the letter from Edward in which he had mentioned the quarrel with Christy Brennan. It was intriguing to speculate about what had happened.

She had, of course, heard Kate's story, and knew that she had arrived to find that Edward had been killed. Kate had never mentioned this letter, though. Perhaps she had even forgotten that it still lay at the bottom of the drawer.

Hope disliked Christy Brennan intensely. She disliked the amused scorn she felt sure she could see in those strange eyes: she disliked the deceptively smooth comments which he made to her, suspecting even the most harmless of concealing a hidden barb, and most of all she disliked the way he had foisted the little half-caste brat upon them.

From a conversation overheard, she knew that she was not his child but had been fathered by this same Edward, who had written the letter and had quarrelled with Christy. The situation fascinated her. One day she would find out all about it.

Meantime, she liked the feeling of power it gave her, to turn over Kate's private possessions, dull as they were. She had known the exact day that Kate had thrown out the photograph of Edward that had previously stood on her bedside table, and she knew precisely where to put her hands on the silver-framed picture of Kate herself which lay in the third right-hand drawer under some scarves.

She picked up the book that lay on the bedside table and studied its title. Poetry! How typically affected. A sheet of paper fluttered from its pages to the floor, and she bent to pick it up.

It was a brief note from Meg, confirming that Hugh would be picking Kate up on the 23rd of December and saying how much they were looking forward to seeing her. It was signed 'Much love, as always'.

Much love, as always! It simply wasn't fair.

Much everything, as always. Why in the world did everyone seem to think so much of her?

Hope replaced the letter and the book and left the room, calling to Kamau for coffee as she went to sit on the verandah.

This, she thought, was how it should be. It was quite ludicrous that she, a fully qualified, Froebel-trained teacher, should be the subordinate of someone without a single certificate to her name.

People in this country were so ignorant that they didn't recognise the value of qualifications. Anyone would think that Kate was her equal, when all she possessed was a huge helping of untrained enthusiasm and a personality that blinded parents to the true facts.

Not that she envied Kate the school. The idea of working for the rest of her days filled her with horror. Marriage was her goal, not teaching—but still it irked her to think that Kate had authority over her. Her still-unmarried state was something that preyed upon her mind more and more heavily. Had anyone prophesied in those first heady months when she had whirled from one social event to the next that three years later she would still be a spinster, she would not have believed it.

But oh, she was glad now that all those lesser men had fallen by the wayside, for she had a bigger quarry in her sights now. Everyone said that Andrew Honeywell was destined to move up the promotional ladder. Even a knighthood would not be out of the question, and her head swam at the thought. She could make it happen, she felt sure. Admittedly, he was obsessed by Kate, but surely even Andrew must in the end realise that his cause was hopeless? And when he did, she would be there.

Her biggest ally was the fact that Andrew was entirely unused to being pursued. He had gone from public school to university and thence to BEA in the Administrative Service, and in no walk of life had women predominated. He was shy and unsure of himself with them, which perhaps was why he was so enamoured of Kate for she treated him without a hint of coquetry.

Andrew himself was the first to admit his inadequacies in this field. Light, flirtatious banter that other men seemed to find so easy stuck in his throat. His collar grew too tight, his feet and hands too big.

This is why, on entering Gladys Cannaway's house on Christmas Eve, he was relieved to see Hope there. George Cannaway was an engineer with the Railway whom Andrew did not know well. Now that more and more Europeans were pouring into the Protectorate, different social circles were forming and though on the whole relations between Railway and Government had improved over the years, this particular circle was not one in which Andrew had so far moved.

Gladys Cannaway terrified him. She was one of

the leading lights of the Amateur Dramatic Society, and a very masterful, self-confident lady. He would have been even more terrified had he realised how hard Hope had worked to ingratiate herself with Mrs. Cannaway, with Andrew's invitation to this event her main object.

His first, horrified gaze seemed to encompass nothing but strangers. Then Hope moved forward to greet him.

"I mustn't monopolise you," he said after they had been sitting on the dim verandah for some time. "It's not fair of me."

Hope touched his arm gently.

"Oh, please don't say that." Her voice was low and intense. "I've never made any secret of my admiration of you, Andrew. You could never be unfair to anyone, not in your whole life. Truly, sitting here quietly with you is so wonderful—so relaxing and peaceful." She gave a light laugh. "There doesn't seem to have been much peace *chez nous* recently."

"Because of the child?"

"Oh, it's wrong of me to complain. I never have, you know. Not one word have I uttered to Kate." She laughed again. "You shouldn't be such a sympathetic listener, you know. You make me say things I ought to keep to myself. It's just that I'm so *worried*."

"Why?"

She seemed to hesitate, pleating the material of her skirt between her fingers before answering.

"The school means so much to me."

"Hardly more than to Kate."

"Then *why*—?" She broke off, leaving the sentence unfinished. She looked swiftly at Andrew then down at her lap again. "No, it's wrong of me to talk so," she said. "I've never been disloyal and I don't intend to start now."

"Do you mean that the school is suffering? I've heard none of the parents complain."

"You've spent a considerable time out of Nairobi recently, Andrew. And I ask you, would they complain to you? Everyone knows how you feel about Kate."

"And finds it a great joke, no doubt."

"*I* don't! I've suffered too much myself to find such a thing amusing, I can tell you. I can't laugh at people like Kate does, somehow. Oh, I don't mean to imply that she laughs at you, Andrew!"

"I'm sure she does," Andrew said drily.

"Not in my presence. I won't allow it. Oh, look—Gladys is organising a game of charades. This should be amusing!"

Andrew looked hunted.

"I *hate* charades!"

Hope stood up and held out a hand to him, laughing roguishly.

"Come, I'll look after you. No one's going to eat you."

She leaned forward and smiled up at him provocatively, the scent of lily-of-the-valley wafting towards him.

"I shall feel such a fool," Andrew protested.

"Such nonsense—and you the most handsome man in the room!"

Andrew's ears flamed and he coughed nervously, but in spite of the embarrassment the flattery pleased him. Gladys Cannaway smiled as she saw them approaching together.

Miss Abandon-Hope is doing well, she thought. Someone ought to warn that poor young man.

It was, Hope thought, the most enjoyable party she had ever attended, for Andrew stuck to her like a limpet and eventually escorted her home. Perhaps even more pleasing than this was the exchange which took place in Gladys's bedroom where the ladies had gone to repair the ravages caused by the games she had organised. Hope was patting her hair in place, sitting at the dressing table, when in the mirror she saw Mrs. McDonald come into the room. The two McDonald girls had been at the school for the past term.

Hope turned and smiled at her.

"Mrs. McDonald, I have to congratulate you on your representation of Boadicea! Really, I thought I should die laughing."

"Oh, I'm no actress. I simply did exactly as Gladys told me."

Waiting her turn at the dressing table,

Margaret McDonald came to perch on a chaise-longue close by.

"I'm glad to see you here, Miss Skinner," she said. "I've been hoping for the opportunity to say how happy my girls are."

Hope came to sit close to her, placing her hand on Mrs. McDonald's arm and leaning towards her earnestly.

"I'm so very glad to hear you say that, Mrs. McDonald," she said in a low voice. "I do assure you, none of the girls in *my* class have suffered."

"I don't think I follow you—"

"Miss Carswell, of course, *has* had her mind on other things and it would be folly to deny it, but she's promised me that next term the school will come first." She gave a little laugh. "As I said to her—just in play, you understand—I should have to write 'Could do better' on her end-of-term report!"

"But she's always seemed so dedicated."

"And at heart she still is, Mrs. McDonald. If you hear any rumour to the contrary, I do beg you to contradict it immediately. Oh, she's all taken up with this little black girl at the moment, of course, but I can't see it lasting."

"Black gel?" The woman who had taken Hope's place at the dressing table and who had been silently applying *papier poudre* throughout Hope's conversation with Mrs. McDonald turned to join in. It was Mrs. McTavish whose daughter had left the Hill Academy last year and was now in Edinburgh. "I had haird something of the sort. Do you mean to tell me she takes lessons with the other gels?"

Hope gave her tinkling laugh again.

"She's only tiny, Mrs. McTavish. She won't be actually joining the school for three or four years yet."

"Has Miss Carswell taken leave of her senses? Do you mean this arrangement is actually pairmanent?"

Hope shook her head sadly, as if the whole thing was beyond her understanding.

"She won't be talked out of it, I'm afraid. I find it all quite astonishing! One can only assume that she likes being woken in the night and having her sleep disturbed. How she thinks she can be fit to teach the next day, I can't imagine—but you know Kate! There's no talking to her once she gets a bee in her bonnet."

"Aye, she was always full of the strangest ideas." For a moment Mrs. McTavish seemed willing to leave the matter there and returned to her toilette, but then another aspect of the case seemed to strike her. "Do you mean to tell me," she said in tones of amazement, "that the wee gel actually *sleeps in the house?*"

"Where would you expect her to sleep?" asked Mrs. McDonald.

"In the boys' quarters, naturally."

"She actually has a bed in Kate's own room—" Hope began.

"Never! That's going too far."

"I can't really see why," said Mrs. McDonald, rising to take the stool vacated by Mrs. McTavish. "Live and let live is my motto."

Hope stood up and smiled sweetly at Mrs. McTavish whose lips were clamped together with outrage. Side by side they made their way back to the drawing room.

"They've no idea how to behave, some people," Mrs. McTavish said. "She's no class at all, that Mrs. McDonald. I know the part of Edinburgh she comes from, and I can tell you my mother wouldn't have hired a maid from that quarter."

"Breeding will out," Hope said piously.

"How right you are, Miss Skinner. I must confess I'm astonished at Miss Carswell. I don't think it's generally understood that the wee gel actually lives in the house."

For a moment she stood on the threshold of the drawing room, head erect, nostrils flared.

"Standards must be maintained," she said. "This could be the thin end of the wedge."

Soon after Christmas, Kate heard of an experienced governess who was looking for a job, and she moved swiftly to engage her. It seemed that her dream of opening a kindergarten class was about to come true. It would, she thought, be the simplest thing in the world to erect another wooden classroom alongside the others, and the expense involved would be small. Plans went ahead for opening the new class after the Easter holidays. Hope seemed less enthusiastic than Kate would have expected, but she was not actively discouraging.

It was a blow when, thankfully just before the new classroom was put up, Kate received a brief letter from Miss Jephson saying that, after all, she found herself unable to take up the appointment.

"How can she do such a thing?" Kate demanded furiously. "There's not a word of explanation! It's unbelievable—she was so enthusiastic when she came here to see me."

Hope smiled her little smile and shrugged, as if the whole matter were of no concern to her. She had other things on her mind. The pursuit of Andrew was going very well and she had high hopes of his declaring himself by the end of term. It gave her a great deal of pleasure to imagine breaking the news to Kate to whom she had played down her growing friendship with Andrew. It would represent a triumph on several levels, she felt. Even though Kate had no wish to marry Andrew herself, Hope felt sure that she would feel deeply his defection to her. That was how she would feel herself, anyway.

With her mind thus occupied, Kate's problems were of only minor significance and she hardly turned a hair when to Kate's chagrin she heard that the Railway Company were reviving their own kindergarten and that none other but Miss Jephson was to run it.

"I simply don't understand this," Kate said. "The Railway have always taken a kind of proprietory interest in the Hill Academy—now one would think they were trying to do me out of business! They could at least have given me some prior warning. And as for Miss Jephson, I should like to think I need never clap eyes on her again."

Looking back afterwards, this incident seemed to Kate like the first small pebble that begins a landslide. Until that point, the short history of the school had recorded nothing but forward progress. She had been the darling of girls and parents alike, receiving nothing but plaudits and congratulations. Now, suddenly, complaints began to filter through to her—complaints which she felt were justified, for there was no doubt that Hope's mind was not on her work these days. She tried a gentle mention of her disquiet, but it merely served to increase Hope's hostility and no improvement was discernible.

When Andrew called one evening towards Easter when Kate was at home alone, she welcomed him gladly. It seemed a long time since he had been to see her. In her mind he was bound up with the early days of the school with all its attendant hopes and fears, and it seemed quite natural to pour out all her worries to him.

"I feel like writing to Mr. Villiers about this Railway school," she said. "I feel very aggrieved about it, since they knew perfectly well what my plans were. But on the other hand, there seems little point. It's a fait accompli now, or very soon will be. I was hoping for at least ten more children next term, so it really is a blow—added to which no less than three sets of parents have decided to send their daughters home to boarding school. I can't think what's got into everyone."

Andrew looked uncomfortable.

"I should have thought the reason was obvious," he said.

"Not to me. Nothing's changed here."

"That's not quite true, is it?"

"Well, if you mean that Hope isn't pulling her weight, I can only agree."

Andrew was silent, but there was something about him that expressed disapproval. Kate felt moved to explain further.

"She doesn't spend any time in lesson preparation any more, and seems quite uninterested in the children's progress."

"I assure you," Andrew said, "Hope is far less critical of you than you are of her."

Kate looked both amused and outraged.

"I should hope so! I seem to be doing half her work as well as my own. I don't consider she has any grounds to be critical."

"There are two sides to every question. It's not my job to mediate. But Kate, as for people taking their children away from you, you must realise that not everyone agrees with your taking that child to live with you."

"Don't call her 'that child'! Really, Andrew,

199

you're sounding stuffier and stuffier, as if you're turning into the perfect government servant before my very eyes. Patsy is a bright, affectionate little girl, and I fail to see how any intelligent adult could object to her. Those that do must be devoid of any kind of Christian charity."

"You're always so dismissive of people who don't agree with you! They don't have to be monsters to think that a European girls' school is no place for a native child."

"They *are* monsters, if that's what they think."

"Nonsense, Kate. They're good, well-meaning, charitable people who happen to have a view-point different from your own."

"Yes," Kate said slowly. "Yes, on the whole they are well-meaning and charitable, aren't they? That's what is so strange. They all look after their servants when they're ill and make clothes for orphans and raise money for missions. Why is my action so different? I think it's because their kind of charity merely involves stooping from a great height to dispense bounty to the poor, heathen savages. It's the idea of lifting one of the said poor, heathen savages to a position of equality that makes their hackles rise. Well, they'll just have to get used to the situation. Patsy is staying."

Andrew sat looking exasperated, saying nothing. Kate made an effort to change the subject.

"Tell me your news," she said. "It's ages since you've been here. I gather you've been squiring

200

Hope about recently—I do wish you'd give her a friendly hint to pull her socks up a bit."

He moved uneasily in his chair and his ears went pink.

"I wish you were as loyal to her as she is to you," he said. "Actually, I—I came to talk about her. I—we—thought you ought to be the first to know. Hope and I are getting married at Easter."

Kate said nothing, but stared at him with her mouth open.

"St. Stephen's Church," he said, as if this added confirmation.

"Oh, Andrew," she said, in tones of disbelief. "Oh, Andrew, are you really sure?"

"Naturally I'm sure! Hope warned me that you might be a little jealous that I'd transferred my affections, but of course I said that was nonsense."

"You're really happy? You love her?"

"She—she's a very lovable girl, Kate."

"Easter is so soon. I wish you would give yourself longer to think—"

"You don't like her, do you?"

Kate hesitated.

"To be honest," she said at last, "not very much. Andrew, we've been friends for a long time, and I've always been fond of you—you know that."

"I know you've always said so, but I don't know how sincere you were. Don't think I haven't realised that to you I've always been a figure of fun."

Kate flushed bright red.

"That simply isn't true! Is that what Hope told you? Oh, I've teased you, I know, but only in fun and only out of affection. I've never said anything about you behind your back that I wouldn't want you to hear."

"I've made up my mind, Kate. Hope is a sweet, loving girl and I'm sure we shall be happy."

"Then I can only give you my best wishes. I imagine she will be leaving me?"

"You're so unfair to her! Quite frankly, I was hoping that she would leave because with my promotion imminent we shall be moving into a large house in Parklands where I shall be expected to entertain, but she stood firm and said that she couldn't let you down. She won't think of leaving you until you have found a replacement. Though, of course," and now not only his ears were red but his entire face, "she would sleep at home."

"Of course," agreed Kate, gravely.

It was during the Easter holidays, after the wedding and the departure of Hope and Andrew to Mombasa for their honeymoon that Christy called, unexpected as always, to find her sitting on the verandah. There was a strange stiffness about her—an air of hopelessness and despair which he had never seen before, but she roused herself to greet him warmly.

"Christy, how lovely! I've never been so pleased to see anyone before in my whole life."

"Has something happened? You look sad."

"I am sad. I had a cable today to say that my father died suddenly of a heart attack."

"Kate, I'm so sorry—"

Miserably she sat with her head down, rubbing at some invisible spot on her skirt.

"I don't feel anything, Christy. Isn't that terrible? That's what makes me sad—the thought that we were so closely related. There could have been so much love between us, but there wasn't. And now there never will be."

"Sure, no one can will themselves to love where no love exists."

He spoke as if the words were not merely spoken to comfort Kate, but as if they had some deeper significance. She looked at him but as always his expression gave nothing away.

"It's been a bad day," she said. "There was something else."

"What was that?"

"I went into town this morning to send a cable to my aunt—it was she who let me know about my father—and at the door of the Post Office I bumped into Mrs. McTavish. You remember Mrs. McTavish, don't you?"

"The salt of the airth? How could I forget her?"

"I wished her good morning, of course, in a perfectly normal way—after all, I've known her for years—and she turned her head away and

203

ignored me. I thought perhaps she hadn't heard me, or was abstracted, and I thought nothing of it, but then we found ourselves standing next to each other at the counter and it seemed she'd suddenly decided to talk to me after all. Christy, she harangued me for a full five minutes—all about my wickedness in taking Patsy to live with me and bringing her up just as if she were white. She seems to think that every African servant in Nairobi— more, the whole of the Protectorate—will take this to mean that they are every bit as good as their masters, and will lose all respect for us, and so on and so on and so on. Can you believe it? She accused me of being a jumped-up newcomer who imagines she knows all there is to know about the native, whereas it is Mrs. McTavish and her ilk who really understand how they should be treated."

"And how's that?"

"They must be taught that the European is their superior in morals, education, industry, etc. etc., for only thus will they retain their respect."

"What did you say?"

"Nothing. Nothing! I just stood there, my arm in a vice-like grip, absolutely speechless, opening and shutting my mouth like a landed fish. She covered so many points that I simply couldn't find the words to start. When she had finished, I murmured something satirical about being delighted, as always, to hear her point of view, and tottered out."

She smiled briefly as she said this, but Christy sensed that she was not far from tears.

"Sure, the silly old cow," he said inelegantly.

"Christy, she's not right, is she?"

"Never in this world. She might perhaps get away with it now while the native still is unsophisticated, but in future years, what then? Respect has got to be based on a surer foundation than that."

"She's certainly wrong about one thing. The more I learn about their ways, the more I realise that I know nothing about them. She said, among other things, that they're congenital liars and totally unreliable and can never be trusted to do what they're told or turn up when you tell them, and of course I know that all too often she's right. They tell us what they think we want to know and hate answering direct questions—and as for time, well, I've suffered too often not to know that it means nothing to them. I've become angry, too, yet I always have the strange feeling that their truth and our truth are different. They march to the rhythm of a different drum, as it were."

"I trust my gunbearer with my life a dozen times every safari," Christy said.

"I trust Kamau, and Mwangi and the others too. But they're mysterious, Christy, don't you agree? I always think they—"

"*Memsahib!*" Kamau was in the inner doorway, his eyes round and gleaming. "*Iko shauri mbaya ya Memsahib* Hudson."

"Oh no, not again!" Kate was on her feet. "Christy, thank God you're here. Will you come with me?" She looked at her watch. "Patsy is at a birthday party at the Jarvis's, next door to Louise. Thank heaven some folk treat her as a normal child. I'm due to collect her shortly."

"It's a very bad *shauri, memsahib*," Kamau repeated.

Christy questioned him rapidly in Swahili.

"I know nothing," Kamau said in reply. "Kiriri said that the *bwana* struck the *memsahib* many times and that there was much blood."

"Have you a first-aid kit?" Christy asked Kate.

"Louise has one."

"Hurry, then."

"Thank God you're here," Kate said again as together they hurried up the road. "Heaven knows what we'll find. Ronnie could have done anything."

"He was drunk as a rat at the Norfolk earlier on, shouting the odds because no man there would put a hand in his pocket to buy another drink for him. I don't know a soul who's not sick to death of him."

"Oh, hurry, Christy," Kate said, breaking into a run. "God knows what we'll find."

The small house looked peaceful enough, drowsing in the heat of the afternoon sun. Before they reached it a sound made Kate turn, and approaching them she saw one of the station buggies driven by a wild-looking Indian with a red turban.

For a moment she stood looking at it curiously, and in that moment Christy leapt up the verandah steps in two bounds. Kate turned and followed him. The moment he opened the door she heard the flies, their sound a high-pitched, angry buzzing.

Christy paused, stiffened and moved swiftly across the enclosed verandah into the small room beyond, Kate only a second or two behind him. She had reached the door to the living room when he reappeared, blocking her way.

"No," he said. "No, Kate, don't come in— please, stay there. There's not a thing you can do for her."

But she had already seen into the room and she turned white at the sight that met her eyes. There was blood everywhere—on the walls, on the floor, and most of all, soaking darkly into the Indian rug where Louise was lying. One side of her face was battered, unrecognisable, her brains spilled out upon the floor, and her limbs were spread at an unnatural angle. The airless room was filled with the buzzing of the flies. The sound seemed to reverberate in Kate's head, pulsating and throbbing, louder and louder, at a pitch that made her want to scream.

For a moment horror and disbelief made her incapable of movement, then, with a strangled cry, she rushed outside, overcome with nausea, and, oblivious to the driver of the buggy, she vomited helplessly into the flowerbed by the verandah steps.

When, finally, she had control of herself she tremblingly wiped her mouth on her handkerchief and looked towards him.

"What do you want?" she asked.

The man spat a stream of betel-nut juice over his shoulder.

"I have come to take the *memsahib* to the station."

"She—she won't be going."

"I am to go back? Who will pay me?"

"You'll be paid." A thought struck Kate. "Wait," she said.

She took a breath and once more went up the steps to the house pausing fearfully at the threshold.

"Christy?" she called.

He straightened up from the task of covering Louise with a blanket taken from the bedroom.

"Is anyone about?" he asked, his face ashen under its tan. "Any servants? Any sign of Hudson, or the child?"

"I haven't seen any servants, or Ronnie. I imagine that Julie is at the same party as Patsy, next door."

"Louise was leaving. She has a trunk packed in the bedroom."

"She would never have gone without Julie. I suppose she planned to pick her up from the party and go straight on to the station. Christy, I've kept the *gharri* here in case one of us should go down to the police station."

"That's a good idea. You go, Kate. I'll stay here in case Hudson puts in an appearance."

"I'll call in next door and ask Mrs. Jarvis to keep both Julie and Patsy until later."

"Off you go, then."

Kate climbed up into the buggy, still shaking uncontrollably. She looked back at the shabby little house, looking just as she had seen it many times, and found it impossible to picture what scenes of violence and passion must have taken place there. It was an unbelievable nightmare, too horrible to be true.

Yet it was true. Louise was dead and Ronnie must have killed her. He had found her in the act of leaving him, waiting for the mule buggy to come for her.

Where had he gone? She feared suddenly for Christy. What she had seen in the room must surely be the work of a madman.

When she returned with a European policeman and one native constable, Christy was sitting on the front steps. He got to his feet at their approach.

"Any sign of Hudson?" the police officer asked.

Christy shook his head.

"The cook says he ran off in that direction—" he waved in the general direction of the Athi plain —"which means he could be anywhere."

"I must go and get the children," Kate said, as the men made to go into the house.

Halfway towards the track something made her look back towards the house. Christy's face was turned in her direction.

He and the policeman were standing at the top of the steps and he was talking, but even as he did so he lifted his hand towards Kate and for some obscure reason she felt comforted. It was an unfinished gesture—the sort of signal that implied he would be seeing her soon. She raised her hand in reply and continued on her way.

When he finally came, it was late—so late that common sense told Kate that she should put him out of her mind and go to bed.

Many times she had lifted her head to listen for him, but the only sound to be heard was the whirring of the crickets and the hissing of the pressure lamps. Several times she rose, and taking a lamp in her hand she went through to the room where the little girls were sleeping. They were both breathing peacefully, their limbs flung out in the abandonment of sleep. Julie had not seemed unduly disturbed by the fact that unexpectedly she had come to stay with Patsy. She had accepted Kate's vague explanations without question, both children finding great amusement in the fact that Julie had to borrow one of Patsy's nightdresses. They had played together happily, becoming

210

uproarious and over-excited before Kate had finally managed to settle them down.

Patsy occupied her own room now and another bed had been moved in for Julie. Kate stood looking down on them, sleeping as if they had fallen in mid-game, one so dark and the other so fair. Julie had smooth hair, braided into two short pigtails, with darker eyelashes fanned on to flushed cheeks. A pretty child, Kate thought. She bent to straighten one leg which was thrust outside the mosquito net.

There was a sound from the sitting room. Kate moved back, taking her pool of light with her, but it was merely the breeze causing the branches of an acacia tree to tap against the roof. She was being foolish, she told herself. Christy would not come now.

If he had gone with the police to track Ronnie Hudson down, he could be miles away. The cook had indicated the Athi plain, but this meant little for he could have turned west towards Ngong, or south, to follow the railway track to Mombasa. In each direction there were dangers: herds of buffalo, or the odd, marauding lion. And game pits, dug by the natives. And the natives themselves.

She sat with clasped hands, too tense to read or to think clearly. What a day it had been! First the news about her father, then the encounter with Mrs. McTavish and now Louise's violent, horrifying death, which had reduced all other worries in Kate's mind to nothing.

It had been such an ugly, brutal end to someone as pretty as Louise. She would have been happy before it happened. Kate could imagine her packing her clothes neatly, for she was deft and neat in all her movements. She would have been frightened, of course. Her heart would have been pounding, her cheeks flushed, but her underlying emotion would have been excitement for without doubt she had been going to Gerard.

What had made Ronnie come home just then? He had been drunk, Christy said. Supposedly that was it. He would have been incapable of opening the store.

It hurt a little that Louise hadn't told her that she was going, but impatiently she brushed this thought aside. She would have written to me, Kate thought. Grief was a physical ache, far more acute than the pain she had experienced at the news of her father's death. She felt as if a giant hand had seized and twisted the heart in her breast.

There were footsteps outside in the darkness and a knock at the door. With a gasp of relief she moved swiftly to open it, and she flung herself upon Christy as he stepped inside.

"Thank God, thank God," she said, her head against his chest. "I couldn't bear the loneliness."

For a long time he held her, his arms like a refuge she had sought for years, but then other

212

thoughts pressed upon her and she drew away from him.

"Did you find him? You look exhausted! Have you eaten? What about a drink?"

He spun his wide-brimmed hat on to the chair and ran a hand through his hair.

"First a wash, I think—then yes, a drink, please."

"Whisky?"

"Sure, that sounds like heaven."

She poured water from a large pitcher into a basin, gave him a towel and left him, going to pour a drink both for him and for herself. She asked no more about the hunt for Ronnie Hudson until he was sitting down with the glass in his hands.

"We found him in a gully towards Mbagathi," he said.

"Was he drunk?"

"Not then. He says that he was when he attacked Louise. He didn't mean to hurt her, he says. The shock of finding her about to desert him made him lose control."

"He admits that he killed her, then?"

"By accident, he says. He didn't know what he was doing."

"What will happen to him, Christy?"

He shrugged and took a long drink of his whisky.

"I suppose the charge will be manslaughter, rather than murder. White men don't hang in Africa—he'll go to prison, I expect."

Kate got up and walked distractedly about the room.

"He's horrible—a monster! If anyone deserved to hang—"

"A male jury would think it a crime of passion, no doubt."

"I'll have to keep Julie, at least for the time being."

"Has she no relatives in England?"

"Not on Louise's side. Ronnie has a mother, but Louise would hate to think of Julie going to her. She never cared for her."

Christy set his glass down and stood up.

"Come here," he said softly. "Would you ever stop pacing around the place like a lion in a cage?"

He reached out and caught hold of her, pulling her close, so that once again she was held firmly in the circle of his arms.

Sudden tears overwhelmed her. Helplessly, she sobbed against his shoulder, only barely conscious of his hand stroking her hair and of the feel of his lips moving over her temple.

"I'm so sorry," she said at last, trying to pull away from him, scrubbing at her eyes with a handkerchief pulled from her sleeve. "I'm not usually given to tears."

"Sure, why wouldn't you cry? It's been a bad, bad day."

He took the scrap of linen and lace from her and with infinite tenderness wiped her eyes, one hand holding her chin, tilting her face towards

214

him. For a long moment he studied her while neither of them moved.

"I love you, Kate Carswell," he said.

Kate stared back at him, hardly breathing, not knowing if he meant it, not knowing if she wanted him to mean it. Slowly, as if it were the most natural thing in the world, he bent to kiss her.

His lips felt cool and light on hers. It was hardly more than the kiss of a friend; then suddenly they were cool no longer, but searching and demanding. He kissed her eyes, her temples, her cheeks, the hollow beneath her ear. And answering him, there was no restraint in her. As naturally as if they had been fashioned for the purpose, her arms went round his neck and she strained towards him.

It was as if all the emotion of the day had somehow contributed to this—that this was the culmination that she had known must happen. There seemed nothing now but Christy. Her life before this moment suddenly seemed meaningless. Her only reason for living was here, with him, in his arms with his body pressed against hers. She felt that she was drowning in sweetness, as if this and only this could eradicate the horrors of the day.

"Can't I have it in words?" he asked, his brogue softened to the point where the question seemed like a kiss itself.

"I love you," she gasped. "I love you, Christy."

Again she reached up, this time to stroke his face and caress the scar that gleamed white across his eyebrow, and again he bent to bring his lips down hungrily on hers.

This was no moment to remember her conclusions about love—that it was an illusion that never lasted. This was no moment to remember Christy's reputation. This was a time of surrendering to sensations which until this moment she had only dreamed of, half-fearfully, half-expectantly. This was a time of revelling in the feeling of hard lips on soft skin, a time of wanting and of giving and of asking no questions, extracting no promises.

When later they lay with their arms around each other, quiet now and at peace, Kate found herself looking into Christy's strange, light eyes, only inches from her own. Suddenly shy, she looked away from him, seeing the lamp and the shadows it made in the corners and the clothes they had scattered.

Christy, she thought. All the time, Christy! How totally astonishing—yet wonderful and inevitable, too. Whoever would have thought—whoever could have begun to *dream* that there could be such oneness? The end of loneliness! Was that possible?

"What are you thinking, Kate?"

Every word a caress, she thought. Hadn't she always felt it?

"Thinking?" Smiling, she turned her head to look at him again. "I'm incapable of thought. Is it always like this, Christy?"

"No!" The curt denial reduced to unimportance the women she knew were in his past. "Never before, Kate. Never, never."

"I want so much to make you happy."

He pulled her to him roughly.

"We can be happy, Kate. We can be, if only—"

He broke off and Kate looked at him questioningly. For a moment he said no more and in some distant part of her consciousness she felt the first, chill breath of warning.

"If only?" she repeated. "If only what, Christy?"

He levered himself away from her and half sat up, his bare shoulders gleaming in the lamplight and the mat of hair dark on his chest.

"Kate—Kate, will you listen to me and try to understand? I love you. I've loved you for a long, long time. I never meant to tell you, though."

She gave a breathless laugh, pushing the unease away.

"I wasn't exactly encouraging, was I? I never lost an opportunity of telling you that the school was the only thing that counted with me."

"It wasn't only that." He reached for her and held her close to him. "Kate, I have to be honest with you. I've kept quiet about my feelings, because there's not a thing I can offer you: nothing that you'd accept, anyway."

She pushed herself away from him and looked into his face.

"What do you mean?"

"I'm not free. I can't offer you respectability."

"You mean you're married?"

He nodded sombrely.

"How can I explain to you? It was a mistake from the first. In a year we were hating each other —destroying each other. To leave the country was the only way out of it, for marriage is a life-sentence in Ireland."

"You deserted your wife?"

Her imagination conjured a picture of a young Irish girl, a shawl over her head, hungry children around her knee.

"I've given her all she ever wanted of me—a wedding ring, the right to call herself Mrs. Brennan, money at regular intervals."

"You should have told me."

"I've never talked about myself."

"You *should* have done! Have you children, Christy?"

"No. She wanted children cluttering the house even less than she wanted a man."

Sadly, Kate looked at him.

"Poor Christy," she said.

"Not any more—not if I have you."

Thoughtfully, she turned from him and sank back against the pillows.

"On what terms, Christy?" she asked softly. "Like this? Odd, stolen, secret nights, with Patsy in the next room?"

"We'd harm no one. Sure, nothing and no one can alter the way we feel for each other."

With a sudden movement Kate threw off the bed covering and reached for her dressing gown. Jerkily she moved away from the bed, tying the belt as she went.

"Don't you *see*, Christy, that how we feel doesn't enter into this? I believe you when you say that you love me. I love you, too. Of course that's important, but it doesn't mean we can forget everything and everyone else. I'm not desperate for marriage for the sake of it, or for respectability for the sake of it, but it's something I can't ignore."

"Because of the school?"

She whirled round to face the bed.

"Yes, of *course* because of the school! Imagine what a field day the Mrs. McTavishes of Nairobi would have."

"And they're important?"

"The school is important. You know how much it means to me—how for all these years it's absorbed every bit of my attention, all the energy and effort I've put into it."

He said nothing, but leaned back on his elbows looking at her, his eyes boring into her. Inside her body she could feel the weight of sadness forming again, the sadness that had melted away in the heat of their passion. The wild, abandoned creature who had clung to him so closely only minutes before seemed already to have distanced herself from Kate Carswell, the determined and dedicated teacher.

Christy, too, seemed to be undergoing a sea

change. The lifted brow seemed inimical now, not amused any more. He flung himself from the bed, stepping lightly with his hunter's tread across the room to reach for his clothes.

There was a violence in the way he moved, in the jerky pull he gave his whipcord trousers, the thrust of his arm into his bush jacket, his foot into his leather boot.

"You're angry," Kate said. "I'm sorry—"

"I thought you were bigger than this."

"The school is bigger than I am."

"The school, the school!"

"You're not being fair to me."

"Sure, I hope Mrs. McTavish is a great comfort to you—"

"*Christy!*"

For a moment he was still. She could have sworn there was a smile on his face, yet harsh lines were drawn from nose to mouth and she quailed before blazing eyes.

She had wanted to run to him, but he seemed like a stranger now. He did not look as if he loved her.

"You're not being fair," she said again. "You must have expected me to feel like this, otherwise you would have told me earlier that you were married. You know I have to think of appearances."

"The speed of your reaction was disconcerting, to say the least." He laughed bitterly and shook his head. "It didn't take a moment's reflection,

220

did it? And there was I thinking that tonight really meant something to you."

"It did."

"But not enough. The bloody school comes first, even though it's dying on its feet—"

"It is *not*! Any setbacks are only temporary: that's why I have to fight and keep on fighting."

Fully dressed now he looked at her once more before turning towards the door. And now she did run to him, holding to an arm which was stiff and unyielding with its anger.

"Christy, please! I can't bear to part from you like this."

"I shan't be bothering you again, Kate. Spare me the plea that we can still be friends."

She loosened her grasp on him and stepped backwards, appalled by the anger and the hurt she could see in his face.

"Oh, Christy," she whispered.

But he had gone.

11

HOPE returned from her honeymoon with a slyly demure air of consequence and self-satisfaction, as if it were now confirmed beyond all question that she was Kate's superior in every way. It was an attitude Kate might have tolerated more easily had she not been so aware of the short-cuts Hope was now taking in her work, but much to her relief the situation was short-lived. A Miss Rose Fawcett applied for employment as a teacher and proved to be not only experienced but also lively and enthusiastic. Hope departed, unwept, and Kate and Rose settled down to live and work amicably together. It seemed to Kate that a new era had dawned.

The parents seemed to sense the change in the atmosphere and beamed with approval once more. The voices which had been raised to criticise Patsy's introduction into the household were, if not silenced, then at least muted. There were no more mass desertions by pupils, and Kate relaxed and began to make plans again.

"I've every hope that I shall be able to enter girls for the Junior Oxford examination very shortly," she said to Meg on one of her infrequent visits to Nairobi, this particular sortie made to enable Hugh to complete the purchase of a motor car. "I've had a most encouraging reply from the examining body. By the time Janet comes to me we might even have achieved the Senior Oxford. Which reminds me—have you decided yet when Colin is to go home?"

"Home!" Meg gave a brief, mirthless laugh. "Why do we persist in calling it that? Home to Colin is a farm in Kiambu, not a wretched little red-brick preparatory school in Brighton. I'd give ten years of my life to keep him here."

"He'll come back."

"But we'll have lost so much of him."

"He must be educated, Meg."

"He *is* being educated. He absorbed reading by some sort of natural process and has read everything he can get his hands on ever since. If only he could come here, to you."

"Heavens above, I'm not equipped to teach boys who want to enter the professions."

"The only profession he's interested in is farming. Oh, I take your point, Kate. I know he must go, and so does Hugh, but we're putting it off until the last possible moment. We've decided to keep him here until the summer of 1914, when he'll be ten. It's late for prep school, I know, but not *that* late. I suppose we're luckier than many. Hugh's sister is quite happy to have him for the holidays—but when you think of the length of a boy's school life, Kate! How can I bear it? It's not as if I can go home very often with our finances in the state they are."

"I thought you were pleased with the price you got for your coffee."

"We were pleased with its grading, but prices on the London market aren't good."

"And now you have the expense of the motor car."

"We can't afford it. We definitely, positively can't afford it—but try telling Hugh that! He was as excited as a boy coming in today to pick it up, bless his heart."

"It will be a great boon to you."

"I can't deny that. It will cut down our journey to town considerably, though I shudder to think of the dust. Kate, how well Patsy is looking! She's a changed child from the little waif I first saw."

Meg was looking through the open door to the garden as she spoke and Kate, following the direction of her eyes, smiled as she saw Patsy, Julie and Janet trotting happily about the garden helping Mwangi to water the flowers.

"They are all so much of an age. Do you realise it's a year since she came? And Julie has been with me nearly six months. It all goes so quickly."

She shied away from the thought of Christy, who for the same length of time had come nowhere near her. If she kept herself from thinking of him, it was possible to persuade herself that it had been a momentary madness, regrettable and best forgotten.

"With Ronnie's appeal being dismissed, she

could be a permanent fixture, I suppose," Meg said.

"Yes, he wants her to stay." Resolutely Kate turned her back on memories and the glimpse of happiness Christy had seemed to offer. "I don't mind having her. She's no trouble—a sweet, well-behaved child, and great company for Patsy. Ronnie seems convinced that he'll be released earlier rather than later, though I'm sure I don't see why he should be."

"You'll all be coming for Christmas, of course—"

"Oh Meg, how we impose on you."

"Rubbish! I shall have a girls' dormitory for them all—and Colin will be like a sheik with his harem. Kate, do you hear anything? Is that or is that not the approach of a combustion engine? I do believe that my carriage awaits—and do you know, I'm every bit as excited as Hugh!"

Vera Lamton was thin, pale, shy and very new to Africa. She felt she had been honoured by the invitation to the sewing bee at Mrs. McTavish's house and she sat very quietly hemming a laundry bag (to be sold in aid of the Scots Mission at the Railway Institute Bazaar), listening avidly to the talk that was going on around her.

Servants, it seemed, were a very mixed blessing, and many were the laments for the Mollys and Mary Janes that had been left behind.

The Njeroges, Njugunas, Mwangis and Kamaus were, it seemed, poor substitutes.

Food was another subject that provided much material for discussion: when it came in, whether vegetables from the farm at Kabete were always as fresh as might be expected, and whether the meat in the market was hygienically butchered.

"You must remember, Mrs. Lamton, always to wash your salad in permanganate of potash," said Mrs. McTavish. "And never leave the boiling of water to the sairvants."

"Have you children, Mrs. Lamton?" asked a large, smiling lady who seemed to be feeling the heat judging by the number of times she had to lay down her sewing and fan herself vigorously with a copy of the *Standard*.

"Two," Mrs. Lamton said. "A boy—Frederick—at the kindergarten, and my little girl —Dorothy—is at Miss Carswell's school. They both seem very happy."

Conversation languished as Mrs. McTavish rang a bell briskly to summon the houseboy with a tray of coffee and biscuits. Sewing was for the moment abandoned, and when Vera accepted her cup and chose a piece of shortbread, she was gratified to find that one of the younger members of the party had apparently made the effort to cross the room to engage her in conversation.

"I'm glad to meet you," the newcomer said. "We were introduced, but I expect you were confused with so many people here. I am Hope

Honeywell. I do hope you will be happy in Nairobi."

"How kind of you. I'm sure I shall." Vera went a little pink with the effort of speaking to a stranger. "It's all very strange, of course. I suppose you have been here ages."

"Ages and ages," Hope agreed. She took a delicate bite of the shortbread, her tongue flicking an errant crumb from her lips. "I was *so* pleased to hear that your little girl is happy at the Hill Academy—pleased, and very relieved. I used to teach there myself before my marriage and the rumours I have been hearing have quite upset me."

"Rumours?" Vera looked perplexed.

"I know it's silly of me, but I can't help feeling as if I still belong there." Hope laughed guiltily. "I still think of the girls as *my* girls, even though I've left them. I suppose it's a case of 'once a teacher—'."

"I've heard nothing but good of the school," Vera said.

"I *am* glad. Mrs. McTavish—" Hope raised her voice a little, since their hostess was standing nearby, a plate of scones in her hand. "Mrs. McTavish, Mrs. Lamton was saying how pleased she is with the Hill Academy. Isn't that good news, after all our fears?"

Mrs. McTavish sniffed.

"Your loyalty does you credit, Mrs. Honeywell. I still think it a scandal the way that

227

black gel mixes with our own bairns on equal tairms. It'll lead to nothing but trouble, mark my words."

"I didn't know there was a black girl there," Vera said, wondering why this should be of such importance, but surprised nevertheless.

"Miss Carswell has more or less adopted her. Such foolishness! As if such a girl can ever become part of the European community—as if such a girl would *want* to!"

"Miss Carswell had the best of intentions," Hope murmured.

"And are we not told that those pave the road to hell?"

Hope stood up, smilingly offering her seat to Mrs. McTavish.

"There's so much you can tell Mrs. Lamton," she said. "So much good advice you can give her. Do let me pass the scones for you, Mrs. McTavish—no, really, a pleasure, I insist."

"Such a lovely gel, Mrs. Lamton," Mrs. McTavish said, looking with approval at Hope. "I wish I could say the same for Miss Carswell! Misguided is perhaps the most charitable thing one can say of her—though really in my view it's hardly strong enough when you consider the responsibility of her position. I felt I had to act when I haird she was about to open a kindergarten class, which—and you may well think I am exaggerating, but I assure you I am not—the wee black gel was to have attended!

Luckily for everyone, my husband is not without influence in the Railway."

Hope drifted away, well satisfied.

She had seen little of Kate since she had resigned her post at the school. This did not mean that Kate was absent from her thoughts: quite the contrary. Hope found herself thinking more and more about her as the weeks and months went by.

She had done her best to get to the bottom of the affair regarding the quarrel between Edward Matcham and Christy Brennan, but Andrew had been cagey and would only admit that much had been unexplained. Under pressure he agreed that there might have been reasons for thinking Christy guilty of Matcham's death: Kate had so believed at one time, he thought, but must have long since dismissed the idea in view of her friendship with Christy.

Discussing Kate with Andrew was like probing a sore tooth, for the fact was, Andrew still loved her. It was incredible, but true. She had found him gazing mournfully at a picture of her that had appeared in the paper when, with her pupils, she had staged an entertainment in aid of the new children's hospital, not only when the paper first arrived, but later, in secret.

Hope had been aware for some time that he was bored with her. After eight months of marriage his boredom seemed to fill the house each evening like the mist which rose from the

Nairobi swamp. Sometimes, unawares, she caught a look of bleak despair on his face, a look quickly replaced by the polite smile of a stranger.

Sitting opposite to him night after night, pretending not to notice that he could hardly bear to drag his attention away from the book he was reading to answer her when she spoke to him, she felt that hatred was growing inside her like a foetus in the womb.

Not that she had any first-hand experience of that situation. Each month, in the beginning, she had hoped, but had always been disappointed. If her brother's wife could do it with such regularity, then certainly she should be able to! Now she was less hopeful. Perfect as she was in her own eyes, even she did not expect an immaculate conception.

It was not Andrew she blamed, however, but Kate.

Christy staked out the carcase of the zebra he had shot earlier in the day and when the moon came up, he and the two Germans settled down to wait for the lions to approach it. The porters had built a stockade for them from thorn bushes, not to protect but to conceal the hunters.

The night was thick with stars, crackling with tension which was only enhanced by the uncounted noises that broke the silence—the call of frogs and crickets, of anonymous rustles and grunts. And always there was the pinging of the mosquitoes.

One of the Germans moved and swore softly, hushed into silence by his friend. Christy and Juma, his gunbearer, were old hands at this game. They sat as if carved from rock, their only movement a tightening of their fingers on the triggers of their rifles when a distant lion coughed.

The cough came again, but this time it was further away. Christy expelled his breath slowly and imperceptibly, resigning himself to a long wait. Holy Mother, but the mosquitoes were a pest! He willed himself to disregard them. Concentrate on something else, he told himself, like that stinking zebra, its stomach distended with gas, its stripes faded by the moonlight to shades of grey.

Bushes crouched silently like living, waiting creatures, more menacing than the two shapes that suddenly materialised close to the kill, causing the hunters to draw in their breaths. But it was only a pair of hyenas come to bury their snouts in the entrails of the kill, snuffling and grunting and snarling at each other. Then they, too, melted away and the night was left again to the mosquitoes and the tree-frogs.

Think of something else, Christy told himself again. Kate? No, not Kate. Anything but Kate. She was hopeless, a lost cause, a straight-laced, holier-than-thou school-ma'am who had no idea how to give or accept love. Sure, it seemed that night as if she were the most generous woman that ever breathed. She had a smile that could charm the heart out of a man and a spirited way of talking that seemed to promise union of heart and mind as well as body. But there wasn't a man alive who could compete with that bloody school —not unless he was whiter than white, purer than pure, with a marriage contract in his pocket that would satisfy all the old biddies in Nairobi.

He would not think of Kate, or even visit her again. He would think of the future.

Was this to be all there was? The hunting, the tracking, the endless waiting? It had been meat and drink to him—was still, up to a point, yet there was sometimes a feeling of futility and emptiness.

He was tired of pandering to the demands of clients. These two Germans, now—he didn't really care for them. They were moody and quarrelled between themselves. He would get them back to town and go off on his own somewhere, up to the harsh, lonely country of the Northern Frontier. Or to Uganda. Anywhere.

And then, what? What was the alternative to hunting? He had been too long in the wild to imagine living in a town. Farming? Perhaps that was it. Perhaps he should spend the money he had managed to save on a few thousand acres in the sunlit uplands. He could build a house—grey stone, with a shingled roof . . .

Oh, *Kate*!

He was away for a long time, going south with the Germans towards Tabora where he left them and paid off the porters and Juma, who was to take the horses back to Nairobi. He took the Lake steamer from Mwanza to Jinja with the intention of going up the Victoria Nile to Lake Kyoga to shoot crocodiles—always a reasonably lucrative operation—but he fell in with an old friend and allowed himself to be diverted to the Ruwenzori Mountains where, he was assured, there was a fortune to be made from minerals just lying waiting to be picked up.

There were no minerals, or none that he could get his hands on. He turned his back on the mountains and at last began the long journey which was to bring him back to Nairobi over a year since he left it.

The difference in the town astonished him. Sixth Avenue was a wide, new thoroughfare which had been cut at right-angles to Government Road and was planted with jacaranda trees, and already there were new buildings springing up along it. The New Stanley Hotel was finished and stood on a commanding corner where Sixth Avenue met Hardinge Street. Almost opposite it was the Theatre Royal.

Garvie's Bioscope and Tea-room had opened to excellent business and one could drink and dance at the Travellers' Club or even drive out to the Clairmont on the Kiambu Road.

There were more motor cars now on the streets

of Nairobi, and Christy stood for a while in thoughtful contemplation of a Ford box-body with the name of a safari firm emblazoned on its side which stood in the back courtyard of the Norfolk Hotel. He sucked a tooth pensively as he walked slowly round the vehicle. It would come to this, of course. He could see that such a contraption would have its uses when it came to transporting tents and equipment, but he shook his head as he pictured its passage up mountains and across rivers and gullies. It could never replace the horse or a man's two feet, he thought. Not in Africa.

In spite of all the other, newer, places of entertainment, the Norfolk Bar was as noisy as ever. The personnel changed a little, Christy thought as he looked about him, but never the atmosphere which always seemed charged with energy, as if the strange, colourful people who crowded in from the farming districts were dedicated to cramming a year's carousal into the few short days they spent in town. They swilled the beer, shouted the gossip from one end of the bar to the other, guffawed and argued and slapped backs with an intensity that almost amounted to religious fervour.

Christy realised with surprise that it was nearly Christmas. He had lost count of the months in his travels, but a few garish decorations over the bar and a dried-up tree that had been dragged in

234

and now stood drooping in the corner awoke him to the fact.

"That," said one farmer in flapping khaki shorts, a flamboyant scarf at his neck and a wide-brimmed *terai* on the back of his head, "is *no* Christmas tree." He stabbed a finger towards the corner as he spoke. "It's second best, like everything else in this bloody country."

"Why don't you go home, Jack?"

"Too many girls waiting for him with paternity suits, old boy—"

"Rubbish! I'm on the verge of making a fortune. Ostriches are the thing, old chap. Absolute gold mine. No trouble to rear and the feathers fetch a fortune—"

"There was I, with the trunk waving over my head and two tons of ivory in spitting distance, all of them flapping their ears like fury—"

"A spark from the railway did it: five hundred acres of wheat up in smoke—"

"He sat all night in the privy listening to the lions outside. Couldn't move, old chap."

"It doesn't change much, does it?"

A voice in Christy's ear made him turn. A tall, rangy, red-haired figure stood there. Christy grinned at him delightedly.

"Pete Wainwright! Sure, it's good to see you."

"You've been gone a long time."

"Too long. I hardly recognise the place. What have you been doing with yourself?"

Wainwright grinned.

"Oh, this and that. Have you any plans?"

"Not yet. I gave myself a break from bloody clients who demand the earth, but a man must eat. I shall have to organise myself and see what work there is around."

"I could put something in your way." Wainwright placed a large, meaty hand on Christy's shoulder. "In fact, Christy, me fine boy, you and I could make a good team. Bring your beer over to the verandah where we can talk."

Hundreds of new settlers had arrived during the past year, he said, and all needed stock.

"It's sheep they're going for, up in the highlands," he said. "They've brought pedigree stock with them in many cases, but everyone knows now that they'll die like flies unless they're crossed with hardy native stock. So where do they get native sheep from?"

"The Masai?" hazarded Christy.

"Right. But the Masai want cattle in return—they're not very interested in shillingis. My plan is to go up to Somalia and buy cattle there, bring them all back to Laikipia to trade with the Masai for sheep which we then sell to the Europeans in the highlands. We can't fail! There should be a good profit at the end of it—and no bloody clients you'd have to sell your soul to."

"We'd be months away from Nairobi."

"When has that ever bothered you? The place is beginning to look like Tunbridge Wells, anyway: I can never wait to get out of it now everyone's so damned respectable."

"I don't know, Pete—"

"I don't need to spell it out for you. This is going to be a bloody dangerous exercise for all sorts of reasons—stock thieves, game, the terrain: you know the difficulties as well as I do. I need someone like you, Christy."

Christy grinned.

"Now, isn't that the truth? Well, I'll think about it, Pete."

"Why the hesitation? We'll make a fortune—"

"I doubt that. It sounds like fun, though."

"Then why—?"

"I don't know. There's something I have to look into first."

"A woman?"

"Maybe."

He sat brooding over his beer after Wainwright had left him. He'd changed his mind about seeing Kate on an average three times every day: now the moment was upon him and still he could not decide. What was the point of it, after all? Better, perhaps, to stay and drink with the boys, to swap stories and drink some more until, beyond thought, he could drop into his bed.

But even as he gave himself this advice, he was getting up from the table, going down the steps, hailing a rickshaw. Suddenly, having at last decided, he could not get to Kate quickly enough. His heart was pounding as if he were a love-sick boy. He had no idea what he would say, what he would do, what she would say to him; he merely knew that he had to see her and that all this indecision was so much play-acting.

He sat motionless in the rickshaw, nervously biting the inside of his cheek, unaware of the words being grunted out by the rickshaw men—one pulling and the other pushing. They were praising him for his strength and his virility, for the bigger the flattery the bigger the tip, but this evening their song fell on deaf ears.

It was an anti-climax to find the house in darkness. Without hope, he banged on the front door, but there was no reply. He prowled round to the back. No lamps were burning anywhere. All was still and silent and deserted.

He sank down on the steps of the verandah, the cloying smell of the shrub which Kate called yesterday-today-and-tomorrow drifting towards him, bringing back with pain the times he had sat there before.

It was almost Christmas. He should have known she would be gone—to Kiambu, he supposed, where she always went for the holidays.

He gave a bitter, mirthless little laugh. So many hours of inward debate to end like this!

Something white gleamed at the foot of the steps and he bent to pick it up. It was an inch-long piece of chalk and he turned it over and over between thumb and forefinger as again he debated.

To follow Kate to Kiambu or to agree to join Pete Wainwright? What was the point in seeing her? he asked himself again, as he had asked himself so many times. Her answer would be the same. The school still existed. Nothing would have changed.

Gritting his teeth, his face tightened into a mask of despair, he hurled the chalk into the depths of the flowerbed, got to his feet, and strode away towards town.

"It all seems to be drifting away from me," Kate said to Meg as they strolled among the coffee. "It's all coming to an end, bit by bit."

"You've had ups and downs before."

"Not like this. It's as if everyone—even people I've considered my friends—has withdrawn from me. I don't know why. I don't seem to be accused of anything. I can't stand up and defend myself because there's nothing to defend myself from. It's as if everyone knows something about me that I don't know—as if I've contracted some dreadful communicable disease that no doctor will tell me of."

"Kate—Kate! How you always exaggerate! You still have pupils."

"A diminishing number, and no new ones coming along. I haven't a hope of being able to keep going once the new Government school opens."

"They'll want teachers."

"Perhaps. Sometimes I think I would like to do something quite different."

"Different? You?" Meg turned and smiled at Kate. "I can't somehow imagine it."

Kate said nothing and for a moment they walked in silence.

"Is it Patsy?" Meg asked at last. "Do people still object to her?"

"Some do, I think. They think that I have strange, liberal ideas that will lead to total disruption of the way of life we enjoy—at least, that's what I imagine they think, but no one comes out in the open. All the slurs made on me are so intangible, just as if there were a whispering campaign. Oh, tell me I'm being stupid, Meg! I expect I am. I've always believed that basically people are kind and well-meaning. It's ridiculous to feel persecuted like this."

"I don't know," Meg said slowly. "In a small community, it's amazing the harm that one or two malevolent women can do. I've seen it before."

"Well, I'm forced to admit defeat. Yes I am, Meg—there's no point in closing my eyes to it any longer. Fortunately I have a small income my father left me. It's only a pittance, but I shan't starve while I think what to do next. In the New Year I shall tell my few remaining loyal parents that they must make other arrangements for their children after the next school year."

"But what about you? Where will you go?"

Kate came to a halt.

"I've thought of England," she said. "Home. But just as you said when talking of Colin, I can't think of it as home any more. My roots may not have been in Africa for long, but they seem to have gone very deep."

"Come here," Meg urged.

"Oh, Meg! I can't keep flying to you whenever I'm in trouble."

"Why not? You could lease a corner of our land, build a little house, teach the girls. Hugh's talking about building a school for the labour, too. Maybe you could get that started for him—perhaps train an African teacher." In her enthusiasm she clasped Kate's arm. "You could keep chickens, grow things—oh, there are all sorts of possibilities."

"Yes." Kate's face brightened as she considered them. "Yes, of course there are. One thing I've always wanted to do, Meg, is translate legends and folk tales into Swahili. I don't believe anything has been written for African children yet. That would be something really worthwhile, wouldn't it?"

"Certainly it would."

Meg smiled to see it happening yet again—the subtle transformation that took place whenever

Kate became fired with enthusiasm. With one accord they fell into step again.

"I think you ought to consult Hugh before you go offering people portions of land, though."

"He'll be delighted, especially if it means that we have no worries about Janet's education. Anyway, you know we all regard you as a member of the family. He's been worried about the fact that you seem down in the mouth. You know, he always had the feeling that eventually you and Christy would make a match of it—but you haven't mentioned him for ages."

"I haven't seen him for ages. But, anyway, Christy is already married." Kate's voice was carefully neutral. "He's in no position to make a match with anyone." They walked in silence for a few minutes, turning to retrace their steps towards the house. "I'd love to live here," she went on. "It's so peaceful and spacious and beautiful. But oh, Meg, how I hate to lose that school! It was all such a lovely dream once, and now it's all fading away."

"A door will open, Kate. Perhaps 1914 will be the beginning of something new and exciting for you."

Full circle, she thought. A handful of girls in a back room.

Broodingly Kate looked at the six pupils in front of her. They ranged from Patsy and Julie, both aged six, to Moira McDonald, who was fourteen. It was an impossible range for one teacher, but she had urged Rose Fawcett to apply for a post at the new school and had, in a way, been relieved when she had gone as it would have been difficult to keep on paying her salary.

It was surprising that she had as many as six girls left, Kate thought, though Moira was only there because in September she was going to Scotland to boarding school, and Dorothy Lamton was going back to England. The two Riley girls were being sent to South Africa, so for all of them it had not seemed worth while making a move to the Government school.

It was July—cold, sunless, as if the weather were in tune with her thoughts. And it was not only the demise of the school that was depressing. Events in Europe were disquieting, with Belgium and Germany squaring up for a fight that would inevitably involve Britain. And that would involve the Protectorate, for the border with German East Africa was not many miles away.

Two solemn-faced men from the Railway Company had been to see her the day before, wanting to see the school in order to assess its suitability as a temporary military hospital. It had brought the situation home to her in a very immediate and frightening way.

She felt isolated from the community around her. It seemed a long time since anyone had called —a far cry from those early days when Andrew had dropped in almost every day, eager to offer his services in any capacity she cared to name.

And Christy.

She drew in her breath sharply and rose to her feet, even though all the children were occupied, none at that moment needing attention. Unnecessarily she went to bend over Julie's shoulder, murmuring encouragement. Anything, anything, to stop herself thinking of him.

Was there ever a woman more foolish than she?

No, no—surely the blame was not entirely hers? He had been so quick to fire up, so oblivious to any point of view but his own. Even so, if he were to walk in through that door, she thought, I wouldn't let him go again. But there was no chance of seeing him walk through the door. He had said he would not see her again, and he had meant it. He was lost to her.

He was, at that moment, quite literally lost to everyone. Pete Wainwright stared across the shimmering plain, his eyes screwed up against the glare of the sun, wondering what had happened to his partner and piously putting up a prayer that marauding tribesmen had not been tempted to violence by the sight of the herd of sheep Christy had been driving this way.

They had arranged to meet at this point, close to a dried-up river bed where a few trees cast a welcoming shade. Pete had expected Christy to be at the meeting place before him, since his journey had been slightly shorter, but finding nothing but lion-coloured grassland inhabited only by zebra and gazelle, Pete had outspanned the oxen, ordered a *boma* to be built for the sheep in his care, and settled down to wait.

Towards evening a runner had come to the camp from the direction of Nakuru, a paper in a pouch round his neck. It was a note addressed to Christy from the District Officer, but Pete tore it open anyway. When a message has been brought by hand for over a hundred miles, the usual niceties no longer seem valid.

"Dear Brennan," he read. "With a war in Europe now imminent, a telegram has arrived here from the War Office ordering you to report immediately to your regiment. I have the telegram here, for safe-keeping.

"The m.v. *Strathallan Castle* leaves Mombasa on 1st August, the boat-train leaving Nairobi on the previous Wednesday. I can only suggest that you return as soon as possible, calling in at my office en route so that I may deliver the telegram."

Pete whistled softly. They had been in the bush for two months now and were totally out of touch with world events. Imagine Christy a soldier! Yes —now he thought about it, of course he had been in the Boer War, hence the scar—hence, in fact, his presence in Africa. He must have remained on the Reserve.

But to leave Mombasa on the first day of next

month! It was virtually impossible. Only by leaving almost at once could they arrive in Nairobi in time for the boat-train. Only if Christy came now, this moment, was there a chance of it. And still the plain before him was empty.

His eyes sharpened. He was wrong. Far, far away, on the skyline was a smudge, a moving mark that kicked up dust, wavering in the liquefying heat. It looked as if, after all, Christy would be in time.

Two days later the school closed its doors for the last time and Kate, together with Kamau and all his supporters, was beginning dispiritedly to clear up ready for packing and her eventual removal to Kiambu. She was emptying a cupboard in the schoolroom, making a pile of books to be thrown out and stacking others that she wanted to keep, when a tap on the door heralded the appearance of Margaret McDonald.

"You look so busy, I hardly like to tell you what I've come for," she said.

"I'm glad to see you."

Kate's pleasure was genuine. Margaret McDonald was a woman who had remained friendly when others had fallen by the wayside. She had a dry sense of humour and a dislike of pretence and humbug that Kate had always appreciated.

"I'm rounding up helpers," she said now.

"For what?"

"To feed the hordes that are pouring into town. I didn't know there were so many men in the country, and they're all coming to volunteer for the Army! Nobody knows what to do with them. The King's African Rifles don't want them. They're totally untrained, of course, with nothing but their vast enthusiasm and patriotism to recommend them."

"What are they going to do?"

"My dear, you wouldn't believe it! They're all having the time of their lives, forming themselves up into private armies. The Boers from Uasin Gishu have turned themselves into Arnoldi's Scouts, and there's Bowker's Horse and Monica's Own, after the Governor's daughter—a more raggle-taggle, swashbuckling collection of men you never did see. And apart from them, the boat-train leaves today, with all the men going back to join their regiments. Proper soldiers, I mean."

"What do you want me to do?"

"Well, there are a lot of comings and goings at the station, as you can imagine. Some of us are going down to man a coffee stall there, with sandwiches and things. Everyone's been baking like anything. Will you come and help behind the counter? It should all be rather a lark—still, I can see you have plenty to keep you busy here."

Kate looked despairingly into the cupboard and down at the pile of books on the floor.

"This is depressing beyond measure," she said.

"Actually, I'd love to come. What time do you want me?"

"Two o'clock. I'll collect you in the trap. There's a train from up country due in at three and it's sure to be full of men coming to enlist. Mrs. Bowden is going to begin setting up the stall with a few helpers then, for there's bound to be pandemonium by the time it comes in. As many as come in will be catching the train to get to the coast."

She bustled away, stirred and excited at what was taking place in the town, and not too apprehensive about the future.

The situation was every bit as confused as she had described, Kate found. They drove in the McDonalds' dashing little trap down Sixth Avenue and found it milling with activity in the area of the New Stanley Hotel and Nairobi House, which appeared to have been taken over for some kind of recruiting campaign.

Men in wide-brimmed hats, their shoulders slung with bullet loops, some on horses, some on foot, hung about aimlessly. A fearsome-looking character with a hat bearing a whole, snarling leopard's head stood outside the New Stanley, legs apart and hands on his hips. He seemed to be giving some kind of rallying speech.

"There's Mr. Bowker," Margaret McDonald said. "He's recruiting men for Bowker's Horse. All I can say is 'thank heaven for the KAR'!"

At the station half a dozen women were already

busy at the coffee stall and they greeted Kate's and Margaret's arrival with relief.

"Everything's ten cents," Mrs. Bowden said. "It seemed the easiest thing—"

"My scones are worth a deal more than that."

"I *know*, Mrs. McTavish, of course they are, but we're not out to make money, are we? Kate, you come down this end next to me. I'm afraid we've had to tie the teaspoon to the tea-urn, we've already lost so many. You will take care to keep the netting over the sandwiches, won't you? The flies are awful, though not so bad as they would have been in the hot weather."

The natives, as always with plenty of time to stare and watch and wonder, hung about the station making baffled comments to each other. So many extraordinary things were taking place, actions which had no precedent. The Indian station master looked equally helpless. He was used to the platform being crowded for the arrival and departure of each train, but not like this— not crowds of men hung about with bedding rolls and kitbags with not a hope of finding room for them all.

The train from up country came in with a whoosh and a puff of steam and a surge of noise from the platform. Kate poured tea and took the proffered money and passed plates of cakes and sandwiches.

There seemed a never-ending supply of

customers. The women grew sweat-stained and dishevelled, and more sandwiches were sent for.

For a moment there was a lull. Cups were collected and washed. Kate collapsed on a sack of grain and wiped the back of her hand across her forehead. It would all start again soon, for the hour of the train's departure was coming close and everyone expected a last-minute rush. Margaret was dispatched for more food and Mrs. McTavish, overcome, retired from the fray altogether.

And here they were, the late arrivals, strangers all, yet somehow alike: hard, tough, weather-beaten men, with calloused hands and far-seeing eyes, wrinkled at the corners. What would England make of them, Kate wondered, in their khaki shorts and their ten-gallon hats?

The train gave a tentative wheeze, and a whistle blew. There was movement everywhere, and surely far too many passengers? They would be packed like sardines!

Kate sighed and eased her back, as doors slammed and the press around the coffee stall grew less. The train wheezed again, and it was then that Kate saw Christy sauntering down the platform away from her, a bedding roll on his shoulder, one arm around Millie.

The station master was shouting at him. Kate called his name and ran round the stall oblivious of the people who stood in her way. She dodged round a pile of sacks, narrowly avoided falling over the legs of an old African who dozed against the wall, and cannoned into a woman who was walking backwards, waving as she did so to a young man who leaned out of the window.

All the windows were crowded with men, and now there was no sign of Christy. The train had swallowed him and nowhere could she see him. But Millie was there, still yards away.

Kate ran towards her unimpeded now, but already the train was moving and the noise was such that Kate's voice could not be heard. Millie laughed at her, shaking her head, miming her deafness, while impotently Kate stood and watched the carriages slide past her.

"What was it you wanted, love?" Millie asked, the last carriage gone and calm restored.

Kate shook her head.

"Never mind," she said.

Slowly she walked back to the coffee stall.

251

12

THE farm was their kingdom. The girls knew each corner of it and it provided all they needed: privacy, recreation, companionship. They rode its ways like three young princesses when their lessons were done, conscious that beyond its bounds events were taking place that were of interest to the adults but to them significant only because Hugh Lacey had gone to fight in Europe, leaving the farm in the hands of Meg and Kate.

Of far more consequence to the children was the small animal orphanage which housed a motherless dik-dik, that most enchanting of creatures, birds with broken wings, and even, for a short time, a baby cheetah. There was the squatter village on the far boundary, close by the river: an alien world from which came a never-ending supply of drama, concerned with life and death, feuds and fertility. Above all there was the world of their own imagination which turned the open spaces into Sherwood Forest, or a field of battle, or the setting for King Solomon's Mines.

They were shabby princesses, for there was no money for new clothes—or, indeed, for much besides. Food was basic and repetitive. Meg was heard to say that once the war was over she doubted whether she would ever again be able to look a Cape Gooseberry in the face, but vegetables were plentiful and Colin kept them supplied with game for the pot, even if imported luxuries were non-existent.

The war, though it deprived Meg of her husband, had granted her one boon. Colin had stayed in Africa after all—rather too grave and responsible for his age, but an invaluable part of the small family at Mawingo.

The problems of wartime living were manifold. It was impossible to export coffee due to lack of shipping space. The Army had requisitioned many of the cattle. Sheer survival was the order of the day—a relentless fight against the encroaching bush, so that at least there would be some semblance of a farm for Hugh to return to, in spite of shortage of labour and lack of money.

Meg worried a little about Colin. She felt he was too over-burdened by responsibility for a boy his age. Perhaps he should have gone to boarding school, war or no war. Here his preoccupations were not whether or not he was to be picked for the house football team, but if he would be able to shoot the porcupine that had been ravaging the vegetable garden, or if the small remaining acreage of coffee would be picked on time. Kate —for all her protestations in the past—gave him lessons as well as the girls, and she welcomed the task because he was thoughtful and intelligent and asked interesting questions. For Latin and mathematics he rode over to the mission three times a week.

There were several parallel worlds operating at the farm, Kate sometimes thought. There was that inhabited by herself and Meg. Together they worked and planned and worried, coping with unforeseen emergencies and crises of all kinds for which they were totally untrained. There was the child left for dead outside one of the squatter's huts—a girl of fourteen or so. Four times she had been put outside, and four times she had crawled back, for the Kikuyu firmly believed that a death inside the hut made the whole house unclean. Kamau—old and unwanted by the Army, still cooking for Kate and now for the others—had brought her to the house, where she had been nursed back to health. There was the time when the wife of Kitoro—the farm *nyapera* or headman —had sickened and died, simply fading away like the withering head of a flower, responding to no medicine that anyone could provide for her, even the hospital in Nairobi where Kate took her one wet and windy night in the teeth of opposition from Kitoro. It was a *thahu*, he said. She had displeased the spirits.

There were stock thefts, and blight, and lazy, untrained labourers whom they were forced to employ in place of the more responsible men who had gone to the war. Some of those pressed into service were scarcely more than children.

Inevitably the world of the squatter village

impinged on their own, but still it was a world apart. Its inhabitants regarded Meg as all-powerful, and indeed many of them called her 'Mama'. They came to her with their sores and their sicknesses and their requests for extra *posho* or meat or tobacco. Sometimes she wrote letters for them, and sometimes they asked her to settle disputes. But by and large it was a secret world, a mysterious world, for no Kikuyu likes to reveal too much.

Kate recognised, too, the separate world in which the girls lived. She taught them on the jasmine-covered verandah each morning and for the most part they were open and responsive, learning each at her own rate, all different, each very much an individual. But hurt one, and they were all hurt. A reproof concerning unlearned work or an untidy page, and their expressions grew strangely similar—closed and secretive. Though none of them had moved, it seemed somehow as if they edged closer together. It was a case of all for one and one for all, and this maxim was painted on a poster which hung over the three beds that stood side by side.

Julie was particularly protective of Patsy. Physically Julie was taller than either of the others, though all were close in age, and was as pretty as any ten-year-old girl could be, who wore a double *terai* on hair that was scraped back in two pigtails, and had scratched knees beneath patched, overlong shorts. She had a clear skin, a freckled nose, and a face that looked as if it would break into a wide smile, even when it was in repose. Her nature was warm and friendly. She expected people to like her because, on the whole, she liked them.

Patsy was different. It was not, Kate thought, because of the colour of her skin, for here on the farm she met no one who made her conscious of it. It was simply because, metaphorically, of the thinness of it. A hurt animal would put her off her food for days, while many an evening Kate would discover her shedding tears over the fate of some fictitious heroine. Yet she was no milksop. Angry and fierce, quivering with passion, she would defend the cause of the weak against the strong, the underdog against the oppressor.

She read voraciously and had amply fulfilled all Kate's predictions about her capabilities. Neither Julie nor Janet was unintelligent, but Patsy far outstripped them in her school work, and there was no moment when Kate regretted the choice she had made to bring the child up as her own. The loss of the school still brought its moments of sadness, but her hopes were on Patsy now. Perhaps there was a purpose in it all, she thought. Perhaps all her efforts were meant to be directed towards this small girl, who so obviously had the potential for greatness.

Her story would be unlike Kate's own. She would have nothing but encouragement, Kate resolved. She should have the best—an English university, paper qualifications that no one could deny, the chance to *be* somebody, to do something really worthwhile that would make her a force to be reckoned with in the Africa of the future. Yes—even though African women had no importance to their menfolk apart from their ability to produce children and work until they dropped, Patsy would be the first of a new breed. It was a privilege, she felt, to have this clever, sensitive child delivered into her hands, as malleable as the clay on a potter's wheel.

She had asked about her origins. Kate attempted to answer her questions as truthfully as possible. Her mother had been a young and beautiful girl, she told her, who had died tragically at Patsy's birth. Her father had been a European.

"He was a man I loved very much," Kate said.

"So you took care of me for his sake?"

"For *your* sake. Because you were small and defenceless and had no one. And because for some peculiar reason I loved you on sight, poor deluded fool that I was, little knowing that you would grow up to be as artful as a waggonload of monkeys, plaguing me with questions when you ought to be in bed and asleep."

Julie's questions were easier to answer now that Ronnie had been killed in Tanganyika fighting against the Germans, thus turning him into a dead hero rather than a convicted criminal. There was talk of Julie going home to her grandmother 'after the war', but Kate, remembering the formidable lady she had seen on board ship, cherished the hope that this idea would die a natural death. Julie was a child of Africa now, accustomed to freedom and open spaces and sunshine. Kate was convinced that life with the elderly Mrs. Hudson would provide none of these things, and very little love, either. She hated to think how Julie would suffer if she were forced to part from Patsy and Janet, not to mention Kate herself.

By 1918 it was hard to imagine the normal world, where men ran their own farms and families were united. Hugh had seen action in France, but had been posted to Brigade Headquarters, much to Meg's relief. All the girls were very proud of him, particularly when the news came through that he had been awarded the Military Cross for his actions on the Western Front, and Patsy in particular thought of him far more than any of the others dreamed. He had been so kind to her in those days before he went away—so gentle. Yet he was strong and brave. It must, she thought, be the most wonderful thing in the world to have a father like that.

Colin was the next best thing. He could be kind, in an off-hand sort of a way, though usually he behaved as if the actions of the three girls were beneath his notice. At fourteen, he was almost a man. Yet because of Patsy's intellectual ability, Kate began including her in the English literature lessons she gave Colin in the afternoon, and while

Patsy pretended to find this a bore—since the other girls would have thought her mad if she had not—in fact they became the high-spot of her day.

Colin knew that he would be sent to England to school once the war was over, but he knew, too, that he would be back. This was where he belonged—this land where the sun soaked through his skin and into his very blood and where the air was filled with the smell of dust and leleshwa bushes, woodsmoke and the bleating of goats. Meantime he was content to work about the farm, to hunt with Kitoro's son, Kimotho, who had become his friend, and to debate questions of history and literature with Kate. It amused him, the way young Patsy strived so hard to put her oar in. She wasn't a bad kid at all, he thought. Too sensitive, of course. She reminded him sometimes of a gazelle in the forest, nose quivering, about to leap off in springing bounds at the least disturbance. There was no doubt, however, that she was sharp as a needle. There were times when he forgot that she was scarcely older than young Janet—spoiled, pretty, wayward Janet—and would talk to her as if she were his equal. He had no way of knowing that Patsy relived those times, over and over, cherishing every word.

The improving news from Europe came at a time when Meg had begun to wonder if she could go on for one more week, let alone months. The years without Hugh had seemed endless, the problems of keeping the farm running almost insuperable.

She came back from a shopping trip to Nairobi in high spirits one day in October of 1918.

"There's a wonderful feeling of optimism about," she said. "For once there seemed nothing but good news talked of on the Norfolk verandah. And, oh Kate, the jacarandas are out in Sixth Avenue—such a lovely sight. You'll never guess who came bustling into the Norfolk while I was having lunch, so full of consequence. None other than Hope Honeywell! She seems to be a real Queen Bee these days—something to do with welfare, I understand—and she's designed herself a smart military uniform, rather like the WAACs but a little more dashing."

"Well, Andrew is on the War Council, isn't he? I suppose they are important people these days."

"The way Hope was flinging orders about, one would have thought she was winning the war single-handed. But who cares, just as long as we *are* winning it? I can't believe that perhaps Hugh will be home soon."

It was a year before he came—older, thinner, but delighted to be home and full of plans for getting the farm back into full production.

"Look at him," Meg said to Kate, smiling affectionately at the sight of her husband standing on the edge of the verandah and looking out over his acres with an ecstatic expression. "Did you ever see anyone look so contented? No one would think we had an overdraft the size of the national debt."

"I don't suppose money seems very important at this moment," Kate said.

She herself was struggling against a feeling of anti-climax. The war, which had seemed to be going on for ever, was now over, and for that she was thankful. Yet there were times when she felt she was still waiting for something to happen: times when she ached with a sense of loss—for the school, for Christy, for life itself which seemed to be passing so swiftly with nothing to show for it.

The idea of building a small house for her on a corner of Mawingo Estate was resurrected. It would be a new life for her and the girls, she told herself. She would raise chickens and a pig or two.

But the restless feeling persisted, in spite of the fact that her days were full and that no more beautiful site could have been chosen for the house. From its verandah she could look across miles of undulating land. There was the forest to the right, the beehive huts of the village at a lower level to the left, the vivid green of the banana trees making a contrasting splash amidst the more muted colours that dominated the immediate landscape.

By 1921 she had a garden that blazed with colour; geraniums and carnations and zinnias and chrysanthemums all flowering together in the strange and profligate manner of Africa.

She never could raise any enthusiasm for her chickens, but working in the garden did much to quieten the strange feeling of waiting that still raised its head at intervals. It seemed sometimes as if some question had been asked but remained unanswered, but for once on this late, lambent afternoon in January, the restlessness was quiescent, soothed by plans she was making for the school Hugh was about to open for the children of his labour. As she weeded and thinned, savouring the smell of the earth and flowers, she thought again of the scheme she once had for producing an African child's first reading book.

She was turning over possible stories in her mind as she stood, trowel in hand, rubbing her aching back absently as she looked down over the valley. A path snaked down the hillside from the village to the road below and from it another path had been cut leading to the house, skirting the coffee bushes. It could only be travelled on foot or on horseback. It was too rough and narrow for the motorised traffic that was becoming more and more common on the road below.

It was the golden hour that she loved the best: the hour of long shadows and deeper colours and a stillness that made sounds carry with startling clarity. She could hear the voices of half a dozen women walking in single file up the path, digging tools in their hands, round-headed babies bobbing on their backs.

Behind them, just in view, was a man on a horse. For a moment her heart seemed to falter, then it continued beating so strongly that the pounding of it filled her head and made her senses swim.

At this distance it was impossible to distinguish features. He was a big man, she could tell that, dressed in khaki, a wide-brimmed hat on his head. He did not look like any of their close neighbours. The horse, too, seemed unfamiliar. She swallowed, forcing herself to be calm. It could be anyone, she told herself. Anyone at all.

Every man wore khaki. It might be the new vet: hadn't Hugh mentioned a sick cow? It might be one of Hugh's friends taking a short cut, or it could be a stranger. The country was full of them since the war. The Soldier Settlement Scheme had attracted newcomers and it was all too easy for them to lose their way, for there were no signposts and few boundary markings to distinguish one man's land from the next.

Still she watched and her mouth dried as the possibility hardened into certainty. Who else held his head like that, as if he didn't give a damn for anybody?

"Christy?" she whispered. Then louder, joyously, "Christy!"

The figure on the horse waved an arm above his head and she flung down the trowel and ran to him, laughing, crying, uncaring of the curious looks of the Kikuyu women or of the years and the anger that had separated them.

Christy slipped from the saddle and held out his arms to her and with the tears of joy wet on her cheeks she flung herself into them, knowing with certainty that the question had at last been answered and that this was what she had been waiting for.

"So long—so many years! You didn't write. I didn't know if you were alive or dead."

"I heard at the Norfolk that you were here—still not married."

"No, no." Kate brushed this aside. "Oh Christy, let me look at you." She reached up and touched his face, the scar that lifted his eyebrow, the corner of his wide mouth, the face that she now knew she would love for ever. "Why didn't you come to say goodbye to me? Why didn't you write? I knew that you'd gone—I saw you at the station, too late to speak to you. I thought my heart would break. Why did you go without a word?"

He held her hand against his face.

"Kate, I did write, I swear it. It was a long, long letter, written on the ship, posted in London the moment we docked."

"It didn't reach me. I heard nothing."

"I addressed it to the school—"

"It should have reached me. There was a great deal of confusion."

"Kate, I *swear* I wrote! When I heard nothing from you in return I thought that was the end of it. Sure, you'll never know how I tried to forget you."

"But you're here! I can't believe it."

"Is that your house up there?"

"Yes—Hugh built it for me and I live there with Patsy and Julie. Come. You'll love them, Christy. Patsy has grown up beautifully, and she's just as bright as we always thought she would be. And as for Julie, she's pretty as a picture, just like Louise."

"What happened to Ronnie Hudson?"

"He was killed at Tabora. Christy, why did it take you so long to come home? You are well, aren't you? Not wounded?"

"No, not wounded." He laughed down at her. "Questions, questions! We've all the time in the world to talk. Let's go and meet those girls of yours. If I'm not mistaken one of them at least is up there waiting for us."

Kate looked towards the house again, and now she could see a small figure on the skyline looking down the path towards them. It was Patsy, who had been a witness to everything—Kate's flight, the repeated embraces, the love that was evident in the way that Kate had touched the strange man's face.

Her lips were parted, her eyes wide with

excitement. Had Colin been there to see her instead of in England at school she would have reminded him even more strongly of a gazelle— a small bushbuck, perhaps, quivering with anticipation, nerves tight as fiddle strings.

Her father, Kate had told her, had been a man she had loved, a long time ago. The unbelievable thing had happened. Her father had come home.

Patsy was not the same innocent child who had romped through the war years, untroubled by the fact that her skin was darker than that of the other girls. She was twelve years old now—would, in fact, be thirteen in less than two months, on the day in April which Kate had arbitrarily declared her birthday—and she understood things that had previously been hidden from her.

Such as the fact that she had a touch of the tar brush. She had first heard that expression from a newcomer to the country, the wife of an ex-airman who had bought the Rowleys' farm whose acres marched with Mawingo Estate. Meg had been entertaining her to tea, and all had been politeness and charm, the three girls passing cakes and speaking when spoken to.

To their relief they had at last been dismissed and joyfully they had run from the sitting room out on the verandah and down the steps towards the stables—all except Patsy who, on the top step, had turned back to retrieve one of her books which she had left on a chair.

266

"The little dark girl," she had heard the newcomer say. "There's a touch of the tar brush there, unless I'm much mistaken."

Meg's voice had been cool as she replied.

"Patsy is part-Kikuyu, if that's what you mean."

Slowly Patsy had turned away and, clutching the book to her bosom, had tip-toed down the steps. It was a horrible thing to say, she thought. It made her feel dirty, as if she ought to wash herself more. The fact that she was part Kikuyu had never been hidden from her, but this was the first time it had occurred to her that it was something she should be ashamed of.

Now she knew better.

There were some, of course, who treated her no differently from the way they treated the other girls. The north-country couple who had come to live at Rivermead Estate, over in the Thika direction, were down-to-earth and kindly, and she felt at ease with them. There was a big family of Danes five miles to the east who made no distinction at all. But often people adopted a special tone of voice when they spoke to her as if the effort to regard her as a normal human being in spite of the colour of her skin was almost too much for them. And some people, like the tar brush lady, tried not to notice her at all, as if the very sight of her made them uneasy.

So, warily, she had kept very quiet all that first evening that Christy had spent with them, and it did not surprise her that he did not immediately acknowledge her as his daughter, for this was another thing she had learned. People were appalled at any sexual union between black and white, and when it occurred, it was spoken of only in whispers. She did not understand it, but she accepted it, and it seemed sufficient to explain both Christy's and Kate's silence on the issue.

It didn't matter. *She* knew!

With Julie breathing deeply and regularly in untroubled sleep, Patsy lay and listened to the sound of voices which came through the thin wall of her bedroom. Words were indistinguishable, but still she listened, for the sound they made was like a pattern, the light, vibrant thread of Kate's voice mingling with the deep, musical tones of Christy Brennan. Her father.

He hadn't belonged to the ranks of 'Them '— those people who had to try very hard to be pleasant to her. He had looked at her with special interest, had drawn her out about her interests, the book she was reading. He had seemed to like her even better than Julie, and that was amazing, because everyone liked Julie best.

Oh, she was so glad he had come! She didn't care that it had to be a secret. She was good at secrets.

Breathless with elation, she hugged herself. His voice, she thought, was like—was like—

She searched her mind for a simile sufficient to cover the situation and finally found one.

It was like molten gold, she thought dreamily, her eyes closed. A voice like molten gold. Still smiling, she slept.

"I knew nothing about the school," Christy said. "It was at the Norfolk I heard you were here— that you still had Patsy."

"I can imagine what all the boys in the bar said about that!"

Christy was silent for a moment.

"What in the name of all that's holy are you going to do with the child?" he asked softly at last. "Where will she belong?"

"With me—where else?"

Kate, who had been sitting on the skin that lay before the fire, her head resting against his knee, turned round eagerly to face him.

"She has such a brain, Christy. I wonder where from? I should hardly have thought that was a legacy from Edward. Anyway, there it is, whatever its origins. I can imagine her setting Oxford by the ears in a few years' time."

"So she's your cause now, is she, Kate? She's taken the place of the school."

"What do you mean?"

"I've seen that look on your face before, only then you were telling me that the school in Nairobi was the most important thing in your life."

She sat back on her heels, and looked at him steadily.

269

"I was wrong. I've learned to—to go on without you, but I haven't learned to live without you, Christy. Not in all this time."

"So do we go on together?" He took her hand in a hard, painful grip.

"Oh, please." The intense whisper seemed to fill the room.

"No matter what the world says?"

"No matter what."

"And you won't mind that the doors of Muthaiga Club are barred to you for ever?"

"Nothing matters, except—*dammit!*" Her voice soared in anger and she brought her fist hard down on his knee. "Damn you, Christy Brennan, you're laughing at me! What have I said that's so funny? You're enough to make a saint lose her temper, and heaven knows I've never claimed to be that."

"Oh, darlin', darlin'." Only half repentant Christy gathered her up on his knee and held her close. "It's just that whatever you do, you do with all of you. That little face of yours, wasn't it just pleading for martyrdom? Would you ever settle for plain, ordinary marriage, like other folk?"

"But you're married already."

"No more. You asked me earlier what had delayed my return so long. The fact is that I was called back to Ireland."

"To see your wife?"

"To bury her, poor soul. She died of the

270

influenza, just as neat and tidy and friendless as she'd always lived. D'you know something, Kate, I never before felt guilt at leaving her for she never wanted anything of marriage but the ring on her finger, but there at her funeral it was a different story. There wasn't a soul at the graveside who cared, one way or the other."

"That was sad."

"All I felt was guilty. Guilty because I left her, guilty because I couldn't feel sadness, guilty because I couldn't leave Ireland quickly enough once I'd paid a duty visit to my father and step-mother."

"Christy, I know nothing of your past life! How strange that seems."

"Most of it is best forgotten. It's the future that matters now. Will you marry me, Kate?"

Bemused, Kate shook her head.

"I can't believe this. I must be dreaming!"

"Would you be after wanting to see the death certificate?" He held her away from him and slanted a hard, questioning look at her. "It was signed, all legal and above board, I promise. No question of foul play."

"Christy!" She put her arms around his neck, forcing herself close to him again. "Don't hold the past against me."

"But will you marry me?"

"Of course I will."

She felt, as he kissed her, like a butterfly must surely feel when emerging from the chrysalis—a different being from the drab, sensible but vaguely discontented creature who had stooped to weed the garden, trying to convince herself that the children and the chickens were sufficient to fill her life. What a fool she had been! What life was there without Christy?

"I have such plans. Let's buy a farm, Kate, somewhere in the high country. I used to dream about it when I was in the trenches."

"No more hunting?"

"I've seen enough killing."

"But what do you know of farming?"

"I was brought up on a farm, with cows and pigs and horses. And, heaven knows, I've talked to enough farmers since I came here twenty years ago. Let's build something, Kate. Let's add our ten cents' worth to this wonderful country."

"It's a hard life."

"Don't I know that? But oh, it'll be a good life, with you beside me." He settled himself more comfortably in the chair, Kate held in the crook of his arm. "I had this picture all the time I was away, of a grey stone house with cedar shingles, set in a garden with the forest behind, and all around lush pastures for the cows. And I could see acres of wheat ripening in the sunlight, and in the distance the sort of view you get only in Africa—hills beyond hills beyond hills. Oh, it will be hard, all right. Up in the icy dawn and never a moment without something to fill it. And crops will fail and cows will abort and the labour will drive us mad. But think of the satisfaction, Kate. Think of hacking all of that out of virgin bush and being able to look at it one day and think: this I did. This I can pass on to my sons."

"Sons?" Kate spoke the word on a quick intake of breath. "Christy, I'm thirty-nine. Oh, the time we've wasted!"

"Don't let's waste any more. Are you with me, Kate?"

For a long moment she looked into those strangely light eyes, alive now with the intensity of the passion he put into the question.

Was his anger as quick to flare as it always had been? Had he changed during these years of separation? Had she?

It didn't matter. She didn't care. She was being given a second chance of happiness and this time she was going to grasp it with both hands.

"I'm with you," she said.

Part Two

1921–1927

Part Two

13

"NOW look," Julie said to Patsy, speaking softly into the darkness of the last night they were to spend together at Kiambu. "You will try not to get into any of your states while I'm away, won't you?"

"Of course I will." From the adjacent bed, Patsy's voice was equally soft. "I don't get into states any more."

"No." Julie considered the reason for this and could think of only one. "It's Christy, isn't it? You're glad he and Kate have married."

"Mm." Unseen, Patsy smiled to herself. She felt safe now that Christy had joined their household. Protected. There was a new softness about Kate which made life less of a strain, and while Patsy still tried her best to fulfil all Kate's expectations for her, she somehow felt as if the pressure had been taken off a little—as if even if she produced work which was less than her best it would not now be noticed quite so readily. "I wish you didn't have to go, though," she added.

"Gosh, so do I."

Julie's voice was full of longing, for the summons which had at last come from her grandmother had been a surprise to all of them. So little had been heard from Mrs. Hudson that they had been lulled into a false sense of security. Now, it seemed, she was determined that her granddaughter should be sent home to be educated.

"Just imagine me at a boarding school," she went on.

"It sounds fun in books," Patsy said.

"Not so much fun as being here—as going up to the new farm with Kate and Christy. Oh Patsy, I don't know how I'm going to bear it!"

"If you were very naughty, they'd probably send you back."

"I've thought of that. It's not knowing people that's going to be the worst thing. And thinking of what's going on back here. You will write to me, won't you?"

"Of course I will. Don't forget about being naughty. People get expelled from schools. In books it happens all the time."

"It will widen your horizons," Kate assured Julie briskly, attempting to put a good face on her departure. "And you can come back just as soon as your grandmother allows it."

They were all in tears when finally they waved her off at the station, Meg having driven them into Nairobi. Christy had already gone up to the land he had bought on the slopes of the Aberdare Mountains, to build a mud and wattle hut as a temporary dwelling for them and to begin on the Herculean task of clearing the ground. Once Julie had gone there was nothing to keep them in

Kiambu, so the final packing was completed and Kate, Patsy, Kamau and Mwangidogo set out by ox cart to drive to the promised land.

It was a daunting exercise, but hot and exhausting as it was, both Kate and Patsy were entranced by the journey, particularly the sight of the mountain which revealed itself to them briefly on the second evening, its peaks wreathed with mist.

"I'm glad they called the country Kenya after the mountain," Patsy said.

Seeing the beauty of the snow-capped summit, Kate could only agree. The new Crown Colony had an auspicious name if nothing else.

"It's the end of the world," Patsy breathed when, after two overnight stops at outlying farmhouses, they first saw Christy's acres. Forest covered the mountain slopes behind them and before them was the vastness of the Rift Valley, Lake Naivasha shining like a jewel in the sunshine to the east.

"On the map they call it the Aberdares," Christy said.

Nevertheless, Patsy's name stuck and the farm became known as World's End.

Farm? It was uncleared bush, nothing more, sparsely wooded on the lower slopes but thickly forested where the hills rose higher. The land would first have to be cleared for the plough, trees felled, stumps rooted out, undergrowth cleared.

"When we actually build the permanent house,

I thought of putting it over there," Christy said to Kate, indicating one of the few level stretches on the entire farm. "Then you'll be able to see the lake from the verandah. There's no problem about water. There's a stream on the western border—one day I'll stock it with trout."

Early on, Christy was brought face to face with the problem he had heard others debating endlessly in the bar of the Norfolk Hotel. If the Government wanted to encourage settlement, why, then, did they not take more positive steps to persuade the local populace to work on European farms?

"I suppose you can understand the Kyukes' point of view," he said somewhat grudgingly to Kate. "To them, working in the fields is women's work—*their* job, as warriors, is to defend the tribe, or so they've been brought up to believe for century upon century. It must seem unworthy, not to say dull, to wield a hoe instead of a spear."

But understanding them did not prevent the explosions of rage that erupted when he found that half his labour had downed tools and walked off the job, or had quarrelled with the Kitosh tribesmen, or had somehow succeeded, against all the odds, in breaking the *jembes* he had supplied.

When his first one hundred acres was cleared, he planted maize. It grew readily enough, but at the railhead there were no proper facilities for grain storage, and even when the crop finally arrived at the coast for onward shipment, it then had to be graded which meant further days in storage when, in that hot moist climate, weevil quickly developed.

It was a bitter disappointment to Christy to find that his first crop, apparently satisfactory and transported to the coast at high cost, was found to have too high a moisture content to fetch much of a price. He swore, kicked a milking bucket, and tried again.

It was the cattle which interested him most. He had bought a dozen native cows—humped-backed, scarred, unbeautiful creatures, and one grade bull. It was not nearly enough, but it was a start. Eventually he planned to run a herd of graded-up Ayrshires, feeling instinctively that no matter how the fortunes of farming fluctuated, a cattle farmer would be able to weather all storms better than most. Which did not mean that a cattle farmer had no problems. He had to contend with East Coast fever, red water fever, ana-plasmosis, contagious abortion, not to mention the ravages made by hyenas and leopard. Christy dipped his cattle and hand-reared his calves up to three months old. He built stout pens to prevent cows wandering off into the forest to drop their calves. Those early years were composed of work from sun-up to sun-down, yet he felt he had never been happier.

He tackled the problem of drying his maize by improved methods of harvesting. It was the old

Somali he had made his *nyaara* who had to break the news to him one golden December morning that a large family of baboons had wreaked havoc over a huge area of the crop.

Was it all worth it? Yes, yes, yes, he told himself, for each day there was Kate to come home to, to talk with and laugh with and argue with. Patsy, too, was a delight to him. She had taken to him from the first, it seemed, which was fortunate. He had been afraid that she might resent him.

The mud and wattle *banda* was replaced by the grey stone bungalow with the cedar shingles. The rooms were sizeable but there was no luxury about it, for any money made at the creamery was ploughed straight back into stock or improvements on the farm. The chairs were comfortable, but they were a motley, second-hand assortment, and the old sofa had seen better days. Packing-cases covered with cretonne served as small tables, and bookshelves were nothing more than planks of wood kept apart by the same grey stone which had been used to build the house. There were not enough of them. Books overflowed in piles on to the wooden floor, mixed with seed catalogues and Government pamphlets. Skins were the only rugs, but the fire that burnt in the huge stone fireplace at the end of the room on chilly nights was only a reflection of the warmth that Christy experienced now that he and Kate and Patsy had become welded into a family.

As for Kate herself, she felt rejuvenated, charged with energy and enthusiasm, all the lethargy of her last days at Mawingo forgotten. Teaching Patsy was, as always, her first concern, but this did not prevent her helping with the morning and evening milking for Christy and she soon realised that only the presence of one or other of them ensured that the job was carried out properly. Without supervision, hands remained unwashed, buckets unscoured.

The vegetable garden was her charge, too. Almost anything grew with ease, but all too often bushbuck nibbled the young shoots. There were frustrations, but so many compensations, like the transformation made by the rain after drought, when the forest quivered into new life. Like the occasional convivial evening with friends. Like the incomparable view over the valley, the distant lake glinting far below like a tiny sapphire. She often heard the rainbird and she always thought of Hugh and what he had said that day so many years before. It was hard to remember that time when life seemed devoid of hope. Now she felt full of it—reborn, wildly in love, not only with Christy but with the country.

Patsy was happy, too. She missed Julie sorely and wrote long, weekly letters to her: but now that she had a father, she felt complete in a way she had not done before.

The secret was one she still hugged to herself. She understood that it was not something she

283

should talk about. It was a well-known fact that Robert Brewster, who was a tall, rangy, raw-boned man who lived some miles away to the east of them, had taken a comely Kikuyu woman into his home, but it was not a thing that anyone dreamed of mentioning. Robert dropped in quite frequently and was greeted and entertained as a friend, but no one ever said to him "How's Wanjeri today?" She was a part of his life that no one mentioned. It proved to Patsy that cohabitation between black and white was inherently bad.

Even so, she brought herself to mention the subject to Christy one day early on in their occupation of the farm, albeit obliquely. He was in the cowshed studying the records of milk yields, only half-conscious that Patsy was hovering beside him as if undecided whether to go or stay.

All at once she blurted out: "I know all about it. Who my father was."

"What?" Christy was miles away. There was a distinct and inexplicable drop in the milk yield which was worrying.

"My father," Patsy persisted. "I know all about it."

Christy frowned at her absently, scarcely taking in her words.

"Is that right?" he asked casually. Then, realising what she had said: "Did Kate tell you?"

"She told me it was someone she loved."

"True enough. It was a long time ago."

He had returned to brooding over his records.

"Thirteen years, to be exact."

"Hm?"

"Thirteen years. That's how old I am."

He looked at her properly then, and smiled.

"You don't tell me! Thirteen years, eh? Sure, it seems no time at all. A little skinny thing you were, all hair and eyes, when I dumped you into Kate's arms."

"Was my mother pretty?"

"Beautiful as a young fawn— just as you are, Patsy darlin'."

The *nyapara* appeared at this point with a long tale of incompetence among the labourers, of work not done and implements lost, and Christy swore and went striding out of the cowshed with the conversation already forgotten.

"It'll be our secret," Patsy whispered passionately to his departing back view.

Familiarity had not dimmed the hero-worship which had begun on the night she had listened to his voice rising and falling the other side of her bedroom wall. To her he was larger than life. He seemed to hold the entire farm in the hollow of his hand, to draw them all together. There was more laughter in her life now, and Kate was more approachable.

Approachable, but still adamant that Patsy was to have every advantage which had been denied her. The teaching of Latin presented a problem.

The subject was essential if Patsy was to go to university, and it was the one thing that, even with the help of textbooks, Kate felt unable to tackle. She approached the White Fathers who ran a mission some way up in the hills, through the forest, and managed to persuade Father Guilbert, a short, swarthy Frenchman, to give Patsy lessons. Patsy took an immediate dislike to the man.

"He's perfectly hateful," she wrote to Julie. "His eyebrows meet in the middle and he has little rubbery red lips in the middle of a beard as black as a horse's tail. I can't understand a single word he says and he gets cross and shouts and waves his arms about."

Julie's reply, though sympathetic, was more concerned with her own problems.

"Your Father Guilbert sounds awful, but he can't be any worse than my Miss Havergal. We call her 'Havergal-every-morning-for-breakfast'. I think that's rather funny, don't you? I am doing my best to be naughty enough to get sent home, but so far have only managed to be given hundreds of lines. I shall have to think of something really big. Actually, school isn't so bad —it's the holidays that are the worst. Grandmother expects me to be clean and tidy at all times, which is very hard, and also I have to read aloud to her in the evenings, which is even worse. I wish I was better at being naughty."

The horror of Julie's situation—exiled, forced

to wear dresses, required to read dull books aloud to an even duller grandmother—haunted Patsy. Sometimes she would climb up to the forest to a point where she could look down on the little grey house beneath her and broodingly she would sit on a fallen log and stare at it and at the rolling land that surrounded it.

Sounds carried easily in that clear air. She could hear the jingle of the cow bells, the voices of the herdsmen, Kate calling to Kamau. The thought of the world away from the farm was terrifying. Why did things have to change? She wanted to stay like this for ever.

Kate, on the other hand, worked relentlessly for change. The school for the children of the farm workers was one of her primary projects, though the first schoolmaster they employed was a disappointment. He was supposed to be a trained man, but Kate thought him a bully, and a lazy, incompetent bully at that. She gave him notice, and he departed, at the same time as the loss of a new calf was discovered. There was no definite link between the two, but no one on the farm had any doubt that there was a connection.

There followed a short period when she taught the children herself as best she could, but one evening while they were sitting on the verandah, a slim, good-looking young Kikuyu appeared, neatly dressed in navy blue trousers and a sparkling white shirt. He introduced himself as David Ngengi, son of a neighbouring chief, and a trained teacher who would very much like to work at World's End. Kate warmed to him immediately. He was an unassuming but obviously intelligent young man, with an alert face and a ready smile.

"I think he's just the sort of man we want," she said to Christy afterwards.

"Then sign him on at once, for the love of heaven. You're wearing yourself out, dashing between the milking shed and the school, not to mention the sick parade each morning and Patsy's lessons."

So David moved on to the farm, and Kate was pleased because he was popular with the children and his class grew. Occasionally he consulted her. At first she would invite him on to the verandah and would offer him tea or beer, but he never accepted. Smilingly, he stood a little aloof— always polite, always respectful, but apparently determined to keep his distance.

Christy approved of him. He said that David was enough to make him take back all that he had ever said about mission boys, for until that point he had dismissed them all as being too high and mighty to buckle down to a day's work, too pleased with themselves to make good employees.

Patsy, by then sixteen years old, regarded David Ngengi with curiosity and would like to have made a friend of him. There were many questions she would like to have asked him regarding his upbringing and ambitions. Once, when he was standing in front of the house talking to Kate, his gaze flickered towards the place where she was standing, and she thought there was interest in it, as if he would like to talk to her, too: but days later, when by chance they met in the forest, he seemed concerned only by the thorn that Patch, the terrier that went everywhere with her, had picked up in his foot. They conversed in brief, awkward monosyllables before going their separate ways.

Nevertheless, she was as sorry as Kate when one evening, only a year after he arrived, David announced that he wanted to leave.

"I am to go to England for further training," he said, in his stilted, accented English. "The Missionary Society has arranged it."

"Then we can only congratulate you," Kate said. "Though we're very sorry to lose you." And she knitted him a sweater as a parting present.

Patsy retreated to her fallen log, hugged her knees, and looked down at the farm. She felt strange these days—half fearful, half expectant. There were times when, in the evening as they sat indoors, she wanted to fling herself on Kate and Christy, to hold them close and implore them never to make her go away from them. At others, she saw herself as a creature apart, misunderstood by everyone, destined to walk a lonely path.

Her books no longer satisfied her. She poured out her heart in letters to Julie and felt vaguely irritated by her replies because she seemed so taken up by school—even resigned to her grandmother, although she never ceased to write longingly of Kenya. There was an aunt who was kind, cousins of her own age. It was all right for *her*, Patsy thought discontentedly.

Kate worried about her moodiness.

"She needs friends of her own age," she said to Christy.

"Then ask Janet Lacey to stay in the school holidays."

"That's a good idea. I'll write to Meg immediately."

And when Kate saw the two girls riding over the farm together, and heard the house ringing with their laughter, she felt happier. There was nothing seriously amiss with Patsy, she thought. She was growing up in difficult circumstances, that was all.

14

YOUNG wives, arriving with their husbands to take up Government duties in Nairobi, were warned by the older hands about Hope Honeywell, the wife of the Secretary for Native Affairs.

"Basically," Mavis Fairbrother told little Anthea Moore, "you have to remember two things. Always behave as if any word falling from her lips is Holy Writ: and bear in mind that no flattery is too fulsome for her to swallow. Never, never argue, or contradict—"

"Oh, I wouldn't!" Anthea was young and shy and horrified at the thought.

"You'll be tempted, believe me."

"Actually," Anthea said breathlessly. "I thought she seemed rather sweet at dinner last night."

"Oh, she's sweet all right! Just as sweet as a boa constrictor. Don't be fooled by the sugary manner, my dear. If any of us lower orders offend her, she goes in for the kill as surely as a striking snake."

"Herbert said that Mr. Honeywell seemed pleasant to work for, though a little withdrawn—"

"It's a wonder he hasn't withdrawn from life

291

altogether, being married to Abandon-Hope. Oh, he's not a bad old stick, though he's awfully stuffy and a bit humourless. Getting put next to him at a dinner party can be trying—it's uphill work making conversation, I can tell you. By the way, you do know that you have to call on them, don't you?"

Anthea gulped. She had married Herbert for better or for worse, but had never dreamed that the 'worse' could encompass an ordeal such as this.

"Do we have to?" she asked helplessly.

"I'm afraid so. You must pay calls on the Chief Secretary, the Secretary for Native Affairs and the Financial Secretary. You can get away with signing the book at Government House. You have had cards printed, I suppose?" Wordlessly, Anthea nodded. "Then it's all frightfully easy. You wait until six o'clock in the evening when everyone's likely to be on the golf course or in the Club, then you race up to the house, give the boy two of your husband's cards and one of yours, and the job's done."

"But suppose they're not on the golf course or in the Club?"

"Then you will be proffered a glass of inferior sherry and will have to exchange banal remarks about the weather and the servants before tottering off, bathed in the glow of achievement."

"Oh Mavis, I wish I had your assurance!"

Comfortingly Mavis patted the younger woman's arm.

"It comes, my dear, it comes. If I were you, I'd get the calls behind you as quickly as possible, then at least Abandon-Hope can't criticise you for *that*, even though there's every chance she will find something."

"I hope to heaven that they're both out," Anthea groaned. "Oh, please God, let them be out."

Her prayer was granted: the Honeywells were at the Club. It was a lucky chance, for Andrew was not a Club man. He played neither golf nor cricket and did not much enjoy sitting and chatting over a drink—not unless the subject was shop.

Hope complained bitterly that he took her so infrequently, for she liked to cast her eye over newcomers and catch up on the gossip. She was, she confessed to women of her own age, just the *teeniest* bit worried about the class of person who was coming into the Administrative Service since the war. Oh, on the whole the men were perfectly acceptable—of good family and education, just as they had always been. Just as Andrew was. But the *wives*! Well, of course, it didn't do to be snobbish and no doubt the whole class structure in England had undergone a vast shaking-up process, but could it be right, she asked, to send women to outposts of the Empire when quite plainly they were unused to ordering a staff of servants? One could always tell, Hope said.

If memories of the semi-detached house in Swindon where she had been born, where one untrained housemaid did the rough work, where the family ate dinner in the middle of the day, ever troubled Hope, then she gave no sign of it. Her voice had changed from those early days. Her vowel-sounds were now strangulated in the accepted upper-class manner. She sat on committees and chaired meetings, all with the deceptively honeyed sweetness which made it difficult to oppose her and often left opponents speechless, devoid of a suitable reply to stem the inexorable implementation of Hope's will.

The Honeywells lived in quite a grand house in Parklands. It wasn't as grand as Hope would have liked—not, for instance, as large as that of the Chief Secretary—but for a government house it was very good, mainly because the Director of Public Works had long ago, for the sake of a quiet life, given up all hope of opposing her requests for repairs, redecoration, new furniture and the like. It had been bad enough when she was forced to communicate with him by letter or by a personal visit. Now she was on the telephone and could plague him several times a day if she so desired. It was easier to capitulate. On this particular evening, he had seen the Honeywells enter the Club, had groaned and immediately retired to the fastness of the men's bar wherein no woman was allowed to set foot.

One look had assured Hope that there was no one quite of their own status present, and she was forced therefore to join Mavis and Alan Fairbrother who were sitting with a couple unknown to her. Andrew trailed a few paces behind her, uneasy about forcing their presence upon junior staff to whom it might be unwelcome, but gloomily aware that his wishes were unlikely to be consulted in the matter.

The unknown couple were introduced as Mr. and Mrs. Maurice Hobbs who were on a visit to Nairobi from their farm in the Aberdares. Maurice Hobbs was exactly the type of man that Hope most admired: tall, blond, blue-eyed. He had an erect, military bearing, and she was not surprised to find that until recently he had been an officer in the Coldstream Guards.

Selma Hobbs was a lady. Thin and languid, she regarded the world with a high-bred distaste almost as great as Hope's own. Mavis Fairbrother found her irritating and was only entertaining her since their mothers had been at school together. For once she was quite glad of Hope Honeywell's help in keeping the conversation going.

"Very remote, the Aberdares," Hope commented. "Do you not find it a lonely life, Mrs. Hobbs?"

"Quite desperately," Mrs. Hobbs admitted.

"Maurice has only brought me to Nairobi because I was literally about to expire from boredom."

"Oh, come now, Selma! You can't complain that there's nothing to do." Maurice Hobbs spoke impatiently.

"Well, of course, if you enjoy drenching cows and coping with labour problems, then life must be one long party." She drew on her cigarette and lazily blew the smoke out without inhaling. "For myself, I prefer other pleasures."

"But such beautiful country!" Hope's sympathies were almost entirely with Mrs. Hobbs. She could imagine nothing worse than being incarcerated on an up-country farm. However, Mr. Hobbs was far too attractive to be alienated by agreement with his discontented wife, so she favoured him with a sunny smile. "And farming must be such a satisfying occupation!"

"Frustrating, too," Andrew put in, drily.

"Do you know that part of the country, sir?"

"Not well. Actually I'm due to go on tour in that direction very soon—Naivasha, Gilgil, Nakuru."

"It is, as Mrs. Honeywell says, very beautiful."

"But devoid of social life," said his wife.

"Selma, that's nonsense! We had dinner at the Brennans only last week."

"Kate Brennan is one of those remarkable women who are madly devoted to home and hearth. Do you know her, Mavis? At dinner the other night she was positively euphoric because she had managed to get some exotic type of flower to grow in her garden. I'm afraid such pleasures leave me cold."

"We know Kate Brennan well," Hope said. "Don't we, Andrew? Such a delightful person I always found her, though it's many years since I have seen her."

"They have both been very kind to us," said Maurice. "Naturally, as a newcomer to the country, there is much I needed to know."

"I find them depressing," Selma said. "Oh, not in themselves, poor dears. I mean, they are cheerful enough, heaven knows. But to think they have been farming for four years and still have so little to show for it! They are pathetically pleased with their frightful house. Kate goes around looking like a stable boy, with no idea of fashion or style. I look at her and I ask myself: is this what I shall look like in a few years' time?"

"But she's happy?" Everyone looked at Andrew in surprise. He spoke with a rough, abrupt urgency, as if the answer mattered to him.

"Oh, blissfully, poor darling."

"Then she's not so poor."

"Andrew was very fond of Kate once upon a time," Hope said with gentle, affectionate amusement. "Oh yes you were, old boy! No need to blush! Tell me, Mrs. Hobbs, is Patsy still living with them?"

"Yes, indeed. Extraordinary, isn't it?"

"Quite extraordinary. She must be sixteen or seventeen. Goodness me, how the years fly!"

Some time passed while the Hobbs and Hope told each other how very mistaken Kate had been, how no good would ever come of it, what problems were bound to arise. They smiled upon each other, all in perfect harmony, while Andrew took up some office matter with Alan Fairbrother, and Mavis sat back and watched with some amusement the sight of Hope Honeywell putting herself out to be pleasant. For what purpose, she wondered?

When Andrew finally managed to catch Hope's eye and rose to leave, cordial farewells were exchanged and both Selma and Maurice pressed them to make a short diversion on their forthcoming up-country tour to spend a weekend with them.

"It would be a positive favour, I assure you," Selma said. "I can't tell you how I long to see a congenial soul. It would give you an opportunity to see Kate and Christy, too."

"That would be delightful. How very kind of you."

"What a very pleasant woman," Maurice Hobbs said, after Hope and Andrew had gone.

"I found her most agreeable," Selma agreed. "I do hope they decide to come."

Mavis smiled and said nothing. To her way of thinking, Selma Hobbs and Hope Honeywell deserved each other.

Kate was feeding the chickens when she saw the unfamiliar car approaching the farm, jouncing and bouncing over the ruts and pot-holes. She was surprised but undismayed, for visitors at the farm were rare and always welcome. She could not for one moment imagine who these visitors could be. Such a smart car was certainly unusual. She and Christy owned a decrepit Ford box-body, as did most of the farmers round about. This was something far more grand, though after its journey up the track, hardly any cleaner.

She set down the *sufuria* in which she kept the chicken feed and wiped her hands on the back of her riding breeches, suddenly conscious that she was wearing one of Christy's old shirts and that her hair which was normally kept reasonably neat on top of her head had chosen this moment to come down. Ineffectually, she put a hand to it, then laughed at herself. If these people had missed their way, which seemed likely, then her appearance was hardly going to matter. If they were long-lost friends, then they ought to be equally indifferent. She was totally unprepared to meet a long-lost enemy.

Hope was all graciousness, full of explanations. They had been staying in the area, she said—couldn't bear to pass without calling—were so anxious to hear all Kate's news after so long. Andrew, after a gruff greeting and a quick handshake, stayed in the background.

Kate declared herself delighted to see them.

"Andrew, I've long wanted to congratulate you on your new position," she said. "Didn't I always say that you would do well?"

Hope put her arm through her husband's.

"Better things are ahead," she said. "Everyone thinks so well of Andrew."

"Hope, please!"

He looked embarrassed as, shepherded by Kate, they walked round the house and up the steps to the verandah, Hope still with her hand through Andrew's arm, presenting a picture of connubial bliss. She was dressed in a sleeveless, apple-green linen dress and from pictures she had seen in the paper Kate recognised it as being the very latest style.

"How nice you look, Hope," she said.

"Why, thank you." Hope patted her shingled head. "We're none of us getting any younger, of course, but I do feel that it's a duty to make the best of oneself, don't you agree? Andrew does so like to see me looking my best."

"Yes—well—" Kate laughed and spread her arms wide. "I'm afraid you caught me in my working attire. Never mind—do sit down and take a look at our lovely view while I get Kamau to make some tea."

"Kamau?" Hope squealed and clasped her hands. "Not *our* Kamau? You mean to say you've kept him all these years? How do you manage it?"

"I wish you'd tell Hope the secret," Andrew said dourly. "Our servants come and go with infuriating frequency. Well, well—this must be Patsy."

Patsy, hearing voices, had emerged from the living room within, and shook hands politely.

"Keep our visitors amused while I go and clean up a little," Kate instructed her. "Please excuse me. I'll be with you in a moment."

To Patsy it seemed a long moment. It took her no time at all to come to the conclusion that Hope was one of 'them '—the people who spoke to her in a special voice as if she were mentally deficient.

Although Kate had shown her to the verandah, Hope drifted inside to the living room, chattering gaily, exclaiming at the number of books, peering at a watercolor which hung by the fireplace. Kate, returning, suddenly saw the room through Hope's eyes. What a make-shift, hotchpotch it must look, she thought. Really, something must be done about the clutter. Perhaps some more shelves—another cupboard—

"My dear, such a *lived-in* home!" Hope gushed extravagantly. "Sometimes I think ours is just *too* perfect—but then I always was a perfectionist, as I'm sure you remember."

Kate could not bring herself to reply to this, and merely smiled politely. She had combed her hair and changed her blouse and felt a little more mistress of the situation.

301

"Kamau is serving tea on the verandah," she said. "Shall we return there?"

Conversation over the tea-cups was not strained, for Hope talked on happily in the new voice that Kate had not heard before. She talked of dinners at Government House, of the entertaining she was called upon to do, of the perfectly divine dressmaker she had found, just at the corner of Sixth Avenue and Government Road.

"And my dear, he would make for you if you mention my name, I have no doubt of it. I really can recommend him most highly."

"I shall remember that," Kate said gravely.

Inadvertently her eyes met Andrew's. He was looking at her with exactly the same look of longing and adoration that she had seen for so many years, long ago. It was strange, seeing those eyes in a face grown prematurely old and weary. Uncomfortably, she turned away.

"Of course, I don't suppose you do much entertaining here," Hope went on. "Life must be dull—in fact Selma Hobbs tells me it is quite unbearable! I really admire you, Kate, the way you stick it out."

"Are we to see Christy?" Andrew asked abruptly, cutting her short.

"I'm afraid not. He's gone to Naivasha today. He'll be so sorry to have missed you."

"How lucky that you stayed at home instead of going with him, or we would have had a wasted journey and that would have been simply too, too disappointing for words," Hope said.

"I don't often go," Kate said. "One of us has to be here for the milking—"

"My dear, I can't *tell* you how I admire you! When I think of what might have been—all you gave up! I broke my heart when I heard how the school had failed. After all the efforts we put into it! It's simply too, too sad that you find yourself living like this."

"Living like what?" Kate enquired pleasantly.

Hope shrugged.

"Well, it's hardly luxurious, is it? A nice little house, as these up-country houses go, but not what you might have expected. I just wanted to let you know how *very* much I admire you."

"So you've said," Kate commented drily.

"And I mean it. Every word. When I consider the comfort of my life compared to yours—"

"Hope, be quiet."

Andrew's curt, authoritative voice cut across her words and for an instant there was silence.

"I *beg* your pardon?" Hope said at last.

"I said, be quiet. I've sat here and listened to you patronising Kate until I can take no more. You've only to look at her to know that she has no need of your pity or of anyone else's."

"Andrew—" Kate began uncomfortably.

"I see." Hope spoke with barely controlled anger, her face scarlet. "I see it all. It's always been the same. It makes no difference what I do—how much I strive to give you a perfect home—how I try to make you happy—"

"Look—please—" desperately Kate floundered for something to defuse the situation.

Andrew stood up and strode to the edge of the verandah. "We'd better leave," he said.

"Please," said Kate, teapot in hand. "Have some more tea."

No one replied. Hope looked from her husband to Kate, and back again. She felt angry and bewildered. How had this exercise gone so wrong? It was meant to demonstrate to Andrew how dowdy Kate had become, how totally unworthy she was of the devotion that she suspected he still felt for her. Equally, she had looked forward to reducing Kate to a state of helpless envy at what she must surely realise was their elevated position. Andrew turned round to face Kate.

"I apologise for my wife," he said, speaking with difficulty.

"There's no need for that, really."

"She can't understand how anyone with so few of this world's goods can still be so happy. For you are happy, aren't you, Kate?"

"Yes. Very."

"I'm glad."

Without another word, he went down the steps, his back stiff and straight, leaving a silence behind him, a silence broken only by strangled gasps of anger from Hope.

"I've no doubt Andrew is tired after his tour," Kate said diplomatically. "It must all be a great strain for him."

"Of course." Hope stood up, patted her hair, straightened her skirt. "His job is of tremendous importance. The responsibilities are quite enormous." Her voice had resumed its normal tones of cloying sweetness, the anger apparently forgotten. "You must forgive his outburst. I'm going to insist that he has a complete holiday, just as soon as it can be arranged."

"What a good idea."

Hope smiled.

"It's been heavenly to see you, Kate. After all, we were colleagues for so long. Please remember me to Christy—I'm so sorry not to have seen him."

"He'll be sorry to have missed you." The lies we tell, Kate thought, in the name of good manners.

"Such a colourful figure, I always thought. Of course, I was amazed when I heard that you had married him."

"Oh?"

"Well, you did think at one time that it was he who killed Patsy's father, didn't you?"

Her words hung in the air like tobacco smoke, and for a moment she stood and smiled at Kate as if she could see them there and was enjoying the sight of them. Kate looked into her eyes and was appalled by the naked malice she saw there.

"Andrew will be waiting for you," she said coldly.

Without a word Hope turned to leave the verandah.

"What did she mean?" Patsy's words had an edge of panic as they tumbled from her the moment Hope had disappeared round the side of the house.

"She wanted to upset me, that's all. Of course Christy didn't kill anyone."

"But she said you thought that he killed my father!"

"Heaven knows where she got that piece of information from. Surely Andrew wouldn't have mentioned it." She put her arm round Patsy and drew her down beside her. "Don't look so worried, darling. She said it to make mischief. Can you imagine Christy killing anyone?"

"She said—she said *he* might have killed *my father*! I don't understand."

"Christy and your father were friends—partners. Your father was killed while they were on a hunting trip and for a while I was crazy enough to think that Christy might have had something to do with it. It was ridiculous—a stupid, unfounded suspicion on my part. Of course Christy had nothing to do with it."

"But I thought—I thought—" Patsy could get no further and Kate looked in bewilderment at her stricken face.

"What is it, Patsy? You believe me, surely?"

306

"You should have told me before!" There was anger in her words, a bitter accusation.

"But you didn't ask me. I thought you were satisfied with all I'd told you. I explained about your father—that he was someone I loved, was going to marry."

Patsy's face seemed to close up, to become mysterious and secretive.

"Patsy, what is it?" Kate asked again.

"Nothing." Her voice was sullen. "I hate that woman. She spoke to me as if I had a mental age of two."

"Hope was always foolish. Malicious, too. She tried to hurt us both, Patsy—for heaven's sake don't let's give her the satisfaction of succeeding."

"You don't understand."

For a moment Patsy stared down at her lap, her mouth set, then in a flash she was gone, flying from the verandah and racing round the house and up into the forest.

Worriedly Kate stood and watched her: then, defeated, she sighed and shook her head.

307

15

WITH growing bewilderment Kate read the note that had been delivered to her at the breakfast table, brought to the farm by one of the boys from the Catholic Mission.

"Christy, listen to this," she said. "It's from Father Guilbert. He says that it's two weeks since Patsy went to him for a lesson. I simply don't understand it. I saw her ride off myself, twice this week."

Christy, pouring thick cream on his porridge, looked up from under his eyebrows with a twist of a smile.

"Maybe the child awarded herself a holiday."

"She's not a child! She's nearly eighteen, and she knows perfectly well how important it is that she's up to standard by next year."

"She's never liked the man, has she? Or Latin, come to that."

"That's not the point." Kate laid the paper flat beside her plate, smoothing it with irritated fingers. "She's intelligent enough to realise it's a means to an end. I wish you'd speak to her, Christy."

"Me?" He looked up in surprise. "Now why in the world would you say that? It's months since

308

she took a blind bit of notice of anything I had to say."

Kate said nothing, realising the truth of this. But she, too, had seemed unable to reach Patsy recently. She ate and slept, sat at her books, moved about the farm, but somehow seemed remote from them. Suddenly, at meal times, Kate realised that she and Christy were making conversation as if Patsy were a silent, difficult guest. If they succeeded in forcing a contribution from her, all too often it was monosyllabic, dismissive, scornful.

"Maybe she has a perfectly logical explanation," Christy said, resuming his breakfast. "And even if she hasn't—well, she works hard, Kate. It's not right to drive the child to the point that she feels the weight of the world on her shoulders."

"I do wish you'd stop calling her a child! She's a young woman."

"It's never easy growing up, and for Patsy it must be more difficult than for most. Now haven't we said that often enough to each other over the last six months?"

Kate banged her clenched fist down on the letter.

"We've made allowances for her until we're blue in the face. I'm really angry about this. She knows that she must keep working—that it would be criminal to let up now, when all she's wanted is almost in her grasp."

"I'm not sure what Patsy wants any more. I have the feeling she isn't, either."

"Oh, it's not just the education that's important." Kate was following her own train of thought, hardly listening to him. "I'm thinking of her entire future. She must get out into a larger world where she's accepted for what she is. I ask you, what can she do here? She can't live as a recluse for the rest of her life. There's no occupation open to her in Nairobi. It's essential that she gets away and becomes part of a young, intelligent group of people with wider horizons."

"Sure, you don't have to convince me!"

"She must see it for herself, a girl as bright as she is."

"Ask her," Christy said. "Here she is now." Kate felt a pang as she watched Patsy approaching them through the garden to the verandah where they sat at breakfast.

There's nothing of her, she thought. She's skin and bone. Can she be ill? That might explain the lack-lustre attitude that seemed to have taken over her mind and spirit these last months.

Patsy herself dismissed any such suggestion.

"I'm perfectly all right," she said wearily, pouring herself some coffee. "Honestly, you do fuss—"

"I've had a letter from Father Guilbert."

"You have?" She looked grimly amused. "I might have known the jungle drums would beat sooner or later."

"But I saw you go off to the lessons!"

"I'm afraid I found a comfortable rock by the stream and contemplated nature for an hour or so."

"How could you?"

Patsy sighed as if the questions were tedious beyond bearing.

"I've had all of Father Guilbert I can stand. He's a nasty, sadistic little man with an inflated ego."

"Don't be so infantile and absurd! You know how much this means to you You'll never get into a university without Latin."

Patsy flicked a blank, uncaring glance at Kate's angry face.

"I don't know that I want to, if Father Guilbert is the price I have to pay."

"Of course you want to. You always have done."

"*You* always have done."

"You must write a letter of apology."

"But I'm not in the least bit sorry."

"It was discourteous, to put it at its very lowest."

"I just want to be left alone," Patsy said coldly.

But in spite of her determination to be as miserable as possible, to disassociate herself from Kate's and Christy's world that had once, when she was small, seemed to cocoon her in comfort and security, she could not help a stirring of interest in the letter which arrived from Meg.

Colin, she told them, had at last come back from Agricultural College, seven years since he had left the country as a boy of fourteen.

"You can imagine how delighted we all are," she wrote. "He hasn't changed a lot, except that he's over six feet tall and has a moustache which Janet pronounces 'divine'! Before starting work, Hugh is allowing him time off for a hunting trip, and he wants to know if he can stop off on the way back to spend some time with you. Would that be convenient?"

Kate seized pen and paper to reply immediately that there was nothing she would like better, but Patsy's feelings were more ambivalent. She felt nervous at seeing Colin again, and on the defensive. How she had looked up to him, all those years ago! He had been kind, in a lofty way. He'd better not patronise her now.

He'd be polite to her, of course, but would he *like* her? She didn't see how he could. It would be awful, knowing that it was duty and good nature alone that was to throw them together.

She took to staring at herself in the mirror and trying different ways of doing her hair. She hated the feel of it, so wiry and coarse. One day she pinned it in a roll at the nape of her neck.

"That looks pretty," Kate said.

Patsy scowled, giving a hollow laugh, and Kate fought down a feeling of irritation.

"I mean it, whether you choose to believe it or not. Look, Christy's going into Gilgil tomorrow

—let's go with him, you and I, and buy some material for a dress for you."

"Would you make it?" Patsy asked, with deep suspicion.

"We could get Dharamshi to do it."

"He's not much better than you are."

Keep calm, Kate counselled herself. Patsy had, after all, resumed her Latin lessons and seemed to be working hard again. In only nine months' time Kate planned to take her to England, where interviews and examinations would take place for her university entrance the following year. It was, Kate well understood, a nerve-wracking, testing time for the girl and heightened tensions would do nothing to help the situation.

For her own part, she had mixed feelings about the forthcoming visit to England. It was almost twenty years since she had left and she was interested to see the changes those years had wrought. It would be good, too, to see Aunt Sophie again—and even better to see Julie and to try to make some sense out of her affairs, for the girl's longing to return to Kenya was undiminished. Now that her schooldays were all but over, Kate could see no reason at all why her wishes should not be taken into account.

Set against all these good reasons for making the trip was her reluctance to leave Christy for months on end. How could she bear going to bed alone with no one to recount details of the day's events to, or to laugh with?

"Don't be worrying about it, Kate darlin'," Christy said, holding her close to him one night as she put some of these doubts into words. "It's months away yet. And can you imagine the reunion, once you're back? Sure, I'll have to be on a diet of those Iron Jelloids that Bob Brewster swears by to build up my strength."

"As long as you don't decide to console yourself with a younger woman."

"Now would I do a thing like that?"

Kate propped herself up on one elbow and looked down at him, tracing the line of his eyebrows, the scar, the strong nose.

"You might, perhaps," she said, a little sadly. "I never did provide you with those sons you wanted."

"And isn't the world grateful for that? Ah now, Kate, will you imagine the rascals they'd have turned out to be." He pulled her close to him again. "Don't be having regrets, darlin', not about our non-existent sons nor anything else. To me, this is life as it ought to be lived—close to the earth with a woman I love. There's no man alive who could ask more."

The new dress, made from pink cotton in a style that Patsy picked out of a year-old magazine, was made by the Indian in Gilgil. She put it on and stared at herself in the mirror yet again, seeing a small face with high cheekbones and large eyes. Her nose was thin, slightly curved, her mouth wide. Not a bad face, she thought.

314

And her skin wasn't really dark—not *black*, anyway. No one could say she was black.

What would Colin think? Oh, who cared? Impatient with herself she stripped the dress off, throwing it across the bed. He wouldn't think anything, she told herself. He had travelled, met all sorts of people. He would treat her as if she were still a little girl, of no experience, which was undoubtedly a true description. In which case, she asked herself, why do I dread the thought of learning about life at first hand? Why am I frightened to death of leaving the farm? I don't want to go and I don't want to stay.

Because life is cruel, came the answer. It consisted of one form of creation constantly preying on another.

One morning as she had sat on the rock by the stream she had seen a butterfly caught in the web of a huge, hairy-legged spider, and she had wept at her impotence as its beauty was extinguished by the deadly strands. It was more than she could bear.

Sometimes it seemed as if life itself was more than she could bear. What was to become of her? She could find no answer to this question.

Colin arrived one evening in March. To Patsy he seemed like a stranger. Thin and tense in her new pink dress, she sat and watched him as he talked to Kate and Christy, and she felt that she had been quite right in her earlier assumption. He would not think anything of her.

She didn't care, she told herself. In only a few days he would be returning to his own territory where people went to races and dances and drove girls in fast cars to wild parties. It was a world she would never know.

He looked unfamiliar with his moustache and his wide shoulders. But then he laughed at some phrase of Christy's and threw back his head in a way remembered; he looked across the room inviting her to share in his amusement, and suddenly she knew that she was not indifferent, that his opinion of her mattered unbearably. Her heart began to beat uncomfortably fast, she lowered her head and picked at a loose thread on her dress.

He must never know, she thought. No one must ever know. It was inconceivable that he would think anything of her.

That first night he talked to Kate and Christy about England and the unfair way Kenya was reported in the London press.

"They've got it all wrong," he said. "They think we're a crowd of play-boys out here. They quote the size of our farms and the fact that by their standards we bought the land for a song. They don't seem to realise that this is virgin land, miles from railhead in most cases, and still more miles from our markets. They don't realise that we have to work with untrained labour. They've no idea of the work and the losses and the heartbreak."

316

"Yet you've come back."

Colin grinned, and once more Patsy saw the boy she remembered.

"There's no country like it, is there? I could have fallen down and kissed the dock at Kilindini. I spent the whole journey from Mombasa to Nairobi looking out of the window of the train with a smile from ear to ear."

They talked of cattle and coffee and cattle again. Patsy watched him talking, noting the play of expressions on his face, the shape of his mouth, the lordly ease with which he lay in his chair, one knee across the other. He's beautiful, she thought. Beautiful. A young Apollo, golden-haired. Who said that? It didn't matter—the term could have been coined for Colin Lacey.

When on the following day they rode into the forest together she was stiff with shyness.

"You don't have to come," she said ungraciously. "I mean, if there's anything else you'd rather do."

"Of course I want to come."

She could not believe him and was unable to counter his conversational attempts with more than monosyllables.

Much of the thick bush beneath the trees—cedars and olives and podocarpus—was impenetrable, but Patsy led him through the ways she had made her own as far as the river. It was clear and cold, springing from its source in the snow-capped mountain, and beside it was a game path where for a while the horses could pass with ease.

In places the river was shallow, bubbling and chuckling over clear, pebbly beds, but in others it slowed to form deep pools where hidden fish made ripples and circles in the water. Lush ferns sprang from the mossy banks and thick clumps of arum lilies showed up white and pure in the shadows.

They tethered the horses and sat together on the rock, Colin unstrapping his rifle and putting it beside him, for there was a feeling of life all around them, hidden but watchful.

"You won't need that," Patsy said. "I've seen nothing more harmful here than porcupine and waterbuck. You wouldn't shoot them, would you?"

She spoke rapidly, scornfully, and she could hear the scorn in her voice and was horrified by it. But then, to distract her, there was a chattering over their heads and a dipping of the branches as, flashing black and white, a family of colobus monkeys leapt above them and was gone.

"Oh, what a place," Colin breathed with delight. "I swear I'll never leave it again."

"Well, you don't have to, do you?"

Colin looked at her thoughtfully and smiled as their eyes met.

"What's up, Patsy?" he asked. "Come on, tell your Uncle Colin. Is it the thought of going away that's bothering you?"

To Patsy's horror and embarrassment she felt sudden tears welling in her eyes. She got to her feet.

"Shall we go on?" she asked.

"Whatever you like."

He didn't really want to talk, she told herself, riding in front of him up the forest path. Why should he? Her conversation must be as dull as ditchwater in comparison with the girls he had met elsewhere.

There was a boy on the farm called Nderitu for whom Kate had a particular affection. When he was very tiny she had treated him for horrendous burns, even worse than those usually suffered by children who were all too frequently left inside the hut without supervision with a fire left smouldering in the middle of it.

Far from resenting the hurt she must have inflicted on him as she anointed his wound and changed his dressing, he seemed to sense that she was doing her best to help him, and he responded by attaching himself to her once his leg was better and he could walk and run and jump again.

He had a wide, gap-toothed grin and an impish sense of humour, creeping up sometimes when she was gardening to tug her skirt, shrieking with delight as she turned and with an assumed ferocity, chased him away. Or sometimes she would pretend not to see him, shielding her eyes to scan the horizon so that he would cover his

319

mouth with both hands to prevent the laughter spilling out, jumping and hopping from one leg to another.

He was perhaps six or seven, and very bright. Kate persuaded his mother to send him to the farm school which was running smoothly these days—perhaps run with less flair than in the days of David Ngengi, but popular with the children and well attended. Thereafter, Nderitu would seek Kate out with a paper held in his hands behind his back ready to whip it before her with pride in his face. Sometimes it would be a row of crudely scrawled letters, sometimes a picture. Always Kate received it with expressions of delighted amazement.

Colin had been at World's End for two days when Nderitu's mother came to the house asking if the boy had been seen there, for he was missing and had not been home to sleep the previous night.

"I haven't seen him for several days," Kate told her. "Can't his friends tell you where he went yesterday?"

It appeared he had not been to school. He had not been to see his grandmother. The woman began to wail loudly, rocking herself backwards and forwards in an agony of grief.

"He is lost in the forest. A lion has eaten him."

A crowd collected and suggestions were hurled dramatically towards the woman. Perhaps he had

320

fallen into the dam, or gone to see his father's sister, or been carried away by baboons.

Christy took charge, silenced the bystanders and listened attentively to the woman as she answered his questions.

"It sounds likely he might have gone to see his aunt in Gilgil," he said finally to Kate. "I'll take her over, shall I? He might have missed his way, and we can't have the poor little beggar out another night on his own."

"How awful," Patsy said as she and Colin turned away from the small crowd, now being dispersed by Kate. "Suppose he *has* gone into the forest—"

"Would he do that?"

"He might. He was adventurous. *Is* adventurous. I'm going to look for him."

Colin joined her and they searched all afternoon but did not find him. Christy, too, came back from Gilgil with no word of him, the child's mother more distracted than ever and talking of *thahu* and evil spirits.

"There must be something else we can do," Patsy said as darkness fell.

"I can't think what." Christy was tired, mildly irritable. "We asked at every farm in the area. I went to three different police posts, questioned people we met on the road. You searched the forest. What else is there?"

"But just imagine . . ." Patsy went no further and did not need to, for they could all imagine a

321

small boy, alone in the darkness and mystery of an African night. A hyrax screeched from the forest—a wild, haunting cry that sounded like a lost soul and seemed to sum up all the unknown terrors out there in the blackness.

Patsy could not eat, could not sit before the fire to talk of other things. She went out on to the verandah and stood with her arms wrapped round her, for it was cool now that night had fallen. She heard the door behind her open and shut, but did not turn round.

"First thing tomorrow we'll look again," Colin said. "We'll go right up to the bamboo belt."

"Where can he be, Colin?" Patsy's voice was strained. "Suppose he's somewhere all alone, cowering in the bush, terrified of every shadow."

"At least he's done something no one else seems capable of doing." Colin was leaning against the verandah post, his face in shadow. "He's made you stop thinking of yourself."

"What?" Patsy froze into stillness. "That's a beastly thing to say."

"True, though."

The hyrax shrieked again and the crickets whirred.

"I knew you'd hate me," Patsy said.

"I don't hate you. I don't know you any more. You won't let me near you—me or anyone else."

The despised, unbidden tears came again and this time, because it was dark, she let them flow.

"I don't know what's the matter with me," she

said, choked with misery. "I don't know who I am or what I want to be."

"Hey—sit down." Colin pulled her into a wicker seat, offered a handkerchief. "Blow. Go on. Blow again."

Patsy managed a giggle. It emerged as a hiccup. "Stop bullying me."

"Somebody has to. Don't you realise you're worrying Kate to death? And you're not doing yourself much good, either."

"I know that. I just feel so—so totally at sea."

"You're alone too much. You think too much."

"There's nothing wrong with thinking."

"There is if it's concerned totally with yourself. What is it, Patsy? Was I right the other day? Is it the thought of going away that's worrying you?"

Patsy sniffed a little more and wiped her eyes.

"Partly," she said. "And partly it's because—oh Colin, where *do* I belong? Look!" She tapped her forehead. "Inside here I'm just as white as you. I've been brought up as a European, I speak like one and think like one. But *here*—" she shot out a clenched fist towards Colin—"here I have what's known as a touch of the tarbrush. And, believe me, just a touch is enough to disbar me from the human race."

Colin took the fist in his hand, straightened out the fingers, smoothed them with his own.

"Things will change, Patsy."

"Will they? I wonder! Kate is sure that

education will make all the difference, but I know that I could come back with all the degrees in Christendom and there would still be only two jobs open to me in Nairobi—I could be an *ayah* or a prostitute. You know that's true! Don't pretend to disagree."

"That's not the sort of country I want it to be."

"There aren't too many like you. Kenya is full of Mrs. Honeywells—"

"Who's she when she's at home?"

"Nobody. The worst sort of settler."

"Most would react as Christy did—as we all did—over that lost child. They're not monsters."

"I know, I know. And they treat their sick and build schools, as we have done. To what end, I sometimes wonder? Will young Nderitu be given the vote if he lives to get through school and go to college?" She gave a short laugh. "Go on—tell me it will take two thousand years of civilisation."

"I can't see into the future any more than you can. All I know is that I'm prepared to work for a country where we can all shake down together—" he broke off sharply. "What's that noise, Patsy? There's a crowd coming this way."

A bobbing lantern could be seen in the darkness and voices were raised in shouts and laughter. Colin and Patsy moved swiftly to the steps of the verandah and Kate and Christy came out of the room behind them.

"*Habari gani?*" Christy called. "What's the news?"

"*Bwana*, the child is found!" It was Onyango, Nderitu's father. He came nearer and stood grinning beneath them, the light of the lamp shining on his teeth and eyes and the planes of his angular face. His head was covered by a shapeless felt hat, torn singlet drooping over torn shorts.

Other voices joined in to tell the story. The child had walked up the mountain to find the God Ngai and had climbed a tree to hide from a rhino. In his fright he had stayed there all night and in the morning there had been mist and he had lost his way.

"Thank God," Kate said fervently, and they all agreed, faces split by smiles, gleaming in the light. *Ndio, ndio,* they said, God had been good.

"This calls for a drink," Christy said when they had gone. "I hope someone tans the little bastard's hide."

"Don't say that," Kate protested. "The poor child must have been punished enough."

"You'll sleep sounder tonight," Colin said to Patsy as they followed the others into the inner room.

She nodded, moved and excited, close to tears again yet at the same time with an unaccustomed lightness in her heart. Nderitu's return was a relief; yet she was experiencing relief of another kind, too. A prisoner released from solitary confinement must feel something like this, she thought. At last she had broken her silence.

Now as she walked or rode over the farm with Colin or sat with him on the verandah there was never silence between them, apart from those times when, all sound suspended, they sat on the rock in the forest and watched a bushbuck pick its way delicately to the river, or smiled to see a wart-hog with three young piglets trotting, tails up, into the bush.

"Suppose I disappoint Kate?" Patsy said one day. "She expects so much of me! Suppose I'm totally unable to do all these great and momentous things for the women of Kenya?"

"You're too damned clever for your own good," Colin said with mock exasperation. "I don't think for one moment you'll disappoint Kate. You'll run rings round everyone, just as you always did when we had lessons together, infuriating little beast that you were. And if I'm any judge you'll be a sensation in other ways, too. They'll think you're like some lovely, exotic flower."

"Oh, nonsense!"

"It's not nonsense, Patsy. You look like a very superior Egyptian princess—regal and somewhat disdainful. If I were an artist I could imagine painting you over and over again, never being satisfied and never growing tired of it."

Biting her lip to subdue her smile of pleasure,

Patsy turned away from him to pack the remains of their picnic with assumed concentration.

There never was a girl more ready to fall in love. Fearfully Kate watched from the sidelines, a chill wind of apprehension disturbing her undoubted pleasure at seeing Patsy happy and animated once more.

"She's frighteningly vulnerable," she said to Christy, lying sleepless beside him. "I wonder if you ought to have a word with Colin—"

"For the love of God, woman, would you ever stop behaving like a demented mother hen? Isn't it you that's been worrying for months because the girl is alone up here without a friend of her own age?"

"But she's in love with him. A child could see it. I do wish Janet had been able to come—"

"And what difference would that have made? If she's ripe for love a whole battalion of troops couldn't change her feelings. He'll be away in a week and in under a year she'll be in England, so stop your worrying and go to sleep."

"But she wants to go to Mawingo to stay. Janet's off to South Africa for a year at business school in August, and there's a party planned for her eighteenth birthday—a combined farewell and birthday party. What am I to say to her, Christy? Would it be wise to let her go? How will the other guests treat her? I couldn't bear it if all this new-found confidence suffered a knock.

Colin's sensible and he appreciates the problem, and he seems to think it would be all right, but I'm not so sure. Yet she wants to go so passionately, I don't think she'd ever forgive me if I refused to let her. I suppose I could write to Meg and see what she has to say. What do you think, Christy? Should we take the risk? Christy?"

He was asleep—which accounted, she thought ruefully, for the uncharacteristically attentive silence. It didn't matter. She knew what his advice would be.

Let her go, he would say. Give her space to grow. Perhaps the advice was sound, but it failed to prevent her feeling of unease.

16

THE rain came, moving in a solid sheet across the valley and crashing down on the farm, penetrating roofs and windows that had before been weather-proof, flooding the garden and bursting the dam.

Kate and Patsy rushed round the house, moving furniture and putting receptacles under the leaks, so that the ping-ping-ping of water dripping into tin baths and *sufurias* seemed to fill the house.

Christy raised both fists to heaven and swore mightily when he discovered the calf-pens awash and found that the gale had removed the roof of the hay-store, completely ruining the hay inside.

There were difficulties about serving food, since the kitchen was a separate hut outside the main house. Kate provided Kamau with a raincoat, but he was old and slow-moving and grew testy and bitter about the elements which ruined his roasts and his soufflés on their journey from kitchen to table. It came as no surprise to Kate when he told her that the time had come for him to take his place among the elders of his tribe.

"I shall go back to my *shamba*," he said. "We have grown old together, *memsahib*."

Well, thank you for nothing, Kate thought amusedly, looking at the venerable, wrinkled face before her.

She was sad to see him go for he had been at the hub of the house since her early days at the Hill Academy, a likable despot for whom she had great affection. She pressed gifts upon him— dresses for his three wives, a box of tomato plants, an old alarm clock and a hundred shillings. There were tears in both their eyes as they wrung each other's hands in parting.

"A hundred shillings is far too little," she said. "He deserves a pension after all these years."

"Any such arrangement will have to wait. I've no more than a hundred shillings to spare at a moment's notice, and that's the truth of it. How I'm to pay the wages I have no idea, for the road to town is all but impassable."

It was not only the difficulty of getting to the bank which made the payment of the wages hard. Christy's dairy herd, built up with difficulty and determination, had been decimated by disease which he swore had been introduced by cattle from the reserves brought in to graze on his land. So occupied had he been by this that supervision of the feeding of the calves had suffered. Herdboys had systematically stolen the milk intended for the progeny of several of his best cows, and three calves had literally starved to death.

He blamed himself bitterly, ranting and raving at his own stupidity in trusting the herdboys.

"Just when we need to build the herd up again! Kate, was there ever a fool like me? I can't even cover costs with fewer than forty milking cows, let alone make a profit."

When Christy finally managed to get through to Gilgil, he came back with a letter from Julie which carried momentous news. Her grandmother had died suddenly in her sleep.

"So I am free to come back," she wrote. "My aunt is kind but has enough to worry about with her large family so would be quite pleased to be rid of me. She is writing to you herself to make arrangements, but if you are willing (and I do so hope you are!) I could come almost immediately. My grandmother has left me a little money, and though it is in trust until I am twenty-one, Aunt Mary sees no difficulty in getting hold of enough of it to pay for my passage out. I can type quite well now, so surely should be able to find a job in Nairobi? Oh, how I hope so! Please, please Kate, do write immediately and tell me if I may come."

"Send the child a telegram," Christy said.

"It will all work wonderfully." Kate was smiling, bright-eyed with pleasure. "She can come and look after you while I'm away in England with Patsy."

Patsy could be heard singing about the house, happy because she would be seeing Julie again

331

soon, happy because the forthcoming visit to Mawingo had been approved, happy because suddenly she felt young and attractive and sure of herself, poised on the brink of something new and exciting.

She did not think beyond the visit to Kiambu. Ever since Colin had left, the thought of him and of seeing him again had filled her mind. Each night as she lay awake, unable to sleep, she relived every word he had spoken to her, and glowed with delight as she remembered his smile, the turn of his head, the lift of a brow.

There had been no physical contact between them, beyond the accidental brushing of one arm against another, or a proffered hand to help her up a steep and slippery path. She had expected no more, though even this had made her pulses race. It was more the shared jokes she had treasured, the knowledge that he was interested in her welfare, that he actually liked her. Oh, even now it made her heart beat faster to remember the quick grin of pleasure he would give in her direction as they watched the antics of the monkeys in the forest, or were startled by the brilliant plumage of a bird.

Janet's birthday was in August. Letters passed between Meg and Kate. Assurances were given, fears set at rest.

"Why don't you all come?" Meg wrote. "It's far, far too long since we saw you, and I'm sure the farm would tick over for a few days without you. Do think about it—it would be such fun."

"Could we?" Kate asked. "It's ages since we had a holiday."

"Not unless I can get someone to come and live on the premises. I can't possibly leave those cows again to the tender mercies of Onyango and Karioki and their partners-in-crime. Bob Brewster might come."

"Oh, do ask him! It would be fun, wouldn't it, Christy? I long to see Meg again. There's no one quite like her."

A letter arrived from Julie's Aunt Mary. There was a sailing in mid July from Southampton, and if this was convenient to everyone, Julie would be on it, arriving in Mombasa on the 4th of August. Patsy was overjoyed at the news.

"So she will be able to stay at Mawingo, too. She'll be in time for Janet's party! Isn't that marvellous? The three of us together again—all for one and one for all!"

Christy discussed the matter with Bob Brewster and, while the matter was complicated by the fact that Bob had other commitments and could not come to World's End until after the date set for the party, arrangements were made for Patsy to go down to Kiambu independently, leaving Kate and Christy to follow a week later. They planned to stay five days at Mawingo—the first holiday away from the farm since they had arrived there in 1921.

"It's like planning a complicated military operation," Kate said. "I'm ridiculously excited about it. You realise, of course, that I haven't a rag that any self-respecting Nairobi matron would be seen dead in? No one wears skirts like this any more, and as for waists, they simply don't exist."

"We can run something up," Patsy said. No sulks now about Kate's lack of skill. She was all energy and excitement and enthusiasm. "I saw in the paper that sleeveless dresses are the thing, and surely, they couldn't be easier, could they? And what am I to wear at the party? I'll need something really smart and grown-up. Look at this picture in the *Standard*—white georgette, with three sloping flounces of white ostrich feathers."

"First catch your ostrich," Kate said. "Somehow I think that might be beyond the powers even of Mr. Dharamshi. I do have some blue silk put away in the chest though, so perhaps he could produce something suitable from that. I bought it years ago, before the war, but never got around to doing anything with it."

"You'll need it yourself—"

"Nonsense, nonsense. Your need is far greater. There's a picture here that looks simple enough —a sort of tunic effect over a swirly little skirt. That neckline should suit you, and you can wear a bandeau of the same material. You ought to have beads—"

"Long ones down to my waist!"

"I have the very thing, given to me by Aunt Sophie for Christmas 1905 and never worn because they were so horribly out of date—and here it is 1925, and they'll be simply perfect."

"Oh, Kate," Patsy breathed, looking as if she had been lit from within. "It's going to be lovely, isn't it? I just can't wait to get to Mawingo to see —everybody again. And Julie coming so soon. It's almost too good to be true."

Kate felt the small chill of unease once again, but she said nothing.

"It's like coming home," Patsy said delightedly, looking round the well-remembered living room at Mawingo. "Only you've put new curtains up."

"The old ones fell to pieces when they were washed," said Meg. "Nothing lasts for ever."

"Come and see our room." Janet, her arm through Patsy's, urged her to the door. "Come on. I've simply *masses* of things to tell you." This last was hissed at her in a confidential whisper. "It's going to be marvellous being eighteen and going away from home. I just can't wait, can you?" Blonde, pretty, blue-eyed, she curled up on her bed and watched Patsy start unpacking. "Daddy's sweet, but awfully stuffy about people taking me out. Harry Winters wanted to take me to the Claremont for dinner and dancing last week, but I wasn't allowed to go—such a swizz! Della Sinclair goes everywhere and she's younger than me. Daddy says I ought to be glad because it shows that he and Mummy care about what happens to me whereas the Sinclairs are usually too sozzled to care one way or the other about Della. I suppose he has a point, but sometimes I wish they'd get just slightly sozzled, enough to take their minds off me for once. Can you dance the Charleston?"

"What?" Patsy turned, her blue silk dress on a hanger.

"The Charleston. It's all the rage. Harry Winters taught me and he's going to bring his gramophone record to my party. I say, is that the dress you're going to wear? It's a lovely colour. I've had a silvery dress made with floating panels —awfully sweet, I know you'll love it. Colin says it makes me look like the fairy on the Christmas tree, but you know him—a typical big brother."

"How is he?"

"Colin? Oh, fine. Patsy, the most wonderful luck! Harry Winters is going to medical school in Cape Town and he's sworn to come and see me and take me out sometimes. Wait till you meet him." She closed her eyes and sighed in ecstasy. "He's simply divine. It's going to be a wonderful party, with all my friends and lots of Colin's friends, too."

A trickle of fear seemed to run down Patsy's spine. What a fool she had been to look forward to this. Now that it was upon her, it seemed the most frightening thing that had ever happened.

"What's the matter? You're not shy, are you?"

Janet was never one to tread cautiously. "You don't have to be. Everyone is awfully nice and there's no danger that people won't be friendly to you because I've told them they've jolly well got to be because you're just like my sister, and so is Julie. Isn't it marvellous that she'll be here, too? I couldn't believe it all worked out so well. Come on, let's go and have some tea. You can finish that afterwards. I can hear Colin's voice—he's come in early especially to see you."

"Is there—" Patsy began, and stopped. She licked dry lips. "Has he anyone special? A girl—"

"Not he. All my friends think he's absolutely divine and even though he's my brother I must confess that he's terribly handsome. But he says they're all brainless little ninnies, which is extremely unfair of him because some of them did awfully well in School Certificate. Daphne Caldwell got three credits. Come on, let's go and see him."

Hugh was there as well as Colin, and he greeted her with affection and asked for news of Kate and Christy. Colin caught her eye and winked at her across the room and suddenly her fears were gone, dissipated in the warmth of her welcome. Everything, she told herself, was going to be all right.

Patsy proved an adept pupil at the Charleston, but Colin showed little talent for it and the three of them became helpless with laughter at his efforts.

During the day he was busy, up at dawn to supervise the milking and finding any number of things to keep him hard at work. The coffee was Hugh's business. There was a vast acreage of it now in bearing and the farm was beginning to look if not prosperous exactly, then well-founded.

The house that Kate had occupied stood empty. A dairyman had lived there during the years before Colin had come home, but he had now moved on to run his own farm. Patsy looked at it, wandered round it, peered in its vacant windows and felt pleasurably nostalgic about the time they had spent there. She remembered lying in her room and thrilling to the sound of Christy's voice, sure that her father had come home to look after her at last.

And he has looked after me, she thought with a pang of guilt. He couldn't have cared more, if he had been my father. I've been such a beast lately.

There was a visit to Limuru races where she backed two winners and cared not a jot that people stared at her, for Colin and Janet flanked her on each side and stared back on her behalf, masking rude comments with false expressions of sweetness, so that once again laughter overcame them.

On the day that Julie was due to arrive, Colin had arranged to go to Thika to look at some cattle that were for sale, including a pedigree Ayrshire bull which he was convinced Hugh ought to buy. He left home to drive in one direction while Hugh took Patsy in the other, towards Nairobi and the station.

Julie stepped down from the train as dirty and travel-stained as anyone else, but there was an indefinable air of neatness and distinction about her. She was hugged and kissed and greeted with rapture, then Hugh held her at arm's length and studied her judiciously.

"I think you'll clean up very nicely," he said.

She cleaned up beautifully. Her skin was creamy, her eyes the colour of dark sherry, her hair lustrous, curling close about her neat head. Excitement and happiness filled her with animation, drew all eyes towards her. Patsy, so long her confidante on paper, felt shy of her— just as shy as she had felt of Colin, for she seemed just as much a stranger.

"You're so grown up," she said to her when they were all in the bedroom together. "You and Janet. I'm still a child—in some ways," she added hastily, for there was nothing childlike about the feeling she had for Colin.

"You're the cleverest of the lot of us," Janet said.

"Cleverness has nothing to do with it, not in the academic sense. You two are wordly wise."

"So will you be when you come back with all your degrees and yards of letters after your name." Julie was unpacking, helped or hindered by the other two.

"You have some *divine* clothes," Janet gasped. "Look at this one, Patsy." She pulled out a flame-red georgette creation. "It's simply gorgeous."

"Aunt Mary helped me to buy it. I needed things for the voyage. Don't forget I had my birthday on board."

"Are you going to wear it at the party tomorrow?"

"Probably. Either that or the yellow one."

"Oh my dear— just look, Patsy. Isn't that ab-so-*lute*-ly divine?"

The blue silk, painstakingly made by Mr. Dharamshi, began to look like something picked up in a street market. Patsy, perched on the bed watching the other two, was swamped by depression, even when Julie dismissed the subject of her clothes and asked about Kate and World's End, and talked of her life in England.

"I never felt warm," she said. "Not once. I swear that school they sent me to was on the coldest headland in the coldest county of England. We used to get icy winds there, straight from the Russian steppes. I just can't believe that I'm here and the sun's shining, and everything's just the same as it always was."

"Not quite," Patsy said. "We're older."

"You should see Colin," said Janet. "He has this perfectly divine moustache—"

"Don't talk to me about Colin! He never came

to see me, all those years we were in England together."

"But you were at school in Suffolk and he was in Gloucester."

"Even so—still, I'll forgive him. I'll forgive anyone anything, I'm so pleased to be back. Can we get changed and go for a ride, just the way we used to? Do you remember that time when we all stopped and gossiped under a tree, and then when we looked up there was a leopard lying there, looking down at us? And the time when someone fired the huts in the squatter village?"

There was so much to talk of and remember. But beneath it all Patsy felt the weight of worry inside her, indefinable, inexplicable. There was no cause for it, she told herself. She was with her friends again. Her best friends.

When Colin came home in the evening and looked with delighted incredulity at Julie, she knew exactly why she had been worried. He gave every appearance of a man who has seen a vision. At dinner—a noisy, convivial meal where the servants joined in the talk and laughter because they, too, were pleased to see all the girls reunited again—Patsy was aware that Colin's eyes were drawn over and over again towards Julie, as if only her presence had any meaning for him.

It forced her into bright, brittle chatter which was meant to amuse, to bring his attention back to her with the same degree of warmth that she

341

had enjoyed over the past few days, but instead she knew that she was becoming shrill.

"You're in tearing spirits tonight," Meg said to her, smiling at her across the table with an edge of worry in her eyes.

She no longer looked forward to the party, even though she was now an expert at the Charleston. She stared at herself in the mirror as she dressed for it, hating what she saw, longing for brown curls and a creamy skin.

"You look lovely," Julie said, coming to look over her shoulder, vivid in her red georgette. "You're so slim. Just look at my beastly curves! I ought to wear a flattener, only I can't bear the thought in this heat."

Patsy could not look at her. She smiled her small, tight smile and said nothing.

Colin danced with her, told her she was looking gorgeous, but looked over her shoulder even as he spoke, searching out Julie's whereabouts. Harry Winters proved to be a dark, curly-haired youth. He was all right, Patsy thought, but nowhere near as handsome as Colin. His cousin, temporarily visiting from England, had come to the party with him. His name was Cedric and he laughed a great deal and had artistic pretensions, telling Patsy that she was arresting and beautiful and that he would give a lot to be able to photograph her.

"In a flame-coloured cloak, I think. Something dramatic, anyway."

Patsy thought him affected and fatuous, but at

least he was attentive and kept asking her to dance, which was better than being left to sit in a corner.

Colin danced once with every girl. He had favoured her no more and no less than the brainless ninnies he had despised so much. But he kept going back to Julie. Patsy couldn't bear to watch them. To her it seemed as if they were encased in a brilliant glass bubble, quite alone with the incredulous wonder of the attraction which had apparently sprung spontaneously between them.

She muttered an excuse to Cedric and went to the bedroom where she poured cool water from the jug on the washstand to bathe her throbbing temples. When would it end? Surely at midnight they would all go?

She heard a light, clear voice singing outside in the passage, coming closer and closer. Julie.

"Yes, *sir*, that's my baby—No, *sir*, don't mean maybe—"

The door opened and Julie came in, her happiness surrounding her like a glowing aura.

"Oh, there you are," she said. "I wondered where you'd got to. Gosh, it's hot, isn't it? I simply had to come and freshen up. Isn't it a lovely party?"

"I suppose so."

Julie turned to look at her.

"Is something wrong? You're enjoying it,

343

aren't you? That Cedric man seems awfully taken with you."

"And Colin seems awfully taken with you."

Julie laughed, a little breathless.

"Oh, Patsy," she said. And again: "Oh, Patsy!"

"Have you fallen in love with him?" Patsy's voice was pleasant, neutral, and she turned away to look in the mirror again as if Julie's reply was only of minimal concern to her.

"I don't know. I think I must have done. I feel so—so *wonderful*." She twirled round on her toes, her arms spread wide, her head flung back in ecstasy, "I feel as if I could dance all night—as if I'm floating up in the stars somewhere. Oh, Patsy." Her voice changed, became low and confidential, as she collapsed on the edge of the bed and hugged herself. "He is rather heavenly, isn't he? I'm so terribly frightened. Suppose he's already in love with someone else? Is he? Do you know anything?"

Patsy turned away from the mirror and looked at Julie. She shook her head.

"I don't know anything about him," she said abruptly. "Why should he confide in me?"

"Come on." Julie stood up and held out her hand. "They're serving supper now and there's a marvellous spread in the dining room. We've been away long enough."

Patsy went with her because there seemed nothing else to do, but she knew that if she tried to eat she would be sick. Cedric was as attentive as ever, but as an audience Patsy was hopelessly inadequate. She could not prevent herself from looking at Julie and Colin.

It seemed that every time she looked up they were dancing together, and hers were not the only eyes that noticed it. People were commenting on it, smiling as if the sight of two such beautiful young people made them happy.

"You can see he's well and truly smitten," Cedric gasped, the words emerging in jerks as he bobbed to the Charleston beat. "Not surprising. Lovely girl."

Patsy said nothing. She wanted to run and hide. For weeks, months, she had dreamed of this party—had imagined the pressure of his hand on her waist, the warmth of the admiration in his eyes. And what had he given her? One brief waltz, soon over, as if it were a duty that had to be accomplished before he could get on with the real business of enjoying himself.

Mercifully the music stopped.

"I must have some air," she said. "Excuse me—"

"I'll come with you," offered Cedric.

"No—" Without waiting for him, she fled.

It happened to coincide with a moment when Colin found Julie pulled away from his reluctant arms by another partner. The dance with Patsy had not been a duty. He liked her very much. She was bright and amusing, as well as being light on her feet, and in the normal course of events he would undoubtedly have asked her to dance many times. She was, he thought, far superior to the feather-brained girls that Janet brought to the house.

But this was not the normal course of events. From the moment he had seen Julie she had filled his thoughts. She was the most beautiful creature he had ever seen. Smiling with pleasure, bewitched by the sight of her, he watched her dancing with the burly young man who had claimed the dance, knowing that in a few moments she would come back to him.

Then he saw Patsy run out into the night. There was something panic-stricken about her flight. He went to the top of the verandah steps and could see the blur of her dress across the expanse of grass, beyond the pool of light which spilled from the house. She was running towards the coffee *shamba*, and rapidly he went after her.

The air was heavy with the scent of jasmine and frangipani. The music and the laughter from the house seemed to have no part in the night. It was an alien, jangling intrusion into the darkness.

"Patsy," Colin called. She had stopped running and was leaning on the fence which divided the coffee *shamba* from the garden. "Patsy, is something wrong?"

He slowed down as he reached her, putting out an arm to touch her. Impatiently, she shook herself away from him.

"What's upset you?" he asked.

"Why should you care?" Her back was towards him, her elbows resting on the fence, but he knew that she was crying.

"Was it that chap Cedric? Did he say something?"

"No." Her voice was full of scorn. "What could he say? As if I would care, whatever he said."

"What, then? Come on, dry your eyes and come inside. It can't be that bad. Look, your shoes will be wet through."

"I don't care about my shoes. Just leave me alone. Go back to Julie."

Realisation dawned slowly on Colin. He opened his mouth, closed it again, shook his head and distractedly ran a hand through his hair.

"We're friends, aren't we?" he said at last, very gently. "I feel as if I've been hit by a cyclone. Be glad for me, Patsy."

"*Glad*?"

She turned round to face him, her arms hooked behind her over the fence, braced against it. Tears were pouring down her cheeks.

"We were so close, up at World's End. You seemed to care about me."

"I did. I do. I hate to see you unhappy."

She relinquished the fence and took a step towards him.

"I'd do anything for you," she said, her voice

low and intense. "Anything at all. I've never felt like this about anyone. It hurts so much."

He reached out to her again, but withdrew his hand before it touched her, angry at himself, helpless and totally at a loss.

"I'm sorry," he said, after a moment. "Oh God, I'm so sorry. Believe me, I wouldn't willingly hurt you."

"Why can't you love me?" The words burst from her and she turned away from him, bent over as if she were in pain, made helpless by a fresh storm of weeping.

Impotently he shrugged.

"You know it's not something one can order."

"Just because I'm not white!"

"It's not that. You must believe me, it's not that at all." Hotly he denied it. "Look, you're very young—maybe you think you love me now, but there are far more deserving men than me around—"

"I'm three months older than Julie."

"Julie—" Colin began, and stopped.

"Go back to her."

"I can't leave you here like this."

"Why not? With luck, I might get eaten by a leopard."

"Don't be an idiot." He took her arm, tightening his grip as she tried to pull away. "Come on, Patsy. You can't stay here."

He propelled her towards the house, but before

they reached the pool of light that surrounded it she forced him to stop.

"I can't face anyone looking like this," she said. "You go on. I'll go round the back."

For a moment Colin stood and looked at her, biting his lips, shaking his head in a gesture of defeat.

"I'm so sorry," he said again. "I've always been fond of you, ever since we were children—"

"So you've said." She had controlled her crying and her voice was high and brittle. "Don't give me a thought. I shall be perfectly all right."

"Shall I ask mother or Janet to come to you?"

"No! I don't need anyone."

Abruptly she turned and ran away from him, round to the back of the house. He looked after her unhappily, then continued towards the verandah steps, not knowing where he had gone wrong but feeling quite certain that he had blundered badly.

The music went on, muffled now, but Patsy could still hear the beat of it—thump, thump, thump. The whole house seemed to reverberate with it. There was laughter, too, and snatches of conversation.

She pulled the bedclothes over her ears to shut it out. She just wanted to sleep, she told worried enquirers. She had a bad headache and felt sick. Perhaps she had eaten something that disagreed with her.

She did not sleep. The hours passed and the noise gradually lessened. Car doors slammed and there were shouted goodbyes. Then Julie and Janet were in the room, undressing with tiny economical movements designed not to wake her, stifling whispers and giggles.

She forced herself to lie still, feigning sleep, until at last the deep breathing of the other girls told her that she could relax—that there was no need for any more pretence.

Life was over, Patsy told herself. She wished that she was dead. She relived those moments in the garden, appalled at the way she had begged for Colin's love. How on earth was she ever to face him again? This was the question that superseded all others as the sleepless hours dragged by.

The loneliness and isolation of World's End had often irked her. There had been many times when she had felt at odds with Kate and Christy, certain that no one understood her or could possibly love her. Now she longed for the farm as if it were a haven, craved to hide herself in those familiar acres, creep into the forest to find solace as she had done so many times before.

She would go. It wasn't so far. If she left at dawn—before dawn—she could walk to Nairobi by the time the up-country train was due to leave. Nothing could be simpler. She would be in Gilgil well before dark and from there it should be an easy matter to find someone who would give her a lift to the farm.

Once this course was decided on she felt a little better. Looking cautiously across at Julie in the next bed and Janet in the bed beyond that, she wrote a brief note by the light of a small torch, then settled back, once more in darkness, to wait wide-eyed for the time to leave.

She would not take any of her clothes, she decided. Just a toothbrush and perhaps a little food. It was better this way. If she told Aunt Meg she wanted to go home it would mean explanations and a bother for Uncle Hugh. There would be arguments and arrangements and explanations, and in the end they would probably stop her leaving. This way she could be gone before the farm stirred, and she need never see Colin again.

She must, after all, have dozed for suddenly she was aware that the sky was lighter and that birds were beginning their chorus. Rapidly she dressed in a cotton dress and woollen jacket, for the early mornings were icy cold. She found bread in the kitchen, and cutting off a hunk put it with two apples in a paper bag which she stuffed into her pocket. In minutes she was letting herself out of the kitchen door—hurrying now, for the day on the farm started early and before long Paulo would be kindling the fire under the big hundred-gallon *debe* which provided hot water for the house, and Njuguna would be emerging from his hut to hawk and spit and scratch himself preparatory to donning his white *khanzu* to take early morning tea to those indoors.

Thinking of Njuguna, she paused for a moment outside, realising suddenly that to take the direct route she would have to pass close to his quarters. Someone was bound to spot her. It would be safer to go through the coffee *shamba* and the forest.

Night was in full retreat now and the trees and bushes which only minutes before had seemed full of menace returned to daytime normality, hung about with spangled webs. Even so, her heart pounded and her eyes darted from one side to the other as she walked. Unexplained noises came from the undergrowth. Somewhere a rainbird was calling, clear and distinctive.

There was a sudden loud crashing on the left side of the path. For a moment she froze, paralysed with fear. She had ridden this way many times and seen nothing more worrying than a bushbuck or tiny dik-dik but now, on foot, she felt frighteningly alone and vulnerable. The crashing noise came again, and in panic she took to her heels, tripping on roots and scratched by trailing branches. Imagination conjured danger behind every thicket. Buffalo, she thought wildly. It could be buffalo.

The path led downward and was slippery with leaves, pitted with holes. Blindly she shouldered her way through a dense bush that grew across the track, turning her head to avoid its whipping

352

branches, ducking to miss the clammy snare of a spider's web.

She lurched sideways as her foot caught in the tangled roots of a tree and almost fell. For a moment she crouched, panting, and could hear nothing over the pounding of her heart, but then she grew calmer as she realised that all she could hear now were the gentle, familiar sounds of the forest: the cooing of a dove, the call of a plantain-eater. Whatever it was that had caused her to panic had apparently gone.

She flexed her foot. She had twisted it when she fell and it hurt a little, but resolutely she ignored it, for it was a long walk to Nairobi and she was anxious to put as many miles between her and the farm as she possibly could before the world was fully awake. The trees were thinning and she could see the sky, pale pink and streaked with gold. She felt ravenously hungry suddenly, and more cheerful, as if her passage through the forest were a test she had done well to pass. As she emerged into rough, uncultivated country, she came to a collection of beehive huts. No one was about, though smoke rose gently from their roofs.

Below was the road and she was glad to see it for it promised easier walking, rough though it was. The pain in her foot had, if anything, increased. She set herself a goal. Once she reached the road she would rest for a while and

353

eat a little bread and an apple. Then she would begin her real journey.

Her foot felt better once she had rested. She saved some of the food and making it into a smaller parcel she put it in the pocket of her jacket, setting off down the road refreshed and at a brisk pace.

Two women, *jembes* in hand, were plodding off to their day's work, the round heads of their babies bobbing behind them. She greeted them and they responded, but guardedly, watchfully, as if she were an object of curiosity. She was used to that. Africans never quite knew what to make of her, for clearly she was not European, yet equally obviously she was not one of them, with her light, coffee-coloured complexion, her clothes and her hair dressed in such an un-African way.

The sun rose and it grew warmer. She took off her jacket and carried it over her arm. Normally this was the time of day when she felt alive, hopeful: but instead, today, this was the moment when nagging doubts started to plague her. Her foot was hurting her, quite seriously. She sat down by the side of the road and considered her position.

She could still go back. She had left the note on the dressing table, but until the girls woke no one would realise that she was gone. Suddenly the whole project seemed like madness. She still wanted to leave Mawingo, but perhaps, after all, this was not the best way of doing it. It had

354

seemed so obvious in the dark watches of the night when she had raged with jealousy and disappointment. Now, with miles still ahead of her and her foot hurting more every moment, it seemed less sensible.

But could she face Colin? He'd probably laughed at her once she'd gone. Just imagine, a little *nusu-nusu* like her, having the temerity to fall in love with him! Why couldn't she have hidden it? Just to come out with it, like that, begging and pleading with him—.

She had to go on. Her foot was swelling now and she could not bear to put her weight on it, but somehow she had to go on.

It was at that moment that she heard the sound of a car. It was a long way off, but the noise of its engine was quite plain in that still morning air. If she stood beside the road, perhaps it would stop—offer a lift to Nairobi. It was coming closer. She stood up and looked towards it expectantly. In this country, everyone helped everyone else. Whoever it was would be bound to stop. It was fate that it should come just at this moment when she was wavering. *Shauri ya mungu*: God had sent it. Hopefully she lifted a hand.

Even in his hung-over state Piet van Riebeeck had seen her from some distance and he had raised his eyebrows and grinned to himself around the cigarette that drooped from his lips, because she was slim and straight and young and seemed to have dropped from heaven, there on the deserted and dusty road.

He pulled up beside her. He was a tow-haired man, jowly and in need of a shave. His face was as red as a new brick wall.

He stared at her with amused astonishment.

"Good God," he said. "It's a Kaffir."

Patsy frowned at him, uncomprehending. Kaffirs, she had always understood, were a tribe that lived in South Africa, many thousands of miles away from Kenya.

"Do you want a ride to Nairobi?" he asked her, speaking now in execrable Swahili.

For a moment she hesitated, for there was something about this man she did not like. But the pain in her foot was worsening by the moment. Going on to Nairobi or returning to Mawingo would be equally impossible if she had to walk.

"Thank you," she said, making up her mind. She stepped forward to open the passenger door next to the driver, but he jerked his head contemptuously.

"*Kwenda nyuma*," he snapped. "Get in the back." For a moment Patsy stared at him with the expression which Colin had likened to that of an Egyptian princess, then lowered her head to disguise her scornful amusement.

"*Ndio, bwana*," she said, with mock humility. She sat down on the back seat of the car and for a few miles they rattled along in silence.

"Mission girl, are you?" van Riebeeck tossed the words over his shoulder with a sneering twist of his lips.

"In a manner of speaking."

This time Patsy spoke in very precise English. He raised his eyebrows and turned to stare at her before giving a short, incredulous laugh.

"My God, man, you think a lot of yourself, don't you? If you want to know my opinion, I think the missions have got something to answer for, giving you niggers ideas above your station. I suppose you think that you're my equal, now that you wear a pretty dress instead of a leather apron and a few beads."

"Oh, never that, *bwana*," Patsy breathed. "I'd never describe myself as your equal."

"I should hope not, man."

He laughed with cheerful arrogance. He was slumped in his seat, his elbow resting on the open window, his thick lips pursed in a tuneless whistle. Patsy stared at the folds of skin at the back of his neck with cold dislike.

"I've got a farm up on the plateau," he said after a moment. "I never employ a mission boy. They're a lazy lot of trouble-makers, if you want to know my opinion."

"And if I don't?"

"Eh?" He half turned again to shoot a suspicious glance at her. His expression was worried, puzzled. There was something here he didn't understand. "You can bet your bottom dollar," he went on, "if there's trouble on a farm, and you've got mission boys on the labour force, then they're the ones that are stirring it up. And why? Because the bloody missionaries give them high-and-mighty ideas, that's why. Take that Dr. Arthur who represents them on Legislative Council. The man's a fool. The only thing they need to know is *hapana kazi, hapana chukula*. No work, no food."

"And that's your opinion, is it?"

"It certainly is."

"Tell me," Patsy remarked conversationally. "What is your opinion on Imperial Preference? Was Joseph Chamberlain justified in resigning on the issue in 1903?"

"What's that? What are you talking about, man?"

"And I should so value your opinion of John Stuart Mill. His views on women's rights were so far ahead of their time, weren't they? Somehow I don't feel you would see eye to eye with him. Nietzsche, now, would be a different case. How do you feel about Nietzsche? He'd be much more to your liking. After all, he believed, as you do, in the creation of an élite—"

"You're mad!"

"Not mad, *bwana*." Patsy spat the word venomously. "Not mad at all." She was leaning forward now. "Just more educated than you'll ever be—"

Van Riebeeck slammed on the brakes and was

358

out of the car before she was aware what was happening. He opened the door, reached in and jerked her out with such force that she was helpless, held by her two wrists in a grip as hard as iron.

"You saucy bloody nigger," he said softly. "You goddamned cheeky black bastard." He drew back his right hand and hit her face so hard that her head slammed back against the car. She cried out and tears sprang involuntarily to her eyes.

"Who's master now, then?" His eyes were round, a very light, clear blue, and they seemed to bore into hers. "Go on, answer me. Who's master now?"

Momentarily incapable of speech she stared back at him, gasping with pain and fright, her ears ringing from his blow. He gripped her by the shoulders and shook her.

"I'd like to thrash you within an inch of your life, you stinking little black whore. Who's the master now? Who? Who?"

Still she did not answer, not in words, but her eyes were full of loathing and as if in reply to this he hit her again. For a moment her senses swam and she sagged against the car.

"Little black whore," he said again, and she could feel his hands on her, moving down from her shoulders, reaching into her dress, ripping the thin cotton.

"Don't touch me," she screamed. "Don't touch me. I'm not a black girl."

"Not a black girl?" Van Riebeeck laughed sneeringly, without amusement. "You're too black for me, man."

He threw her from him using so much force that the breath was knocked from her body as she hit the road. Dust was in her eyes and nose and mouth but she was less conscious of it than of the blows she felt sure were still to come. She tried to roll away, but still laughing he kicked her and she moaned aloud. There was a searing pain in her side. Through half-open eyes she could see his booted feet on the road beside her. They moved and she cringed away from him.

She could hear the scrape of his feet on the road and the beat of the car engine which he had not bothered to switch off. Somewhere goats were bleating. In breathless suspense she waited for the boot to land once more in her ribs, every nerve screaming, but the next sound she heard was the slam of the car door and the increased revving of the engine. Slowly she relaxed. She was alone.

It was only after she had crawled to the side of the road where she collapsed trembling in the shade of an olive tree, that she realised the jacket with her money in its pocket was still in the car. In helpless misery she covered her face with her hands. What on earth was she to do?

Why couldn't she have let it go, all those things

that the man had said? Why couldn't she have taken it submissively, pretended to agree—or at any rate, not have argued? Because she was Patsy Brennan, that was why, who had to prove every minute of every day that she was better than anyone else.

She assessed the damage. Her side ached unbearably and she felt faint with nausea. The prospect of having to move appalled her. She could not imagine being able to walk a yard, let alone the rest of the way to Nairobi, nor yet back to Mawingo.

Now that the morning was further advanced, cars passed in both directions from time to time, but no one gave her so much as a glance. Her dress was dirty and torn, her hair wild.

It could have been worse, she thought after a time. For one moment I thought he was going to rape me.

And then she remembered the words she had screamed out:

"I'm not a black girl."

"What am I?" she asked herself. "Oh God, what am I?"

One thing was certain, she could not go on sitting there. Somehow she would have to find the physical strength to make her way back to Mawingo. The problem of facing Colin and Julie together—such an overwhelming disaster when contemplated earlier—had diminished to nothing in the face of her physical misery.

She stood up and immediately felt so dizzy that it took all her determination to stay upright. Blindly she reached out and clung to the tree. Bushes on the opposite side of the road swam in and out of focus. There were a few goats tethered at the top of a bank and the sound of their bleating grew both faint and resonant as if they were at the end of a long tunnel. The red and dusty road seemed to stretch out endlessly before her, the haven of Mawingo so distant that it was unobtainable. Even so, she would have to try it, one foot after the other, on and on.

If only the pain in her side was not so bad. If only the road would keep still. It seemed to billow up and down, side to side, like a stretch of red water. Water! She would give anything for a drink.

She mustered every ounce of determination and took a few steps. There was the sound of a rushing torrent in her ears, the noise swelling into a roar, overwhelming and extinguishing her. The redness of the road was all around, hurtling suddenly to meet her as she pitched forward to lie unconscious upon it, a small and insignificant heap of flesh.

There was both concern and annoyance at Mawingo when her absence was discovered.

"She's a naughty little girl," Hugh said severely. "What can she have been thinking of?"

"I can't imagine."

362

Meg, usually inclined to champion the cause of any of the children, was uncharacteristically angry.

"She knows that Kate and Christy are due here themselves in a few days. If she does anything to upset that, I shall be absolutely furious. Kate's been looking forward to it so much. It really is very thoughtless of her."

"Thoughtless? It's inexcusable, and damned bad manners. Now I suppose I'll have to drive into town and haul her back. We can't leave her to find her own way from Gilgil to World's End. Kate would never forgive us."

Hugh sighed heavily. His plans for that day had not included a morning drive to Nairobi.

Colin went with him and they looked for her along the road, but found no sign of her.

"She made good time if she's reached Nairobi already," Hugh said.

"Someone could have given her a lift."

"I suppose she'll be waiting at the station."

It was still an hour away from the train's departure time when they arrived at the station, but already there were a number of Africans waiting—women sitting passively on bundles of belongings, babies on their backs. There was a group of old men dressed in the hides and blankets which were now largely discarded in favour of European dress by those who were younger. They squatted on their hunkers, gossiping and taking snuff.

There was no sign of Patsy.

Hugh swore briefly but explicitly as they drove off to search the streets, and when this was fruitless they returned to the station where now intending passengers were assembled for the train. They walked from one end of the platform to the other, and waited until the train had gone, and for some time after, just in case she arrived too late.

"She's disappeared off the face of the earth," Hugh said, his face grim with anxiety. "Where in hell can the girl be?"

17

SHE was not in hell: in fact as she struggled towards consciousness her first thought was that she had died and gone to heaven, for she could hear high-pitched voices singing a hymn. But in the next moment she realised that these were not angel voices, but a choir that bore the unmistakable stamp of Africa—harsh, yet harmonic.

She blinked dazedly. She was lying on a low, hard bed in a bare room, two other beds beside her, both empty, their mosquito nets looped and tied above them. She could remember nothing of her arrival in this place. It hurt her to breathe and her head throbbed, but experimentally she moved it on the flat pillow and it was then she heard the voice.

" *Jambo*," it said.

Patsy blinked and a figure at the end of her bed swam into focus. It was that of a small woman —a European, dressed in a high-necked, shapeless dress of printed cotton. Her smooth brown hair was drawn back into a knot and she wore gold-rimmed spectacles behind which eyes of brilliant blue regarded the girl in the bed with a warm, compassionate gaze.

The woman came nearer, in her hands a thick cup.

"*Kula maji*," she said.

Gratefully Patsy raised her head and drank.

"*Habari yako sasa?*" the woman asked. "How are you feeling now?"

"I speak English," Patsy said. "Where am I? Who are you?"

"My, you do speak it well!" The woman's voice was soft and musical and had cadences unfamiliar to Patsy. "We call this place Peacehaven."

"Peace," Patsy echoed, and closed her eyes again. She gave a long sigh. She had so many questions, but mists of exhaustion seemed to fill her mind, making it impossible for her to frame them.

The singing stopped and in its place she heard the monotone of a man's voice. She was conscious of the stillness of the woman who stood beside her bed. The voice of the man fell silent and she heard a whispered 'Amen' from the woman. A cool hand rested for a moment on her forehead.

"Sleep, child," the woman said. "May God bless you."

Patsy hovered between sleeping and waking, inexplicably conscious of her presence which seemed to fill the room long after she had left it. How was it possible that such comfort and security could come from this insignificant figure —this mousy little woman in her ill-fitting dress? It defied logic, Patsy thought, that she should feel so totally at peace here, only mildly curious about the way she had been brought to this place.

She slept and woke and slept again, her wants attended to by a deft, smiling Kikuyu girl, who brought her fruit and *posho* and tea and washed her with gentle hands.

"This is a mission, isn't it?" Patsy roused herself sufficiently to ask the question.

"*Ndio.*"

"What kind of a mission."

"*Missioni mazuri sana*—a very good mission."

Patsy smiled. This was not entirely what she had meant, but it was a valid answer, she felt.

"You are a Christian?" she asked.

"*Ndio.*"

The girl was kind and attentive and Patsy felt drawn to her.

"What is your name?" she asked.

"Rhoda," the girl said.

All day long Patsy lay in a wholly alien state of lassitude. She could never before remember being so inert, so unwilling to move or make any effort, either of mind or body. She barely thought of her friends and family who would be anxious about her. She wondered more about the small woman who had given her the drink of water and who had left behind her this strange feeling of peace.

It was evening before she came again, and this time Patsy roused herself to ask questions. How did she come to be here? Who brought her? What kind of mission was it?

367

"How good your English is."

"I was brought up in an English family."

"Then I guess it's a lot better than mine. I'm an American, from Rhode Island. My name is Hannah Skipton. I think you'd better tell me how you came to be on the road in such a terrible state."

Patsy began the story haltingly and because, through pride, she could not bring herself to tell of her love for Colin and his rejection of it, it seemed to make little sense.

"These people—Mr. and Mrs. Lacey—were they unkind to you?"

"No, no. Never that. They're the kindest people I know."

"Yet you ran away." Hannah Skipton's eyes were clouded, mildly bewildered. "No doubt you had your reasons. The main thing is to let them know that you're safe. I'll send them a message immediately."

"Do I have to go back there?" The thought threw her into a panic. She wanted to hold on as long as possible to this strange tranquillity.

"For our part, you can stay if you want to. Certainly you should keep to your bed for a while."

"What is this place? Rhoda told me it was a mission."

"And she was right, though none of the established missionary societies acknowledge us. We have come here independently. It was

Wilfred's dream to become a missionary but his views are a little unorthodox. For many years we prayed for guidance, quite unable to see what the Lord had in mind for us, but then through someone who had travelled here we heard of Kenya and how miserable the conditions were in the native quarter of Nairobi, and at once we knew that he was calling us to come here."

Patsy watched her as if mesmerised, trying to fathom this extraordinary aura of strength. She was such a small, undistinguished figure. Small mouth, soft skin—pretty, really, in an un-memorable sort of way, or would be without those round spectacles.

"Where are we, exactly?" Patsy asked.

"On the outskirts of Nairobi, not far from Kariokor. Most missions are way out in the bush, but we wanted to be near town because that's where the greatest misery is. People come in to work, away from their villages, away from everything they've ever known. They come into contact, perhaps for the first time, with crime and vice. It's hard for them to find somewhere to live."

"And you run this as a hospital?"

"More of a hostel. We are not doctors, though we both studied first aid in preparation. We are here to help in any way we can—though first and foremost our task is to preach the Word."

"And how did I come here?"

"Wilfred found you on the road not far from

town. We figured you must have been set upon by thieves."

"So, like the Good Samaritan, he brought me here."

"What else? Now you must sleep again. You were examined by a doctor friend of ours when you first came in and it seems you had mild concussion and two cracked ribs as well as the more obvious contusions. However, there is nothing wrong with you that rest won't cure. We shall let your friends know your whereabouts."

Meg came at once, and any residual anger left her when she saw the bruises on Patsy's face. She was anxious to take her back to Mawingo but Patsy begged to be allowed to stay. Meg remembered that Colin and Julie were at Mawingo, so much in love that their enchantment was obvious to everyone, and reluctantly she agreed that Patsy should remain in this place which seemed to her so stark and comfortless.

Patsy was not conscious of any lack of comfort. She lay inert, happy to sleep, happy to wake, relaxed and peaceful and totally without sequential thought. She saw no one but Mrs. Skipton and Rhoda, but she had been conscious of many comings and goings elsewhere in the ramshackle building.

On her third evening Rhoda indicated that if she wished to be fed, it would be necessary for her to get up and join the others.

370

"For you are almost better now," she said. "I will help you."

Reluctantly, Patsy rose from her bed, the effort to rejoin the world seeming almost too much. In the living room she found Hannah Skipton laying a cloth at one end of a long trestle table while Wilfred was immersed in a book. At her arrival he cast it aside and rose from his hard, straight-backed chair, plunging across the room to meet her and to pump her hand with a great deal of nervous energy. He waved aside her thanks and fussily pressed her into a chair.

Hannah looked up and smiled at her.

"Shadrack is coming," she said. "And Samuel, too I think."

The names meant nothing to Patsy, but she smiled politely. When both men arrived, they proved to be Ugandans from the kingdom of Buganda. Both were on familiar terms with the Skiptons and Patsy was astonished to hear them using Christian names. Never before had she heard an African behave in this way towards a European.

Rhoda brought in a thick, savoury meat stew and they all sat down together, bowing their heads devoutly as Wilfred asked a blessing. Patsy followed their example but she was too busy analysing her emotions to hear a word. It was the first time that she had ever sat down to a meal with Africans; the first time she had ever seen a black face bent in prayer over a meal served to

371

him by a white woman. She was very conscious of the colour of a hand against the white tablecloth, the warm, rich darkness of Shadrack's head which merged into the flickering shadows, highlighted by the candles which burnt on the table.

It was an evening she would never forget. Love was a presence she felt she could reach out and touch. Tension eased away from her and the relief was so overwhelming that she felt sudden tears come to her eyes.

She asked about the mission and how it was run, how it was financed if they had no backing from churches at home.

"We have backing from the Lord," Hannah Skipton said, her eyes glowing with fervour. "He provides for our needs, day by day."

"He dumps groceries on your doorstep?"

Hannah took no offence at Patsy's flippant remark, but instead laughed with genuine amusement.

"You think that impossible? We have good friends and many well-wishers. The Lord works through them. If faith can move mountains, surely it can provide the means to continue His work?"

Such simplicity was laughable, Patsy thought —yet the burning sincerity was impressive. So was this inexplicable feeling of calm, of total acceptance of her as she was: Patsy Brennan, half-black, half-white. Confused, rebellious, restive.

They talked of the work of the mission—of the sick woman and child who had come that day for help, of the man newly released from prison. They talked of plans for enlarging the hostel so that the wives and families of men who left their native villages to work in the town could come to visit them from time to time.

"Children grow up hardly knowing their fathers, and they're impoverished because of it," Wilfred Skipton said passionately. "The belief that love and affection within the family are unknown is patently false. On the contrary, Africans are *all* family feeling! They have little or no loyalty to anyone outside their convoluted family structure. Accommodation must be made available so that the tie between parents and children is not broken."

For hours they talked, and as they did so it seemed to Patsy that a picture she had held out of focus all her life was gradually becoming clear.

When finally she retired to bed, she could not sleep. What of this childish faith of the Skiptons? Religion was all very well, she thought indulgently, but was such total submission of will logical?

And yet—and yet—couldn't it be true that if it was worth anything, it was worth everything? Ever an espouser of causes, this was an attitude Patsy could understand.

Hannah would say that the Lord had a hand in bringing her there, in allowing her to meet with them and with Shadrack and Samuel. Because of them she was more conscious than ever before of the part of her that was African. It was not that it was better or worse than her European side, but simply that it was *there* and could not be denied.

And with this thought came the memory that she *had* denied it. She had screamed in panic to the man in the car that she was not a black girl, as if this would prevent him from harming her.

I shouldn't have said that, she thought wretchedly. Hot tears of shame forced themselves through her closed eyelids. Up at World's End she had asked Colin: who am I? Here, in a tumbledown wooden bungalow which sat cheek by jowl with shacks and hovels made of flattened tin cans and sacks and tarred paper, she felt nearer knowing the answer to this question than she ever had done before.

"If the child is set on it," Christy said, "sure, I don't see that a few weeks can harm her. These Skipton people seem of good character."

"Beyond reproach," Kate agreed.

"And young?"

"Younger than we are, by a long stretch."

"You're always saying she needs more young company—and living without some of life's comforts won't harm her at all."

Kate had just returned from a visit to Patsy at

Peacehaven and was strolling through the coffee with Christy as she made her report.

"It seems so out of character," she said. "This sudden burning desire to devote herself to suffering humanity."

"She was always one for extremes. Let her go, Kate. Growing up is perhaps better done away from those who are closest."

"But she's going away soon enough. And she *must* keep up her studies."

"She's happy, you say?"

"Strangely so, considering how Colin must have hurt her—"

"Ah now, divil of an intention he had of doing so! You can't blame him—"

"Can't I? Only an idiot would have missed seeing it."

"Colin's no idiot. And what's more you love him like he was your own."

"Maybe I do. But that doesn't mean I don't think he was obtuse." She sighed. "Well, perhaps you're right. A break from us and World's End will do her no harm. If the worthy Skiptons would like her services for two or three weeks I suppose it would be churlish to refuse, after all they've done."

"It'll do her nothing but good," Christy said. "Now relax and enjoy your holiday."

Kate smiled and put her arm through his, but below the surface her feeling of unease persisted.

Part Three

1927–1952

18

THE wedding of Colin Lacey to Julie Hudson took place in the golden October of 1927. Julie was married from Mawingo for it was altogether more accessible than World's End, even though it could truthfully be said that most Kenya settlers were ready to travel any distance in search of a party.

The cottage that had been built for Kate was to be their home. Essential repairs had been carried out and Julie and Meg had consulted with each other over furnishings and decoration, so that it now waited for the young couple, clean and bright as a newly minted penny.

Kenya settlers were, on the whole, tough people: nevertheless, many shed a few sentimental tears as Julie joined Colin at the altar. They were a couple of such extraordinary beauty, and were so obviously in love. They seemed to epitomise everyone's hopes and dreams, to reaffirm the possibility of a life free of care in this incomparably fertile country.

Not for them the hardships of the past, their guests thought. For many of them, married life had begun in a tent or covered wagon and the farms which now grew maize or corn or barley or

379

coffee on their ordered acres had been nothing more than tracts of barren land.

Christy, looking less shaggy than usual since Kate had insisted on a Nairobi hair-cut rather than the Gilgil variety, gave the bride away. Kate, standing beside him on the lawn in the reception line, felt happier than she had done for a long time. How could she not be happy on this joyful day? Colin and Julie were made for each other. It had seemed obvious both to themselves and everyone else for the past two years.

That damned bird ought to be singing now, she thought, as she smiled and shook hands with the wedding guests. Now was the time of hope and new beginnings.

Instead, it had chosen the day when Patsy had told them she was not going to England to continue her education, but was going to throw in her lot with Hannah and Wilfred Skipton.

Kate had been hurt and angry, the pain of disappointment forcing her to say things far better left unsaid. She had called Patsy's new-found friends cranks and dreamers, sanctimonious do-gooders with no knowledge of Africa or appreciation of the real contribution Patsy could make to it, if only she went on to university as she had always planned.

"It's the sheer waste of it that angers me," she raged, pacing up and down the room. "I don't doubt that their hearts are in the right place, but to persuade you to cut your education short and join them—"

"No one persuaded me. If anything it was the reverse—they tried to make sure I knew what I was doing. I simply feel it's there that I ought to be."

With an effort Kate damped down her rage and spoke in a more conciliatory way.

"Don't you see how much more authority you would have with some sort of academic status? And *now's* the time, Patsy. It will never come again."

"You don't understand. I find them so compelling."

"So, I believe, was Karl Marx. Wasn't there a time once when you thought of becoming a Communist? And then there was your Muslim period, if I remember rightly. Now, apparently, you want to give up all you've ever worked for for this childish, fundamentalist type of Christianity!"

Patsy said nothing in reply, but turned away from Kate. "I don't know whether I believe all that or not," she said. "I haven't undergone some sort of conversion like Paul on the road to Damascus. Perhaps they're right, or perhaps they're mistaken. I only know that they're *good*. For the first time in my life I felt—" she broke off sharply.

"You felt what?"

Patsy shrugged.

381

"I don't know."

"You're not usually lost for words. I want to know, Patsy. How did you feel?"

"It's so hard to express."

"Tell me!"

For a moment they stared at each other in silence across the room, then Patsy's gaze faltered.

"I felt at home," she said, her voice a whisper.

Kate felt the words like a blow in the face.

"For the first time in your life?" Kate repeated icily, each word very clear.

"In a way. I felt totally accepted for what I am." She took a step nearer to Kate, her hand lifted in a gesture of appeal.

"You've been so good to me Kate, always. Don't think I'm ungrateful—"

"I never asked for gratitude."

"But you wanted me to conform to your idea of me."

"I wanted you to be the best that you could be. You could achieve great things. I know it, Patsy. All your life I've known it. You have an unusually good brain in that silly, stubborn head of yours."

"Then trust me when I say that this way is best for me."

With an impatient sigh Kate turned from her.

"You've known these people how long? Four weeks? Surely you owe it to me to give the whole matter more thought than this. Ever since you've

382

been in my care I've taught you and shaped you—"

"I don't want to be shaped!" Patsy was shouting now, her voice shrill and desperate. "I want to be myself. I don't want to go to an English university where I have to prove myself to be better and brighter than the others, just to get accepted. I don't want to have to make jokes about the colour of my skin, to show what a jolly good sport I am—"

"No one but you makes you do those things."

"You make me, Kate. You make me! You don't mean to, I know, but that's how I feel, with all your talk about my brilliant future, all the pressure you put on me to excel. Don't you see?"

"I see the waste of an intelligence above the ordinary," Kate said stonily. "I see total misunderstanding on your part of all my hopes for you."

The arguments had raged for days but in the end she had gone. Kate, unable to settle to anything else, had gone into the garden to weed with ferocity, her pain and disappointment a physical weight in her breast.

And the rainbird with its descending notes had sung and sung. It had seemed a mockery. All her hopes had been centred on Patsy, and now she had gone. The ambitions would never now be fulfilled.

It had seemed to Kate as she had worked in the garden that day that life had been a series of disappointments. The frustration she had felt when prevented by her father from becoming a teacher; Edward's shocking death; and the failure of the school that had taken his place. Now, after so many years, Patsy's defection. What did it all add up to? A wasted life. No children of her own, no achievement that she could point to and think: this, at least, happened because of my efforts. And still that damned bird was singing!

When she had heard the noise of the old box-body bringing Christy back from the station where he had taken Patsy, she had run to him and he had held her and stroked her and whispered comforting things in that caressing voice of his, as helplessly she had sobbed her sorrow into his chest.

All that was two years before the wedding of Colin and Julie—past history, water under the bridge. Patsy had not come back home. She had settled into the strange ménage in Kariokor, living in Spartan circumstances, never really knowing where the next meal was coming from, but apparently happy. She was, at that moment, engaged in setting up women's clubs for wives living in that overcrowded, ramshackle quarter of Nairobi. Further rooms had been added to the bungalow to provide accommodation for families. Patsy shared her room with a succession of mothers and babies and lived a crowded, communal sort of life which was so alien to anything she had ever known before that Kate found it impossible to imagine how she could bear it, though she had to admit that the mission did good work. She had even come to like Hannah and Wilfred, though she remained sceptical of their wide-eyed idealism.

The breach with Patsy had been healed but disappointment remained—and there was more disappointment, too, that she had not turned up for the wedding although she had naturally been invited.

The reception in the garden of Mawingo was well under way with the noise level rising steadily. Husbands and wives drew apart, luxuriating in the unaccustomed company of their own sex. A roar of laughter rose from a group of men standing by the improvised bar, tankards in their hands. Kate raised her eyebrows at the woman with whom she was happily exchanging garden and farm talk and who had been telling her of her daughter safely delivered of a fourth daughter in Nakuru Hospital.

"That was a good one," Kate said. "Whatever it was."

"Perhaps it was Mike telling them about the telegram Sheila sent from Nakuru after the baby was born," her companion said. "It read: ANOTHER HEIFER SUGGEST CHANGE SIRE"

Kate laughed in appreciation.

"Grandchildren of either sex must be lovely," she said. "I envy you—"

She broke off in mid-sentence, for she had caught sight of Patsy, who was talking with animation and with every appearance of happiness to Colin and Julie. She made her excuses and went over to join them.

"Patsy, you came! I'm so glad."

Delightedly, she hugged her.

"I wouldn't have missed it for the world. Wilfred Skipton lent us his car for the occasion and the wretched thing broke down three times on the way. I thought we would never get here."

"We?"

"Yes—I have a surprise for you." She looked over her shoulder, to right and left. "Where can the man have gone? Oh, there he is, lurking behind that bush."

She darted away and seconds later returned with a slim, dark-suited African whom for a second Kate did not recognise. He gave an awkward little bow and smiled.

"*David!*" Kate reached out and shook his hand warmly. "How lovely to see you again. How are you, and how was England? Do you know, our little school has never been as happy since you left. Are you still teaching?"

"He's only just arrived from London," Patsy said, answering for him. "And he did very well at college. Everyone's terribly pleased with him."

"It was you, Mrs. Brennan, who encouraged

me more than anyone," he said, looking embarrassed at this outspoken praise.

How ironic, Kate thought. I encouraged him and discouraged Patsy, all at one and the same time.

"Come and see Christy, both of you. He'll be as pleased as I am."

They threaded their way through the knots of people on the lawn, stopping for Patsy and David to greet Meg, and if there were curious looks and sideways glances from some of the white settlers, neither Patsy nor David appeared to notice them. There was undoubtedly a new assurance about Patsy, Kate thought. She looked poised and happy and confident.

Christy enfolded her in his bear-like hug and shook David by the hand.

"You're not part of this crack-brained outfit of hers, are you?" he asked him.

"You'd be surprised at the people who drop in," Patsy said. "All the intelligentsia of Nairobi!"

"We met there a week ago," added David. "I felt I should not come here uninvited, but Patsy assured me that I would find a welcome."

"Besides," Patsy said, "I needed someone to drive the car. Beastly thing! I feel quite sure that someone has put a *thahu* on it but David says no, it's just old age and overwork."

"Is it battery trouble?" Christy asked.

"No—the clutch, among other things—"

Kate and Patsy drew away from them a little.

"You look happy," Kate said.

"I am. Very."

"How's the club going?"

"Wonderfully. I wish you lived nearer—I'd rope you in to give lectures on growing vegetables and rearing poultry."

"Thank heaven I don't, then! All I really know about hens is that I can't abide the silly creatures. How well David looks! He's far better dressed than most of the men."

"He bought that suit in London at something called a Fifty Shilling Tailors. He's awfully proud of it. He's teaching at the mission in Kikuyu—for less salary, of course, than a European with the same qualifications."

"I suppose his expenses are lower—"

"Don't defend it! No one cut his tuition fees in half."

"Is he bitter about it?"

"Bitter? David? He doesn't know the meaning of the word. He's like you—mad about teaching, and as long as they let him do that then he's not likely to grumble. He doesn't even grumble about having to carry a *kipande*. He's too good-natured for his own good."

Afterwards Kate mentioned to Christy what Patsy had said.

"It is demeaning for a man like that to have to carry an identity card with his fingerprints and record of work, isn't it? I can understand all the unrest there has been about it."

Christy frowned.

"I hope Patsy's not getting herself mixed up with political issues. If the authorities get the idea that the Skiptons' mission is more concerned with rabble-rousing than spreading the Word, they'll be in trouble."

"Oh, come!" Kate laughed at him. "Can you imagine those holy Skiptons being rabble-rousers?"

"I can imagine them being too blinded by idealism to see further than their noses."

Christy had been worried by all that he had heard at the wedding. Feelings had been running high amongst his fellow farmers about the Indian question. The wretched fellows were actually demanding equal representation on Legislative Council! Christy's observation that they did, after all, outnumber the white man and had for the most part been living in the colony far longer as well as contributing immeasurably to the commercial life of the country, had been greeted with outrage and scorn. Trust a damned Irishman to say a thing like that, had been the overwhelming reaction. He felt half-amused, half-depressed when he spoke to Kate afterwards.

"God knows, I've no particular love for the Indians as a race," he said. "Like the rest of us there are good and bad. The caste system strikes me as particularly obnoxious. But I hate all this lining up in teams—the British here, the Indians there, the Africans somewhere else. No good will come of it." He stared into the fire, glad to be back in his own armchair with Kate's knitting needles clicking rhythmically from the opposite side of the hearth.

"You sound like a prophet of doom."

"A wealthy, educated minority isn't going to rule the roost for ever."

Kate laughed ironically.

"Wealthy?"

"All things are comparative." He was silent for a moment, then changed the subject completely. "Is there something between Patsy and David Ngengi, do you think?"

Kate froze, the needles stilled. Expressionlessly, she looked at Christy and drew in a very slow, deliberate breath.

"I suppose it's what we must expect," she said.

"Of course. What else?"

Kate shook her head.

"I don't know. I keep hoping—"

"Don't. Patsy has made her choice, and to me she seems a new creature. She knows what she wants out of life now."

"And you think she wants David?"

"I don't know. I think that she could do a lot worse. He's an educated man of good character, as we know from experience, and if she married him she would live in a mission environment among both Europeans and Africans. His father is wealthy. I'd take a bet with you that the man has more goats than you've had hot dinners."

Kate said nothing, pensively resuming her knitting.

"If not David, then someone like him," Christy said. "You must expect it to happen one day, Kate."

"If David is in Kikuyu," Kate said, "and Patsy in Nairobi, then they won't meet so very often."

She was not quite ready to give up the dream.

It was two years later that events killed it for ever. The rain was falling steadily and since there had been no money for repairing the roof there were even more receptacles distributed around the house to catch the drips. Christy had come home exhausted after an entire day spent trying to rescue a cow that had fallen off the mountainside in a minor landslip. Kate was out of sorts because Selma Hobbs had summoned her to tea in such a way that Kate had imagined some sort of a *shauri* to have arisen in the Hobbs household. She had braved mud and flood to ride over there, only to find that there was no *shauri*. Selma, it seemed, had simply been too, too bored and would have died had she not had someone to listen to her lamentations.

Now they were both home and bathed and fed, and were relaxing before the fire, whisky in hand, reporting the day's events to each other, both doing more talking than listening.

"Sure, Kate, if we tried one way of raising the animal we must have tried twenty. I tried climbing down but there wasn't a foot- or a handhold to be found. I'd never have managed it without Nderitu. We lowered him on a rope in the finish, and he slung a harness round."

"Five miles in the pouring rain! Urgent, her note said, so naturally I ploughed on—I thought someone must be ill. Can you imagine it, Christy? Calling me out to take tea and listen to stories of how dull and boring Maurice can be, able to talk of nothing but sheep and cattle."

"She's in calf, but praise God seems to be—"

He stopped, for there was a small commotion in the rear of the house and through the back entrance came two sodden figures, barely recognisable as Patsy and David. Kate leapt up to greet them.

"What on earth! How did you get here?"

"A lift by car to Naivasha, another lift in an ox-waggon as far as the Hobbs' farm, and we walked from there. Don't come near us—we're soaked! Oh, that fire looks good."

"Come in you poor, poor creatures. Have you eaten? You must get out of those wet things."

Patsy was laughing, peeling off her raincoat, kicking off her shoes, instantly at home, but David looked ill at ease. Christy got to his feet.

"Come with me, David," he said. "I'll fix you up with something dry to wear."

Patsy watched them go, an unreadable expression in her eyes.

"Dear Christy," she said obscurely.

"That's always been my opinion. Go on, child —get out of that dress for heaven's sake."

Patsy did not move.

"As we came along, David told me a story," she said. "A long time ago when his father was a young man he was caught in the rain—really heavy rain, like this. A complete downpour. He stopped at an isolated border post for shelter, miles from anywhere. There was only one man there—a European of about his own age. He directed David's father into an empty hut for the night and when he was asked for a blanket—for it was a cold, wet night—he was gone for some time. I suppose he was debating with himself what to do. Finally, he came back. At last he had managed to find a blanket for this black man. It was the mule's blanket. It stank of mule and was covered in hairs."

Kate looked at her for a moment, then put an arm around her shoulders.

"The bigoted we have with us always," she said. "Try to remember the farmers' wives who tend the sick, make clothes, impart education."

"Like patriotism," Patsy said, "paternalism isn't enough. It's much easier for us to remember the others."

Us, Kate noted, as Patsy left the room. There was no doubt now where her loyalties lay.

Neither she nor Christy would listen to explanations until both Patsy and David were dry and fed, but at last when they were all once more sitting round the fire, Patsy spoke.

"You must be wondering why we've come like this without any warning. Really there are two reasons." She exchanged a smile with David across the width of the fireplace. "The first isn't a happy thing at all. The Skiptons have been told to leave the country. The mission has been closed down."

"Why?" Kate's voice reflected her astonishment. "Those good people!"

"They were trouble-makers in the eyes of the authorities. It's totally ridiculous, of course."

"There is a degree of truth in it." David's voice was quiet, precise, heavily accented. "They were used, I'm afraid. You know it, Patsy, as well as I."

"It doesn't surprise me," Christy said. "What happened?"

"They kept open house," Patsy began. "You know what it was like there—I've told you before. Anyone could drop in, black or white, and have their say about anything. We've had a wonderful old Frenchman from the Congo staying for the past week. You'd adore him, Kate—he's so wise and funny and gallant."

"Never mind the wonderful Frenchman," Christy said tersely. "What happened?"

"Many of our people's grievances were

discussed, of course," David said, taking up the story. "The house became a meeting place for what the Government regard as subversives. Samuel works for the Kikuyu Central Association and Shadrack writes for *Muiguithania*—"

"What in the name of all that's holy is that?"

"A vernacular newspaper, virtually the voice of the Central Association. Johnstone Kenyatta is the editor."

"Anti-Government?" Kate asked.

"Well, of course!" Patsy was amused. "What else?"

"*You* were involved?"

"I did my share of talking, I admit, but that's all. We all talk the hind legs off a donkey."

"Unfortunately, Shadrack's views are disseminated more widely in the paper," David said, "and the Government has been watching him for some time. Samuel, not to be outdone, wrote letters to the *Kenya Weekly News* on the subject of the *kipande*, and he gave his address as the mission. Foolishly, he used inflammatory language and the police came round to investigate."

"So Wilfred wrote to the paper himself," Patsy went on, taking up the story. "He was enraged by the manner of the policemen who came to see the place and he complained about them bitterly and said that in his opinion much of what Samuel said was valid. His letter was printed over yet another one from Samuel. It was too much. It gave the impression that the mission was a hot-bed of sedition."

"So the Skiptons were blamed?"

"It was easy for the editor of the *Weekly News* to find out that the Skiptons were free-lancing, as it were. If they'd been attached to some recognised missionary society I expect they would have fared better—after all, Archdeacon Burns and Dr. Arthur are very vocal about African interests. But as it was, they were told to go."

"There's no appeal?"

"None. They've already left, for South Africa. Someone with an interest in the shipping line offered them a free ticket, so Hannah was convinced that the Lord meant them to go—and perhaps He did. There must be work in plenty for them down there."

"What about the hostel, and the women's club?"

"I'm hoping that the Women's League will take over the club. The Church Missionary Society are going to run the hostel."

"Will there be a place for you?"

"That brings us to the other item of news," Patsy said, looking across at David again. "I think I'll have to tell you, as David seems to be overcome by shyness. We plan to get married. We've come to ask your blessing."

It was Christy who was first out of his chair, pulling Patsy to her feet and embracing her, extending a hand to David. But Kate was not far behind.

"Bless you both," she said. "Oh, bless you both."

Inwardly she was full of misgivings.

"Christy, is she doing the right thing?" she asked, when they were alone together. "Their upbringing has been so different."

"What else would you have her do? Live celibate for ever? There'll be no Colin Laceys for her, no matter how you might regret it."

"But does she love him?"

"He's a good man—a man of integrity. She seems happy."

Kate smiled at this.

"Yes, I thought so, too. Not feverishly happy, the way she was when she imagined herself in love with Colin, but somehow calm and at peace with herself. I suppose one shouldn't ask for anything more."

Christy grunted as if in agreement but said nothing more until they were almost asleep. Then he spoke out of the darkness.

"I just hope," he murmured sleepily, "that David doesn't imagine that he's getting a submissive, obedient, *jembe*-toting Kikuyu *bibi*. If he does, he's in for something of a surprise."

And so, after all, Kate ended the day with a laugh.

19

"THANK God she didn't marry a farmer," Christy said more than once during the ensuing years. "At least David gets some sort of a salary paid by the Missionary Society."

They had never imagined that times could be so hard. Prices dropped all over the world and it was a disaster not only for individual farmers but for the developing colony. Coffee was the mainstay of its economy, and it was on coffee that Hugh had built up his prosperity. Now its price dropped from a hundred and twenty pounds to seventy pounds a ton in the London salerooms. Since it cost Hugh seventy-three pounds a ton to transport his coffee from railhead to saleroom, it became uneconomical to export it at all and the story was current that in Brazil it was being used to fuel locomotives.

As the depression tightened its grip other commodities were slashed in price. Maize, dairy products, sisal—there was not a farmer who did not suffer, and suffer badly.

"At least it will sort out the men from the boys," Christy said grimly. "All those playboys who thought Kenya was going to give them a nice easy living—they'll be packing up and going home if this keeps up, mark my words. Thank

God I went in for cattle: at least the home market still wants dairy products, up to a point. I'm afraid, though, that there's no hope of the new tractor I wanted."

"I've money saved," Kate said. "Money I was keeping for Patsy's education."

"But we're keeping that for the holiday in England you're always talking about."

It was a fast-fading dream. It had been the one good thing about Patsy's decision not to go to England: that, after all, Kate did not have to leave Christy. One day, she had been saying ever since, they would go together. Have a real holiday —a sea voyage round the Cape, perhaps. Now this was an even more distant prospect.

"When would we be able to leave the farm? We couldn't pay a manager for months on end. Have your tractor, Christy. We can't manage without it."

So he bought it, but felt guilty having done so when prices continued to fall.

"We ought to diversify," he said worriedly. "How about turkeys for the Christmas market?"

"Bloody poultry," Kate muttered mutinously.

Christy's eyebrows shot up.

"Mrs. Brennan," he said with mock severity. "I have noted a marked deterioration in your language of late—"

"I wonder who I caught that from? Think of something else, I implore you."

Mwangidogo caught and killed a snake. Christy

came back to the house to find Kate lost in contemplation of it.

"Would it make a bag?" she asked. "We could send the boys out to scour the countryside—skin them and cure them—make shoes and things. They sell for a fortune in Europe."

"Bloody snakes," Christy said. "Sure the smell of them being cured is enough to turn the stomach of a savage."

At last she got down to writing her stories. They were simple tales of African animals with legends that she had learned over the years, and she wrote them in Swahili to be used in junior schools. The Education Department welcomed them with open arms and she felt like a millionairess when she received ten pounds for the outright sale of her first volume. Immediately she bent her energies to writing more, but for the second book she was offered less. Times were hard, said the Education Department.

These small, spasmodic earnings were a drop in the ocean when it came to running the farm.

"We're getting deeper and deeper in debt to the bank each month," Christy said, coming one evening to join her in the garden. "Are we mad, Kate? What's the point of it all?"

Kate had been cutting yellow chrysanthemums for the house and stood now with a bunch of them in her hands.

"We have each other," she said. "And we're surrounded by beauty. I was thinking just now, when I die I want you to lay my bones just there, under the olive tree."

"Sure, I'll be there before you. You're a spring chicken compared to me—why, what is it? You daft creature, I'm only joking—", for Kate had launched herself into his arms and was straining him to her, not smiling now, her face gaunt with fear.

"Christy, I've nothing but you—nothing! I can't bear the thought of it, being alone without you. Promise me, promise me—"

"What can I promise you?" The flowers fell to the ground forgotten as he cradled her head against his shoulder. "Only that I love you with all my heart and soul, and will do all the days of my life—and after, too, if that's permitted. We've years ahead of us, darlin'."

"Yes, of course." She eased herself out of his arms, picked up the flowers. "One can only live one day at a time, I know that. I'm not usually so foolish. It's simply that I felt as if a goose had walked over my grave just then."

She stood still and looked at the valley that was spread before them, the rolling green acres that dropped to the aridity of the Rift.

"It is beautiful, isn't it?" she said softly. "We'll hang on somehow, Christy. The bad times can't last for ever."

They could, however, get worse. The rains failed and so, therefore, did the cereal crops. The drought was the only reality in their lives. The water in the dam dwindled almost to nothing and the land grew parched and yellow and withered, crumbling to dust before their eyes.

Animals of all kinds, including elephant and rhino, came to drink from the dam for it was the only water in the area. Christy swore at them and fired his rifle into the air to frighten them away, for his cattle needed the precious water, but still, night and morning, they came.

Then the locusts arrived, first a few hoppers that could be ignored, then a cloud-like mass that turned the dry, brittle air into a whirling snow-storm of insects that settled on every scrap of vegetation and left devastation in their wake.

After weeks of anguished indecision, Christy went hunting for ivory, leaving Kate in charge of the farm. Both had known that some such solution was inevitable, but they had postponed the final parting. Maurice Hobbs had at last yielded to Selma's pleas and returned to England. Bob Brewster, ruined after fifteen years of working all the hours God gave, accepted a job in a garage in Nakuru. This meant that Kate had no neighbours nearer than eight miles away.

Alone again, she thought, as she stared across the dried-up acres. She laughed ruefully, for the crux of the matter was that she was far from alone. She was surrounded by the squatter village, by herdboys and their wives and families and aged parents, by the dairy-men and the *syce* and the stableboy. And there was Mwangidogo and the garden boy, Muriuki, and Iringo, the competent but somehow not wholly likable successor to Kamau.

All looked to World's End for their livelihood. All called her 'Mama' and brought to her ailments, and family *shauris*, and long, involved tales of *fitinas* which made the vendetta between the Montagues and Capulets seem as simple as a nursery tale.

Alone? Life would be a great deal simpler if she were, she sometimes thought. There were times when the weight of responsibility seemed a crushing burden.

At least before his departure Christy had insisted that a telephone be installed, which provided a frail and unreliable link with the outside world. And there were visitors who brought her news and gossip. Patsy came sometimes, with her growing family—first James, born barely a year after her marriage to David, then Margaret, closely followed by Christine.

Janet was a surprising but frequent visitor at this time. The only one of the trio of little girls who had grown up at Mawingo to remain so far unwed, she lived a social life of such pace and complexity that Meg and Hugh were inclined to despair. She seemed able to work behind the reception desk of the Norfolk Hotel all day and still find time for tennis and riding and dancing all night, with a perpetually-changing cast of partners.

But she loved her quiet periods at World's End, which she regarded as restoring some sort of balance to her life, and she confided things to Kate which she could never have brought herself to discuss with Meg.

"I think your mother may be right," Kate said drily, after one particular tale of moonlight swimming and near-seduction. "Perhaps it is time that you married."

"I'm waiting for Harry," said Janet. "Harry Winters. He's at medical school in Cape Town, but he'll be qualified next year and then he'll come home and I'll marry him."

Which she did, very prettily, thus providing yet another excuse for a Kenya party of the very finest kind.

It was at this gathering that Kate heard someone mention pyrethrum. So far it was a crop in which Japan and Yugoslavia shared the monopoly, but now the idea was being floated that it could be a good cash crop at high altitudes in Kenya.

Soon its white daisies were appearing all over the highlands and it was the saving of many a farm fortunate enough to be sited at the right altitude. It meant that Christy could come home again, to till his acres and build up his herd. It meant that financial solvency was at last a real possibility.

Every penny went back into the farm. A drier had to be made for the pyrethrum, the roof of the house was at last repaired, and the old box-body was pensioned off and a newer vehicle purchased. Not new, but newer. It was at this time, too, that Christy bought a few Merino sheep, the start of a flock which was to bring him considerable local recognition.

Politicians and nationalists argued in Nairobi about the land. Was it empty bush when the British arrived, as had always been claimed? Or was it land that the nomadic Kikuyu and Masai were merely allowing to lie fallow temporarily? Commissions were set up, reports made. Irate settlers wrote letters to the paper, while secret meetings were held in back rooms in Nairobi attended by men who fretted at being second-class citizens without a vote. Meanwhile, the dancing and the drinking and the polo and the golf went on in European clubs up and down the country.

The invasion of Ethiopia by Italy caused a mild disturbance—a small *frisson* of worry, for Italy's rapid victory meant that Kenya had a Fascist power on its border: all the more worrying to those who took seriously Germany's continued claim for the return to Tanganyika, a territory which had been in British hands since the end of the war. But the average settler was far more closely concerned by the price of pyrethrum or coffee or sisal, by the constant battle waged against the apathy and fecklessness of his labour force, or the latest outbreak of rinderpest, or the club gossip.

Kate, reading every word that the *Standard* had to say about the Italian campaign, shook her head at its wider implications: but even she was diverted by another item of news concerning the opening of a large school for African girls at Thika.

"The principal is to be a Miss Ellen Saunders," she read out to Christy. "I had a girl called Ellen Saunders at my school, but lost touch with her years ago when her parents left the country. Could it possibly be one and the same—yes, listen to this! It says that Miss Saunders began her distinguished academic career at the Hill Academy, Nairobi, before proceeding to Cheltenham Ladies' College. Isn't that wonderful? One of my girls. And now she's to head the first real girls' school in Kenya!"

"You must have instilled the right ideas." Christy grinned at her pleasure.

"Oh, I tried, but my influence must have been small. It was all such a long time ago and many others have taught her since."

"You know what the Jesuits say. Give them a child up to the age of seven—"

"Ellen was not much older than that when I knew her. Oh, I *am* pleased. I shall write to her."

And so, eventually, there was another visitor to the farm—one with whom Kate could discuss matters of mutual interest to her heart's content.

Through Ellen she heard news of other past pupils.

"I exchange Christmas cards with some who are still in the country," Kate told Ellen. "I love to hear news of them. It was such a happy time."

"Happy for us, too. I never did understand what went wrong."

Kate smiled and said nothing, for she saw no point in raising the spectre of Hope Honeywell. She had appeared on the stage and had gone again, Kate thought. There's nothing she can do to me any more.

There was an air of feverish gaiety about wartime Nairobi. Kate, who was there on one of her infrequent shopping trips, remembered the way it was in 1914 and found it hard to believe that this was the same town, for the streets were paved now and the stone buildings of Delamere Avenue, lately Sixth Avenue, seemed to sparkle in the sun.

There were said to be shortages. Sugar was difficult to track down and there was no soap in one of the shops in which she asked for it, but there were no obvious signs of privation. The smart dress shops around the New Stanley seemed to have plenty of stock, and Bazaar Street was more fascinating than ever, with its mixture of spices and dress materials and leather goods.

All sorts of uniforms could be seen, for the town was full of soldiers, either in transit between Britain and the Far East, or posted there to manage the halfway house that the colony had become.

Most looked as if they were in buoyant spirits —as well they might, Kate thought wryly, for the sun was shining, the jacarandas were out all along Delamere Avenue, the hospitality of Kenya settlers was a by-word, and all in all there must be a thousand less favourable postings for any serviceman.

Perhaps less happy were the Italian prisoners-of-war who had been taken to camps up country. It all added up to many more mouths for the country to feed, and farming was booming as even the most dedicated optimist would have considered impossible only a short time before.

When Kate joined Christy for lunch at the Nairobi Club she was pleased to see that somewhere along the way he had fallen in with Colin, and the two of them were together at the bar. They greeted each other affectionately and she made enquiries about Julie and the boys, but although there appeared to be no particularly startling news to report, there was something in his manner which made Kate study him carefully. He's up to something, she thought. She had known him too long not to recognise the fact. He surely couldn't be thinking of trying to join up? Not at his age—or in his occupation! She wouldn't put it past him, though. Something was in the wind, that was certain.

"How's your father?" Kate asked. Hugh had

lately suffered a mild heart attack which had worried everyone, but for some time now had been back at work.

"He seems well. He rides over every day to keep an eye on Reg Dexter's herd—the man next door, you know."

Next door. Five miles away.

"He's joined up?"

"Mm." Colin nodded and raised his eyebrows, a rueful smile twisting his mouth. "And he's older than I am, do you know that?"

"Oh come, Colin—you can't be thinking of volunteering? What on earth can be more valuable than the job you're doing?"

He shrugged.

"I know that's true, really, but even so—one hears of people going, right and left. Steve Rayland has left his estate in the hands of his M'Kamba overseer, and he's looking after things very well."

"So far," Christy said, sceptically.

"I saw Patsy and David the other day. It seems that David's brother has been left to manage the farm up at Molo. He always was a good stockman—"

"Not that nasty, smart-alecky one with the gammy leg?"

"No, that's Reuben. This is Tobias. He's a reliable sort of chap. Small. Very like David to look at."

"What's going to happen when it's all over?" Kate asked.

"You mean 'How you goin' to keep them, down on the *shamba*, now that they seen Paree?' It was a problem after the last war, wasn't it?"

"And this time many more have gone and of those who have stayed, many have been promoted far beyond what they could have expected. I hope we're all big enough to react sensibly. Now there's something you should be addressing yourself to, Colin—making post-war Kenya a better place. That would be far more worthwhile for a man of your age than dashing off to play soldiers."

"Ouch!" Colin pulled a face. "That hurt, Kate. I'm not exactly in my dotage."

"You're just the right age—young enough to be full of vigour, old enough to have a bit of experience of life. Young enough for idealism, old enough to temper it with common sense."

He was grinning at her over the top of his glass.

"Who's been talking?" he asked.

"What do you mean?"

"You can't sneeze in this town without someone knowing you've caught cold. I've spent most of this morning talking to a group of people who want me to stand as an elected member of Legislative Council at the next election. There's going to be one very soon, I'm told."

Kate banged her glass down on the bar with such vigour that the contents were almost lost.

"Colin, that's *marvellous*! Christy, isn't that the most wonderful thing? Isn't Colin just the sort of person we need?"

"What group of people?" Christy asked more cautiously.

Colin shrugged.

"People whose views I agree with, by and large. The *kipande* has to go—I'm convinced of that. There's too much ill-will about it. It's always there, like a grumbling appendix, ready to flare up and give trouble on the least provocation. Then there's the question of African representation. It's pitiful at the moment. The Reverend Beecher is a marvellous advocate for them, admittedly, but the time must come, and come soon, when Africans have a voice themselves. In our own interests, I feel sure that this is so."

"Now isn't the boy talking like a politician already, and he's not even sent in his nomination papers yet?" But Christy smiled as he spoke, thinking, like Kate, that the country would be well served by such as Colin Lacey.

Colin sighed.

"There's a snag, of course. If my platform is to be a better deal for the African, it's unlikely that I'll get any settlers to vote for me. They can't see the wood for the trees, most of them. They'll immediately assume that my main aim is to give the Kyukes large chunks of the White Highlands, which isn't at all the case. I know the money and

411

effort settlers have put into the land, none better, and I also know what would happen to it if Africans with no capital and archaic farming procedures got their hands on it. But I'm also aware that creating a discontented majority isn't in anyone's interest."

"You'll have to box clever," Kate said, looking wise and inscrutable.

Colin gave a small, deferential bow.

"Then pray tell me, oh fount of all wisdom, what I should do?"

"Rule One: mind your manners! Rule Two: concentrate on what the settlers *do* want to hear. You can do that without compromising your integrity. Just think what a pitiful amount of money is voted each year for agricultural experimentation, yet we live or die by our agriculture. From the beginning of the century it's been trial and error. Things are better now, of course, but not that much better. You could campaign for more funds to be devoted to that purpose after the war and there isn't a settler living who wouldn't be behind you."

"And if they ask me my views on African representation?"

"You must *never* lie!"

"No, ma'am." Colin tugged his forelock.

"On the other hand, you could talk very fast and very convincingly about the need to set up proper training schemes for men home from the Army. Soft-pedal on the vote, push the creation of a skilled labour force who can take pride in their achievements."

"Sure now, you'll learn to do that in the twinkling of an eye," Christy said. "Is there a politician living who doesn't tackle an awkward question by answering something completely different?"

"I'm afraid I'm not very devious," Colin said humbly.

"You may well have to learn." Kate spoke decisively, eyes narrowed a little, mind racing ahead. "The important thing is to get you *in* so that a start can be made towards a more equitable society. Oh, make no mistake: I'm not a starry-eyed idealist who thinks we can run before we can walk. I don't imagine that a tribesman straight from the bush can manage to run a complex country in the twentieth century, neither do I subscribe to the view of some woolly-minded people who think that every African is noble and hard-working. We all know that there are good and bad, lazy and industrious. They would hardly be human if this wasn't so. The main thing is to ensure that those who are educated can see some hope for the future. They *must* be given a chance to play a significant part in the destiny of their country. Frustration and insurrection will be the only result if we neglect to do so."

"Shall I fetch you a soap-box, at all?"

"Christy, you agree with me, surely?"

"Indeed I do." Serious now, he reached out to

grip Colin's shoulder. "I wish you luck, boy. You don't need advice from the likes of us, I'm sure, but any help that it's in our power to give, then it's yours."

"Thank you," Colin said, equally serious.

"And remember," said Kate, "this could be one of the few times when the end is so important that a certain amount of—well, *deviousness*—may be justifiable."

"Did you not realise what a little Machiavelli the woman is?" Christy asked Colin, putting an arm around each of them and turning them towards the dining room.

20

"THE talk of women is like the crackling of thorns beneath the cooking pot."

Chief Ngengi spoke disdainfully, and the complaining voice of his eighth wife fell silent, her mouth sulky. She shrugged and, picking up a naked child from the floor, took her leave.

The chief sat very still. He was a small man, with a long, bony face. There was a natural dignity about him that invested him with an authority none could dispute, in spite of his lack of physical stature. Even on the rare occasions he discarded his wide-brimmed chief's hat with its badge in the shape of a rampant lion or lay down his chief's staff with the brass knob, a stranger would instantly recognise him as a man of importance.

Patsy smiled at him, wondering a little at the depth of affection she felt for this wily, devious old man. When David had first brought her to the village she had been as nervous as any prospective daughter-in-law wishing to make a good impression, and the chilly politeness of his welcome had made her think that she would always be regarded as an interloper. Now, fourteen years later, she knew that she held a privileged position. He discussed matters with her that normally he would have considered outside a woman's province, and in conversation she answered him with a licence his wives would deem unthinkable.

She attributed this less to any virtue on her part than to the fact that he was flattered by her willingness, indeed her desire, to hear his reminiscences of the old days, for she found his memories enthralling. He was old enough to remember the days before the coming of the white man and could speak of battles with the Masai and cattle raids. He was steeped in legend and the traditions of the tribe. Patsy had learned much of her Kikuyu heritage from Kate and from questions she had asked from the Africans who worked at World's End, but not until she became part of Chief Ngengi's family did she fully realise the extent of the hold that superstition had on the hearts and minds of the Kikuyu.

She now knew that it was total. Ancestors were not dead and gone, but were part of everyday life. Their spirits had to be consulted before anyone undertook any enterprise, from going on a journey to taking a wife. Illness, the loss of a cow, the breaking of a pot, any misfortune, was the result of the spirits' displeasure and meant that in some way they had to be propitiated.

"I'm just as confused as ever I was," Patsy said when she and David were walking back to the mission station. "In a way there's a—a *validity*

416

about the old ways that seems lacking in the kind of Christianity that's imposed by people like us."

"You are not unique," David said. "We are the confused generation of Africa, you and I. I may be wholly Kikuyu, unlike you, but I, too, am confused, for was I not brought up as a naked little *toto* in a mud and wattle hut? And have I not seen other ways? I have travelled across the sea and lived in a fine, stone-built college and I have seen factories and shops and railway stations so big that they made me gasp with their magnificence. There is much about the old ways that was good, and this we should preserve: but we should be fooling ourselves if we did not realise that there is much that was bad."

"It's not always as easy as some might think to differentiate," Patsy said.

"Perhaps our children will not be confused. They will be wholly of the twentieth century, unlike their father who was brought up with one foot in the dark ages."

David was right, Patsy thought afterwards. James was fourteen now, a fine, tall boy who certainly showed no sign of being confused. He was about to transfer from the mission school to the Alliance High School and she was full of hope for his future. Christine and Margaret were eight and ten. They were pretty, lively girls who had inherited Patsy's lighter skin and were widely admired because of it, unlike James who would have passed for a full-blooded Kikuyu anywhere.

She appreciated that she had much to be thankful for. She enjoyed her life at Kimilil Mission, where she taught the smaller children. Her husband was a man of quiet integrity and had a sweetness of nature that she found entirely admirable. Dr. Webb was head of the small mission hospital which he ran with the help of a junior doctor and a nurse, while Mrs. Webb was responsible for the school, with David and Patsy as her assistants. They were a close community, not so many miles from Nairobi but with no near neighbours, and relations between them all were excellent. In spite of the fact that materially she and David had very little, Patsy could not imagine any circumstances in which she could be happier.

James was happy, too. He knew himself to be privileged. Many of his relations lived in mud huts, whereas although the house he lived in was small, it had stone walls and a tin roof, a tap in the kitchen and even a bathroom.

Moreover, his parents had been educated. That was something he would never underestimate. Whenever there was a gathering of his father's clan, he almost burst with pride when he saw how smart and well-dressed his parents were, in comparison with so many of his other relatives.

He looked forward to going to boarding school. The work would be harder, of course, but he had no fears about being able to cope with it. What excited him most was the prospect of playing in a proper football team, and of learning gymnastics. He knew that he had a powerful body that seemed to answer every demand made upon it, and he felt sure that in this field, if in no other, he would make his parents proud of him.

"You take after me," his Uncle Reuben used to say, pretending to feint and box with him. "You are a strong boy."

Uncle Reuben had not been to stay recently and James was sorry about that, for although he knew that his mother did not care much for his uncle, undoubtedly he brought his own kind of excitement to the little house. There was a vitality in his loud laughter, a feeling of exuberance which James admired. It was, he thought, an awful shame that Uncle Reuben had one leg shorter than the other. If it hadn't been for the accident that had happened when his uncle and his father were small, undoubtedly he would have played football like a champion. Even now, he managed better than most people and he seemed to be able to catch a ball successfully no matter in what direction it came at him.

He had stopped coming, his father said, because he now had a business in Nairobi. Perhaps he had. He had heard others talking and they, too, said that Reuben had managed to make money out of the war, but James was certain there was more to it than that. He had lain awake too many nights with his ear pressed against the thin partition dividing his room from the living

419

room, listening to arguments between his parents and Uncle Reuben, not to know that they had their differences. Once, when some other friends of his parents were present, he had heard real sounds of anger: raised voices, a table overturned, the soothing voice of his father calming everyone down afterwards. It was all to do with politics, James knew that, but he was not very much interested.

Patsy greeted the cessation of Reuben's visits with nothing but relief. She hated the arrogant way he took possession of her home and his sneering attitude towards David's scholastic attainments and his Christian beliefs; and she burned with indignation on David's behalf when Reuben taunted him with being responsible for the accident that had injured his leg so many years before.

"It's sheer nonsense that you should be made to feel guilty," she said to her husband. "Reuben is a headstrong man and I have no doubt he was a headstrong child. If he wanted to climb a tree, I don't suppose you could have stopped him."

"I am the older," David said. "I was in charge of him."

It was an attitude that Reuben exploited to the full.

It was a major operation for the entire family to go into Nairobi together, but one Saturday morning, shortly before James was to start at his new school, they managed it, getting up early to walk to the bus stop so that they were dropped off in Government Road shortly before ten o'clock. The girls, who had been full of excitement in the bus, fell silent and clutched at their mother's hands, unused to the people and the traffic they could now see all about them. James was awed, too, but strode along beside his father and tried not to show it. Nairobi was a very grand place, full of soldiers in uniform and ladies in pretty dresses and farmers, in from the Highlands. There were Indian women like flocks of brightly coloured birds in saris of every hue, and flower-sellers, and newspaper stands.

They shopped in Bazaar Street for the khaki shorts and the white shirts that James needed. He stood, stiff and self-conscious, while the Indian measured him, then grinned with pleasure when the right size was produced.

"We'll need a sweater, too," Patsy said.

He had never had so many new clothes at one time, and he felt proud of his father who was able to take out his wallet and pay for them, every bit as sure of himself as the European who was buying pyjamas further down the counter.

"Our turn now—Mama, you promised," clamoured the girls, as they left the shop.

"All right—quietly now." Patsy took a hand of each and calmed them. "I said we should buy material for your new frocks when we had

421

finished with James. There's no need to make a fuss about it."

"Why don't you take them on your own?" David asked her. "We men will go and buy a new pen so that James has no excuse for untidy work. Shall we meet on the steps of the market in half an hour's time? You'll need money. Here —give me a ten shilling note and take the whole wallet."

"You're very trusting," Patsy said, laughing at him.

"Half an hour—no more! In that time you will not be able to spend so much."

They parted, Patsy and the girls going in one direction, David and James in the other. James carried a bag with the name of the shop which had sold them the new clothes written on the side, and he was conscious of the glory of the contents, as proud as if everyone that passed could see inside the bag and would know that next term he was actually going to the Alliance High School.

They bought the pen and looked in shop windows until the time came for them to go to the market to meet the rest of the family. There was much to see as they stood on the steps and at first they hardly noticed how the time was passing. People of all races were going in and out. Hawkers wandered about outside with trays of tomatoes or oranges or eggs. There were beggars with crippled limbs, and one with a face half eaten away with leprosy.

An elderly European woman with a lined, bad-tempered face came towards them. She was holding a *kikapu* in one hand and as she approached them she shifted it awkwardly under her arm and opened her handbag as if to search for her money. Her head was down and, unable to see where she was going, she cannoned into David.

"*Angalia*," she snarled. "Watch out!"

David, who had not moved from the spot throughout the whole incident, murmured an apology, but James burnt with indignation.

"It was not your fault," he said hotly when the woman had gone.

"Such things are not important." David spoke calmly, determined to show no emotion at this gross injustice.

"But why should she shout '*Angalia*' at you like that? *She* should have apologised, not you."

"There are some Europeans who will never apologise or admit blame. It is as well to recognise that fact. Some are as stiff-necked as the giraffe."

He had hardly finished speaking when the woman was back pulling a European police officer behind her.

"That was the man," she said, pointing to David. "He pushed his way into me and the next moment I found that my purse was missing."

"Madam," David said politely. "You are mistaken. It was you who bumped into me."

"Insolence!" The woman's mouth was pulled down with outrage. "Madam, indeed! A common thief! You will address me as '*Memsahib*'."

"Turn your pockets out," the policeman said. He was a tall man with sandy hair and a face burnt bright pink by the sun.

James felt frightened and his heart began to pound under his rib-cage. He knew his father had done nothing wrong, that the policeman could not possibly find anything with which to accuse him, but still he was frightened. The policeman and the woman represented a force against which his father was as helpless as a child.

"He's probably passed it to the boy," the woman said. "Search that bag."

Dumbly James handed over the large paper bag and the policeman looked inside it.

"Nothing," he said to the woman. "Look— you could have been mistaken. You might have dropped it, perhaps. If this man took it as you claim, he's hardly likely to have gone on standing here on the same spot."

"I am innocent of this charge," David said. His voice was quiet and even, but James could detect fear in him, too. "I am not a thief. I am a teacher at Kimilil Mission School."

"Your *kipande*, please." The policeman held out his hand and instinctively David's hand went to his inner pocket before he remembered.

"My wife has my wallet," he said. "The *kipande* is inside it."

"There, you see!" The woman was shrilly triumphant. "You can't believe a word they say. A teacher, indeed! What will they think of next? Officer, I insist that you take this man to the station for questioning."

The policeman looked at the woman with a cold expression, then back again at David. He was an experienced man and no fool. It seemed obvious to him that the wretched woman had made a mistake—she'd probably come out without her purse in the first place and would find it safely on the mantelpiece when she returned home. Yet it could not be denied that the man had no *kipande*.

It was at this moment that Patsy and the girls arrived on the market steps, out of breath and full of apologies for their late arrival, until Patsy lapsed into a shocked silence, suddenly aware that all was not well.

"Mama, mama—" Grown-up as he was, James could have wept with relief. "Show the policeman Daddy's *kipande*."

"You are this man's wife?"

Patsy, her face very still and watchful, nodded. "I am."

"He says he is a teacher." The man's voice was polite but puzzled. It was obvious that Patsy was no ordinary African and he found it impossible to categorise her.

"That is perfectly correct." Patsy's educated voice, which bore no hint of an African accent, puzzled him still further. "We both teach at Kimilil Mission. What's this about?" Her eyes fell on the woman standing beside him and they sharpened with a look of recognition. "I believe we have met," she said, in a voice that was ice-cold. "It's Mrs. Honeywell, isn't it? You called once to see my guardian, Kate Brennan, many years ago."

"This man jostled me," said the woman, but weakly now, clearly anxious to have done with the whole affair. "I'm prepared to overlook it."

"It *is* Mrs. Honeywell, isn't it?"

But she had gone, muttering vaguely about the need to search elsewhere.

"An apology wouldn't have come amiss," Patsy said for the policeman's benefit.

He smiled uneasily and raised a hand to his cap in a half salute.

"It's as well to keep your *kipande* to hand, whoever you are," he said, as he went on his way.

David said nothing, but stood for a moment looking at the ground before drawing in his breath and looking into Patsy's eyes.

"In front of my son," he said. "In front of my whole family. Accused of being a thief. I was helpless."

"Let's go home," Patsy said gently. "Don't give that stupid woman a thought. She seems to have a talent for making trouble."

"Carry your *kipande*!" David spoke through clenched teeth, more upset than James had ever seen him. "No matter who you are, carry your *kipande*! What can a man do to win respect in this country? I work, I train, I qualify. I am a professional man, a Christian, the son of a chief. And still a woman such as that can accuse me of being a thief!"

The fun and excitement had gone out of the day. Bitterness and despair seemed to ride with them in the bus as they drove away from the town which at the beginning of the day had beckoned with such promise.

Patsy talked quietly to David to dispel the tension.

"I would have recognised her anywhere, though she hasn't worn very well. She's younger than Kate, I believe, but she doesn't look it, does she, for all that make-up? They worked together at one time, years and years ago when Kate had her school in Nairobi. I hated her when she came to World's End. She despised the house and Kate's clothes, and me—"

"I can't forget the disgrace." David's face was averted. He seemed to be whispering to the reflection of himself that he could see in the window of the bus. "The injustice! That a man cannot stand in his own country, harming no one, his son by his side."

"You're the one who always counsels patience and passivity," Patsy said, after a moment.

"You're the one who believes in turning the other cheek."

"There is no viable alternative," said David heavily. "But oh, the disgrace!"

James, straining to hear his words from the seat behind, knew that he had spoken nothing but the truth, and could have wept.

21

COLIN knew he had no reasons for complacency. The opposing candidate, Colonel Ewart Farquhar, was a man well-known in the colony who had suffered through the bad times and prospered in the good. He was, everyone agreed, able to talk the hind-leg off a donkey, and there was no doubt that his oft-repeated opinions reflected the views of many of the less liberal settlers.

He was, however, a man in his sixties, his skin yellowed by malarial attacks, his liver ruined by quinine and pink gin. He could talk all right, but it was a dry-as-dust discourse that had his listeners nodding in agreement only if they managed, against all the odds, to stay awake to hear the end of it.

Colin's appeal was that he looked forward rather than back. Only fools thought that life in the colony would stay the same after the war. Changes were bound to come. Colin's election speeches were positive and exciting, painting a picture of a developing country that would grow ever more prosperous only if all races played a part. His comparative youth and dynamism appealed to the younger men, as did the fact that he, too, was rooted in Kenya. They couldn't imagine him being a 'yes-man' to the Government, which had been the reputation of many of the previous elected members. And if some of the women voted for him because of his looks and his charm and that slow, boyish smile that made foolish matrons want to mother him, then it was very understandable. As Kate said, Colonel Farquhar had all the sex appeal of a stick insect.

Patsy whooped with delight when she read about his victory in the *Standard*, and not even Reuben's sneer could mar her pleasure.

"Oh David, isn't that wonderful?" she said. "It's a beginning. At least we'll have one sympathetic ear in LegCo."

"Only when he is hungry is the hyena prepared to fawn on the lion," Reuben said. "When his hunger is satisfied, he is no man's friend."

"Colin is no hyena," Patsy said evenly, determined not to rise to Reuben's bait. Her heart had dropped when she had heard his voice at the door that day. It had been some months since he had called on them and she had devoutly hoped that his black market activities in Nairobi would keep him out of their way for a good time to come. "Colin has the interests of this country at heart."

Reuben laughed.

"Which face of this country, the black or the white? He seeks only to feather his own nest."

Patsy looked at her brother-in-law who lay in

his chair on the base of his spine, his legs straddled before him, drinking from a bottle held in his hand. She clenched her jaw to control her anger and concentrated on folding the paper very neatly.

"The future will prove you wrong," she said at last.

"The future will prove who owns this land, the Africans or your white friends."

"Your mind is too simple, Reuben. You reduce everything to the matter of colour. Colin Lacey is an African first, a white second. He has done more to improve life for Africans in this colony than you ever will. All you think about is milking them dry for a little extra sugar or flour."

Reuben laughed, not attempting to refute the charge. The reason for his visit that day was to prove to his holy brother how well he was doing in Nairobi. He was dressed in very pale grey flannels, two-tone shoes, a navy-blue blazer and a white panama hat on the back of his head.

"How sad it is," he said to David, "that your *mzungu* wife dislikes me so. I may have only one good leg, but it is a leg that carries me very swiftly in the direction I want to go. She has two legs, but each moves to a different corner. The time will come when she has to choose."

"I have chosen!" There was no disguising Patsy's anger now. "I made my choice years ago, when I married David."

Reuben laughed again.

"You are still on the fence," he said. "And your husband is like a sheep who follows where you lead. You think this *mzungu* friend of yours will make any difference? You think all your talk and debate and letters to the paper and prayers will help one Kikuyu gain an acre of his rightful land back from the *mzungu* thieves?" He spat on the floor beside his chair. "You are wrong, sister. There are many, many men in Nairobi who know the truth. Only when our voices are strengthened by the gun and the knife and the *panga* will we regain our land and the white men will run before us like frightened gazelle."

"Lower your voice," David said, mindful of the girls in the next room. "It's you who are a sheep to follow the lead of men who say such things which go against all that our fathers have ever taught us. It is wrong to set man's hand against man."

"Such a good Christian!"

"I hope that I am. But Kikuyu law, too, forbids violence."

"Besides which," Patsy said, "you underestimate the Europeans. They have sweated blood over this land, some for two generations. They will not run. Do you think that a Government that has caused a mighty army to retreat in the Western desert will let a few Kikuyu thugs drive their nationals out of Kenya?"

"I am not talking of this year or next. I am not talking of a few Kikuyus." He levered himself to

432

his feet and for a moment he stood towering over David and Patsy. "It will be a rising of *all* Kikuyus—all the Njeroges and Kariokis who slave for the *wazungu*." He raised his voice, parodying a British *memsahib*. "Here, *boy*; go there, *boy*; carry this, *boy*! In almost every European home there is a Kikuyu, yes even in Government House we have many of our kin. And when the time comes—" He paused and grinned at Patsy, not speaking, but drawing the side of his hand across his throat in an unmistakable gesture. "And that will be the time that you'll have to decide where you stand, *sister*!"

He laughed again, twitched the newspaper out of her hand, and flung it on the floor. Then, with a contemptuous look at both of them, he limped out into the night.

"He hates me," Patsy said flatly, breaking the silence that lasted for a few moments after he left them. "God knows, there's never been any love lost between us, but I never dreamed that he could be so—so frightening."

"We must pray for him. He suffers much frustration, because of his leg. It is constantly on his mind."

"Stop blaming yourself!" Swiftly Patsy came to sit beside David. "Many people have far worse disabilities and yet manage to make something useful of their lives. He has two wives and six children in the village and obviously makes a comfortable living, whatever it is that he does, yet he's eaten up with bitterness and hatred. He's so—inimical. I feel he would hurt us, if he could. I wish you'd tell him to stay away."

"My own brother? I could never do that." He put his arm round Patsy's shoulders. "I can't believe he would ever hurt you, but he is an irritating man, that I grant you. I understand your point of view."

Patsy laughed, with affection.

"That should be written on your tombstone," she said. "You *always* understand everyone's point of view. You've even forgiven that horrible Honeywell woman."

"I should like to think that you are right. I have tried. Perhaps if James had not been there . . . but at least now I see the incident for what it was—the unpleasantness of one woman, not the entire European race. And the policeman was doing his job, no more."

"One woman, yes." Patsy sighed heavily. "But duplicated a sufficient number of times to add fuel to the hatred of Reuben and his friends. Well!" Briskly she reached for the empty bottle Reuben had left on the floor and picked up the scattered sheets of the newspaper as if disposing of the last remnants of his visit. "God knows, I want a new Kenya after the war, but I don't want it Reuben's way. We'll just have to carry on fighting in ours."

David laughed.

"Your expression was so like Kate's just then."

434

"It was?" Patsy smiled ruefully. "I must say I have noticed a tendency lately to think that I can set the world to rights, alone and unaided. You will tell me if it all gets too much, won't you?"

"None of us can do it unaided. We need God's help."

"Onward, Christian soldiers," said Patsy.

There was a stirring, military rhythm to the hymn and James was enjoying it, singing lustily along with the other Scouts in the Alliance High School troop.

Baden-Powell would have been proud of them. Faces, badges and boots alike shone with cleanliness. Shirts and shorts were pressed. They were a credit both to the Scout movement and their school, and James Ngengi was proud of being one of their number. At sixteen, he was a King's Scout, having gained more badges than any other member of the school in all its history.

He had marched at the head of the parade of Scouts from all over the colony, black and white, and had been entrusted with the Scout flag to carry in a leather holster, the gold-coloured Prince of Wales feathers gleaming against the green background. A shorter, blond boy had carried the Union Jack and they had walked proudly, side by side.

Representatives of all three services were present in the cathedral. Sun filtered through the stained-glass east window and there were flowers everywhere. They reminded James of his grandfather who had told him that in the beginning, when European ways were unknown in Africa, he had believed the custom of cutting flowers and taking them into the house had a religious significance. They had laughed together, for of course they were enlightened now and knew that it was only for the flowers' decorative value that Europeans followed this practice.

Every pew was filled. The Scouts had filed into their appointed pew towards the back, all except James and the boy with the Union Jack who had placed their flags near the choir stalls and taken their place close by at the side of the cathedral. It was a good position for they could see everything that was happening. There were the soldiers and the airmen, and even a few sailors, though Nairobi was so far from the sea.

There were only a few black people present. From his vantage point James could see a sea of white faces, the men dark-suited, the ladies dressed in every colour of the rainbow, their pretty dresses topped by some truly remarkable hats.

The front few pews were reserved for members of LegCo and senior members of the Government. James could see Mr. and Mrs. Colin Lacey. They grinned across at him and his mouth twitched in a half-smile which he hoped the Scoutmaster had not noticed, for they had been forbidden to talk or laugh under pain of death.

Everyone stood as the Governor came down the aisle. He was dressed in his white uniform with a high, gold-encrusted collar and epaulets and he carried his pink-plumed helmet. When he and his wife were installed in their front pew, the thanksgiving victory service began.

It was very grand and impressive. The organ music thundered through the cathedral and everyone sang lustily. There were several clergymen at the front, all dressed in rich colours beneath their snowy surplices. His Excellency read the lesson.

James heard not a word of it, for his eyes were feasting on the spectacle and the splendour of the scene before him. No wonder the Allies had won the war! The congregation knelt to pray, another hymn sung, another lesson read. And now this —this wonderful marching song that somehow seemed to bring everything together: robust faith and pageantry and a striving for the right. James sang with fervour, feeling one with the rest, his eyes shining. And then, suddenly, he faltered.

Why had he not noticed her before? It was because of the hat, of course, for the brim half-shaded her face. They sat in the same row as Mr. and Mrs. Lacey, but further along, she and her husband, a thin man with a balding head and very large, pink ears. There was no mistaking her, for now she was singing with as much fervour as he had himself, her head thrown back, her chin lifted, as if she could indeed see the cross that was going on before and was filled with inspiration by the sight.

She had not looked like that on the market steps. Her face had seemed small and spiteful, her mouth pinched with ill-humour, incapable of being inspired by anything. Seeing her again brought it all back—the awful shame, the feeling of helplessness, and the wholly hateful feeling he had not been able to shake off, that for some reason his father was to be despised for not proclaiming his innocence more vigorously.

A cloud must have covered the sun for the colours of the window did not glow any more. James stopped singing, stopped enjoying the pageant. At the end of the service he stepped up to the choir stalls, knelt to receive the flag, wheeled about smartly, flanked by his colour party, and marched with them up the aisle, but it was mechanical now, not a ritual that filled him with pride.

There was a bus waiting outside to take the boys back to school and James got in it without looking around for his friend, Josiah Mugo, as he would normally have done.

"You were in a hurry."

He heard Josiah's voice as he took the seat beside him, but he kept his eyes on the window and merely shrugged his shoulders in reply.

"What's the matter with you?" Josiah persisted. "Didn't you like it in there with all the *wazungu* in their fancy dress? It was a fine sight, meant to dazzle country boys like you and me."

Josiah had a sarcastic way of talking that amused James, even though he sometimes found himself shocked by it and knew very well that his parents would be even more shocked. Together they were the brightest stars of their year and it was for this reason that they had gravitated together rather than because of any similarity in their outlook. They were rivals, both academically and on the football field, and lately they had both been taking boxing lessons. James was delighted to find that whereas Josiah could easily outstrip him on the athletics field, when it came to boxing he was usually the victor.

"I—saw someone in there," he said, hesitantly.

"A girl?"

In this area Josiah was far more advanced than James. James's experience so far was nil, but according to Josiah he had enjoyed the favours of more than one Kikuyu maiden during the past few holidays from school.

"You talk like a fool," he said. "What girl could I see in there?"

"White girls." Josiah made smacking noises with his lips. "There was one in front of me who looked like Betty Grable, but I could not see her legs—"

"Shut up!" James hunched his shoulder away from his friend, in no mood for this kind of talk.

"Who did you see?"

"That woman." James turned and spat out the words as if they had suddenly become too bitter for his mouth to hold. "I told you about her. She abused my father at the market, and there she was, in that church, singing, as if her heart was as pure as—as the snow on Kerinyagga. She is a fraud, a liar. How can she be a Christian?"

Josiah was laughing at him.

"It's you who are the fool," he said, "to be duped by all this white man's religion."

"But my father believes it, and my mother, too."

Josiah shrugged. He would not be impolite enough to say that James's parents also were fools, but the implication was obvious.

"And the masters at school," James went on. "They are good men. Mr. Thorpe—"

He stopped and turned away helplessly at the thought of his hero, the cheerful extrovert who had encouraged him so much in the field of physical fitness. He knew that Josiah found his admiration—worship, even—a subject for mockery.

"Thorpe is the same as the others," Josiah said scornfully. "Paid to tell lies—paid to convince us that the old ways are wrong and only if we follow their instructions can we make a success of our lives. The missionaries tell us that a Christian must not kill or take a woman in adultery or covet his neighbour's house, but though the masters sit in church on Sunday and bow their heads, how

440

many truly believe? Even as we came out of church last week I heard the wife of Mr. Chambers saying that her house was too small and that next tour after their leave in Britain she was going to make him apply for one of the larger houses that have just been built. And as for Thorpe—the brother of a friend of mine who works as a barman at the Sports Club said that he danced close to a woman who was the wife of another man, not once but many times. So close, he said, that it was surprising he did not get her with child, there on the dance floor. And when it comes to killing, how many did they kill when they were fighting the war? Thorpe has a medal for killing so many Germans!"

"That was different. Anyone is allowed to kill an enemy. Thorpe is a good man."

"Tell that to the husband of the woman he was dancing with." Josiah leant closer, lowered his voice. "They tell us at school that only through education and diligence will we be worthy of equality, isn't that true? They tell us to have patience, to work hard and prove ourselves."

"That is what my parents tell me."

Josiah, once more on the brink of saying what he thought of James's parents, opened his mouth and closed it again.

"Europeans use Christianity to confuse us, that's all—to make us dumb and uncomplaining, like the beasts of the field." He sat back in his seat, his arms folded across the knotted scout tie and lanyard and polished badge, the shoulder knots a gleam of yellow on his dark shirt. "But it won't last. Many of us are growing as clever as they are. We go to church and smile and say 'Yes, sir' and 'No, sir' and ' Of course we are happy to wait another two thousand years so that we can be as civilised as you.' But we will be as false as they are."

"I do not believe that Mr. Thorpe is false." James clung to his image of the beloved games master, unable to form a logical counter to Josiah's argument.

"Is he patient, as we are told to be?" Josiah's voice was searing in its sarcasm and James was silenced, for it could not be denied that Mr. Thorpe hated to be kept waiting or to see time wasted and could give vent to biting phrases if the occasion demanded it. He remembered that Josiah himself had felt the lash of his tongue only days before when by his late arrival on the football field he had kept the whole team waiting for several minutes. But he had never spoken in this way to James, for James was keen and anxious to succeed and more likely to arrive early than late.

"He is good to me," he said stubbornly. "He has helped me with my boxing, even when classes were finished and he could have gone home."

"Because you will bring honour to the school," Josiah said.

Well, James thought, if not the teachers, then what about Granny Kate and Grandpa Christy?

442

They were good people. No one could possibly hate them, even if they were settlers. He said as much to Josiah and then wished he hadn't, because, as he might have guessed, there was an answer to that, too.

"Some are, of course, better than others," Josiah said loftily. "All races are the same, with good and bad, that goes without saying. But your so-called Granny and Grandpa stole our land, whatever you say, and they make sure that a school is on the farm so that they can teach children lies right from the beginning. You are too simple, James, just like your father."

James said no more, even though he could not agree that Granny Kate could have done anything bad and had seen for himself how she sat up late to write interesting stories for the children to read, and how she drew pictures and made apparatus to help them learn. Besides, the bus had arrived back at the school and there would be a good hot lunch ready for the boys, and afterwards a game of football where he was to play on the wing, his favourite position.

They stood in silence behind their chairs at the long tables as the headmaster—grey-haired, gowned, venerable—said Grace.

"Bless, oh Lord, this food to our use and ourselves to Thy service."

James, looking up, caught the eye of Josiah who stood opposite and saw that he gave a conspiratorial and knowing wink before sitting down to begin his meal.

It was taken for granted that James would be circumcised the summer of his sixteenth birthday. He himself was anxious to undergo the ritual that marked his initiation into manhood, and even though the origins of the ceremony were pagan, David was in favour of it because it meant so much in the life of a Kikuyu. It was a time when boys of the same age lived and prepared and suffered the knife together, so that thereafter they were as brothers, bound always to help each other.

Christians were not barred from it though there were certain parts of the preparation for initiation that they were not called upon to undergo. Patsy knew that the ordeal dominated James's thoughts and both excited and terrified him, the terror being not so much because of the knife but because he thought that he might not be able to bear it unflinchingly. To cry out or to show any sign of feeling the pain would bring utter disgrace.

"I know you'll be all right," Patsy told him. But she herself was sickened by the whole prospect and, on the day before the initiation ceremony, she took the girls up to World's End for a week, for this was men's work and there was nothing that she could do for her son but hand him over to the tribe.

444

It took three weeks for James to recover fully from the circumcisor's knife. He had not flinched, he told Patsy proudly, and now that it was all over he knew himself to be a man and he asserted himself with more assurance, spending more time with others of his age-grade in the village and growing a little angry when his parents made enquiries about his holiday homework. Patsy watched him anxiously, growing troubled by the part of his nature that seemed attracted to the world of *thahu* and the witch-doctor.

"It's only curiosity on his part," David reassured her. "It's only natural, after all. It's part of his heritage."

But her uneasiness remained.

"You know it will take hard work for you to get to Makerere College," she said to him towards the end of the holiday. "You're not going to let things slip at this stage, are you?"

"Of course not!" He looked amazed that such a thing could have crossed her mind. "Two years at Makerere, and then Cambridge. Mr. Roberts says he's sure I can manage it." Mr. Roberts was the science master at school, and another of James's heroes.

"That's wonderful. Just stick at it, James, and I know you'll do great things."

And she laughed at herself, realising how like Kate she must be sounding these days. The only difference was that James listened seriously and agreed with her. Thank God he was so uncomplicated, so eager to do well. It was the competitive instinct of the sportsman that helped, of course. He couldn't bear to be beaten.

He went back to school gladly, in spite of his increased freedom at home and a sweet adventure with a plump, laughing little girl of fourteen or fifteen in his grandfather's village. She had allowed him into her hut at night and he had lain with her, not reaching the final, forbidden treasure, for the consequences would have been serious for both of them had she become pregnant, but coming so close that his senses had swum with delight as if he had drunk too deeply of the home-brewed beer. He hoped that no other young man would stake a claim to her while he was away.

Meanwhile, important examinations were looming. He was entering for a schoolboys' boxing tournament. Mr. Thorpe had practically promised that he would captain the First XI. Life was full of excitement, with Uganda's Makerere College just over the horizon.

James Ngengi was a happy young man.

22

THE men came back in swarms from the armed services, full of travellers' tales, each one a hero—or so he became when telling the story of his army career to the tribe back on the *shamba*.

Not many had seen any military action, but even years spent guarding stores or sweeping hospital wards took on a certain glamour when such duties had been carried out in such far-flung places as the Middle East or the Indian subcontinent.

Reuben, sitting in a dingy tea shop, lounging on a chair with only its two back legs on the floor, blew smoke from his cigarette in a contemptuous way towards the man who sat nursing a glass of tea at the table opposite him. He had listened with a sceptical smile to stories of courage under fire as Raphaelo drove his supplies lorry up to the troops in the front line. It might be true, or it could all be lies. All Reuben knew was that the man before him was penniless, whereas he wore a fine blue blazer and a panama hat, which was a great deal better than Raphaelo's army greatcoat.

"So now that you, the warrior, have killed the enemy, what now?" Reuben asked. "Do you go back to the farm to herd the *bwana's* cows?"

His companion shook his head.

"Does a dog eat *posho* when it has once tasted meat? Can a buffalo be held in a cage when once it has lived in the forest? I am no longer a hyena who eats the carcase left by the lion."

"Brave words, Raphaelo, but words come cheap, my brother." For this was one of Reuben's age-grade who had suffered the circumcisor's knife at the same ceremony. "There are many like you and all want work in the town."

"I have entered a training school set up for returned soldiers. In the Army I learned to maintain the lorry I was given to drive. Now I am to learn more. I shall become a garage mechanic."

If he expected to impress Reuben, he was disappointed. The other man merely reached for the crumpled packet of cigarettes in the pocket of his blazer and shouted for the woman to bring more tea.

"Ee," he said when she brought it. "How that woman stinks! So, you are to be a mechanic! Is that the work of a warrior? Is that work for a man who has been to the uttermost end of the earth and fought in the greatest army in the world?"

"It is skilled work." Raphaelo looked sulky, deflated by Reuben's reception of his news. "One day I might have a garage of my own."

"To buy this garage, will you use empty maize husks which your wife throws on the fire?" Reuben brought down the front legs of his chair with a thump and leaned on the table, bringing his face close to Raphaelo's.

"Those schools are set up to make fools of you and those like you," he said. "There has been much talk of them in LegCo. The Europeans saw that there would be soldiers returning and that they would not be content to return to their *shambas*, so they are turning you all into frightened chickens who come for food when the *bwana* calls and scatter when the food is finished, for when the training is done there will be no work for you. And those who do find a job will be paid less than half the wage they deserve."

"There will be work," Raphaelo argued earnestly. "We have been told. There will be much building—schools and houses and offices, and there will be many lorries to be mended as well as more people coming here with cars."

"Lies," Reuben said flatly. "Lies to keep the brave, returning soldiers from making trouble. You have been fooled, my friend. Does the dog that allows the tick to feed upon his blood wait until the tick is bigger than he is before shaking him off? All these stories are so much magic to blind you and keep you from seeing the truth."

"But at the training schools they will feed us," Raphaelo said. "Many of my friends have joined and will become carpenters and electricians and builders. A man must eat—"

Reuben exhaled smoke.

"I eat well," he said. "I have a bottle of white

man's brandy in my room, and my clothes are fine. Have you seen my shoes?" He thrust out a foot towards his friend who nodded slowly and admiringly at the brown and white shoes and the red patterned socks. "I can have a woman at any time of the day that I wish it. And all of this comes to me because I have used my head, not because I have pecked at the scattered grain the white man chooses to throw me,"

"But how—?"

"There are many ways to make money. I own a shop and a beer hall of my own now. During the war, I—sold things."

"What things?"

"Things that people wanted and could not get."

"And how did you get them?"

"I did not wait for others to give them to me, you may be sure of that."

"And what do you sell now?"

Reuben laughed.

"Everything. Shoes, cloth, food, beads. Anything you want to buy. Those things anyone can come and see in my shop, but for other things it is necessary to ask."

"What other things?"

"You want a fur cape for your wife? I have one which was worn by the wife of the Attorney-General at Government House only last week. You want a radio? Blankets for your bed? A gold cigarette-lighter? I have men who work for me.

You are my age-grade brother and you can drive a lorry. If you want work, I can give it to you."

"You steal these things?"

Reuben did not answer immediately but lifted one arm high above his head and snapped his fingers. Immediately, a younger man who had been sitting at another table apparently engrossed in conversation came over and sat beside Raphaelo.

"This is Kimani," Reuben said. "Kimani, have you a man to take Karioki's place?"

The man shook his head.

"The accident was a bad one. The lorry will never be used again and Karioki will be in hospital for many weeks."

"This man can drive." Reuben jerked his chin towards Raphaelo. "It will be easy to steal a car." Raphaelo stirred uneasily and Reuben placed a hand on his arm, his contemptuous tone moderated now so that he sounded soft and persuasive.

"We need you, Raphaelo, and you need work. It will mean a great deal of money for all of us. There is a house where the people are away on holiday at the coast and it is filled with good things that an Indian I know has promised to buy from me if only I can get hold of them. There is not even a dog left at the house to raise the alarm."

"There could be a servant—"

"We know that there is a servant. They have

451

left the *shamba* boy in charge, but he is the uncle of Kimani, and he has arranged everything. He will show us where to break in, and then we will tie him up and he will shout for help after we have gone."

Raphaelo's eyes flickered to right and left.

"Take a cigarette," Reuben said, offering him the packet. "Remember the first time you were with a woman, how your heart beat and you were excited and afraid at the same time? That is how you will feel tonight. But you will find the experience enjoyable and the next time the fear will have gone and the pound notes in your pocket will be fruitful and produce children so that you will grow rich, as I have done. You will be able to buy your own lorry—your own garage. Why wait for Europeans to pay you in *simonis* when you can feel the paper with the King's head on it, as sweet to your fingers as a woman's skin?"

Raphaelo licked his lips.

"Where would I get the car?"

"The Europeans leave them everywhere. Tonight is Saturday—they will be dancing at the Flamingo and the Travellers' Club and Torrs Hotel and the New Stanley. Cars will litter the streets like blossom after a rainstorm. We have many keys—"

"I don't need keys." Raphaelo's professional skill made his voice full of confidence, and Reuben smiled lazily at him through a haze of smoke. "But I did not say I would do it," he added hastily.

"Come." Reuben stood up. "Come to my place and you will see what money can buy for you."

Standing, he was a tall and commanding figure, and his limp, hardly perceptible, gave him a kind of swagger as, throwing money on the table, he left the tea shop. Raphaelo, Kimani and the two men who had been sitting with Kimani followed him. Raphaelo quickened his pace to keep up with Reuben but the others walked several feet behind like attendants to royalty, knowing their place.

It was high afternoon in the street outside, hot and shadeless, with the sickly smell of rotting fruit and meat and spices and latrines hanging like a pall over the jostling crowd. Vendors pushing carts, dented buses with humanity, women in from their *shambas*, bent low with burdens on their backs, knots of aimless, workless young men and the whores who tried to tempt them—the street reeked with them all, bright colours swimming in haze. Yet for all the colour there was a deadness about it—an almost tangible feeling of despair as if these people hoped to get through the day, with luck, but could not see beyond it. It was a different world from the Nairobi of the wide, tree-lined avenues and glass-fronted shops which existed no more than five minutes' walk away.

Reuben sauntered through the crowd with his

entourage, panama hat tipped to the back of his head, and Raphaelo could not help being impressed. He was a fine figure of a man—tall and broad and powerful. There was a smiling self-confidence about him that no one else in the street seemed to possess.

Most of the shops they passed were owned by Indians. Many sold brightly coloured rolls of cloth, and some had a man outside pedalling diligently at a sewing machine. Some sold sticky, fly-blown sweetmeats, or gaudy china and tin *sufurias* and buckets. On a corner an old crone roasted mealie-cobs and in a small area of flattened dirt between hovels men sat on forms and drank tea from thick glasses dispensed by a slattern in a torn and filthy dress.

Reuben limped along the pavement avoiding the squashed fruit, the drunks' vomit, the unevenness of his gait giving him a kind of rakish distinction. He was above it all, a man of importance. They turned into a back street where the hovels were not packed so tightly but were smaller and for the most part made from beaten petrol tins. Even now they had not reached Reuben's shop, for he led them through a maze of alleyways, stinking of urine and of the filth that was piled along the side of them.

At last he stopped before a stone building. It was low and flat-roofed, totally without architectural merit, but in the context of all the lesser shacks it looked to Raphaelo as grand as a palace.

To one side of the building there was a window, large and square and shaded by a wooden shutter hinged above it, propped open now to allow a group of several women to peer inside and see the wares. Brightly coloured advertisements surrounded the window—Simba Chai, Tusker Beer, Crown Bird Cigarettes.

Reuben gestured towards it with his cigarette in a lordly, proprietorial way.

"This is a good little business," he said. "But wait until you see inside."

He led Raphaelo through a central door and down a passage which led to another door covered by a greasy velvet curtain that had no doubt once graced some *memsahib's* sitting room. Now it hung a little drunkenly, many of its rings missing, but with a grand gesture Reuben swept it aside and ushered Raphaelo through to the room which lay beyond it.

His friend gave a long, low whistle of amazement.

"Ee," he said. "Now I can see that you have made much money, Reuben."

The room was about twenty feet long and fifteen wide. Its walls had been painted a dark, blood red. There were forms round each side of the room, and at the far end a shallow stage. The body of the room was filled with chairs and tables, many with slats missing, most leaning at odd

455

angles. The cement of the floor was cracked and the two light bulbs hung unshaded from the ceiling.

"All mine," Reuben said. "All from those *shillingis* you are so fearful of earning."

"What's that for?" Raphaelo asked, indicating the stage.

"Every week there is a dance. There will be one tomorrow, and that is where the band sits. Sometimes I put on a boxing match."

"And this is all yours?"

"All of it—and the rest you have not seen." He pointed to a door beside the stage. "That leads to the back where there are four rooms for the whores."

"This is a brothel, too?"

Reuben winked.

"There was a demand for it."

"The pounds in your pocket must have many babies," Raphaelo said reverently. "Where do you sell the beer?"

"From this place." Reuben turned to show him a space in the wall at the back of the hall which was covered now by a wooden batten. "This goes through to the shop which you saw at the front. At night we close the front shutter and open this one, and it becomes a bar."

"Ee!" Beyond this Raphaelo was speechless.

Reuben slapped him on the back.

"So you'll help us?"

Raphaelo nodded.

"I will try, this one time."

"Of course." Reuben grinned at him. "This one time."

The house was in Karen and the robbery could not have been more simple and, just as Reuben said, the Indian bought all the goods stolen within hours so that Raphaelo was able to count his money with a feeling of disbelief that it had been so easily earned.

Taking the car had been the worst part. Raphaelo had been about to open the door of an old Chevrolet when he saw two policemen approaching and had been forced to melt into the shadows, his heart hammering, until they had turned a corner into the next street. There Kimani had caused a diversion by approaching them and politely asking directions to the nearest Catholic church, saying that he was a stranger from Kampala and wished to go to confession: and by the time they had finished telling him, Raphaelo at the wheel of the Chevrolet was well on the way to the point where they were to meet before driving out to Karen.

The rest was easy. The house was at the end of a long drive, well hidden from the road. Kimani's uncle was waiting to take them to a window he had left open on some previous occasion and it was the work of a moment for Kimani to climb inside, to come downstairs, and to open the front door. The old man was very helpful, making several journeys from the house to the boot of the car with silver and other goods they might have missed without him, and Raphaelo was astonished to see how much the boot of the Chevrolet could hold. A van might have been better, of course. Raphaelo found himself thinking that next time he would try to get a van. Next time? Had he really decided to throw in his lot with Reuben?

There was another bad moment while he sat at the wheel waiting for Kimani to finish tying his uncle up, but the matter was soon done with and the journey back to the shop passed without incident. Together they unloaded the car as quickly as possible. They had driven round to the back where no one was about to see them. The area was never wholly silent. Gramophones blared, drunks quarrelled, goats bleated, cats squawled, but that night it was as quiet as it ever was.

Once the car was unloaded Raphaelo drove it to the European Hospital and abandoned it in the car park with some reluctance, for it had been the fastest vehicle he had ever driven. His share in the proceeds went some way towards compensating him for the loss of it. They came to more than he had ever made before in a week and it was easy to see that before long he could save enough to buy a car of his own.

"I understand now how your *shillingis* grow like maize shoots in the rain," he said to Reuben.

"Brother, you are thinking now like a man!" Reuben clapped him jovially on the back. "Tomorrow night a band is coming and there will be dancing. I might need a strong man like you to help me here, for sometimes men's wits become addled by the beer and they fight each other."

"When will you want me to drive a car again?"

Reuben roared with laughter and hugged his friend to his side with one great arm.

"You have scented blood and are eager for the kill. Have patience, little brother. The police are stupid, but not so stupid that we can strike every night. Besides, in a few days I go home to my village. I am marrying another wife—plump as a partridge, and young."

Raphaelo drew in his breath, round-eyed.

"Ee," he said. "You are a wealthy man, Reuben." And he thought without enthusiasm of the wife he had married long ago before he went away to the war, who had grown scrawny with the years. He might, he thought, find himself another wife even before buying the car.

Patsy, returning from the direction of the mission school at lunchtime, heard Reuben's voice before she entered the house and she checked on the doorstep, her lips tightening with annoyance. It was some time since he had called to see them and she was beginning to hope that with a new wife and his business interests in Nairobi he had no time left for them. But, dismayed though she

459

was, she schooled herself to speak welcomingly to him.

James had returned from school for the short Easter break only the previous day. The mission school did not close its doors until the following day, and Christine and Margaret were staying to eat a quick lunch at school before taking part in the final rehearsal of their Easter play. David was on duty, and Patsy therefore was without his support. She was glad that James was in the house. She had no wish to entertain Reuben on her own, but in spite of this she felt a moment of disquiet when she heard a burst of laughter from James. She did not like to think of him getting on too well with his uncle, whom she felt certain could only be a bad influence.

He was lounging back in the chair as if he had never been away, the hat on his head, a sly grin on his face.

"The bad penny," he said. "Isn't that what you would call me? You see, I always come back."

"How are you Reuben? And your new wife?"

"*Mzuri sana*. Already she is with child. There are some things a man can do even with one leg shorter than the other."

Patsy ignored this thrust and turned to lay a cloth on the table.

"You will eat with us, of course," she said. "I'm afraid David is on duty."

"I heated the meat and rice when I came back

460

from football," James said. "There is more than enough for three."

"How did you get on with the football?" Patsy asked. She turned to Reuben in explanation. "James is helping out with some of the boys while he is on holiday."

"He is very big and tall, my nephew." Reuben thumped his chest. "I, too, am strong. The two of us, we are like the cedars of the forest. If I had two good legs, I would have been the best football player in Kenya."

"I don't doubt it," Patsy said drily. "But think, Reuben—if you'd had two good legs, you would no doubt have gone into the Army and would not then have made so much money out of the misfortunes of other people. So perhaps David did not do you such a bad turn after all."

Her tone was pleasant, even admiring. Reuben shot her a suspicious glance, but decided that she had said nothing at which he could take offence.

"The football was all right," James said. "Some of the boys are quite good."

"But not so good as my fine nephew, eh? Ee —so big and strong you are!"

"It's boxing that I really enjoy. I won the schoolboys' tournament."

Patsy shuddered.

"I wish you'd stick to football. Boxing seems such an uncivilised sport to me."

"When are you going to knock out Joe Louis,

my nephew?" Reuben asked, as, grinning broadly, he took his place at the table.

James laughed, sitting down opposite his uncle. Reuben leaned over and squeezed his upper arm.

"Such muscle," he said. "I am not making a joke, James. There is much money to be made from boxing."

"Money isn't everything," Patsy said tightly, serving out the rice. "James is going to be a scientist. This September he is going to Makerere College for two years, and then we hope that he will go to university in England."

Echoes of Kate again. She understood better now how disappointed she must have felt when her hopes came to nothing.

"A scientist!" Reuben sucked his cheeks in and turned his eyes to heaven, signifying awe and astonishment.

"Well, I'd like to do research into animal husbandry, I think. I am not too sure yet."

"And all the white men will come to ask your advice. Ee! That is something I should like to see —but it is something I cannot believe will ever happen."

"Then you are wrong," Patsy said tartly. "This country is going to need young men like James."

Reuben laughed at her, saying nothing.

"Science is what I do best," James said. "Even better than boxing. But there is so much to learn, sometimes it frightens me."

Patsy smiled at him.

"If you keep on working as well as you have done this year, then you'll have nothing to fear. Tell me, Reuben, how is your father?"

She managed to keep the conversation on strictly noncontroversial lines for the rest of the meal and at the end of it she looked at the cheap alarm clock over the mantelpiece and got to her feet.

"I must get back," she said. Adding hopefully, "Perhaps you'll be gone by the time I return, Reuben. I'd better say goodbye to you now."

"I shall be in Nairobi by the time school is finished," he said. But he made no move to go. He looked at her with eyes that seemed to her to glow with malevolence and again she felt an instinctive stirring of disquiet.

"What are you doing this afternoon, James?"

"I have work to do—notes to make for a history essay—"

Patsy nodded approvingly.

"A good idea, to get the work done early in the holiday."

There was silence for a moment after she had gone as James set about clearing the table.

"I thought," Reuben said at last, "that you became a man two years ago. Was it not your circumcision I attended, or was it that of another young man?"

"It was mine." James looked at his uncle curiously, on the defensive.

"Then how is it that you still behave like a

463

child, listening always to the words of your mother as if you were taking milk from her breast? Do you not get tired of school and books? Do you come into Nairobi so that you can enjoy the pleasures a man enjoys?"

"We go to the cinema sometimes."

"Ee—the cinema." He pronounced the word with the emphasis on the second syllable. "But those women you cannot touch."

James looked uncomfortable.

"I—have been with girls," he said. "There are girls in the village."

"Why do you not come to see me in Nairobi?"

"I am very busy at school. There is not much free time."

"But now there is no school."

"The buses are not frequent."

"You have no bicycle?"

James laughed.

"My father cannot afford one for himself, never mind one for me."

"Ee." Reuben took out a cigarette and lit it, tilting his chair back as he blew the smoke towards the ceiling. "That is a shame. I could give you work that would give you enough money to buy a bicycle in just one night. And for one more night's work, you could buy one for your father, too."

"What work?" Unloading crates, lifting boxes, James supposed. He knew his uncle had a shop and bar. Yet such work hardly seemed to merit payment on such a scale.

"Work that you would enjoy. Work that would seem like play to you. At my bar I stage boxing matches and men pay much money to come and see them."

"Boxing!" Interested now, James sat down at the table again. "Who would I have to fight?"

"No one too good. I don't want my fine scientist nephew killed, do I?"

"But it would be a fair fight? I mean, you wouldn't rig it in my favour? Because that I would never agree to."

"Of course it would be fair. Last week we had Adam Ogot and Kimani Mwendwa."

"They aren't bad."

"Ogot earned ten pounds because he was the winner. Kimani had five pounds."

"You mean, even if I lose—" James's face was alight with interest, but then he shook his head. "No, it's no use. My parents would never agree to it. You heard what my mother thinks of boxing."

"But are you not eighteen years old and a full-grown man? Imagine what you could do with ten pounds—even five." Reuben flicked a derisive look at James's trousers which hung an inch or two short above his ankle. "You could buy new clothes. A blue blazer like mine. Ee—I saw the English cricketers on the cinema arriving in Australia and I tell you, not one of them had a coat finer than mine."

"I need football boots."

"The money would be yours, to spend as you want." But inwardly Reuben was cynically amused. Football boots! The boy was a true son of his father. What woman's head would be turned by football boots? "A friend is coming by here soon to give me a lift in his lorry to Nairobi. You could come with me."

"I don't know—"

With a flick of his hand, Reuben dismissed the subject.

"Never mind. There are other fighters who are not afraid of their mothers."

"I'm not afraid." But still James sat tracing a pattern on the wooden top of the table, unable to decide.

"Are you a child to keep your head in your books even when the school gives you a holiday? Why do you not write a letter to your mother, telling her that you are going to Nairobi with me? You would be back in only a few days with money in your pocket, enough to buy presents for everyone. Is it, perhaps, that you are afraid of the man you will be fighting?"

"I am not afraid," James said again. "But that is something I should like to know."

"Kimani Mwendwa said he will fight any time I want him."

"And he was beaten by Adam Ogot?"

"Last week."

"And I have beaten Adam Ogot. He came to

the school sports day for an exhibition bout and issued a challenge. It was only a game, but I beat him fair and square."

Reuben slapped a hand flat on the table.

"Then you will be ten pounds richer by tomorrow night. What are a mother's fearful words set against that? It is time for the young lion to think for himself."

Still James hesitated and Reuben watched him narrowly. Last week the winner won a purse of fifteen pounds. Kimani would have to be told to keep his mouth shut. But even if he were to be forced to pay the going rate for the job, it would be worth it, Reuben thought, just to pierce Patsy's armour. She had always set his teeth on edge—that cocksure, supercilious almost-white woman his brother had married, who was always so ready with argument.

"You and me," he said to James, pointing first at James's chest and then at his own. "We are of the same kind. Your father's head carries as many ideas as a dog has fleas, but he has little knowledge of the world outside this mission. He cannot see that his young calf has become a bull and can no longer be kept in a small pen. This place is not big enough for men such as you and me. And I tell you—" he leaned sideways, lowering his voice—"I tell you, James, I know a little girl—a little, soft Somali—who will teach you all you want to know about the pleasure of having a woman. She will make the eyes roll back in your head, the strength drain from your limbs."

James's heart began to pound heavily and his stomach felt as if a giant hand was squeezing it. For all his talk of football boots he was by no means averse to the admiring glances that came his way from the opposite sex. But the girl he had lain with in the village had married and he had seen no others that pleased him quite so much. To have the means of acquiring a woman *and* a bicycle was too much even for his filial duty.

"I'll come," he said, the decision made.

A slow smile spread over Reuben's face as he punched James in the chest.

"A young lion," he said.

The room was full of smoke and the stench of sweat, musky and airless. The haze hung in a layer above the level of the men's heads, obscuring the full glare of the unshaded lights. From the improvised ring set up on the stage James was aware of faces, faces, faces, pressing in on three sides, some almost at floor level, others higher, some at the back standing on tables and chairs, the light falling on black skin and wide-open mouths which shouted encouragement or hurled abuse or cheered with delight as one of the fighters landed a particularly telling punch.

Here and there he caught the bright flash of a girl's dress, heard a high-pitched laugh, but he could see from the corner of his eye that the audience was predominantly male. Most were drinking freely. The fight was like nothing he had known before, both more frightening and more exciting. On other occasions at school his friends had cheered him on: but he had never experienced this frenzy, the terrifying pressure that seemed to come over in waves from the men who had placed bets on him, the sheer hate that emanated from the section who had backed his opponent. And the noise! The heat was intense, the sweat pouring down his naked torso above the black shorts he was wearing, but it was the noise that he found overwhelming. His ear drums felt as if they would burst. Reuben was shouting, standing outside the ring, dancing with excitement, waving a towel, but James could distinguish nothing of what was said. His eye had taken a bad knock. Kimani Mwendwa was far from the walkover Reuben had led him to believe and James had been a little disturbed by the fact that there seemed to be a very close relationship between Reuben and his opponent. He had seen them talking together before the contest and there had been something odd about the way they had so patently changed the subject on his approach.

He knew that he was not doing his best. Stagefright was keeping him from moving his feet in the way he knew that he could, sheer nerves prevented him from anticipating Kimani's most predictable lunge.

A bell rang. The fifth round was over.

Back in the corner Reuben wiped his face, handed him a bottle of water, a bucket to spit in. He yelled advice. Watch his left, keep your guard up, move your feet! Bouncing up and down, feinting with his fists, James nodded, and as the bell rang again he danced into the next round with his determination renewed.

Kimani seemed to be lowering his guard, almost taunting him, and James seized the opportunity. The punch connected, the crowd roared. This was better. Suddenly the adrenalin was flowing and James's nervousness fled. He no longer cared whether Reuben had told Kimani to go easy on him. He no longer cared about the noise and the heat. He could almost hear Mr. Thorpe's voice in his ear, giving instructions, foreseeing his opponent's moves. He punched again, a hard right, and Kimani rocked back on his heels. The end of the round found Reuben crowing with delight.

"You're on top of him now! Keep going, little lion—you have him as dazed as if he has been at a beer drink. Watch his left, now. He can be dangerous."

Too keyed up for speech James listened and nodded, eager to be in the ring again, oblivious to everything except the need to finish the fight. Even the knowledge of his parents' disapproval which had lain like a leaden weight in his stomach all day had become of no importance. Only the cheering of the crowd had any meaning for him and the man who had temporarily become his enemy, the man he had to beat.

Two rounds later it was finished. Kimani lay senseless, out for the count of ten, and if he opened an eye before the counting was done, it was the eye away from the audience and only Reuben was there to see. The referee held James's hand aloft, and the relief and delight that filled every nerve transcended anything he had ever experienced before. Matches at school had never been like this. Here there was hysteria—cheers, shouts, boos, a burst of drunken song, a scuffle on the periphery of the crowd as one of the bookmakers attempted to abscond without paying his clients.

James felt like a god—ten feet tall and capable of anything. There was blood running from the cut over his eye but he felt nothing. Reuben dabbed at it with the filthy towel, grinning hugely, hugging his nephew in a bear-like embrace and clapping him on the back. Raphaelo, who had been acting as Kimani's second, came and shook him by the hand.

"A young lion," Reuben shouted. "I said it, right from the start. A young lion!"

"Beautiful, strong man," said a girl, insinuating herself between Reuben and James, rubbing herself against him. Reuben took her by the shoulders and thrust her away.

"Leave him," he said. "I have another for him. But first he must drink."

He yelled for beer, handed James a shirt to put on, and cleared a space for him to sit at one of the tables close to the ring.

The adrenalin still pumped through James's veins. Reuben was right. He *was* a young lion, ready now for the hunt, ready to prowl through the bush on his own without his parents giving their approval for every move he might make: ready for beer, for women, for anything and everything life had to offer. Reuben had the right of it. What was there at the mission that came near to this excitement? Of course Reuben was right! He enjoyed life, swaggered through it, towered above it. That was the way to live—like a giant, not like a dog who could be kicked by any *memsahib* who walked up the market steps.

"Drink!" yelled Reuben, raising a brown bottle aloft, and James drank the unaccustomed beer and felt even more a lion.

The make-shift ring was dismantled and the press of people eased a little for now there was more room in the red-walled cavern where the smoke grew thicker and the smell of close-packed bodies more pungent.

Men he had never seen before came up to the table and praised the way he had fought. They clapped him on the shoulder and bought him drinks. Any small, lingering suspicion that

472

Kimani had conspired with Reuben to throw the fight melted away.

"My nephew," Reuben shouted proudly. "My brother's son. A young lion, I tell you. He grows more and more like his uncle."

And James drank the beer and felt that life was beginning for him that night. He looked around for the girl Reuben had mentioned. He felt only excited anticipation now, his fear completely gone, for this was a night on which he knew that everything would go right for him.

"Where is she?" he shouted to his uncle. He looked around again, surprised at the sudden hush that seemed to have fallen on the room. "The girl," he said again, because suddenly he seemed to find difficulty in shaping his words correctly and he thought that Reuben might not be able to understand him. "Where is the girl?"

Reuben stood up and James, too, got to his feet, swaying a little, holding on to the table to steady himself.

"The girl," he said again.

"Hold your noise." Reuben spoke tersely in a voice quite unlike his usual self-confident bellow and James blinked, uncomprehending. The room was almost silent now—almost, but not quite, for there was a collective whisper of apprehension, a fearful mutter which came from nowhere and everywhere.

Blindly, clinging to the table, James peered through the smoke haze. Men were sitting as if frozen, but there was a movement beside the door, the blur of a white face surmounted by a peaked cap, khaki uniforms.

"Police," someone said softly, and the sibilant whisper was taken up all around him.

James could now see that there was a black constable stationed by the door and that coming towards Reuben was a white police officer and another African constable.

"Are you Reuben Ngengi?" asked the police officer.

"Yes, sir." Reuben had never sounded more respectful.

"I have a warrant for your arrest. I must caution you—"

He got no further for in that second the lights went out. There was scuffling in the direction of the door and shouts of command from the officer, who from somewhere produced a powerful torch and swivelled it in a rapid circle round the room.

"Everyone stand still," he shouted. "Constable, find the light switch."

He moved the torch again and in its beam James saw that the African policeman who stood close to Reuben held a truncheon in his hand and was raising it as if it were his intention to bring it down on Reuben's head. James lunged forward and grabbed hold of the upraised arm, twisting it behind Reuben's attacker. The policeman, taken by surprise, grunted with pain.

The room was still in darkness, this action

having only taken a moment, but the police officer must have seen it all by the light of the torch for he pinioned James in one arm and hit him a glancing blow. The torch was heavy, encased in rubber, and for a moment James reeled under it. Uproar seemed to be going on all round him. There was a fight over by the door, a rush of air as someone opened it, a surge of bodies in that direction. And still no light.

James felt the grip of the police officer slacken slightly as the man turned to yell orders at the constable who was supposed to be finding the light switch, and in that second James shrugged himself away. There was a faint light coming through the open door now and by it he could see that the constable whose arm he had seized was lunging towards him. He shoved him with such violence that he staggered into the crowd, but now he turned and saw that the officer was coming for him again. His reaction was instinctive. He hit the policeman a powerful right to the jaw, knocking him to the floor at the precise moment that the lights came on.

Suddenly the pandemonium reached fever pitch: men pushing their way to the door over other men, others fighting with panic-stricken expressions—out, out, out—they had to get out.

The officer lay on the floor where he had fallen, his head against the edge of the shallow stage. The two African policemen were swinging their truncheons trying to get to James and Reuben, but there were too many bodies in the way.

James felt himself pushed from behind. Reuben was shouting again, pulling him towards the back door, and there was a frightening urgency about his voice although James was unable to distinguish a single word. Then, suddenly, he could feel the cool night air and he breathed deeply, taking in large gulps of it, realising with an overwhelming sense of relief that they had left that hell's kitchen behind them, that the nightmare was over, that surely it had never happened. Nothing felt real.

Reuben was still pulling him, forcing him to run, and behind him Raphaelo and Kimani were urging him along. There were whistles blowing, even a shot fired from the direction of the bar behind them. They ducked into an alley, running fast now, and sufficient of his wits returned to James to make him understand that the nightmare was not over and that he had to follow Reuben wherever he might lead them, for only he knew this area minutely and could find a place of safety for them.

A dog barked at them; a beggar asleep under a wall, wrapped in sacking, stirred and coughed and slept again. Reuben lurched along at a tremendous pace. He was right, James found himself thinking, with two good legs he would have made an athlete.

They were in a maze of alleys and hovels and

James had no idea how far they had gone from the bar. He knew only that they seemed to have worked round in a circle for the shouting and the disturbance that had been behind them now seemed to be coming from some hidden point in front of them.

"Here," Reuben said, coming to a halt in front of a shack that was somewhat larger than most of the others. "We shall be all right here."

It was a *hoteli*—a combined hotel and brothel in which the area abounded, closed and dark, but swiftly opened at Reuben's urgent plea. They went down a narrow passage to a back room.

"You cannot stay here," the owner said. "The police will search."

"If they come, we will hide."

"There is nowhere to hide. Four rooms, no more, and all occupied."

Reuben was silent, thinking.

"Lend us your van," he said. "I'll pay you well, don't worry. I'll pay you now, in advance."

Reaction had set in and James was shivering, close to tears. He heard nothing of the bartering that was going on. He stood by helplessly, longing for home, for his own bed, for the sound of his parents' quiet voices.

At last, it seemed that some arrangement had been reached. James was pushed into the back of the van, unaware that Kimani had melted away into the shadows. A mattress was put on top of him, blankets, cartons, sacks. He heard Reuben

477

and Raphaelo talking in urgent, broken gasps, half-sentences that made no sense to him. Then Reuben crawled in the back beside him and the van began to move.

Thought was suspended. James felt as if he were lost in a nightmare, understanding nothing except that his ordered world had suddenly gone crazy. The longing for home swept over him again and tears came to his eyes, even though he was a young lion, even though he had fought like a giant. How could everything have gone so wrong?

The van slowed down. He heard Raphaelo talking but could not distinguish words. There was a laugh. Someone banged twice on the side of the van and Raphaelo drove on.

"Keep still." Muffled by the layers of miscellaneous junk that covered him, he heard Reuben's voice and obeyed it. It was a relief to have everything taken out of his hands for by himself he would have been incapable of making a decision, and he knew it. He hoped that Raphaelo was taking him home. His mother would know what to do.

He would have to give himself up, he supposed, unpalatable though the thought was. What would they say at school? Would it spoil his chances of getting to Makerere? He hadn't meant to hurt anyone. It was all a mistake. If the policeman hadn't hit him with the torch, if there hadn't been so much confusion, if the lights hadn't gone out, if he hadn't had so much to drink—his head ached with the effort to straighten it all out in his mind. Yes, he would have to give himself up, apologise to the police officer, explain how it all happened. He came from a good, respectable family. Surely this would be taken into consideration.

It felt as if Raphaelo was driving towards Kikuyu. They were going up, anyway, for it was colder than it had been in Nairobi, the air much sharper. He managed to get his head free from the blankets which covered it and he breathed deeply of the night air, feeling clearer-headed every moment. He'd made a fool of himself, there was no doubt about that. His mother and father would be angry, and they had every right to be.

The van was bumping over ruts and pot-holes, the engine labouring. It seemed a long drive, but perhaps the discomfort merely made it seem so. He was lying in a jack-knife position with something unyielding pressing hard against his shoulder.

"Reuben," he said at last. "Are we nearly there?"

"Shut up. Keep hidden." Reuben's answer was curt.

James sighed and covered his head again. They must be taking the long way round to Kikuyu, via Karen and Rhino Park, to throw the police off the scent. Wherever it was, it was a terrible road. Raphaelo was gunning the engine and the springs were hitting bottom. Once he seemed to lose control altogether and the van slipped sideways.

It seemed a lifetime before they finally came to a halt. James felt a rush of cold air as the rear doors opened. He heard Raphaelo's voice talking to someone else in rapid Kikuyu, felt the things that were covering him lifted from him, and he sat up slowly, easing cramped limbs. Reuben was doing the same but was out of the van before him, shaking the hand of the slight figure who stood at the rear.

"Come out," he said to James. "This man will take care of us. His name is Irumu."

Looking about him with amazement, James climbed out of the van, realising as he did so that they were nowhere near Kikuyu. The countryside was quite different. They were in the middle of a forest, surrounded by tall cedars hung with ghostly grey lichens that only grew at high altitudes. No wonder it felt so cold!

The man called Irumu held a small torch at the back of the van, and there was light from dipped headlamps, but beyond this small, illumined circle the darkness was absolute. Moisture dripped from the trees. Somewhere, unseen, a hyrax screamed.

"Where are we?" James asked. "I thought we were going home."

"Home?" There was scorn in Reuben's voice. "Ee—you are either brave or mad. How can we go home?"

"I was thinking as we came along. I shall give myself up to the police. If I apologise to that officer—"

"Say you are sorry, please forgive me, like a good mission boy?" He could see Reuben's mirthless grin half-lit by the torch. "How will that save you from the hangman's rope, my nephew?"

James stared at him.

"I don't know what you mean."

"That man back there. The European. The one you hit so hard—"

"I hit him no harder than I hit Kimani in the fight."

"Perhaps white men have thinner skulls, like eggshells. He fell with his head on the edge of the platform."

"I punched him, just as I punched Kimani."

"The policeman who stopped the truck and spoke to Raphaelo said that the white man was dead."

"Dead?" James's face felt stiff with horror. "No! You must be mistaken. It can't be true." He looked round wildly, from Reuben to Raphaelo to Irumu, begging them to agree with him. "The man said that to frighten you. I do not hit anyone hard enough to kill! Kimani will tell you. Where is Kimani? He was with us—"

"Why should he come here? He did nothing wrong. It was you, James Ngengi, who hit the police officer."

"But not hard—not hard—"

"I think his neck was broken," Raphaelo said. "I have seen a man fall like that before now, when I was in the Army."

"So you see, young lion," Reuben said, "we have to stay here. Unless you want to hang at the end of a white man's rope. Let us go to your hut, Irumu—we need shelter and rest. Raphaelo, you'd better get back for the time being. Perhaps later you will wish to join us. You will find yourself among friends if you do."

"Take some of those blankets," Irumu said as Reuben went to close the van's rear doors. "The nights are cold on the mountain and there are many who would be glad of them."

James stood by and watched them, trembling with cold and shock and fear. None of it was real. Yet there was Reuben in his blue blazer, looking just as usual. He had even brought his panama hat with him and wore it jauntily on the side of his head.

"How long—" he began, but his voice was cracked, his throat dry. He swallowed and coughed and tried again.

"How long will we have to stay here?"

"Here? No more than a night."

"Good." James sighed with relief. He was still frightened: still could not see what would be the outcome of this. But he longed for home, feeling a childlike trust in his parents' ability to help him out of trouble.

"Tomorrow we move on," Reuben said. "Further up the mountain. Irumu will take us to join his friends."

"But when can we go home?"

Reuben threw back his head and laughed.

"On the day that the signal is given, little lion. On the day that the Kikuyu rise up and throw out the white man with *panga* and gun and spear and knife. That's when you'll go home."

Then James knew that he had indeed entered into a nightmare more terrible than he had ever imagined. A nightmare without end.

23

DECEMBER in Nairobi, with the sun beating down on shopfronts decorated with blobs of cotton wool and cut-out cardboard reindeers: with sparks glinting from the quartz contained in the stones of the new office blocks and the windscreens of the cars neatly angle-parked along Delamere Avenue.

It was hot—so hot! The statue of Lord Delamere on his traffic roundabout seemed to gaze more longingly than ever towards the bar of Torrs Hotel. Flowering shrubs shouted aloud in reds and pinks and oranges, and bare-legged, bare-headed housewives checked their shopping lists and pushed damp hair back from their sweating brows.

No one in 1949 bothers about the harmful rays of the sun, Meg thought, as she sat in the car in the shade of a jacaranda tree waiting for Hugh. Who would have thought, when they started excavating Sixth Avenue, that it would ever look like this? No more rickshaws, no more Ali Khan with his riding breeches and whip meeting the trains and hiring out his buggies, no more men in pith helmets and spine pads and double *terais*.

The place was just as colourful, though, in a different way. Up-country farmers still roistered into town and white hunters hadn't changed much except that instead of riding horses they drove workman-like jeeps hung about with canvas water bottles and other esoteric equipment. Sometimes one came across stars of the silver screen resting on the verandah of the Norfolk after the rigours of life on location, and always there were the beautiful and the wealthy, going ever further afield to find a place in the sun.

No one now thought that the colony was unhealthy for children. She smiled as she watched a family walking down the street towards her: three fair-haired boys, all sun-tanned with strong, straight limbs and plenty of vitality, plaguing their mother for ice-creams, dancing round her. They were not unlike Colin's boys, she thought, then laughed at herself for a foolish old woman, for Keith was eighteen and had already started at Agricultural College and Richard and Paul were at the Prince of Wales School, and it was many a long year since they had plagued Julie for ice-creams. It was more likely now to be motorbikes or records or tennis racquets.

It was hard to believe that both Julie and Janet were forty. Forty! She remembered reaching that milestone herself as if it had been yesterday, and now here she was, thirty-odd years on and surely the most fortunate of women. She still had Hugh, and her two children were happily married and living within easy reach of them. The five grandchildren were healthy and intelligent and good-looking. The farm prospered—that was another thing to be thankful for after so many ups and downs—and if there were constant dramas regarding the grandchildren, well, what would life be without them?

What could be keeping Hugh? She looked at her watch and frowned. It was not like him to be unpunctual. Perhaps it would have been better to meet him at the New Stanley Grill as he had suggested, for she could at least have sat inside in the cool of the cocktail bar as she waited. He had offered her lunch there as a treat, because it was rather a special, exciting sort of place where one might run into all sorts of famous people, but she had said that really, she would rather go to the Club. Another sign of growing old! The Club was homely and familiar, the scene over the past years of many quiet lunches as well as wild parties, and one was nearly always sure of meeting old friends there. Besides, she would be able to change her library books.

So she had arranged to meet Hugh at the car at noon. And here it was, twenty minutes past the hour and still no sign of him. They'd had separate errands to carry out. Christmas shopping for Meg: a visit to the bank, the barber and a hardware shop for Hugh.

She looked at the people approaching on the pavement, frowning now, a little anxious, searching for a sight of his lean, tall figure with the nut-brown bald head, the remaining hair that fringed it snowy white. He had been wearing khaki cotton trousers and a sleeveless khaki jacket over a checked, short-sleeved shirt. Several times she thought she saw him, but sighed with disappointment. Half the men in Nairobi seemed to be similarly clad.

Then, incomprehensibly, she saw Colin. What was he doing in town? They had left him at the farm, busy with accounts. He seemed to be searching for someone—her, perhaps? She opened the door to get out of the car, calling to him in an old lady's voice that could not be heard above the sound of the traffic. But at last her waving hand attracted his attention and with a look of relief he started towards her.

Relief—yes, he was thankful to have found her, that was obvious, but at the same time he looked distraught, ashen with grief.

"Mother," he said, and then again, "Mother." He put both his arms round her and held her to him and she knew without it being put into words that something had happened to Hugh.

Holding on to Colin's shoulders she pushed herself away from him and looked into his ravaged face.

"Tell me," she said. "Is it your father?"

Colin nodded, tried to speak and failed. He cleared his throat.

"In the bank," he said at last. "A heart attack. It was over in a matter of minutes."

"I see." Meg felt numb, strangely calm. "When?"

"Oh—an hour or so ago. No one knew where to find you. They phoned me. He couldn't have suffered very much."

"Thank God. You'd better take me to him, Colin."

"Get in. I'll drive you."

Meg opened the door and sat down inside again, smoothing her skirt, winding the window up a little, for even on a hot day she disliked to feel the wind whistling past her ears.

"I—I can't seem to take it in," she said faintly.

She looked over her shoulder to the parcels on the back seat of the car. There was a book for Hugh—a new one, by a favourite author—and a dressing gown. She had hesitated so long between the navy-blue with white polka dots and the maroon with blue polka dots that the young woman in the Nairobi Emporium had become a little frosty, making no secret of the fact that she considered Meg a tiresome old woman.

"They said I could change it if he didn't like the colour," she said.

And for some inexplicable reason it was this that made her cry.

At least she has a grave, Patsy thought.

For her there was nothing. No news, no certainty: just an aching, unbearable loss. Yet as she stood by the graveside in the City Park

Cemetery, seeing Meg's grief—controlled now, but none the less apparent—seeing Colin's pain and the tears on the faces of Janet and Julie: seeing Kate's sorrow and the way she and Christy had somehow drawn even closer together as if Hugh's death were a reminder that one day they, too, must be separated, she knew that it was better to have hope, even if that hope were only the most tenuous thread.

There were times when she felt certain that James was alive somewhere, and if that feeling was right, then surely he could not divorce himself from them for ever. He knew that they loved him. Nothing could alter that—not the most heinous crime in the world, and nothing and nobody could ever convince her that James had intended to kill the policeman.

If it hadn't been for Reuben! Instinct had always warned her that his influence would be disastrous in one way or another. She forced a shutter down in her mind. This was not the time or the place for hatred.

A large crowd had assembled to mourn Hugh Lacey. He had many friends of all races. His old headman stood only a pace behind the family, his face seamed by age and sorrow, and there were many other black people present. Workers from the estate, men he had dealt with on the Coffee Board, even a few politicians he had met through Colin. Troublemakers, some of the settlers called them, but he had enjoyed meeting them and talking with them. Patsy could see the Indian from the saw-mill, a well-respected Asian lawyer, two others who looked like clerks. And there was Hugh's dentist, Ravi Dev.

By far the greatest majority were those of his own kind, however, some who had come to the colony at the same time, their fortunes fluctuating with the fortunes of the country. They had worked hard, had ploughed back everything they had made into their farms, had weathered good times and bad, and asked nothing more than the fate that had befallen Hugh: that they should be allowed to work until the moment of their death, and that thereafter their bones should rest in the soil of Africa.

The coffin was lowered into the open grave and people stepped forward to scatter earth upon it.

Barbarism, Patsy screamed silently within herself, the reality of Hugh's death hitting her for the first time. She had loved him, that nut-brown man with the dry sense of humour and the piercing blue eyes, who had always been as kind to her as if he were indeed her Uncle Hugh, as she had always called him. No, no—anything was better than the awful finality of soil falling dully on polished wood. Only when she stood over James's grave would she give up hope that one day he would return to them to fulfil the promise of his boyhood. Until then she would cling to her faith, however frail a thing it was.

It was never warm in the forest. They lived high up in the mountain where the trees pressed so close that only by following game trails could they move from one place to another. They were always on the move, sleeping for a few nights in quickly constructed shelters, then pressing on.

James was numb with misery. For a few days he walked like a man in a daze, stumbling in front of Reuben through the maze of bush and creeper, the paths sometimes no bigger than the trail a dik-dik would make. He was astonished at the number of men and women they met with each night. It was a whole new, secret world, up there in the forest.

The ways of the other men were wholly alien to him. They were, he quickly found, the dregs of society—all outcasts for one reason or another. It had been a shock when Reuben confessed to him that he himself was wanted for armed robbery, and he shrank in horror when his uncle, hugging him to him in the familiar, one-armed embrace, introduced him to a matted-haired ruffian as a 'fellow murderer'. That night as he lay down to sleep beside Reuben, he ventured to speak of it.

"It was not murder," he said in an urgent whisper. "It was manslaughter. In English law there is a difference. They would not hang me."

"They would not hang you for killing a European policeman? Such clever lawyers my young lion must have for his friends!"

"But we can't go on living like this!"

Already James was miserably aware that he was almost unrecognisable as the bright-faced schoolboy with such high ambitions. His clothes were filthy and he stank. He had found lice in his blanket and knew that it was only a matter of time before they were transferred to his person. Soon his hair would be long and matted and full of the vermin, just like all the other men who drank beer and snored around the fire and spent their lust on the women who brought food for them, passing them from hand to hand.

"Be patient," Reuben counselled him. "We will not have to live this way for ever. Soon we will reach a camp and you will meet a man who will explain everything."

"I would rather take my chance and go home," James said.

Reuben reached out a mighty fist and gathered up a handful of James's shirt, hauling him close so that their faces were only inches apart.

"Don't try it," he said. "You may be the son of my brother but I would kill you myself if you attempt to leave the forest. These are desperate men. We are all desperate men. We stay together as one group and one day you will rejoice that we have done so."

Oh yes, James thought bitterly, staring sleepless into the night. The day when all Europeans will flee in fear. As if anyone could take that idea seriously!

As the days passed he learned a little more about the group. Not only were they criminals, fugitives from the law, but they were virulently anti-white. Well, he might have known as much, he told himself, after all that Reuben had said, but somehow in spite of everything he had not quite appreciated the bitterness of their hatred. He heard again the theory that Josiah had put to him: that the white man's religion spread lies for the sole purpose of corrupting the Kikuyu people and that mission and farm schools were there only to indoctrinate children, to turn them away from their tribal practices, to weaken their national identity.

"That's why the Kikuyu Central Assembly have started independent schools. Now we teach our own children."

Prudently James kept silent, but he had heard of the independent schools and doubted very much that their teaching was better than the education given to him at a mission school.

"What about hospitals?" he argued.

"It is a well-known fact that injections are given to make women barren and men impotent."

"But many Europeans treat Africans on the farms. You must know that is true—"

"It is those women who are the most dangerous, for they present a smiling friendly face to us and many Africans are duped into thinking that they wish us well. It is the *memsahibs* who shout and strike us and write bad things on our *kipandes* who are good for our cause, because we can look at them and see them for what they are. It is the smiling ones who must first be destroyed."

"Destroyed?"

"Chopped down like vermin. We must kill and kill and kill again, not only the Europeans but the Africans, too, who persist in their loyalty to the British. There are many chiefs on our list— hyenas, all of them: scavengers who feed on the scraps left to them by the *wazungu*. We will cleanse the country of all of them and then the Europeans will take fright and the land will be ours again."

"I am to have Chebili farm," said a filthy, thin-faced man wearing nothing but a blanket. "I have already paid two thousand shillings. Once I was a herdboy there."

"And I am to have Worldiend." The voice came from a man who was hidden in the shadows at the other side of the fire. James's eyes tried to pierce the darkness to find him. "I, too, have paid. Worldiend is a good farm with many, many good sheep and cattle."

James felt Reuben's hand gripping his arm, signalling silence, and he said nothing.

"You were wise," Reuben whispered when they lay down to sleep. "Keep silent about your European connections. The old man and woman at World's End are not your business—they must take care of themselves. I go now to take the woman because Muthengi has finished with her. Do you want to take a turn after me?"

Dumbly James shook his head. He lay on his back and looked up at the thick curtain of branches that formed the roof of the improvised hut in which he slept. Moonlight filtered through them, pure and white. He thought of praying as he had been taught as a child, but he could not. Evil was all around him, a tangible, frightening force, and it seemed more logical to believe in the spirits of which his grandfather had spoken rather than the God in a white nightgown who seemed so distant and irrelevant at this moment. Was his grandfather one of the chiefs on the list? It seemed likely. His relations with the Government had always been good.

The old people would say that by killing the policeman he had brought a *thahu* upon himself. Nothing but bad things had happened since that moment, so perhaps they were right after all. Perhaps he should be cleansed by a witch-doctor, a *mundumugu*, which would make everything all right again. But there was no wise *mundumugu* here, no one he could turn to. He thought of Mr. Thorpe and a shaft of longing for the old days pierced him so painfully that he turned and buried his head in his arms. To be at school again, vaulting over a horse in the gym, climbing a rope, leading his team on the football field. How wonderful that would be!

And to go up to the platform to receive his

certificate—to be applauded because he was one of the few boys to go on to Makerere College, his parents in the audience, smiling proudly.

Secretly, noiselessly, he wept.

Time meant nothing. They stayed in one camp for several weeks and they ate well there for they were not far from two European farms and sheep and cattle were stolen regularly. Women brought them food from the squatter villages. James realised with amazement that this group was part of a huge network stretching all over the land occupied by the Kikuyu and he learned that there was hardly a village anywhere that did not possess a safe house, like that of Irumu where he had slept that first night.

"But *when* is all this going to happen?" he asked Reuben again and again. "How long must we live like animals?"

There was never a satisfactory answer.

"We are waiting," Reuben told him. "We will know when the time has come. Word will be sent to us."

All his sophisticated veneer had long since gone. He had clung to the blazer but it was unrecognisable now, torn and dirty, one pocket hanging only by a few stitches, a lapel almost entirely detached. The hat had gone many months before, and with it the boisterous bonhomie that James had in the past found attractive, even though he had been aware that it was not only his mother who considered Reuben a worthless character.

His arrogance, which previously had the virtue of possessing a kind of panache, became overbearing, and he quarrelled fiercely with one or two of the men who had been the group's nominal leaders before his arrival. Tempers grew short and one night there was a fight between Reuben and a man known as Kali, the Swahili word for 'fierce'. General Kali, he liked to be called.

Pangas flashed in the firelight, the quarrel breaking out with all the suddenness of a summer storm, and while other men broke up the fight and held the protagonists until the spirit had gone out of them, the aftermath was an uneasy peace during which James decided that come what may, he would try to leave the forest and find his way down the mountain.

He waited until a night when women had brought up beer which was drunk with the evening meal of meat and *posho*, the meat being cut from the carcase of a pedigree bull stolen from a farm just below the forest line.

When it seemed to James that everyone was asleep, he rose silently to his feet and melted away into the trees surrounding the clearing in which they were camped. But he had gone only a few yards when a figure stepped from the shadow of a huge tree and gripped him from behind, holding a *panga* at his throat.

"Where do you think you are going?"

Eyes bulging with fear, the *panga's* blade cold against his skin, he said the first thing that came to his mind.

"I was looking for a woman."

The guard threw him to the ground and stood over him.

"You speak lies. There are no women in this direction."

"I thought—"

"You thought you would run away. You are a fool. Your life would be over, and not only your life but that of Reuben, your uncle. And your mother and your father and your sisters—all would be killed. Your head is full of facts, like seeds in a gourd—names and places and the paths we take. Would we let you go and spill those seeds to the white men so that they would take root in their heads?"

He laughed as he saw James's fear, and prodded him with the *panga*.

"Perhaps I am the fool, to let you live tonight. But I am Reuben's man, not Kali's, so I will give you one more chance. Go back to your bed and sleep, and learn to give your heart and mind to us, because very soon now, we will be the masters."

So James went back to his bed. But he did not sleep.

They were waiting for something—not the day when they would be told to rise up and kill all

Europeans, for that was remote, even to true believers, but for something more immediate. James could feel the tenseness in the air, the atmosphere of expectancy. And then the word went round: "He is coming, he is coming."

Into the clearing came an old man driving some goats in front of him. He was a small man, quite bent, but there was a wiry strength in the corded legs in spite of the grey in his hair. He was dressed in the old, traditional Kikuyu way, in monkey skins, his ear lobes split to hold large round plugs, a skin cap on the back of his head.

Clearly he was a man of great importance. He was given beer to drink and food to eat and after he had finished he stood up and gave his orders.

The day was advanced by the time the preparations were completed, the light receding rapidly. An archway of leaves was built and the eyes of a living goat were plucked out and impaled on thorns at each side of it.

Now it was fully dark. The leaping fire threw the black faces that surrounded it into relief. The goat bleated horribly as it was hung upside down, its stomach slit open and the contents of it mixed with powder spilled from a horn which the old man had brought with him.

Still he had not finished with the goat. It was cut down and skinned and a hole made in its thorax.

James watched in appalled fascination as a newcomer to the group was propelled forward, and he covered his mouth with his hand as he saw what the man was compelled to do. He had witnessed many scenes of degradation since he had been with this group, but never anything like this.

He turned and saw Reuben beside him.

"Will they make us do this?" he asked.

"I have already eaten this oath." Reuben was panting with excitement, his eyes white and staring in the darkness.

The man who was taking the oath uttered no protest but did exactly what he was told to do. He inserted his penis through the hole in the goat's thorax and held it in his left hand. With his right he took one of seven sticks which were on the ground by his side and these, too, were inserted into the hole. By the time it was over he had sworn to obey orders to kill anyone, or the oath would kill him, even his own family, if he were called on to do so. He had sworn that if called out by the brotherhood at any time of the day or night, he would rise up and answer the call without question. He had sworn that he would destroy the property of the European, his natural enemy. And he had sworn to drive every white man from the soil of Kenya. Seven oaths he swore, repeating seven times:

"May this oath kill me. May this seven kill me. May this goat kill me."

Then the basin containing the bitter mixture was presented to him, and seven times he took a mouthful of the liquid and spat it first to the left and then to the right.

"I will not do this," James said softly to Reuben.

But Reuben was beyond thought, beyond hearing. He was one with the hushed mass of bodies who were witnesses of this horror and participants in it, bound together by this mystic oath which all knew to be more powerful than any individual.

Now an old man was being pushed forward, and he was protesting. No, no, he was saying. He would not use his manhood for such a thing. He had taken the old oath, and that was good enough. This one was too much.

He was pushed to his knees and in the end, to the accompaniment of threats and jeers, he took the oath.

Wildly James looked around him but there was no escape, for others pressed in on him on every side. He knew that his turn was coming, that it was now only a matter of time. However reluctantly he, too, would be forced to his knees, would undergo this degradation, would take the oath.

The educated part of him recognised it as a repulsive, pagan rite which would shame him and the entire Kikuyu nation. But was defiance worth dying for? Save yourself, an inner voice said. Take the oath. Repeat the empty words. What does it matter?

A shudder of fear shook him even as arms reached out for him and he knew that he was lost. For no Kikuyu could eat such an oath and be unaffected by it. The core of superstition that lay at the very heart of each one of them made it a certainty that from this time forward, the brotherhood had claimed him.

24

FOR a few months after Hugh's death Meg had stayed at the farm, outwardly calm, pleased to receive guests, happiest when her grandchildren came to see her. But there was a curious blankness at the heart of her life. Nothing seemed important any more. She felt as if she, too, were waiting for death, merely putting in a few years before it would claim her.

Kate and Christy had asked her to stay with them at World's End but for some reason she was reluctant to go, not through any lack of affection for them—indeed, her friendship with Kate was one of the strongest threads which bound her to life—but simply because she felt that if she were ever to come to terms with Hugh's death, then it would be here at Mawingo where they had lived in such happiness for so many years.

She was lucky, she kept telling herself. She had Colin and Julie and the boys on the doorstep, and Janet and Harry with their family only a few miles away in Muthaiga.

It was not until she was drinking coffee on Julie's verandah one morning, half-listening in the vague way which had become a habit with her to talk of friends who were coming to stay and dinner guests that Julie had to entertain, that something seemed to click in her brain and the world came slightly more into focus.

"My dear girl," she said. "What must you think of me? How on earth have you managed in this tiny place for so many years? The solution is obvious. You and Colin must move into the farm and I will come here."

Polite protests were made but Meg brushed them aside. The solution *was* obvious, and she was ashamed that she and Hugh had not moved into the cottage years before. Her only excuse was that while Hugh was alive they, too, had frequent guests.

"We've loved it here," Julie assured her. "Honestly, never once did it occur to us. We did build on another room, after all."

"But this sitting room and dining room are tiny compared to mine at the farm. A straight swap is the answer. It will make it imperative for me to have a good clear-out, which is something I've been meaning to do for ages."

There were no protestations from Colin. The idea seemed to make good sense to him, but he did have another suggestion as well.

"Go home to England for a bit," he said. "Have a complete change. It's ages since you saw the relations."

"Oh, I don't know—"

"You could fly. It only takes twenty-four hours. Or on the other hand, a sea trip might do you good."

504

Without Hugh? She couldn't imagine it. Imagine being one of those lone women, talking to other lone women, not liking to order a drink or knowing how much to tip the stewardess.

"I'm a helpless creature," she said, seemingly at random.

"Helpless?" Colin asked. "You? Who was it shot the snake when it got into Janet's bedroom when she was a baby? Who went on foot safaris over the Aberdares? Who climbed a tree and waited three hours for a family of lions to go home?"

"That was different," Meg said.

She had sighed and got on with clearing out a house which contained the memorabilia of fifty years, changing her mind every day or so about the suggested trip; but eventually she had gone, and was glad she had done so, for Hugh's sister and her husband were old now and it seemed unlikely that any of them would ever meet again.

It was October before she flew back, and when she had recovered from the journey she found herself anxious at last to pay the long-deferred visit to World's End.

Nothing had changed there, except that inevitably Christy and Kate had grown older though they were as energetic as ever, Kate spending a great deal of time in her garden.

"It's looking beautiful," Meg said.

"Yes, isn't it. Did I tell you I won a first for my antirrhinums at the Nakuru Show? I feel guilty about it, actually, for most of the credit goes to Muriuki. Our pyrethrum did well, too."

"Doesn't it feel odd," Meg mused, "not to be worried about money?"

"Well, we still don't ever seem actually to *have* any. But you're right. One doesn't worry any more. Not that one ever did, really."

"How lucky we were, being poor in a country where it didn't matter. Nobody thought anything about home-made clothes and second-hand babies' perambulators, did they? I remember once telling an aunt of mine that I had bought one for Colin at an auction for five shillings, and she shook her head and said 'Poor child, poor child. What a dreadful start in life.' Which reminds me, he wanted me to ask you how your protégé Nderitu is getting on."

"Still lecturing at Makerere. He seems to be doing very well. Any particular reason?"

"Colin thought he might be interested in sitting on some Commission about education."

"I'm sure he would, particularly if it's to do with the Kikuyu schools. I don't like the sound of these independent places, do you? They seem like hotbeds of sedition, to me. I think we could do with a sane man like Nderitu to look into them."

"What a lot he has to thank you for!"

"I couldn't be more glad we were able to help. It's very satisfying, knowing that we happened to have the money available just at the right time. We couldn't have spent it in a better way."

"That was the year you were going to England on holiday."

"Oh, well," Kate shrugged. "I don't regret it. Tell me about England, though—I simply can't imagine what it must be like now. When I left, there were still horse-drawn buses and cabs and a housemaid was paid twenty-five pounds a year and we all wore those dreadful cast-iron corsets. Things have certainly changed for the better."

"Well, they've changed—some for the better, some for worse. But the country is as lovely as ever, Kate."

Kate smiled.

"I expect it is. Sometimes in nostalgic moments I remember things like church bells across a meadow, and woods full of bluebells, and I wonder if I'll ever see such things again. And Piccadilly Circus, the Horseguards, and the Lord Mayor's Show! Oh, sometimes I just long to see it all."

"Why don't you get Christy to take you?"

"He means to, he means to! But there's always something more pressing, like a new tractor or another stud bull or miles and miles of fencing. Christy had to re-fence the land on the east border, and I'm sure it must be gold-plated, the amount it cost. Now we're told we need a new generator. This one is certainly erratic, to say the least. Don't be surprised if you're plunged into darkness in the middle of your bath or at any other time equally inconvenient. I've distributed candles and matches everywhere, just in case."

"Your new curtains are lovely."

"Do you like them? I felt wildly extravagant when I bought them, but do you know, they are the first decent ones I've ever had? I had the most unworthy longing to be able to dangle them in front of Hope Honeywell, though on the other hand I can conceive of no circumstances that would make me ask her across my threshold. Not that there's any chance of her coming now. I hear they've retired to South Africa."

"And about time, too. Andrew must have been a long way past retiring age."

"He stayed on because of the war, I suppose. Funny how he never really achieved all the things we thought he would. Do you remember, we thought he would become a Governor and have a handle to his name? He seemed to—to diminish in stature once Hope got her hands on him."

"She would be enough to diminish anyone. I was rather amused when I heard they'd settled in Natal. Hope did nothing but moan about the servants here and how frightful Africans are in every way, yet she can't face life without them."

They laughed a little and were silent, content to sit and look at the view, sharing memories and observations and family gossip as they occurred.

"How is Patsy?" Meg inevitably asked. "Have they heard anything about James?"

"Nothing. Talking of people diminishing in stature reminds me of David, except he has done just the reverse. He's been truly magnificent since James disappeared. He has the sort of shining faith that saints are made of. I don't think Patsy could have kept going without him."

"Poor girl. It must have been frightful for her."

"Christy is sure he's up there, you know." Kate jerked her head in the general direction of the forest and the mountain. "He's been talking to his *rafikis*. They say all the stock-thieving that's going on is because of gangs in the forest."

"What a horrible thought!"

"Christy says—" Kate began, then broke off.

"Christy says what?"

"Oh, nothing really." It was pointless recounting such vague, insubstantial rumours. It would only frighten Meg and perhaps spoil the few days they had together, and it wouldn't do much to calm her own nervousness, either. "He doesn't know any more than anyone else."

What Christy did know was that stock-thieving had increased to such an extent that it had become a major and costly problem. There had been an outbreak of grass fires, too, in the area around World's End. Christy used his old skill as a hunter to make investigations and he felt quite certain that the fires had been started deliberately.

A few days after Meg returned to Mawingo, there was a meeting of local settlers in Gilgil attended by government officers and Christy had put this theory to them. The government officers had laughed him out of court. He was being grossly alarmist, he was told. And one of the men from Nairobi had taken him on one side after the meeting and spoken quite sternly about the demoralising effect of such talk.

"The main thing that demoralises me," Christy said, "is knowing that there are these so-called Mau Mau gangs in the forest but that the Government doesn't take them seriously."

"My dear fellow, of course we acknowledge their existence, and I don't doubt that they are to blame for some of the things you mention. But I assure you that the strength of the gangs is greatly exaggerated. I mean to say, how could the scores of people that are said to be in the forest actually *live*?"

"The women take them food. And haven't they had untold numbers of the cattle around here—including my prize bull? Sure, that must have been the most expensive beef any man ever ate."

"When did stock-thieving *not* exist in this country? Really, my dear chap, I do assure you your fears are groundless. The matter is under control."

That conversation took place early in 1952. In March, the hut of a chief known to be loyal to the British Government was set on fire and his decapitated body was discovered nearby. In April, prize cows belonging to the Bennetts who farmed close by World's End were hamstrung and had to be shot. Three days later another farm was broken into while the occupants were away and two rifles stolen.

"And still the Governor won't admit that something serious is brewing." Kate, reading the account of the burglary in the paper, flung it away from her in disgust. "What's the matter with the man?"

"He doesn't want to rock the boat," Christy said. "He's retiring soon, isn't he? And doesn't he have the royal visit coming up in a couple of months? Sure, he'll not want to do anything to make Princess Elizabeth change her mind about coming here."

He sighed heavily and walked to the front of the verandah where he looked out over the apparently peaceful landscape, his expression bleak.

"Such a fight we've had, Kate," he said. "And now this—this fifth column at our backs. Maybe I should have stuck to hunting."

"It's a little late in the day for regrets. And I don't think you have any, if the truth were known."

He laughed ruefully.

"No, I don't suppose I have. For good or ill, it's been a lot of fun, hasn't it?"

Kate went to join him and put her arm through his.

"I know I must sound awfully His Excellency-ish, but I can't believe this disease is terminal.

These gangs, whoever they are, can't be representative of the majority. Think of all the Kikuyu we've known. Old Kamau. Mwangidogo. Karanja. Muriuki. David. Nderitu. Thousands of them. Rogues, some of them. Lazy, too. But not evil. Not like this."

"There's talk of oathing. That's serious, Kate."

"There's talk of all sorts of things. Oh, I *know* it's serious, Christy, I'm not denying it, and what we're to do about protecting our stock I don't know. But we'll have to think of a way because no one is going to do it for us, that's certain."

Reluctantly, Christy took to wearing a gun when he went out on the farm and he made sure that his hunting rifles were locked up safely.

The Princess and the Duke came for their historic visit and stayed at Treetops where, in the morning, it was revealed that King George VI had died, so that when the couple flew out of Kenya that same day, the small Dakota that took them on the first leg of their homeward journey was carrying the Queen of England.

"So now His Excellency can die happy," Kate said, hearing the news of their safe arrival on the radio. "The sooner he goes and lets the new man get on with governing the country, the better for all of us."

Mau Mau activity seemed to shift from their immediate area which was some relief, even though they appreciated that there was no cause for rejoicing. Cattle and sheep were still being mutilated in the Nanyuki district, the other side of the mountain, and there were even more grass fires.

"I can't bear to think that James is part of that murderous crew," Kate said one evening when the radio had been giving them the usual ration of bad news. "My heart bleeds for Patsy and David. There was such promise in James."

"I heard it said that the gangs in the forest are just waiting for the whistle to blow, and then they'll come and drive us all out. James could yet end up as Prime Minister."

Kate shuddered.

"Don't joke about it," she said.

Christy looked surprised.

"I wasn't," he replied.

It was October before the new Governor arrived, and only nine days afterwards he declared a State of Emergency.

"Well, thank heaven for that," Kate said. "Now, perhaps, we'll get some action."

And her remark was echoed all over the highlands of Kenya.

Meg was reading the same report in the East African *Standard* when she heard Julie's step on the verandah.

"Anyone home?" Julie called.

"Come in. You're just in time for coffee. Have you seen the paper?"

"I haven't had time to read it all, but I heard a report on the radio." Julie came in and sat down at the table, pouring herself a cup of coffee. "They said that Jomo Kenyatta's been flown out of the area. And spiriting the Lancashire Fusiliers down here seems like a good move. Far better to stamp on it hard before it really gets started."

Meg sighed and laid the paper down.

"Pour me another one, there's a good girl. I have a horrible feeling that the stamping hard should have been done at least a year or more ago. I hate the thought of it. This has been such a peaceful place until all these frightful things started happening. I simply cannot comprehend how the Kikuyu, who place so much value on stock, could mutilate animals in this way. After all, stealing is understandable, if regrettable—but this! It's a bestial thing to do, yet the Government has consistently played it down. Christy has been trying to get some action for ages."

"Colin, too. Actually, it's Christy and Kate I wanted to see you about—well, Kate, anyway. I wondered if you'd remembered that it's her seventieth birthday next month."

Meg pulled a face.

"Good Lord, what does that make me? What a very nasty thought. What are you planning?"

"A really good party, we thought. Heaven knows, we need something to cheer us up." She finished up her coffee. "Look, I can't stop now —I'm just on my way to Nairobi to do my stint at the hospital canteen, but I thought I'd mention it to you so that you can do a bit of pondering. We should mark the occasion in some way, don't you agree?"

"Certainly we should. A party would be a good idea. Whom should we ask?"

"That's partly what I want you to ponder about. Colin said ask everyone that has ever known her, but that seems like a pretty tall order. I wouldn't know where to start. Can I leave the list to you?"

Meg smiled at her, reaching already for a pencil.

"It will be a pleasure," she said.

"Meg's asked us over on my birthday," Kate announced as they sat at lunch. "She phoned this morning. As it falls on a Sunday she says all the family will be there, and she's asking Patsy and David and the girls. I told her that the last thing I wanted is for anyone to make a song and dance over it. I'd rather forget the whole thing, if the truth were known—but it would be nice to see everyone again, wouldn't it?"

"Very nice," Christy agreed absently, scanning the newspaper as if lunch parties were the furthest things from his mind. He had himself been the recipient of a phone call from Meg the previous Wednesday afternoon when it was a well-known fact that Kate would be attending a meeting of the local East African Women's League. They were planning a surprise of some sort, it appeared. He was charged with the job of ensuring that the invitation was accepted. No excuses would be recognised.

"Well, shall I tell her we can go? I didn't like to accept without asking you."

"Mm?" Christy raised his eyebrows at her and Kate could have sworn that he was amused at something. But then again, it had always been difficult to tell. "I don't see why not," he said after due consideration. "Yes, tell her we'll be glad to come."

"You're sure? You don't sound terribly keen."

For in spite of the round-up of Mau Mau leaders, the mutilation of cattle had continued, and Chief Warahiu, a man who was fiercely loyal to the British, had been murdered. Patsy and David were fearful now for Chief Ngengi. What a world it was—what an awful, awful world!

"Now why in the world wouldn't I be keen? A day away from here will do us both good." He cleared his throat and returned to the paper. "Perhaps you'd like a new dress for the occasion," he added after a moment.

Kate stared at him in amazement. In all the years she had known him, he had never seemed particularly aware of the way she was dressed. Bush shirts and riding breeches appeared to please him as much as silk and lace and had been a great deal more practical in her life on the farm.

"A new dress?" she echoed.

"That's right. You know, those things that women wear—"

"Very funny." Kate looked at him suspiciously. "I am acquainted with the word. I'm just totally amazed that suddenly you should think it necessary for me to buy a new one simply to have lunch at Mawingo."

"I thought as it was your birthday—"

"But Christy, you promised me that book about orchids! I'd so much rather have it than a dress. I've found the most fascinating variety I never saw before, only a yard or two into the forest—"

"What the *hell* were you doing in the forest?" Christy roared at her. "I told you not to go anywhere near it."

"Muriuki was with me. I'm sorry, Christy. I suppose it was silly, but we only went a tiny way up the trail. I wanted some of those lovely ferns for the rockery. Things have been fairly quiet lately."

Even so. Christy reached out and took her hand in his. "Kate, promise me you'll be careful. That was a foolish thing to do—there's no need to court danger."

"I know. I'm sorry."

"So I should think."

"And you will buy me the orchid book?"

"If you behave yourself."

"I don't think you have any idea how expensive it is!"

517

"And wouldn't I buy you the Koh-i-noor diamond if I could?"

Kate leaned over and gave him a brief kiss.

"I know you would, bless you, but fortunately for you the summit of my ambitions is a book on orchids. Illustrated, please. So I'll give Meg a ring and say we'll love to go to lunch, shall I?"

Two days before the event Christy announced that he had errands in Nakuru and asked Kate if she would like to go with him.

"Shouldn't one of us stay to man the battlements here?" she asked.

"Musa can cope. Damn it all, he'll have to be here on his own for the whole day on Sunday."

"Well, in that case I would rather like to come. I want to go to Speke Groceries and I badly need a few things from Howse and McGeorge. I swear our entire labour force must be plastered from head to foot with mercurichrome, the amount I got through last week."

"You might take the opportunity to have your hair done." Christy's voice was off-hand, but Kate whirled round to face him, a suspicious frown on her face.

"Have my *hair* done?" She made it sound as if he had suggested cosmetic surgery at the very least. "Christy, what is going on?"

"Holy Mother!" Christy exploded. "Why should anything be going on, at all? Wasn't I talking to Jane Marshall down at the Post Office and didn't she say the one thing she missed about living up here was not being able to get her hair done every week? Sure, it looks fine to me but I thought maybe you'd enjoy it, as a special treat . . ."

His voice trailed away helplessly as Kate stood and laughed at him. She went to him and put her hands on his shoulders, looking up into his face. It was the colour of old leather, seamed and craggy and utterly beloved. His hair was white but still abundant, his eyes as clear as ever, their brightness undiminished. As she had done so many times before, she traced the scar with the tip of her finger.

"It was a lovely idea," she said. "If there's time, I'll think about it."

She felt unwontedly smart as they set out for Mawingo the following Sunday. Her hair had been cut and set by the wife of one of the new settlers who seemed to take a remarkably phlegmatic view of the wave of violence in her recently adopted homeland, seemingly far more agitated by Kate's rejection of a proferred blue rinse than by rumours of attacks that circulated around the salon.

Kate wore a pale-blue linen dress of a classic design which she had bought from an expensive shop in Nairobi in a fit of unusual extravagance. The saleslady had assured her that it was a style that would never date, which was certainly a good thing since the purchase had taken place ten years previously.

"You look beautiful," Christy said, as they were about to start out.

"Beautiful? At seventy? There's prejudice for you!" But she smiled and was pleased.

Once on the main road the going was easy, for now they could drive on tarmac made by Italian prisoners-of-war. It meant that a day trip to Mawingo was a simple matter, not the complicated excursion that it once had been.

They passed through the township of Naivasha and onwards in the direction of Nairobi, across biscuit-coloured plains where zebra and giraffe grazed. Mount Longonot and Mount Suswa rose dramatically to the west, and to the east were the foothills of the Aberdares merging hazily into the blue horizon. The road climbed upwards and there, below them, was the Rift Valley.

"Let's stop a minute," Kate said, and immediately Christy pulled in to the side, a little way off the road. Together they stood on the edge of the escarpment and gazed in silence.

"It doesn't matter how many times you see it, does it?" Kate said at last. "Every time is the first."

Steeply the land fell away to the rocky floor of the valley, shimmering thousands of feet below in the heat haze that blurred the distant hills and mountains. It was a stark scene, painted in shades of ochre and umber, oils slashed on a canvas so large and magnificent that the human eye could not encompass it. Those purple hills that were its furthest boundary must surely be some magical, mythical country, Kate felt, that would retreat as one neared it. To her it seemed a beckoning Shangri-la, always mysterious.

"Is it the vastness?" she asked Christy now. "Is that what stuns me whenever I stand here and look at it?"

"It's the essence of Africa. Grand and untameable."

Still they stood and gazed, smelling the dust and the sun on the bushes around them.

"To think," Kate said, "that when I came to this country I was full of ideas about making a contribution to it. The arrogance! As if anything that any of us can do makes one small mark. It was here a million years ago—it will be here a million years after we've gone." She turned to Christy. "Maybe that's the appeal of this place. It's the timelessness of it. Nothing's changed in this valley for generations. And it's true of all of it, really. We'll pass and the dust will blow over our tracks and there'll be no sign of our passing."

"Now isn't that the most arrant nonsense I ever heard? How can you stand there and say that?" Christy was robust in his disagreement. "In fifty years we've eradicated diseases that had Njeroge and his *totos* dying like flies only a generation ago. And think of the agriculture! People have invested fortunes in building up disease-resistant strains of wheat and maize and cattle and everything else. The Masai have stopped killing off the Kyukes at the least provocation—"

"I don't mean those sort of things." Kate shook her head helplessly as she turned away to go back to the car. "I can't really explain what I mean. I suppose I'm taking much too personal a view. The school—Patsy—so many things! I had such dreams. I wanted to usher in some kind of millennium where black and white lived together in harmony. That's where the arrogance lay. All I've done is struggle along from day to day, achieving little, making mistakes all along the line. And now this hateful Mau Mau business which threatens everyone, black and white alike. Sometimes I feel that life has been one constant trudge uphill with the god Ngai standing on the top of it hurling rocks down with the sole purpose of dislodging us."

"Come on!" Christy propelled her more briskly towards the car and shut the door on her firmly. "The sooner you're at Mawingo with a gin in your hand, the better for all of us."

They continued on their way, in the heart of Kikuyu land now. The land was green and fertile, the landscape one of rolling hills, the green broken by the red earth of the *shambas*, the brilliance of a random flowering shrub, and round, thatched huts. There were women, as always bent under their loads, and almond-eyed donkeys pulling water cars. And here was a mission church with girls in pale dresses and men dressed in their best making their way towards it. A skinny urchin by the roadside waved and grinned at them as they passed, and Kate waved back.

"Everything seems so much as usual," she said, smiling. "I'm quite convinced that Kenya is going to live through this. I have the highest hopes for it. Changes will have to come. We must get people to think constructively when the Emergency is over. The trouble with settlers is that they *will* take up entrenched positions. I suppose it's their very inflexibility that makes them so dogged and determined—otherwise they wouldn't have lasted five minutes in Africa. But now, surely, they will see that frustration builds up such a head of steam that it's bound to burst out somewhere. Somehow attitudes will have to change—"

Christy smiled to hear the note of determination once more present in her voice. No doubt the silence that followed this speech meant that she was formulating a letter to the editor of the *Standard*, or perhaps thinking of meetings and discussions she could arrange with the Women's League. But whatever lines her mind was running on, it was distracted by the sight of the number of cars she could see outside the farmhouse as they approached Mawingo by the track leading from the main road.

"However many people have they asked?" she

demanded in amazement. "This isn't just the family!"

Christy, his eyes bright with amusement, brought the car to a standstill outside the house.

Immediately they were surrounded by a surge of people: Meg was in the forefront, of course, and Colin and Julie and the two boys who were still in Kenya. And Janet and Harry, with their children, Celia and Robin. And Patsy, David, Christine and Margaret.

There on the verandah waiting for the family greetings to be finished was Ellen Saunders, her erstwhile pupil, and an unfamiliar, sandy-haired woman who greeted her warmly and announced that she was Agnes McTavish on holiday from her hospital in the Congo. A grey-haired matron introduced herself as Nellie Carstairs, née Mortimer. There were others, too, from those far-off days of the Hill Academy. Maud Rankin, now a grandmother. Margaret MacDonald, now Nicholls, married to a Community Development Officer in Uganda. Frances Morcombe, who had been the naughtiest girl in the school but was now married to a bishop, and others temporarily forgotten but now remembered.

And there were the Bennetts who farmed at Cedarwood, next door to World's End, who had breathed not one word about attending Kate's birthday party.

"We couldn't be left out," Steve Bennett said, kissing her soundly. "You saved our sanity, our

524

marriage and possibly our lives when we were total greenhorns. Happy birthday."

"This is too much—too much," Kate said, overwhelmed. "It's so wonderful to see you all— *Nderitu!*" For suddenly she had caught sight of the tall young African who had been the little boy pulling at her skirts so many years before. He had kept in the background until this moment, but now stepped forward and she took both his hands in hers. "Nderitu! You surely didn't make a special journey from Kampala."

"I came with Mrs. Carstairs and Mrs. Nicholls. They were kind enough to give me a lift."

"All that way! I'm so delighted to see you— and so proud of you." Distractedly she turned towards Christy who was coming towards her with a glass in his hands. "Thank you—I need this more than ever now. It's all too much for a woman of my advanced years."

But her eyes were bright with happiness as she turned to talk to first one and then another old friend.

Julie and Meg had between them prepared a vast cold buffet, and it was served by the Mawingo servants who were enjoying the occasion as much as anyone. To a man they shook Kate by the hand and thanked her for having a birthday.

"There is much to be said for their reverential attitude towards the old," Kate said.

"I have long thought so," Meg agreed.

"You know, this is quite the most wonderful day of my life!" Kate sat down beside her old friend to eat her lunch. "Christy knew, didn't he? All that talk of new dresses and hairdressers. I should have known that something special was in the wind. It was a lovely thought. How you contacted all these people I shall never know— or why they all came."

Janet had brought her plate of food over to them and sat on a stool close by.

"We couldn't let the occasion pass," she said. "We all owe you so much."

"*Owe* me?" Genuine amazement froze Kate, her fork halfway to her mouth.

"Before you came your old pupils were saying that you marked them for life—and I must say they're an impressive bunch. Matron of a native hospital, headmistress of the girls' school, all those big wheels in the Women's League. And then there's that provincial commissioner's wife from Uganda, and the other one—they both seem so involved with their husbands' work they probably do as much good as all the others put together. Not to mention the bishop's wife!"

"I remember when she put a frog in Hope Honeywell's desk. Hope Skinner, as she then was."

"Oh, *how* that endears her to me," murmured Meg.

"Ripples in a pool," Colin said, coming with Nderitu to sit on the floor at Kate's feet. "Little

526

did you know how the tiny one you made with your school would widen."

"Tiny it certainly was. I had no idea! I thought it was all finished and forgotten long ago."

"Without you I'd still be herding goats," Nderitu said.

"Rubbish!" This Kate refuted altogether. "You have the sort of intelligence that would rise to the top in any society."

"But you were there with help when I needed it."

"And I've never forgotten your astute advice before I put up for LegCo," Colin said.

Kate put her plate aside and folded her hands. "Do go on," she said. "I'm beginning to enjoy this. It's rather like being able to read one's obituary notices."

"Actually, you were an absolute beast to me," Janet put in. "You made me miss a picnic once because I hadn't learned my French irregular verbs. Would anyone care to hear me recite the pluperfect of *conduire*?"

"Not just now, dear. But you may fetch me another glass of this rather nice wine."

"Just so long as you don't fall flat on your face before Colin's speech—"

"He's not going to make a speech? Colin, really, there's no need for that—I do beg you! We all know that you're a politician now as well as a farmer, but truly speeches are not called for."

Colin, however, would not be put off. It was

some time later, when all were in a mellow mood after food and wine, that he called for order. Everyone crowded in from the verandah. Some found seats, others perched on the arms of chairs or sat on the floor.

He was middle-aged now, thickset, still fair-haired, still good-looking. He was quite aware of the fact, not being a fool. He enjoyed making speeches, being the centre of attraction, but this did not detract from the fact that he had a genuine desire to serve and a passionate love of Africa. He had matured into an impressive figure, Kate thought now, as he stood on the hearth-rug. She leant towards Meg.

"You must be proud of him," she whispered. Meg nodded, smiling.

"Shipboard romances are notoriously short-lived," he began. "But there are exceptions. I met Kate on a ship in 1906, and I've loved her ever since—"

Kate's mind went off at a tangent. *Impossible*, she thought—forty-six years! Where has it all gone? And nothing accomplished, nothing at all!

But here was Colin talking of the old days: of the Hill Academy, and the war years on the farm when she had taught the Lacey children as well as Patsy and Julie, of the school on the farm, of the textbooks she had written that were now in standard use in schools.

"I've talked enough," Colin said at last.

"Kate's been a wonderful friend to us all, and really one can say no more. So we all clubbed together, Kate, and we've bought you a present which we hope you—and Christy, too, because after all, he's not such a bad chap—will enjoy. We hope you'll accept this with our love and our fondest wishes for many, many more happy birthdays." And he extended his hand, in it an envelope.

Kate, a little tearful now, dabbed at her eyes.

"I'm overwhelmed," she said. "Totally, totally overwhelmed. Just seeing you like this is more than enough of a present for me."

But even as she spoke, her mind was registering the envelope and thinking, Good—it must be a book token! That means I can have not only the orchid book but the new one on East African birds. Or maybe a book of verse by that new poet, Dylan Thomas. It was time she came to grips with it, she thought. Some of what she had read she had liked, but some needed more careful study. On the other hand, if it were meant as a present for Christy, too, then the bird book would be better. Poetry wasn't something he had ever learned to appreciate.

All this went through her mind in the seconds it took to thank Colin and open the envelope. She extracted the contents and looked at it wonderingly, for she had never seen anything like it before. It had a stiff paper cover, dark blue, with a bird-like design in the corner over which were written the letters BOAC, and inside—

She looked sharply up at Colin.

"BOAC?" she said, incredulously.

"It's an airline ticket," Colin said. "Two of them, to be exact." Kate saw that there were, indeed, two dark blue folders in her hand. "For you and Christy to have a holiday in England."

And then, indeed, she was rendered speechless. Blindly she turned around, looking for Christy, and he came and put his arm round her and she clung to him, both laughing and crying.

"You knew," she said accusingly. "All along, you knew."

"No, no, I swear I didn't. I had no idea what the present was to be."

"We've arranged for someone to take care of the farm. A really good man. You can go for as long as you like."

"Could they be trying to tell us something?" Kate asked Christy, laughing. "Thank you, thank you, every one of you. This really is the most exciting day of my life. I thought that being seventy might prove quite insupportable, but so far it's wonderful."

The talk and the laughter continued as Kate and Christy circled the room, thanking everyone individually. Patsy—thinner, quieter, hugged them both.

"We haven't had a chance to talk," Kate said. "Come up and see us soon, all of you."

"We will," Patsy promised. "I worry about you, so close to the forest."

"I don't imagine Kimilil is a particularly salubrious place at this moment. But just for one day, let's forget Mau Mau." Patsy nodded, but even as she did so, Kate knew that her words had been hollow, useless. None of them could forget it. Knowledge of its existence lay like a canker at the heart of the brightest day.

Resolutely it was ignored as the reminiscences of times past were brought out to be laughed at, and finally Kate found herself alone with Meg in a quiet corner.

"You shouldn't have, you know," she said. "But oh, what a magnificent present."

"The sum kept growing and growing. There was talk of giving you the money to spend as you wanted, but Julie wouldn't let us. She said it would only go on a pedigree bull, or something."

"I daresay she was right. Oh Meg, you've made me so happy, you and your family. Don't think I haven't realised how you've been missing Hugh all day."

"If he'd been here, he would have made the speech," Meg said. "Colin may be an accomplished speaker these days, but Hugh wouldn't have delegated that job to anyone."

"Hugh helped me so much back in those first

531

awful days. It's strange how some things stick so firmly in the mind. I remember that he told me my life wasn't over. I was twenty-four, and quite convinced that it was. In some ways it seems like only yesterday. There was a rainbird singing. Tell me," briskly, she returned to the present, "should we fly home now or wait until the spring?"

25

"WHY can't we go down now?" James asked. "We know that the farm is empty. If, as you say, the cook has eaten the oath then he will let us in and it will be an easy matter to steal the guns."

"Wait," Reuben said.

A dozen of them had hived off from the original gang. For some time they had been on the other side of the mountain, but Reuben, undisputed leader now that General Kali was in command of the whole network of gangs in the forest, had led this small party back to their earlier camping grounds. Last night they had slept in the place where James had eaten the oath. It had not troubled him. Eighteen months of living like a wild creature had changed him to the point where not even his own mother would have recognised him.

It was, perhaps, inevitable that the bitter hatred felt by his associates would worm itself into his bloodstream. Each night he listened to the tales of cold-blooded exploitation they recounted, and because in so many cases they were tinged with truth he was able, more and more often, to say: "Yes, yes, thus it happened. This, too, has been my experience." The memories of kindnesses received and confidence shared receded and became blurred and distorted.

It was for his own ends that Mr. Thorpe had encouraged him to do well—no doubt his would have been the credit, had James brought honours to the school. Perhaps it would have meant promotion for him.

As for Colin Lacey, pretending to further the cause of African representation in LegCo: he was hedging his bets, that was all. He must know that soon would come the night of the long knives. He was merely ensuring that there would be a place for him in the Kenya of the future.

And his own father? A dupe of the missionaries, deluded into believing that they had the true faith. His mother? Half-white, thinking like a European.

So the distorting mirror was tipped to reflect a deepness of despair that James had never dreamed of. The woman on the market steps whose image had haunted him since the days of his boyhood became all white women. Those who arrogantly shouted 'boy' at men old enough to be their fathers, who spoke derogatory words about their servants to their friends, neither knowing nor caring if the servants could hear them; those who condemned their cooks and houseboys to cold, unlit, insanitary quarters, became the standard, the archetype. It was all too easy to forget the others—or even if one remembered, it could be dismissed coldly as paternalism.

From this it was but the smallest step to the realisation that all white men were the enemies of all black men. And those Kikuyu—those many, many Kikuyu—who did not agree, then they, too, were enemies and must be cut down.

It was only in dreams that James remembered another way of life, a time when he said grace before meals and sat at a table for his food. Sometimes he would wake in the forest, possessed by a terrible despair because in his dreams he had been back at home and there had been kindness and laughter and soft voices, and books to read and the excitement of a football game in prospect. But swiftly the dream disappeared, to be replaced by the endless talk and the waiting and the savage raid that brought its own excitement.

He did not hesitate now to take his turn with the women who brought them food from the squatter villages. It did not matter which one. He knew the names of very few of them.

But even now, changed man though he was, he could not see the sense of killing unless it was strictly necessary. The signal had not yet been given for the Mau Mau to descend from the mountain and slash the Europeans to pieces. Some said that this would come on Christmas Day when all men would be too occupied by eating and drinking to be on their guard, but so far it was just rumour and speculation. Deep in the secret places of his heart he hoped that it would not be necessary—that they would realise the impossibility of their position and would go, having seen the ease with which their herds of cattle had been decimated.

The order had come for them to steal fire-arms and they had achieved a good haul from Cedarwood Farm, just along the ridge. Now it was the turn of World's End.

"It would be easier while it is light," he persisted. "Before the old couple return home."

"We will wait."

Only James was ever bold enough to argue with Reuben who was now known as General Panga. But even he knew that it was impossible to make him change his mind once he had determined on a certain course of action. He did not understand the other man's thought processes on this occasion. Nothing would be easier than to go down now. The old people had been away all day. The cook was about, and the headman, but until milking time the farm was unusually deserted because it was Sunday. The gang could be in and out before there was any trouble. The headman was not a Kikuyu, but could be disposed of if he objected. The cook had eaten the oath. Why the delay?

From this outcrop of rock in the forest they could see the roof of the farm and the track which snaked down to the main road. Nothing moved. A tongue of forest pushed down into the green hills to their right. Between it and the house there were sheep grazing, the noise of their baa-ing coming to them quite clearly in the still, warm air.

Some of the gang were sleeping. James glanced at Reuben to see if he, too, had dropped his guard but he saw that his gaze was riveted to the track, his eyelids drooping, his mouth half-open. There was a tenseness about him, the same feeling of expectancy that James had noticed on other occasions. Like the time the chief had been killed. Like the time they had entered the home of the European who lived alone a little to the north and had slashed him to death in his bath.

That was it, of course. Even now the realisation tightened his stomach with a sudden shock. Reuben *wanted* to kill the old people below. And everything that James had known and been in the past before he had become one of the brotherhood seemed to harden and coalesce, so that he saw clearly that Reuben was wrong and that he was wrong, and the oath was evil. Not for the first time, he looked wildly round for somewhere to run to, but he knew as he did so that he was many, many months too late. The oath and the brotherhood had him in a grip of iron.

Kate lay back in her seat in the car with her eyes closed, for she was very tired now. She was smiling, however.

"Oh Christy, wasn't that the most marvellous thing that could happen to anyone? Quite literally, I've had the time of my life. And so much to look forward to! Won't we have fun?" She turned her head on the back of the seat and opened her eyes to look at him. "You were a wretch not to warn me."

"Meg told me it was to be a surprise."

"It was that, all right." Kate was silent for a moment, then she sighed. "Dear Meg! My heart breaks when I see her, Christy. I admire her strength so much. I can't imagine that I could ever be so strong."

Christy reached out and squeezed her hand briefly.

"If it's any consolation, my father lived till ninety-three and I'm as strong as an ox. Now close your eyes and have a nap and we'll be home before you know it."

"Oh, sleep's out of the question. I'm far too excited."

But she did drift into a pleasant semi-conscious state, sitting up and blinking as the car turned into the track off the road. Dusk was falling, the sky a deep rose fading to the palest pink. There was a light on in the house and a faint drift of smoke from the chimney.

"I hope Iringo hasn't cooked a proper dinner," Kate said. "I couldn't eat a thing."

"Didn't you tell him not to?"

"I can't remember. I meant to. Surely he would have the sense to realise we'll have eaten an enormous lunch? There's half a cold chicken from yesterday. I'm sure he'll have come to the conclusion that's more than adequate. He's usually good about that sort of thing. We are lucky with him, aren't we? I'd trust him to the hilt."

"Even so, from now on we're going to have him out of the house with the doors locked before we eat our dinner. Colin was warning me today that old and trusted servants are known to have let gangs into houses."

"How horrible it is! Quite unbelievable. But at least we can be sure of Mwangidogo."

Christy grunted in reply.

"What does it mean?" Kate asked.

"Just that the only thing you can be sure of in this country is that you can't be sure of anything. Heaven be praised, at least someone has lit a fire under the boiler even though it's Muriuki's day off. It'll be good to soak my old bones in hot water."

"Mm—lovely. And lovely to be home. It always is, isn't it? But oh Christy, what a wonderful, wonderful day. I'll remember it till the day I die."

She was leaving the car as she spoke, greeting Simba the cross labrador-ridgeback who went everywhere with Christy, going into the house through the kitchen.

Iringo greeted her warmly.

" *Jambo, memsahib*. Has the day been good? What is the news of *Memsahib* Lacey? And *Memsahib* Patsy?"

539

And no, he had not prepared a big dinner.

"Just vegetable soup and the cold chicken with salad, for at the house of *Memsahib* Lacey you always eat a great deal. And to follow I made the lemon mousse that the *Bwana* likes."

"*Mzuri sana*, Iringo. That was very good. And now you may go, for we are not ready to eat yet and can serve ourselves later. *Kwaheri*, Iringo."

Christy stretched and rubbed his back.

"I think I'll go and have that hot bath I promised myself."

He went off to the bathroom, but not before he had securely locked and bolted the back door and checked the one leading to the verandah.

Kate followed him through to the bedroom and took off the blue linen dress, putting on a warm housecoat because it was so much cooler at this altitude.

Christy had his bath and changed into his pyjamas and dressing gown. Throughout Kenya, farmers in Molo and Subukia and Rumuruti, on tea estates in Kericho and the flat wheatlands of the Plateau were doing the same, for it had become a tradition, first to bath and then to eat dinner in dressing gowns. Contentedly, still warm from the glow of her wonderful day, Kate sat down in her usual armchair, Simba lying on the rug beside her.

"You don't want to eat for a bit, do you?" she asked Christy. "I thought I'd read."

Christy went to the window and pulled the curtain aside, looking out into the blackness.

"That must be the first time I've come home and not gone straight to the milking sheds," he said. "We are getting old, Kate. I simply didn't think of it, if you can believe that."

"Musa can cope with what's necessary. Don't worry about it, Christy. It's been an exhausting day."

Christy stood for a moment as if toying with the idea of going to the sheds even now, dressed as he was, but then let the curtain drop and came to sit by the fire.

"What about this trip, Kate?" he asked. "Tell me everything we're going to do."

"Now," said Reuben, his voice thick with excitement. "Go now, nephew. Go to the front, to the verandah. Knock at the door. Call out to them. Make sure that they know it is you, James Ngengi, who calls, and they will rush to open the door to welcome you like the prodigal son."

"And you will be there?"

"We will all be there, our *pangas* sharp. All twelve of us—eleven without you. But you are the most important of all."

"Why not use the cook? He has eaten the oath."

"They have grown wily, the Europeans. They have learned to distrust the voice of a servant calling in the night. It must be you. Only you are the key that will unlock the door for the rest of us. Go now—go on!"

James stood up, rising out of the tangled undergrowth. He was a tall figure, broader now than when he first took to the forest. His clothes were in rags, his hair wild and matted.

He had sworn to obey. He had sworn the most terrible of all oaths and he was helpless in the face of it, not human any more but an automaton with no other choice before him but to carry out the orders of the brotherhood.

The others were behind him. It was dark now and there was no moon, but he felt the presence of them. They moved silently as they had learned to do, down, down, past the milking sheds, nothing now between them and the house.

They fanned out, some skirting the house in one direction, some in the other. They melted away into the shadows and for a moment James stood alone as he looked at the house.

Why was he hesitating, he asked himself? They were only Europeans in there. Two white people who meant nothing to him any more.

"Go on." Reuben had emerged from the shadows once more, another man at his heels. "Go to the verandah. We shall hide there until the door is opened."

James moved forward slowly and silently, up the steps of the verandah. The big double doors were shut and bolted, that went without saying. On each side of them there were windows, one imperfectly covered by the curtain that Christy had disturbed only minutes earlier. Stealthily James looked in through the crack.

Granny Kate was facing him, sitting forward in the way she always did when she was interested and engrossed in the subject under discussion. She'd sat like that when he had told her about his desire to go to Makerere, his longing to do scientific research. Granny Kate—

He hadn't called her that, not once, when he'd been thinking about coming down from the forest. He'd thought of them as two old Europeans. But there she was, talking and laughing, picking up a book from the table beside her, sobering suddenly as the dog lifted its head, pricked up its ears and looked towards the verandah door.

She was frightened. You could tell that by the way her face froze, the way her hand flew to her throat. It would have to be now, if he were to do it.

If? He had sworn. He had to do it.

"Go on," Reuben urged quietly from his unseen position in the shadows.

They were all evil. All the white people. There would never be any justice in the land until they were driven out, seven times he had sworn it.

Grandpa Christy had got to his feet, had turned towards the door. *Evil*? He had lifted James on to a horse, had carried him on his back, had shown him how to fly a kite. Granny Kate had looked upwards and had laughed and clapped her hands and had hugged him and taken him home and given him chocolate cake and read the *Just So Stories* to him.

"*Now*," hissed Reuben.

James licked his lips.

"Get your guns," he screamed. "Don't open the door. The Mau Mau are outside. Get your guns—get your guns—get your guns—get your . . ."

"By the time you come back it may be over," Patsy said.

She looks almost as old as I do, Kate thought. She's suffered so much. All the years of worry about James, then the tragedy of his violent death.

"I wish you were coming, too. You need a change more than anyone."

Patsy shook her head.

"No, this is for you and Christy. Besides, my place is here. It always will be."

"Mine, too. We won't be away for long. I don't suppose Christy will ever be convinced that anyone else can look after his precious livestock."

"Colin says that Philip Whatsisname—the man who's going to look after World's End—is very good. Absolutely reliable."

"So I'm told."

"He took care of the Watsons' place over at Njoro, I believe."

"Yes. They were very pleased with him."

What *are* we talking about? Kate asked herself. The words were a smokescreen for their thoughts, nothing more.

"Patsy," she said, breaking through it. "You must put it all behind you. He was so brave! What James did—it was unbelievable. We owe our lives to him."

"There was evidence that he was involved in other killings," she said tonelessly. "Fingerprints everywhere, the police tell me."

"But in the end, so brave. None of us knows what awful pressures were put on him. That bestial oath!"

"I'm glad they got Reuben. David prays for me. He hates my vindictiveness."

"We can't all be Davids. But he's right, Patsy —bitterness can only corrode from within. There's altogether too much bitterness. Think of the girls." Kate's voice lightened, and she leant forward a little in her chair. "Christine and Margaret. Such lovely girls, Patsy, and so bright! Think of their future. Why, by the time they—"

"No!" Patsy held up her hand. "No plans— not any more. Where the girls are concerned we'll live a day at a time and do as David does, leave the rest to God." She sighed heavily, as if the prospect did not fill her with optimism.

Kate sighed in agreement. What cause was there for hope? No sooner was one gang caught than another made its presence felt in an even more horrific way. No one slept safe any more, black or white. Women went shopping with guns at their belts and little children could not play outside their own houses.

Nerves on edge, Patsy jumped at the sound of Kate's fist coming down with a heavy thump on the arm of the chair.

"What are we *doing*, sitting here like this with faces as long as fiddles?" Kate rose to her feet and went to the edge of the verandah where, as she had done so many times before, she stood and gazed at the beauty of the scene before her. "Just look at it, Patsy. It's worth fighting for, you know."

Patsy joined her at the rail.

"I know," she said.

"And that's what we'll have to do, all of us who love the place." She stood up a little straighter. "Black, white, settler, missionary, official—the whole damned lot of us. We can't sit down and let the powers of darkness and death take over, can we?"

"No one thinks they'll win in the long term. But what sort of a country will it leave?"

Kate's lips tightened.

"Christy and I need a holiday and I'm going to see that we get one. But we'll be back because *someone's* got to clear this mess up and build a decent country out of the ruins."

Patsy found herself at last able to smile.

"I dare say you'll be wanting to have a hand in that," she said.

"Well, naturally!"

For a while they stood there in silence, Kate's expression softening as she sniffed the blossom-laden evening air of her beloved garden.

"Will you look at it?" she said. "See that sky? Was ever a country so lovely?" She put her hand through Patsy's arm. "There really ought to be a rainbird singing."

THE END

Other titles in the
Charnwood Library Series:

Other titles in the
Charnwood Library Series:

Other titles in the
Charnwood Library Series:

Other titles in the
Charnwood Library Series:

Jane Eyre	*Charlotte Bronte*
The Pilgrim's Progress	*John Bunyan*
Lord Jim	*Joseph Conrad*
Great Expectations	*Charles Dickens*
Oliver Twist	*Charles Dickens*
A Passage to India	*E. M. Forster*
North and South	*Mrs. E. C. Gaskell*
The Wind in the Willows	*Kenneth Grahame*
Far From the Madding Crowd	*Thomas Hardy*
Jude the Obscure	*Thomas Hardy*
The Mayor of Casterbridge	*Thomas Hardy*
Tess of the D'Urbervilles	*Thomas Hardy*
The Go-Between	*L. P. Hartley*
Fiesta	*Ernest Hemingway*
For Whom the Bell Tolls	*Ernest Hemingway*
Brave New World	*Aldous Huxley*
Captains Courageous	*Rudyard Kipling*
Aaron's Rod	*D. H. Lawrence*
Sons and Lovers	*D. H. Lawrence*
Women in Love	*D. H. Lawrence*
Nineteen Eighty-Four	*George Orwell*
Kenilworth	*Sir Walter Scott*
Catriona	*R. L. Stevenson*
Kidnapped	*R. L. Stevenson*
Gone to Earth	*Mary Webb*